"HANG ON, KID!"

As he said it, he took a tight wrap on the lines of the four-horse hitch and the boy, glancing ahead, grew pale. A hundred yards away a line of mounted Indians in full war paint blocked the stage road, their leader holding up his hand, palm out, in the halting-sign.

"Like I said, kid," muttered Monk Gurley, *"hang on."*

With the low-voiced warning, the old man yelled at his horses and drove them straight at the warriors, crashing the heavy stage into, and on through, their squealing ponies before they could react to get them out of the way. The rest of it went swiftly worse.

Recovering, the Indians raced their mounts after the stage. Strangely, they did not fire a shot, nor even unboot their rifles. Looking back, Monk grunted.

"That's bad, they mean to feather us. Low on powder I reckon. Hold your fire till they're hand-close, kid."

The Indians—they were Wind River Cheyenne—came on, whipping out and notching arrows to their squat war bows, their yelping wolf cries standing the cold sweat out on the young shotgun rider's forehead.

Other *Leisure* books by Will Henry:
ONE MORE RIVER TO CROSS
YELLOWSTONE KELLY
RED BLIZZARD
THE LAST WARPATH
WHO RIDES WITH WYATT
CHIRICAHUA
JOURNEY TO SHILOH
MACKENNA'S GOLD
THE CROSSING
THE BEAR PAW HORSES
SAN JUAN HILL
DEATH OF A LEGEND

WILL HENRY

THE HUNTING OF TOM HORN

LEISURE BOOKS NEW YORK CITY

For my sister
AUDREY ALLEN STEWART
a gallant lady

A LEISURE BOOK®

February 1999

Published by special arrangement with Golden West Literary Agency.

Dorchester Publishing Co., Inc.
276 Fifth Avenue
New York, NY 10001

"King Fisher's Road," "A Mighty Big Bandit," "Isley's Stranger," and "The Hunting of Tom Horn" were previously published in *Legends and Tales of the Old West* © Western Writers of America 1962.

ISBN 0-8439-4484-6

Printed in the United States of America.

FOREWORD

The following stories do not conform to the unwritten Law of the Old West. All the men are not valorous, nor all the women without virtue. These are stories of uncertain heroes, clean-cut ladies, talkative undersized cowboys, devious preachers, fumbling gunfighters, brave bullies, honest sheriffs, crooked criminals and a whole host of infamous calumnies against the "code of the frontier" as it has been so courageously delineated from Ned Buntline to Zane Grey to John Wayne and Warner Brothers.

Even with fair warning the reader will not be able to tell the heroes from the villains in these stories.

Worse yet, right will not always win, nor wrong go down in defeat.

Life, as she was lived out there a hundred years ago, wa just about as shiftless and no-account and downright unreliable as today.

So with these stories.

They don't stay inside the accepted fencelines, they don' follow the herd, they don't come out right in the end and most of them don't even start off right in the beginning.

They just drift. Like tumbleweeds. Or tipi-smoke. Or the far thin cry of the coyote.

TRES LOBOS, N. MEX. W.H.
1962

CONTENTS

The Oldest Maiden Lady in New Mexico

I

The shabby cadaver in seat four dozed fitfully. Betimes it snored, betimes it snorted. In between, it breathed like a wind-broken horse. From his vantage in seat sixteen, across the aisle, Euphemistic Smith observed to his companion.

"I declare that's the gustiest one preacher I ever listened to. You reckon the altitude's got him, Windy?"

"Nope," said Windy.

"The pure air mebbe?"

"Nope."

"Likely it's the smoke, then. What with that corn shuck of yours added to the cinders blowing back from the stack and that cob pipe them two Mescalero squaws are trading off on back yonder—phew!—it's something fierce in here."

"Nope," said Windy.

"Could be the lung fever?" asked the wizened cowboy hopefully. "Or mebbe some eastern kind of the epizootic?"

Windy shook his head.

"Nope," he said.

Euphemistic walled his one good eye at him. It wasn't as though he was mad, it was more like he was furious.

"Well," he gritted, "if it ain't the altitude, nor the air, nor yet the smoke, and he ain't feeling poorly, what in tunket *is* the matter with him?"

"Him asleep," said Windy Red Horse, and turned back to staring out the rattling, dirty-paned window.

His white companion studied him, wondering if murdering an Indian came under the same statute as doing in a regular human being. He decided it might get a man up to six months, if done cold-blooded the way he had in mind. Accordingly, he dropped the idea and went to counting telegraph poles on his own.

Things got pretty quiet in the little wooden coach. The Mescalero squaws let their pipe go out. The other half dozen rough-garbed ticket holders catnapped, or allowed their talk to fall off to drowsy monotones. The lone lady white passenger sat motionless in her seat with eyes apparently for nothing but the endless New Mexico landscape.

Without warning, the bullet whined across the mesa.

It smashed through the preacher's window, spat past his up-tilted nose, lodged with a vengeful smack in the pine backrest of the vacant seat beside him. Splinters flew. So did the reverend. For him it was but the matter of an eye flick from nostalgic daydream of far, fair Peoria to the underseat company of his disreputable straw suitcase.

By Tophet, thought an admiring Euphemistic Smith, that pilgrim preacher could certainly galvanate. He had got under cover faster than a lizard off a hot rock. Euphemistic hadn't seen anything move so swift and shameless since the night Hardpan Halloran had gone to treat his saddle gall in the dark and got the horse linamint out of the bunkhouse medicine chest instead of the bear oil.

The little cowboy's interest in the eastern preacher's speed went not unshared. His high-booted countrymen in the coach, none of whom had so much as twitched at the bullet's entrance, now bothered to sit up and take notice.

The ability to act swiftly under fire never went unrecognized in a society of western men. That preacher could move. Such an instant sense of decision was an important asset in the frontier community. It had to be saluted. Euphemistic Smith supplied the eulogy.

"Feller's no ordinary coward," he said.

A few affirmative nods closed the incident for the briefly interested male passengers, but the lone lady in the rear of the coach continued to stare as if enchanted at the musty regions of the seat under which the reverend had vanished. Long after the men had tilted their hat brims back over their eyes, she was still waiting for the missing man of the cloth to reappear. Eventually her vigilance was rewarded.

The reverend's nose made a cautious reconnoissance over the top of his valise. It was followed by a pair of askant brown eyes, anxious and uncertain as a kicked dog's.

At this point it was a five to one doubt that he would have been coaxed to emerge any farther had not Euphemistic Smith noted the young lady's interest in the matter. Euphemistic was the hopeless gallant, the complete chevalier, the incurable Eros and Psyche back to back. What his friend Windy Red Horse more accurately described as, "heap big fool." With a reassuring look for the young lady, he arose to defend the reputation.

"Reverend," he proclaimed, squatting on his heels in the aisle and addressing his remarks "soda voche" so that everybody in the car could hear them, "you can come out now. That there bullet wasn't nothing to worry about. Just old Susie Doklinny full of high purpose and *pulque* juice. This here train gets shot at twice a week regular. Which is to say every time it makes the run up to Silver Mesa from the main line. You see the roadbed cuts through the reservation just along here and them da—them dastardly Mescaleros continues to take it personal. Especially old Susie. She's past seventy and ain't never surrendered. Says Geronimo was a sissy and Cochise a squaw. Claims there ain't been a male Apache in these parts since Mangas Coloradas. Long as there ain't, she reckons it's up to the women to keep the war with the U.S. going."

The preacher came out from behind the suitcase and from under the seat. A conservative man, he stayed on his hands and knees, keeping his head below window level.

"Do you mean to tell me, brother," he inquired, "that the native Indians hereabouts are in the habit of firing at will upon peaceful citizens and, indeed, upon the United States mails?"

"Well, it's true, Reverend, that this here train is carrying some mail for Silver Mesa. Six letters and a pint of bitters for Ma Johnson. Likewise, saving for my friend Windy and them Mescalero squaws yonder, we're all the rest of us entitled to vote for President. All the same, old Susie ain't trying to wing none of us, nor yet bust Ma Johnson's bottle. It's a private fight 'twixt her and the train."

"You are saying, sir, that this old Indian woman tries to shoot a railroad train, per se?"

"I didn't say nothing about Percy," denied Euphemistic, "but she sure does aim to center this here railroad train, yes sir."

"Incredible," said the eastern preacher.

"Worse then that," said Euphemistic Smith, "it's downright hard to believe. However, it's the truth. Likewise, it's the truth we're a mile up the line now. It's plumb safe to stand up and set down in your seat agin."

"Well—"

The tall young clergyman eyed the bullet hole in the window above, shook his head, still clearly needed a clincher. Euphemistic was ready with it.

"Parson," he said sternly, "if you don't rise up and walk you might as well take the next train back to where you come from. Folks out here don't hold with kowtowing to no Apaches. Give a second chance, they might win."

He kept this advice low-pitched so as not to humble the preacher beyond need. But courtesy and counsel were wasted alike. The reverend stayed put. Unhappily, Euphemistic Smith threw in.

"All right," he said, getting up. "I done told you old Susie didn't mean no permanent harm. Took sober, she's sweet as a desert peach. She ain't kilt no peaceful citizens I know of, leastways not sober, she ain't." He paused, wagging his head in genuine sadness. "As for the United States mails," he concluded dispiritedly, "what in he—what in heaven's a bullet hole to a bottle of bitters?"

Still wagging his head, he returned to his seat. Here his friend Windy met him consolingly.

"You like old dog chew bone no teeth," the big Indian said. "Try hard but nothing happen."

"Go to heaven," said Euphemistic, and went back to counting telegraph poles.

This left the big-eyed young lady in the rear of the car the only white person in New Mexico still interested in the pilgrim preacher from Peoria. The latter directly became aware of that interest and made some belated shrift to restore the ministerial dignity in the face of it.

Arising rump first, like a cow, he soberly tipped his hat to the lady. Then he fussed with the suitcase under the seat, as though examining it had been his original reason for diving behind it. Straightening, he tipped his hat a second time, swallowed, bobbed his head nervous and red-necked as a turkey gobbler, turned around and sat down.

Proper respect had to this extent been returned to the cloth, when its wearer's eyes fell again upon the fracture-rimmed bullet hole in the window glass at his shoulder. Groaning shamelessly, the preacher sank back beneath the level of the sill, quivered and lay quiet. Presently he was snoring as draftily as when old Susie Doklinny took her biweekly shot at the Silver Mesa Mail.

This retreat to Morpheus was the smartest move he could have managed. It provided Psyche the opportunity to tiptoe up the aisle to Eros, or, viewed with calluses, Miss Abbie Gresham the chance to sneak up the car and slip into the empty seat behind Euphemistic Smith.

"Euph," she said, "ain't that the new preacher going up to Eagle Nest?"

"I reckon it is, Miss Abbie," answered the little man. "But he won't be let to light long enough to prove it. He's plumb spineless. The boys will rawhide him back down the hill inside forty-eight hours."

The "hill" was the switchback stage road that went from railhead at the mining town of Silver Mesa, to the high valley cattle country above. In that valley up there, there was nothing but half a dozen big ranches, eight, ten thousand cows to go on them, two, three dozen cowboys, chuck wagon and horse wranglers to sit company with those cows. Then there was likely thirty-five or forty little nesters, white, Mexican and mixed blood, scattered out in the stunt timber, with perhaps fifteen or twenty other people bunched up in the town proper. It was a high and a far and a wolf-lonely place, and Eagle Nest was as good a name for its crossroads store, mud-chinked saloon and gaping-windowed, unpainted residential district as any man was going to invent.

Abbie Gresham knew both the boys and the hill Euphemistic Smith was talking about. Glancing now over at the sleeping preacher, she took a sudden resolve that this time no boys were going to rawhide no preacher down no hill. Not if Abbie Gresham could arrange it otherwise. And Abbie allowed she could.

"Mr. Smith," she said, "you got any part of your winter's pay left, or did you blow every cent as usual in your annual spring stroke of nobility toward that poor ailing maiden aunt of yours in Juarez?"

"Why," said Euphemistic, "as a matter of fact I *have* got an estate of ten dollars remaining to me. I hid it out for mad money, then forgot where I'd put it."

"Very well," nodded Abbie. "I am prepared to offer you an opportunity to escape the odium of going back to the Rafter G uncleaned. I will give you three to one that the boys don't buffalo this here sky pilot like they done Parson Skiles."

Euphemistic studied the odds, then their cross-aisle subject.

"I dunno," he said, scratching the unshaven arroyos of his chin. "He's a mite bigger'n Skiles. And a heap younger. Got fair bone but lacks substance. Moves nice though. Hard to make out, really, what's under them sacky clothes. I mean for flesh. For spirit he's ganter than a botflied colt."

"Put up," said Miss Abbie, "or shut up."

"Now wait just a dogbone minute," protested Euphemistic, and got up and went over for a closer look at the sleeper.

"No sir, by jings," he announced, coming back. "It don't figure no way you look at him. I allow there's more sand in one of Windy's biscuits than in that there sky pilot's craw. Ain't that so, Windy?"

The dark-skinned Apache boss of the Rafter G chuck wagon stared at his cowboy friend. He decided to pass the professional insult but not the point of discussion.

"Put-um money where mouth is," he grunted.

"Why you mealy-brained Mescalero, I'd ought to—"

"You'd ought to ante up," Abbie Gresham cut him off, "or get out of the game. If you don't like the odds, we can improve them."

"Heckfire!" snorted the little rider, "it ain't the odds, Abbie. You know better'n that. It's your Paw. You dang well remember what he done the last time he caught me taking odds off'n you. That was the time you give me the Dominicker rooster and nine to five. You tooken the Rhode Island Red, all the time knowing my bird had fell off the roost and like to bust his leg since I seen him last. Not to mention having come down with the rheumy-eyed roup likewise."

"That's a bald-faced lie! I didn't no more know that bird had the roup than you did!"

"Mebbe not, but you sure as sin knew a lot more about who turned him in with them thirty-six hens the day afore the fight, than I did!"

"You always was a bad loser, Euph. And poor pay too."

"Now you listen here, Abbie Gresham, you ain't jaspering me into nothing. You know your Paw's dead set agin gambling in any shape, along with bosky morals in general. Why for you figure he built that cussed schoolhouse to look like a church? And why for you figure he keeps importing these here preachers to try to fill it up Sundays? He ain't been making no money doing it. No sir, he don't cotton to the sporting chance and I ain't abouten to give him no more excuses for docking me another thirty days' pay. Not for you nor any other middle-age spinster in New Mexico. Now you trot back and set down, you hear me?"

Abbie Gresham eyed him hostilely.

"It's for a fact I'm single," she finally said. "But I will be roped and throwed for a slickear, if I'm a spinster!"

"You was twenty-three this spring," said Euphemistic accusingly. "What does that make you, a blooming debyootanty?"

"It don't make me no old maid."

"Hah! My ma had five kids time she was your age."

"Yes, and look at the sample of same setting here fifty-two years old and don't know there's any other letter but 'X' in the alphabet. And wouldn't know that, happen he didn't have to, to sign up for his forty a month and found."

Euphemistic took that tragically. He scrunched down like a wet dog that has just tried to slip into the warm kitchen and had the door slammed on his nose. Abbie had a heart as hard as summer butter. She melted down and ran all over him.

"Oh, Euph!" she cried. "You know what I mean. I don't want to get married and have no kids till I can be sure they'll be book-larnt and brung up halfways fit. Paw's got the same notion. That's why he built that school to look churchy and why he keeps bringing in preachers. He knows Eagle Nest can't afford no regular teacher, so he goes on along fetching in these sky pilots from back east, hoping one of them will hair-up and stand off the locals long enough to bring *some* education into the valley. Religion? Pshaw! Mord Gresham ain't got no more religion nor a Mescalero medicine man. It's education he's after, and me too. Now you going to ante up, or ain't you?"

"Well," allowed Euphemistic Smith, "eddication's like mother love, or a married lady's morals. A man don't dast question neither one in public. You come out agin eddication you just ain't going to get elected in this country. Same with sky piloting. A man might better stand in favor of being kind to horse thieves or giving free *tequila* to the Injuns. I'd druther run on a ticket of kicking stray dogs and pistol-whipping little old ladies than to utter a deroggerary word about book learning or Bible preaching."

He paused, scraping at his chin again.

"It's no bet, gal. That slat-ribbed galoot yonder don't stand a leppy calf's chance of wintering through in Eagle Nest, but I ain't taking your money all the same."

"All the same you ain't being honest either, are you, Euph?" asked the gray-eyed girl. "Admit it, you're yellar."

"Clean through," grinned the little cowboy. "When it comes to betting agin Mordecai Gresham's old-maid daughter, I ain't got the gumption of a squashed toad."

The two eyed each other while the wooden coach swayed and bounced over the mountain roadbed and the ore cars rattled and banged their empty bins along behind the coach and, up ahead, the ancient diamond-stack locomotive hissed and sparked and made its usual threat to blow up on the Silver Mesa Grade.

"Well," said Abbie Gresham softly, "if you won't bet into my raise, how about staying in the game just for old time's sake? You know, Euph, sort of to keep the other players honest."

"You mean back your bet on this preacher feller agin Clebe McSween?"

"I didn't say nothing about Clebe McSween."

"You don't need to say nothing about Clebe McSween. He's going to be there when this here preacher lights down whether you say anything abouten him or not. Besides, he likely knows your Paw sent for this new one. Ain't much goes on around Eagle Nest Clebe don't know."

"Well, he don't know about Paw sending for this preacher because Paw didn't send for him—I did."

"*You* did?"

"I sure did. Paw, he don't even know this preacher's alive. I ordered this one out all by my lonesome."

"Abbie, your Paw will peel the hide right off'n you. You know he don't cotton to nobody giving no orders saving himself. Not even you."

"This here preacher ain't Paw's affair, he's mine."

"I'll plead you was took temporarily unsanitary," said the worried cowboy. "I'll tell your Paw you was took with a fever in town. I'll say that you been out'n your head for forty-four hours and that Doc Abernathy said to keep you dog-chained in a dark room for ten days before—"

"You will do no such thing. I'll handle Paw, but I may need a little help with Clebe. You know how he is."

"Lord, Lord," moaned Euphemistic Smith, "who in the whole south half of New Mexico don't?"

"You're with me then, like always?"

"Here." Euphemistic reached inside his hatband and dug out the limply folded ten-dollar bill. "Take the blasted money. You can have my horse and saddle too, and my book of Spanish geetar lessons and—"

"Euph, I don't want nothing but your moral support. Now calm down and act your age. I ain't asking you to take an ax haft to Clebe. I just want your word you won't sandbag me, happen I have to bet my pile on the preacher."

Windy Red Horse turned from his window and impaled his small friend with a pure Apache look.

"Missy Abbie mean all you got do keep him big mouth shut," he translated disgustedly.

"That's it!" cried the girl delightedly. "Thank you, *schichobe*." She leaned quickly forward, placing an airy kiss on the huge Indian's cheek, and was gone back down the aisle before Euphemistic Smith could haul in his breath to cuss out either one of them.

"*Ho-hah!*" grunted the startled redman, feeling his cheek. "How you like that? She call me 'old friend' in Apache. By gols, that something!"

His white companion slid low in his seat, pulled his shapeless hat far down over his injured expression.

"Brother," he seethed, "it for sure as sulfur smells bad, is!"

II

The Silver Mesa Mail topped the grade, smoked and clattered on across the juniper and piñon flats toward the town at a kidney-pounding eighteen miles an hour. All its passengers, save one, were subdued by now. Even Windy Red Horse and the Mescalero squaws had joined the white brother in the state of somnolent shock induced by the daylong deadliness of the Mail's wounded goat lope over the best unballasted roadbed west of El Paso. Every other tie was a different size and they were all laid without benefit of fill, right as they were pitched down off the construction cars. The rails were reclaims from a dozen other short-line mining camp runs, and had more kinks in them than a cold bronc's back. You had to be young to ride the Silver Mesa Mail and stay conscious. Abbie Gresham was young. And she was still studying the leggy preacher she had ordered out all the way from Peoria, Illinois, in the United States.

He certainly had graded herd-run for get-up, she decided. And, though mightily fast afoot, he wasn't sizable enough to brace up to Cleburne McSween, nose and nose. Which same was not altogether surprising since Clebe took a size 20 shirt and a 13 boot.

This preacher fellow, though, he did have something about him.

He stood fairly tall above his bunions and didn't pack any excess tallow. He was rangy, sort of. With wrists like the knucklebones on a four-year-old steer, and hands the size of stove lids. Gangly, yes, and lanky, yet he had got around like a broom-swatted cat when old Susie had shied that rifle shot through the window. Somehow, from some vestigial shred of female devilment going back to the watery days when the world was young and men, to their gentle mates' eternal delight, were still men, Abbie Gresham wound up her inspection of the new sky pilot with the distinct suspicion that the good Lord had not cut the gawky figure of the Reverend Able John Arkwright precisely to fit the cloth.

Lulled by the she-animal fascinations inherent to this deduction, she, too, was presently asleep. The next time she saw her personally imported apostle in action was in the matter of his boarding the stage for Eagle Nest.

The Eagle Nest & Upper Valley Stageline Co., Fat Jaime Gonzalez, Prop., had its entire corporate assets—one prehistoric platform wagon and four harness-broke saddle broncs—lined up and ready to go in front of Ma Johnson's boardinghouse when the Mail chuffed up to the depot and died on schedule—seven hours and fifty-five minutes late.

The regular passengers for Eagle Nest, Abbie, Euph Smith and Windy Red Horse, were quickly off the train and piled aboard the "Eagle Nest Express." But the new preacher had overslept the stop and, when he did wake up and stampede out onto the freight dock, failed to recognize the contraption over in front of the boardinghouse as a stagecoach.

It was, Abbie Gresham allowed, a reasonable confusement.

That particular side-seat platform wagon was a crossbred sort of a Spider Surrey designed originally to double as a pickup hack for hotel or resort passengers and, with the single side-facing rear seat removed, as a hearse in communities lacking the stature to supply enough business to warrant the genuine article. With its nine-by-three-foot bed, its black leatherette top, Brewster green fringe, Burgundy red body panels, chrome yellow gear and scrofulous cowhide curtains, it was a miscarriage of coach-crafting justice which no mortal born east of Dodge City could ever hope to connect with a western U.S. stage-line operation. Not if he stood on that depot platform until Silver Mesa grew wings and sprouted a halo. Or the Republicans got elected in Texas.

''Yoo-hoo, Reverend!'' Abbie hallooed across Main Street in a mountain contralto trained to outbellow a mother cow at the branding fire. ''Over thisaway by the boardinghouse!''

Her friendly grin faded as she saw the long-shanked preacher wave back and smile and start across the street in the direction of another house which was not of the boarding variety.

''No! no!'' she called. ''Not there! not there! Over here, you danged foo—'' She stopped herself short of the sacrilege and drew breath to start over again. But it was too late. Fat Jaime had waited all he had a mind to.

With a Chihuahua squall for his wheelers to proceed ''*mas pronto*,'' he laid about the ears of his leaders with a fifteen-foot Durango bullwhip which he handled like a schoolgirl's quirt.

His four mismated chargers hit their collars cowboy-style—from a droop-headed doze to a back-humping run in three jumps—and the Reverend Arkwright was left strangling amid an acrid cloud of horse dust and disillusionment, smack in the middle of Main Street. The manner in which he emerged from this eclipse made *cantina* talk in Silver Mesa from then until snow flew.

With no outcry of foul play, in fact with no audible complaint whatever, he proceeded to run down on foot a four-horse hitch of prairie mustangs in full gallop. Once abreast of the platform wagon's front wheels, he seized the seat-box handirons, vaulted up beside Fat Jaime, relieved him of the lines by direct action. Then he lifted all four horses practically clear of their tugs and threw them back on their haunches for a 26-foot sliding stop which flung Fat Jaime down between the wheelers, Miss Abbie into Euph Smith's lap, and set a local record for dead-run haul-ups which Fat Jaime spent the rest of the summer trying to equal and never did come closer to than 38 feet. And even doing that he turned over the wagon and killed eleven chickens and a sleeping dog. While the chickens didn't matter, the dog was a good friend of Fat Jaime's, and the little Mexican stager never did outrightly forgive the *yanqui ministro* his patent responsibility for the affair. However, that was six months later.

For the present Fat Jaime lay where he had fallen between the quivering rumps of the wheel team. There, eyes tightly closed, he kept muttering over and over again, "*Madre Dios, cuatro caballos, cuatro caballos!*"

"Now, friend," the tall Yankee preacher called down to him in a pleasantly diffident voice, "if you will cease importuning the Lord and climb back up here, we shall call for Divine guidance and embark at once for Eagle Nest. Ah no, friend—" he remonstrated, as Fat Jaime crawled back up and reached for the lines. "The Lord and I shall pilot this chariot the remainder of the way." Whereupon, and before his companion could object, he tossed the prized bullwhip into the dirt, clucked gently to the leaders, advised the shaking wheelers to labor for the Saviour and sent the surprised hitch into a honey-smooth road lope that would have done company credit to any six Wells Fargo horses ever foaled.

"*Quita!*" breathed Fat Jaime. "I don't believe it."

And with that Spanish-American disclaimer, the run to Eagle Nest was under way.

Behind the rocking driver's box, the owner of the grayest, blackest-lashed eyes in the Territory of New Mexico clung to the iron handles of the side seat and wondered joltingly how tandem life in the parsonage might be.

On the box, itself, the object of her intentions had his mind set hard upon the more Christian work of putting the fear of the Lord into the waiting wilderness folk of Upper Valley. It was clear, thought the Reverend Arkwright, that the hour for local redemption had grown pressing late. If these isolated lost souls were to be reaped and gathered in time, all haste would be required with the harvest.

Jutting his considerable chin, Parson Skiles's replacement again chided his wiry teams to increase their labors, guided their gallant response around the first hairpin turn of "the hill" and on up the steepening track beyond. Six hours later, nearing the brisk summer midnight, the little mustangs topped the last rise in Jackpine Pass. Easing over the summit, they began the glad trot down the long valley straightaway toward the distant twinkle of the red coal-oil lantern hung both as a public service and a business announcement in the single unscrubbed window of Mestizo Marie's Soledad Saloon.

Thus to Eagle Nest determinedly astride the driver's box of the regular stage from Silver Mesa, came the Reverend Able John Arkwright. His entire high purpose was to get himself behind the altar in the least possible time. But with him came Miss Abigail Kate Louise Gresham. And her entire purpose was to get him in front of same, with the likewise proviso as to no unnecessary delays.

Looking first at the new sky pilot, then at the maiden lady heiress to the Rafter G, Euphemistic Smith cocked his good eye at Windy Red Horse and said, "I will give you ten to one, and you take the preacher."

Replied Windy Red Horse, after due study of the odds and the specimen upon which they were offered.

"No thanks. Me no bet-um on dead horse."

III

Able John Arkwright stood in the middle of downtown Eagle Nest watching the two little dashboard lamps of the Rafter G buckboard disappear into the darkness of the Upper Valley road. When they had done so, he turned to survey his new parish, a feeling of some measurable loss pervading him.

He could not account for this feeling except to imagine it might be because the homely small man with the grotesquely bent legs had been kind to him on the train. It could certainly not be the gargantuan Indian nor the gray-eyed girl for whom he suffered these pangs of parting. The former was about as sociable as a sawlog and the latter, from the grammatical crudities of her speech and the sunburned straightness of her figure, about as exciting as a seventeen-year-old boy.

No, it must be the diminutive fellow with the weasel's face and baleful-fierce eye. "Euph" he had heard the girl call him. The Indian was Windy, the girl, Abbie. She was obviously the daughter of the man who had corresponded with his missionary group in regard to a schoolteacher-pastor for the mountain community of Eagle Nest, New Mexico; a place so remote that not even the Postal Department knew where it was, all mail for Eagle Nest being simply sent to Silver Mesa stamped "Please Forward." As with the U.S. Mails, so with the Upper Valley stage-line passengers. They were forwarded and deposited at Eagle Nest strictly c/o General Delivery. After that it was up to them.

Turning now to examine these conditions of delivery, Able John shuddered and set his long jaw.

Nothing could be as bad as this place appeared to be.

It had to be the long train ride. Or the strain of driving up "the hill." Or the nervous depletion of the demented old Apache woman firing at him through the coach window. Perhaps it was even the unexpected lonesomeness caused by the three Rafter G people leaving him so abruptly upon his obstinate refusal of the girl's warm insistence that he come along and stay at her father's ranch. What she had actually said was, "Paw will be mightily shook if you don't show on schedule," but he had understood her to mean that her father was expecting him to share the Rafter G bed and board, as had Parson Skiles and the others before him. But Able John Arkwright was otherwise determined.

It was his opinion that the common mistake of his predecessors had been to permit too close a relationship with these strayed New Mexican lambs. The successful frontier pastor was the one who could stand apart from his sheep yet be ever ready with his rod and his staff to comfort them while, at the same time, his ministerial dignity served as a constant reminder that he was the shepherd and they, surely, but the flock.

The Reverend "Able John" as he liked to think of himself—it was friendly yet held the important reserve—was not quite the eastern Ichabod these rough people had plainly taken him for. He knew, or directly sensed, that he had made a poor start in diving under the train seat. If the paramount dignity were to be restored, the soonest start was the best one.

He had also overheard Euph's reference to the local Brom Bones. The threat here was patent. If he were to rise above it, he would need to be extremely agile in mind as well as motion. Fortunately, his teachings had provided for just this emergency.

The trick, according to his course in missionary practices, was to get in the first smite with bullies of this stripe. There was nearly always a lusty Ned-raiser like Cleburne McSween to be dealt with in the uncultured outland community. The ways and means of handling such muscular troublemakers were severally set down in the instruction booklet furnished Able John with his doctorate and his train ticket: "*The Modern American Apostle: a Manual of Useful Advice to the Neophyte Minister in His New Life Upon the Trans-Mississippi Frontier; Conveniently Indexed and Arranged For Handy Reference.*"

Able John now felt in his frock coat pocket for the reassurance that the slim volume was still there. It was, and he took a good stout grip on it, feeling immensely fortified thereby. Then he took another look at Eagle Nest.

"Lord God of Israel," he pleaded aloud, "gird up my loins."

IV

"As Heaven is my witness," proclaimed Mestizo Marie, "I will swear it. Ask Sanchez. Or Hardpan. Or Del Norte. They were all here."

The two new patrons of the Soledad to whom she spoke, a long tall cowboy and a wide short cowboy, turned to stare at the three named witnesses.

"It's true," said Hardpan Halloran, overstocked on thirst and sold out on credit at the moment. "I seen it. Anyways, you know Marie don't lie. Not a woman of her standing, no sir."

"No more beer, Hardpan," said Marie. "Not a drop till you pay up. And you ain't talking to no shorthorn strangers. Mile High and Stumpy wasn't calved last week, nor out of no winterfed cows. Next witness."

Sanchez, a slim, appealingly dangerous-looking Mexican with teeth the texture and brilliance of Raritonga pearls, put down his *tequila*, testified softly.

"*Es verdad, Señores*. What *La Patrona* has said, this is precisely the manner in which it came to pass."

"Del Norte," demanded Marie.

The squat Mescalero chief, who could not be served the fruit of the bottle and who sat in a far corner of the barroom spearing peaches out of a Number 2½ can with a ten-inch wooden-handled butcher knife, answered stoutly for the State.

"*Ho-hah*, you betcha."

The Irish-Indian-Mexican, née *mestizo*, proprietress of the Soleded drew a prideful breath.

"*Quita!*" she exclaimed, "imagine it! A man of the church, even though but a *yanqui padre* and not of the true Faith, coming into a dungheap like this and asking to be put up for the night. It don't hardly seem possible."

"By gum," agreed Stumpy, "it sure don't. Seems like a man in his business oughten to know a red li—say," he interrupted himself hopefully, "you reckon the pore critter's color-blind?"

"Not hardly," doubted Hardpan Halloran, self-made student of the mother tongue and only man in Upper Valley owning and operating a dictionary. "When the feller first come in, he bows to Marie and says, 'Excuse me, sister, but I seen your rubious beacon from afar and was given to hope I might find lodging where it shone.' Now I will give you a wrote-out guarantee that that there 'rubious' don't mean green. I ain't aiming to dispugn no innocent sky pilots, mind you, I'm only saying this here one is full aware of what color makes a bull mad."

"Son of a gun," said Stumpy. "Even if you allow he's plumb igorant of the facts of life, you got to admire his gall. It ain't been six months since Parson Skiles give up the Holy Ghost and here's this new feller all set to step in and start spouting the same sentiments which got Skiles shagged off down the hill on such a high lope. I'll swan, ain't Old Man Gresham ever going to get it into his rock head that the folks up thisaway ain't in the market for salivation?"

"Dunno," opined Hardpan. "Mr. Gresham's a tolerable determined man. Long as the supply of preachers holds out, I reckon he'll keep sending east for refills. Appears to me, though, like they was getting perilous close to the bottom of the keg. This here new one is some gant. I'd say he was wintered through on prickly pear and catalog paper."

"Another preacher in Eagle Nest," muttered Stumpy, still shaking his head. "That's the third one in less'n two years. It ain't Christian."

"Nope," agreed his friend Mile High, "but it's the Gospel. Iffen Marie says she seen it with her own two eyeballs, you got to accept it as ipso fatso evidence."

"*Your* credit is still good," Marie informed him dourly. "You don't need to be spraying none of that two-bit slickum around here. What'll it be, Mile High? The usual?"

The tall cowboy stood scratching his head, still thinking about that new preacher walking square into and asking to be rented a bed in the only—well, in the only double-duty saloon between Silver Mesa and Socorro.

Finally he gave it up and nodded to his hostess.
"Yup. Two beers and a buttermilk chaser."

V

Able John strode on beneath the starlight.

Underfoot, the red dust of the Upper Valley road made no sound. Overhead, the mountain night returned the complement of velvet stillness. Able John had never listened to such a big quiet. Not in his entire life had he been so close to actually feeling the presence of the Maker. There was something in the black wine of the air, the buttressed peaks ragged against the encircling sky-line, the lantern-bright wink and glitter of the stars, the scent of sage and pine and summer hay standing, flower-dotted, in the rail-fenced meadow that put a man more in mind of his God than all the words and warnings in both Testaments.

The experience of his brief journey by wagon road in the held breath of a summer's night 7,000 feet up in the piñon country of southern New Mexico was a revelation to the loose-striding young preacher from Peoria.

Nothing in his Bible studies had prepared him for this over whelming contact with the works of the Creator. Twenty-six years a farm boy in the palm-flat cornlands of the Illinois River bottoms had converted but not convinced him. This was his virginal realization that the Lord actually had created the earth. It was a sobering yet a wondrously exhilarating discovery.

Nonetheless, his time for spiritualizing was limited by temporal demand.

At 7,000 feet, even of an August night, the air grows sharply chill near one A.M. Also the lithe young body, no matter how stimulated, grows weary at last. Able John had not known true rest in the eleven days by stage and rail from Peoria to El Paso. Now, although the psyche soared, the soma plummeted. He was vastly relieved to see ahead the gaunt, wind-leaned structure of the Upper Valley district school.

Going in by the unhinged gate, he started up the grassy path. He walked but a few steps, then faltered. Putting down his straw valise, he straightened to peer uncertainly at the abandoned building.

At first it appeared as desolate of life as the hinder surface of some frozen planet, yet, as Able John watched, its gelid lone someness began to thaw.

To begin with it was the inquiring friendliness of a small tufted owl calling *tah-hoo? tah-hoo?* from its sentinal perch inside the tilted belfry. Then it was the chittering flutter-about of several curious, sharp-eared mountain bats drawn from their raftered roost within the building proper. Lastly it was the bright returning peer of the two tenant pack rats poised on the dusty threshold, undecided as to what the bony apparition in the outer yard might be, but determined to welcome its arrival into their cloistered lives, regardless.

Able John was restored of his strength.

"At least," he recited under his breath, "I am made to feel not as a stranger here." He tried to think of the appropriate scripture relating to man's communion with the birds of the air and the beasts of the field but could not. After a moment he smiled and said aloud.

"I thank you, small friends. May I enter within? I have traveled from afar and am sore wearied."

At the sound of his voice the pack rats vanished, the bats skittered away, the owl left the belfry and floated off into the night. They will be back, thought Able John, and picked up his suitcase, pleased to suspect he would not lack entirely for creature companionship through the remaining dark. It was when the sun-grayed treads of the doorstep complained beneath his ascending weight that the surmise was given certain confirmation.

The growl was low, animal, and unfriendly. It came from directly inside the partly open door, for the rusted knob of which Able John had been about to reach. Instead, he wheeled to flee.

But the brute within had gotten his scent by now. The warning growl became a whine of entreaty. The plea was accompanied by the thumping of a plumed tail upon a wooden floor.

"A dog?" said Able John. "Abiding in this manless haunt?"

His reply was another whine, another series of hopeful tail thumps.

He found a sulfur match in his frock coat pocket. Striking and cupping it, he put his head in at the door.

Lying before him in a dark welter of its own blood was an emaciated blue merle and mixed brindle sheepdog of ancestry as varied as his coat color. But wherever found, and in whatever hues, the sheepdog is always and unmistakably the sheepdog. Able John knew the type. He knew also, before the match sputtered out, that this particular sheepdog had need of human friend beyond ordinary measure.

"Just so, boy," he said quietly, easing in past the door and stepping over the dog. "Have faith while I search for light."

Presently his eyes adjusted to the inner gloom of the school house and he saw at its far end a rickety teacher's desk and chair, backed by a blackboard and a yellowed wall map of the world. Going forward, he rummaged in the musty top drawer of the desk and was rewarded with three Parker crayolas, a broken pencil, some several assorted marbles and a confiscated slingshot, twenty or thirty dried beans, an empty bottle of cinnamon oil, a rabbit's foot, a compoundly fractured yardstick and, as he had hoped, a stub of tallow candle.

Lighting the candle, he returned to the dog.

"Seek and ye shall find," he told him, and bent to examine the shattered leg.

It was a cruel wound. Some hours old, it was apparently caused by a rifle or revolver bullet. The radius, or front longbone of the left foreleg was very badly broken near its juncture with the humerus or upper arm of the shoulder. The dog had been able to reach the site with his tongue, hence minimum infection had developed. But to reduce the fracture and to splint it in such manner as to prevent crippling or, indeed, to prevent gangrene and so save the leg at all, was going to require the help of both the Lord and Able John's limited medical education.

Like most missionary-evangelists sent out to the frontier, he had received elementary instruction in minor surgery and asepsis. But this poor brute's nearly sundered limb would have challenged a Harley Street physician. Yet he was God's creature and Able John the Lord's servant. Inasmuch as ye have done it to the least of these . . .

Able John reached for and opened his suitcase. Inside was revealed the spartan store of church, school and personal books, small linens, past life reminders, and the heterogeneous oddments of medical and dental supply which composed his workaday arsenal for the spiritual assault on Eagle Nest and Upper Valley.

He selected swab, splinting stick, wound compress and bottle of carbolic. Then he removed his coat, tore his shirt into yard long bandage strips. With that he was ready. Placing his big knuckled hand upon the watchful dog's head, he inquired softly.

"Art with me in spirit, good dumb and faithful friend?"

The dog whined, licked the ever-so-easy hand, lay back upon the floor and was still.

"Trust in the Lord," said Able John Arkwright, and took up his swab and bottle of carbolic.

VI

"Honest to mercy, Clebe, I tooken the shovel and went out yonder to do what you told me. But he was plumb gone. There wasn't nothing in sight but a line of bleedy tracks staggering off over the ridge."

Cleburne McSween scowled, gulped down the greasy beef *taco* which was his eleventh for breakfast that morning, and said, "You're a liar, Clyde. I belted that critter good. He went down like he'd been stricknined. Cripes, he wasn't no farther from me than you could throw a yearling bull. Now you get on back out there and bury him like I ordered."

Clyde, the baby McSween, only fourteen and six-two, tucked his chin stubbornly against his brisket.

"Cain't do it," he insisted. "Critter's gone."

Clebe shoved back from the table. He fetched down the family scattergun from over the kitchen door.

"All right," he said, "let's see how far he's gone."

Clyde hesitated.

"You want I should call in Collis or Chauncey?" he asked.

"Naw. They both went off afore sunup to chouse them *ladino* steers out'n the north cedar brakes. Where's Cyril Charley?"

"Messing with that tick-bit sick elk he found and drug in on the woodsled. I'll swear, Clebe, that Cyril Charley he ain't exactly took with the brights."

"No," agreed Clebe, kicking open the door, "he ain't. But what he don't savvy about doctoring livestock and running a critter's track line you could paint on the head of a pin with a barn brush. Go fetch him. He'll do, short of somebody with good sense."

"Sure he will. But I wisht, all the same, that he would leave off lugging home and fooling around with all them pore sick and crippled wild things. It gives a feller the fantods."

Clebe uglied-up his scowl.

"Clyde," he said, "I done told you we ain't entering him in no first-prize pupil contests. Now you go fetch him like I done told you. We got to track down that chicken-killing Injun sheepdawg afore he gets out'n the county."

"I'm agoing," said Clyde. "But I still say he was a right nice little Apache sheepdawg, and no stock-killer. No sir, not him. I wouldn't have minded having him for my own dawg."

"No," accused Clebe. "Nor you wouldn't have minded giving him a leg-up and a boost on his way over the near hill, neither!"

"That's a brockle-faced falsehood! I never teched him!"

"Clyde."

"Huh?"

"You going to fetch Cyril Charley, or ain't you?"

"Sure. But you shouldn't have shot that little dawg. He was only hongry and alooking for a bait of grub."

"All right; he should of looked somewheres else than my pullet roost."

"Yeah? Well, you should've looked at his tracks afore you pulled down on him, too. They wasn't the same as them under the roost. Them was coyote tracks 'neath that pullet pole."

Clebe set himself.

"You aiming to tell me I don't know a dawg track from a coyote print, boy?" he rumbled, narrow-eyed.

Clyde took heed. He weighed his older brother on the

hoof and carefully. After a cautious bit he shook his curly head. Clebe was still Clebe and had him by three inches and sixty pounds.

"No sir," he replied. "I'm aiming to go out and fetch Cyril Charley. What horse you want, the black?"

"Naw, he's stove. Get the bay."

"Yes, sir." Clyde was out the door, bawling toward the haybarn back of the corral, in something like two seconds.

"Cyril Charley? Cyril Charley? Where the blazes you at? Th'ow a hull on Clebe's bay and lock the barn. We're agoing coyote hunting."

VII

Able John yawned, stretched, winced, sat up.

Sleeping in the rat-filled straw of the openfront horse shed out behind the schoolhouse, with nothing but a splint-legged sheepdog to keep him warm, had not conduced to a limber awakening. Yet once the eyes were opened, once the realization of the waiting work returned, all small problems vanished. There were also the pure glories of the morning, itself, to give confidence. The mountain sunshine and birdsong, taken with deep breaths of juniper and pine air and spiked with the perfume of artemesia sage and gramma meadow grass, would have stirred the pulses of a corpse. Able John thrilled to these heady aromas and scintillations all about him and called out to his companion:

" 'Wake! for the Sun, who scatter'd into flight
The Stars before him from the Field of Night
Drives Night along with them from Heav'n, and
strikes
The Sultan's Turret with a Shaft of Light!' "

The dog looked at him as though to say he was downright sorry he hadn't had a good night. Able John patted him on the head. "Omar Khayyam, the FitzGerald translation," he explained belatedly. But the dog didn't care. In fact he wasn't very strong for the Rubiyat or Omar in any version.

"*Aaarrrowww,*" he whined, and reached out his sound paw. Able John accepted it, and they shook with feeling.

"Well," said the latter, "the good Lord gave us this shining day to improve. Let us now see how we may reward Him for the opportunity. What was it the poet said:

" 'Think that day lost whose low descending sun
Sees from thy hand no worthy action done'?"

The dog didn't know what it was the poet had said, nor, for that matter, what the preacher had said either. So he just cocked his wise head and whined again and the answer suited Able John right fine.

With some slight difficulty he got himself up from the wrinkled hay, and the dog, obeying the example, managed a brave three legged arisement of his own. At his first gingerly step to follow Able John off, however, he yelped at the sharp reminder from his stiffened wound. Able John looked around, returned swiftly to take him up in his arms.

"Lean thou on my heart," he advised him, and started on around to the front of the schoolhouse.

Inside the structure, he made a bed of his coat on top the teacher's desk and put the dog carefully upon it.

"Abide there," he said. "Anon, we shall forage abroad for sustenance. Presently there is other work to do."

He paused, surveying the bat litter, pack rat tracks,

spiderwebs, dry rot and roof leak water stains of the once respectable Upper Valley District School. The prospect firmed his blue unshaven jaw, put the light of battle into his kindly brown eye.

"Rest thou in good comfort," he said to the dog. "We must consider what is to be done to refurbish this abandoned house of the Master. It must be once more habilitated for the study both of the Saviour's words, and those of learned man, himself. Be of firm belief, friend, and lie tacit. I shall return forthwith."

"Well, now," contradicted a rough voice from the front door way, "I reckon that ain't rightly so, stranger. Seeing as how you ain't going no place, how could you be acoming back?"

Able John wheeled about, more as though he had been stabbed than startled.

"Oh, I beg your pardon, brother," he quavered at the towering black-haired human brute posed just inside the door. "I fear I did not hear you come in."

"You ain't going to hear me got out, neither, less'n you rustle your backside out from atween me and that chicken-killing dawg," said Clebe. "Now get!"

With the order, he elevated the ten-gauge double he carried, bringing it to bear on Able John's navel.

"All right, boys!" he roared. "Come along in; the tracks end here."

Able John gasped again, as two more human animals the general pelage and proportion of the first, clambered in through the front windows to flank the shotgun toter.

"Good Gawd," said the younger of the two newcomers compassionately, and peering at Able John's ribby torso. "He's ganter than the pore dawg hisself. You hongry and homeless, too, mister?"

Able John's limpid brown eye fired up. He swept a lank arm accusingly at Clyde McSween.

"Young sir," he informed him, "you are in the house

of the Father; therefore take not His name in vain.''

''What'd he say?'' Clyde appealed to Clebe.

''Pore critter's addled some,'' answered the latter. ''Thinks this here is a church. Belfry fooled him most likely.''

''Don't give a hoot what fooled him,'' put in Cyril Charley.

''He's a sure enough heller on boarding up busted dawg laigs.'' He stared past Able John at the neat splinting of the sheepdog's broken forelimb. ''You a doctor, mister?'' he inquired with slack jawed admiration.

''Of Divinity,'' admitted Able John modestly.

''It's a kind of candy,'' Clebe explained aside to Clyde. ''Sort of like fudge, only white. Got nuts inside. I et some Abbie slang together onct. It weren't bad.''

''Sure!'' enthused Clyde. ''I remember that batch. She give me a chaw of it too. Light and floaty as angel spit, it were. Say,'' he asked respectfully of Able John, ''you a sure enough candymaker, mister?''

''I am a minister of the gospel,'' replied the latter, and stiffened to stare them all three down.

They didn't stare worth beans.

''Holy Moses!'' thundered Cleburne McSween, ''Old Man Gresham's brung in another sky pilot!''

Clyde bobbed his head in dubious agreement, but Cyril Charley backed off.

''Ain't got no clawhammer coat,'' he charged suspiciously.

Able John turned to the desk. ''Excuse me,'' he said to the dog, and took up the coat from beneath him and donned it with consummate dignity.

''By jings!'' cried Clyde, mightily pleased, ''it's a clawhammer sure enough!''

''Yup,'' admitted Clebe, ''no denying it. I reckon he's the real article, all right.''

''Aw shucks,'' mourned Cyril Charley, ''that's

mighty hard doings. I'd hoped he was a people doctor and could smarten me some for cutting on them animiles of mine."

"Hellsfire," said Clyde, "you cain't have everything."

"By damn," affirmed Clebe soberly, "that's so."

At the first echo of the profanity, Able John threw up his hands, pulpit-style, and laid into them.

"Brethren," he demanded sternly, "was not this desolate shelter once called the Upper Valley Community Church?"

The brothers McSween thought it over, finally nodded, yes, it had been so called. On Sundays, that was. Other five days of the week it had been the Upper Valley District School, and on Saturdays the Eagle Nest Township Meeting and Dancehall.

Able John inclined his lately unshorn locks.

"No matter," he said, "about the other days of the week. Did not Brother Skiles hold services here of a Sabbath?"

"He means did Parson Skiles preach here on Sundays," Clebe explained for the other two, and all three then nodded together that, yes, this had, indeed, also been the case.

"Well, then," inquired Able John severely, "would not this fact of prior devotional usage still render this humble building the House of the Lord on Sabbath days?"

The three deciphered this at length, then nodded once more in family unison that perhaps this assumption might additionally be granted—on Sundays.

"Very well!" triumphed Able John, a righteous gleam in his soft brown eye. "And precisely what day is this one upon which we stand foregathered here?"

Clebe frowned thoughtfully, and started a careful count on his fingers. Clyde and Cyril Charley watched him, their lips moving laboriously with his. Four times the leader of the McSweens remade the count. Each time it came out the same. In the end he could not deny the patent truth.

"By Gawd, boys," he announced to his waiting brothers, "he's got us fair and square. Hats off and no more cussing."

The three stood awkwardly for a moment, big hats doffed to chest levels. Then Clebe put his hat back on and gestured with the shotgun.

"Amen, Reverend. It being Sunday don't save the dawg. Get out'n the way."

The chill steel clinking of the ten-gauge's two big outside hammers being put on cock ran a rash of goose bumps up the knobby spine of Able John Arkwright. But he stood to the age-old oath of Aesculapius as though he had invented it.

"As the Lord is my witness," he proclaimed, spreading his gaunt form to shield the patient on the desk, "ye shall not bring harm to this poor dumb beast of the field."

"How's that?" queried Clebe.

"If you mean to shoot the dog, sir," said Able John, "you will have to shoot through me to do it."

Clebe scratched his head, studying the angle.

"Cuss it all, Reverend," he said at last, "way you're standing don't much leave a feller much choice. Reckon I got to drill th'ough you to hit paydirt in the dawg. Mind you, it ain't nothing personal."

"Friend, you wouldn't do it!"

"Now, now, no need to fret, Reverend. I ain't agoing to rush you. Take your time. I'll count three. *One—*"

Able John broke and bolted.

Racing around the desk he threw one arm about the wounded sheepdog, set the other desperate hand to opening the desk drawer in an instinctive search for some weapon of defense.

Clebe shook his head.

"Hiding ahint the critter don't change nothing but the order in which you get blowed apart, Parson. *Two—*"

"Dang it, Reverend," urged Clyde, "do as he says. That double is bored fullchoke both tubes. She's loaded with Number 1 buck. You will look like somebody drove a snubbing post th'ough your brisket, sideways."

"Hold on, Clebe," objected Cyril Charley in turn. "We had ought to make mortal certain he ain't a doctor afore you splatter him. It'd be a sinful shame to waste a doctor."

"Hesh up your mouth," said Cleburne McSween, and took aim.

Able John threw a last despairing glance at the contents of the desk drawer. His choice of weapons lay between the remnant of broken yardstick and the contraband slingshot. The possible combination of the latter with one of the dusty marbles among which it reposed—huge, kiln-fired "clayies," as big as horse chestnuts, and bullet-heavy—tempted him momentarily to combat. But he was the servant of the Lord and this was the Sabbath. Bloodshed was out of the question. He put aside the passing weakness and stayed strong. Forcing the slingshot out of mind, he committed both arms to holding the dog, returned his trust sonorously to its proper channel.

"Desist!" he exhorted Clebe. "In the name of Sweet Charity, lay down your arms!"

"Yes," said a dry voice from the same doorway which had admitted the principal McSween. "And if Sweet Charity don't work, try Abigail Gresham."

It was Clebe's turn to spin about as though hit in the hip with a hayfork.

"Abbie!" he shouted.

"Cleburne McSween," she ordered softly, "put down that shotgun."

Clebe firmed up.

"I ain't agoing to do it," he said. "That Mescalero mutt kilt them barred rock pullets you give me for my birthday. I'm agoing to cut him in two. Asides, you know the law on stock-killing dawgs. It ain't a matter of my choice."

"Well," answered Abbie, setting her trim feet, "we'll just make it a matter of your choice, right now."

The two stood glowering at each other, the man six and a half feet of splendid bearlike muscle, the girl a scant five feet of slender mountain cat grace. It was the first *for real* time Able John had noted the ashy sheen of her flaxen hair, the slatey glow to her gray eyes, the charcoal black of her thick lashes. Additionally, it was his primal discovery of some lines other than angular to her figure. He watched her, an alien demand of mundane desire growing within him. Feeling it, he flushed a rose madder red. As he did, Abbie struck petulantly at the calf of her riding boot with her small Mexican quirt.

"Well?" she stabbed at Cleburne McSween.

"Now, cuss it all, Abbie—"

"You want to cuss it all, go out in the yard. This here is the Lord's house."

She threw Clebe the prim rebuff but it was to Able John to whom went the appended flutter of dusky lashes. Then, to nail down the lid on the new preacher not missing the point, she repeated the maneuver—with gusty sighs added.

This time everybody got the idea.

"By Tophet!" hollered Clebe, "you lay off batting them lashes around, you hear? You want to auger religion, all right, we'll auger religion. But any time you figure it's more piousful to be making goo-goo eyes at some pistol-neck sky pilot than to be scatter-gunning a

Injun sheepdawg in church, you got to prove it to me! Meanwhile, you just remember you're engaged to Cleburne Cletis McSween. Providing you don't want parts of new-imported preacher blowed all over yonder blackboard, you won't be forgetting it again neither!''

With the outraged threat, Clebe banged the butt of the old ten-gauge on the floor for terminal emphasis. He got it too. The jolt jarred off the worn hammers on both barrels and the big bored double blew a hole through the roof overhead, out of which squealing, dayblind bats were fogging for the next five minutes.

The explosion, together with an eyeful of dislodged Chiropteran guano from above, sobered Clebe. It was not in him to apologize directly to any man in front of Abbie Gresham, but he did his second best.

''Hang it to Hades!'' he yelled lamely, ''them was my last two shells!'' And with the string-halted imprecation, he stormed up the aisle past Abbie and slammed on out the schoolhouse door. Only when the subsequent pounding of his horse's hooves had died away down the road toward Eagle Nest, did the Reverend Able John Arkwright release the cringing sheepdog and his own longheld breath.

''Hallelujah!'' he said.

''Amen,'' echoed Abbie Gresham.

But the way she lowered her tomboy's voice somehow failed to match up with the way she let down her sooty lashes.

By the time Able John understood the disparity, it was much too late.

VIII

From its low-water mark of the first morning, when Abbie Gresham unabashedly rescued him and the fugitive sheepdog from the pursuing vengeance of Cleburne McSween, the tide of Able John's fortunes in Upper Valley altered swiftly. It fell immediately and much lower.

Hardpan Halloran allowed he had never seen anything in New Mexico drop so fast, unless it had been the price on Billy the Kid's head the morning after Pat Garrett caught him asleep at Pete Maxwell's. Euph Smith agreed, announcing that the odds on the Peoria pilgrim sticking it out in Eagle Nest, after bucking Clebe McSween in front of Abbie, had sunk to a hundred to one. And no preacher money in sight at that price. Other available sentiment in the valley ran along similar dismal lines. Clebe catching his girl making eyes at the new reverend had guaranteed that the old record for running circuit riders out of Eagle Nest would be broken six ways from Sunday. From next Sunday.

Mostly, the boys at Mestizo Marie's gave Able John twenty-four hours to live—in Upper Valley.

Nobody messed into McSween family plans and improved his chances of making it through the winter.

The McSweens were mountain people. A fire-headed, hard-eyed, hog-poor lot, they made their clannish way acting as New Mexican receivers for Old Mexican beef products imported in the original longhorned container. Terms of delivery were damp, conditions of import, nocturnal. Their supplier was Estaban Sanchez, he of the Raritonga teeth, and Estaban's source of moonset steers from south of the Rio Grande seemed as sufficiently vast as his entire home state of Chihuahua, which indeed it was. It was a chancy partnership, and one of lean returns, its operators making just about enough to meet the mortgage and keep a bottle of *tequila* in the house. But at least it wasn't honest.

Clebe, bull-voiced head of the tribe since old Wiley McSween had gone under the past spring from a self-prescribed tonic of two quarts of uncut tarantula extract, taken to ward off the chilblains which he had never had but might get sometime, was not really a mean or bad man at heart. Trouble was, he had never got down to his heart. He did his thinking with his head and in Clebe's case this could be interesting. Old Wiley used to say that Clebe's head was stuffed with 50-50 sawdust and cement. And that given thirty days to do it, he still couldn't figure out how to pour creek water out of a wet boot with directions printed on the heel. And Clebe was the smart McSween.

This combination of bedrock head, behemoth body and inbred belligerence made him about as safe to handle as a black Spanish bull. To get between him and where he might be going was deemed as sporty as standing barefoot in front of a trail herd stampede. Or crimping dynamite caps with your side teeth. Crossing Clebe McSween was as bound to lead to the rigors of mortis as shooting yourself through the roof of the mouth with an 8-gauge goose gun.

So it was that the betting at the Soledad Saloon was all on the six-foot five-inch grizzly bear from the Bar-K, and none at all on the buggy-whip-built preacher from Peoria.

It was only a matter of details. Such as where and when and by what weapon. But the reverend himself, not knowing he was a dead man, carried on as happy as though he had his whole life in front of him.

Out at the old schoolhouse-church, bright and sunrisy the following morning, the sparks began to fly. The clang of hammer and rasp of saw was heard from dawn till late, last light. Beyond the sparks, some dust was astir. Wielder of the flying broom and banging dustpan was Abigail Kate Louise Gresham. Pale blond hair done up in an Apache headcloth borrowed from Windy Red Horse, slim body drowned in a size-38 *mestizo* squaw dress, hastily bargained for from the cowhipped hostess of the Soledad, the Rafter G heiress was drawing more stares than an albino badger with two heads and a sweet temper. Not in the memory of the most saddle-bent of the valley elders, drawn from the Soledad at the news of the reconstruction going forward out at the old schoolhouse, was there any recalling to mind of Miss Abbie in a dress. On top of that, to now see Mord Gresham's tomboy daughter waving a broom like any regulation female, when the only other dust she'd ever raised had been from the bucking-strap end of a salty bronc, was more than most of the boys could accept without moral reinforcement. They left Abbie and Able John to their shoveling out and shoring up, and ambled back to town for the necessary hair of the dog.

As for Able John, he was too busy ripsawing, jack-planing and draw-knifing with the carpenter tools Abbie had ordered Euph and Windy to tote in from the Rafter G, to notice what the sunny-eyed girl was wearing. The big thing was to get the old building made decent for the first service come next Sunday.

"Till that there fate is accompleed," growled Euph disgustedly to Windy, "it don't look like the critter will glance slanchwise for nothing short of the Second Coming. Even then," he added acridly, "I reckon Jesus would have to show up on the handlebars of a bicycle rode by a tame bear, to draw so much as a walleyed blink. I give up."

Euph's dour forecast was unexpectedly strengthened by the sudden rattle of horse's hooves on the Upper Valley road. He and Windy shaded their eyes against the climbing sun, winced, started hunting a suitable hole. They knew that tall black and its 265-pound rider and, moreover, suspected they knew what brought them hammering up to the schoolhouse in a lather fit to shave. But they were wrong. Clebe had not come loaded for sky pilot, nor did he mean to have any preachers for breakfast. He only stepped down off the black and walked up to Able John, reasonablelike.

"Good," he said, eyeing the house-cleaning operation approvingly. "It looks right nice, Reverend. Saves me a heap of augering too. You see, I just come over to tell you to get the place all curried and brushed for next Saturday night. I've decided me and the gal's getting hitched then. What time you want to make it, along about sundown?"

Able John hung his head, sort of shamed, or anyway, stubborn, and mumbled that the matter of setting a time lay in the province of the bride.

But Clebe demurred.

"Let's leave Providence out'n it," he said. "I aim to have Abbie here. Don't let that part of it th'ow you. Now, what time you want to announce us man and wife?"

Able John took a sidelong look at Abbie Gresham and slid his lantern jaw out a careful notch.

"Well, brother McSween," he started to object, "I cannot truthfully—" but Clebe cut him off by dropping a hand the size of a coal scoop to the scarred wooden butt of the big Sam Colt in his belt, and Able John said quickly, "Anytime you say, brother, anytime you say!"

Abbie, herself, too flabbergasted by the sheer brass of Clebe's proposal to rebuttle it right off, now started barking back.

"Now just a danged minute, Cleburne McSween! I ain't said I would marry you next Saturday, or any other Saturday. Far as I'm concerned, you can go shinny up a cactus tree. I won't be rushed into marrying nobody!"

"Rushed!" roared Clebe. "I give you a ring six years gone, and you ain't even give me a kiss for it since!"

"I'd ought to give you a kick for it. That infernal thing turnt my finger green up to my elbow. Lucky I didn't get the lock jaw from it, you big barn owl!"

"Well, it don't matter now. Me and you's marrying up sundown next Saturday. That's my mind."

"Your mind? Clebe, you ain't got no more mind nor a mud coot. I've see'd more brains in a lightning-struck sheep than you got. I wouldn't marry up with you if you was the last man in Upper Valley."

Clebe's color dunned off into a slatey gray, colder than the inside of a sleet cloud.

"You're gonna marry up with me, gal, if I have to *make* it that I'm the last man in Upper Valley. You read my sign, gal?"

Inasmuch as he padded out the allusion with a chuck of his shaggy head toward the Reverend Arkwright, Abbie read his sign all too well. She knew she daren't push him another inch. But, like any man, she reckoned he could be led where he wouldn't be driven. She thawed into a spring melt of smiles. She lowered her small golden head. She upped and downed her long black eyelashes. Then she trembled and sighed and let one tiny tear roll down her suntanned cheek.

"Aww now, Abbie, that ain't fair!" groaned Clebe.

"Cleburne," she murmured, "we had ought not to fuss like this in front of the new reverend. It ain't fitting for a couple aiming to get wedded in his church. Now you just be patient and give a girl time."

"How much time?" asked Clebe, a cunning gleam of suspicion burning far back in his deepset eyes.

"No nice girl sets a date in less than thutty days."

"After six years!"

"Cleburne, you saying I ain't a nice girl?"

"Hecksfire no, Abbie. It's just that—"

"Thutty days, Cleburne."

Clebe glared at Able John, squinted again at Abbie Gresham, tried to ferret out any hint they were hazing him from his blind side. They weren't, he decided, and nodded in ponderous agreement to the girl's ultimatum.

"Thutty days," he rumbled.

He took up the fingers of his callused paws and began to toll them off under his breath. Pretty quick, he had it figured.

"That's four weeks from this coming Saturday," he announced. Then, eyeing Abbie. "I'll be here, come sundown. See you are."

As he finished with her, he somehow separated his three-pound revolver from its holster, all in the half-second process of easing around to face Able John. Twirling the heavy weapon on a forefinger of a size to make it look like an eight-ounce pocket derringer, he concluded the maneuver by poking its gaping bore into Able John's midsection deep enough to strike oil.

"Thutty days," he repeated ominously, and turned away and went for his horse.

IX

Clebe, if he had no ordinary intelligence, possessed nonetheless the feral instincts of a he-mustang. He knew when his herd leadership was being put in jeopardy, and when his favorite filly was being led to wanting to rub noses with the new horse from over the hill. Accordingly he did not wait for Abbie's thirty days to elapse before going to work on Able John Arkwright.

His method appeared innocently guileless and was, in fact, fiendishly effective.

Clebe's was the outlaw dog-wolf's philosophy of survival: if you can't eat it or bury it, defile it. Knowing that overt violence would only increase Abbie's regard for the pilgrim sky pilot, he set craftily about the task of contaminating the latter without touching him.

At first service the following Sunday, the mixed cowboy and Spanish-American flock that showed up to hear the miracles of the Old Testament explained, Peoria-style, was cautiously, even politely, curious. But the restive sons of the saddle, remembering his dive under the seat on the Silver Mesa Mail, and led on by Clebe, soon began rawhiding Able John's tender spirit unmercifully. His subsequent thundering of the Lord's word could not drown out the echo of Susie Doklinny's rifle shot. Clebe saw to that.

In the middle of a perfectly good sermon, the hulking boss of the Bar-K would unbend his bulldog legs and rear up from the back pews to inquire in his rutting buffalo's bellow how the Lord branded his critters. Did he use a regular stamp iron, or a running iron? What did the brand itself look like? Was the Reverend burned with it himself? If so, where? And, granted he was, would he mind showing it to some of the boys out back of the horse shed after Sunday school? Poor Able John did not know how to handle these questions from the floor, except either to answer or ignore them. When he tried the former, the other and perfectly goodhearted cowboys would begin to rise up and get in on the ride. When he tried the latter, Clebe would whip out his .45 and demand to be recognized on penalty of Coltsmoke. Faced with this choice, Able John could not win for losing. Yet, to his credit, he fought on.

Through it all Abbie Gresham remained loyal and it was she, who, on more than one occasion when the boys had Able John scripturally surrounded, would charge into the dust and do some chapter and verse hog-tying of her own. Such proved her ability at these "rescue sermons" that a good lot of the rawhiders allowed she was a better sky pilot than the Reverend himself. It was out of sheer respect for her that they quit cowboying Able John after the second Sunday service, and even gave up Indian-raiding him after the third.

These raids were noisy, harmless affairs. But such was the perfect mimicry of Apache yells and such the wondrous quality of Winchester marksmanship displayed in them, that they always ended with Parson Arkwright digging in under the teacher's desk pulpit and refusing to emerge until the cavalry had arrived.

Abbie could not convince him it was just the boys whooping it up for his benefit. Yet through these, as in all the other assaults upon his wavering spirit, she continued to stand undaunted between him and total defeat in the field. While she was about it, she threw everything in the Book of Eve at him by way of getting him to recognize the light of love and pop the legal question before the thirty days were up and the sunset showdown with Clebe McSween at last arrived.

Able John apparently couldn't even see the title on the outside cover, let alone read the fine print on the shamelessly exposed inner pages.

"It's downright brazen the way Miss Abbie's been gunning for that chicken-livered sky pilot," was the way most of the valley folk viewed the fruitless chase.

"Yes, and her promised with a storebought ring, and everything, to Clebe McSween for going onto seven years too!" was the response which usually accompanied the critique.

The concluding opinion, in any case, was unanimous.

Clebe was a powerful ugly critter once he was put on the prod. If he wound up by calling out that pale-bellied parson, there would be some preacher-tracks laid down a sight longer than those he made in running down Fat Jaime's stagecoach in Silver Mesa.

Meanwhile, what Able John's closed mind would not admit his open heart could not keep out. He was slipping and simply did not know the symptoms. Even so, he hung tough.

He attributed the chills and fever he enjoyed when

Abbie glanced his way, or brushed on purpose too close to him, to their mutual enthusiasm for the refurbishing of the Upper Valley schoolhouse, and he would not weaken beyond the point of saying an extra prayer each night for the Lord to help him keep his mind on the school's construction, and his eyes off Abbie Gresham's.

The fourth, fatal Saturday drew near. And Abbie broke down.

Unable longer to risk the mounting odds against Able John realizing what ailed him in time to save her from the 265-pound pride of the McSweens, she played her sleeve ace.

It was the oldest card in the marked deck of Dan Cupid. Abbie dealt it out with understandable, if slightly singed, confidence. The first hint Able John had of it was when Euph Smith found him buying his frugal week's provender in the Eagle Nest general store.

"Reverend," advised the little cowboy, "you had better light a shuck up the road and get back to minding your own store."

"I beg your pardon," said Able John.

Euph gave him the squint-eyed stare.

"Clebe and his gang are out yonder to the schoolhouse. They're decorating up the church end of the place something scandalous."

"What!" gasped Able John.

"Yes sir. Miss Abbie's done give in for good. She's up and told Clebe she'll go th'ough with it right square on schedule."

X

Able John's loping stride ate up the distance between town's edge and the Upper Valley schoolhouse. It was all that "Lazarus," (from being raised from almost certain death), the mending three-legged sheepdog could do to keep him in sight. That preacher was in a hurry.

As he sped along, Able John assured himself that it was not that Abbie Gresham had decided *actually* to marry Cleburne McSween, which lent feathers to his size-twelve feet. He admitted that he had not believed, in the beginning, that the dear, gray-eyed child would go through with it. That such a mountain Circe would take unto her virgin breast this loutish rustic who, according to evil report, purloined the kine of others for a living, had never seemed possible. But even now that the monstrous event seemed certain, and mightily imminent, it was not the factor that explained his speed. The fact that McSween and a band of his big-hatted cow-chasers were desecrating that part of the schoolhouse reserved unto the Lord was the primary impetus that carried him galloping through the picket gate and up to the rehung door of the little church-school.

Once inside, he beheld a vision of sacrilege not surpassed by the excesses of Sodom and Gomorrah combined.

Like an outraged lion of Old Judea, Able John Arkwright charged the milling knot of McSween-men intent upon stocking the Sunday altar behind the pulpit desk with every brand of bottled sociability that Mestizo Marie and the private cellars of the Soledad had been able to provide.

At his brush-snorting advance, the saddle-tanned friends of the groom drew back from their handiwork, revealing the altar area transformed into a commendable replica of the backbar in the Painted Lady Saloon in Silver Mesa.

It was, in artistic fact, a triumph of authentic native handicraft. But Able John was in no mood to appreciate *ars gratia artis* as practiced among the untutored cowherds of south central New Mexico. The Lord's House had been defiled. The Divine Lightning must now be called down in punishment upon the defilers.

Able John set his heels, slid to a hock-burning stop. He flung up his hands in dramatic application for a writ of celestial brimstone. Nothing happened. He stood, transfixed, upraised hands motioning in a mute plea for someone up there to come on, do something. But no one did. The interested cowboys watched, fascinated.

"By jings," said one of them presently, "I believe he's been strick with a stroke."

"Naw," denied another. "He's only pumping up pressure to make a speech. He'll open up in a minute and start spouting scripture all over the place."

The next moment Able John did manage to get his arms down and his mouth open. But before he could begin issuing any wholesale damnations, Clebe jammed his .45 barrel between his teeth.

"Reverend," he said, "you'd best use any spare strength you got for brushing up on the "I do" oration. Don't waste no lung power lecturing me and the boys for readying up the meeting house to give Miss Abbie the dangdest wedding ever th'owed for any white woman in New Mexico."

The chill of the cold steel against his incisors took all the spunk out of Able John. As best he could, he mumbled around the weapon's muzzle that he would appreciate being excused. Clebe nodded that this was reasonable, and removed the Colt. Before holstering it, however, he spun it expertly, dropped its business end floorward, thumbed off six shots into the planks around Able John's feet.

"Just to help you remember the ceremony's set for tomorrow night, sundown," he nodded. "You'd better have your part down pea-pod perfect. One off-note yelp out'n you, and I'll blow you futher apart than Susie Doklinny's last three teeth. You savvy my smoke, Parson?"

The parson savvied his smoke.

"Yes, sir," he answered, "sundown tomorrow night," and crawdadded up the aisle, backward, as fast as he had just dashed down it, frontwise.

At the door he reversed the order of rearward march just in time to see Lazarus, who had been peeking in cautiously, pull his head back and disappear like a coyote caught reconnoitering a chickenhouse. The dog's conservatism struck a responsive chord in Able John. Ducking quickly around the doorjamb to cringe with him against the outer wall, he reached down a comforting hand.

"Blessed are the meek," he said hopefully, "for they shall inherit the earth."

"Aaarrroww?" said Lazarus.

"Oh," replied Able John, "excuse me. Matthew, v, 5: New Testament."

Lazarus thought about it a minute, then shook off the reassuring hand and crept back toward the edge of the door. Taking another side-eyed peek around the jamb, he flinched and jumped back. He snorted and sneezed, to get the smell of the dreaded McSween out of his nostrils, then put an urgent paw on Able John's pants leg and whined softly.

An all-night elocution in Illinois English could not have spoken with more moving force of the existing need for prompt evaporation from that vicinity of one wandering Apache sheepdog and one strayed Peoria preacher.

Able John read dog-sign as well as he did McSween-smoke.

Raising the rejected hand, he recited a little lay scripture with the lines put real close together.

"He that fights and runs away
May live to fight another day,

But he that is in battle slain
Will never rise to fight again."

So quoting the text for the next retreat, he slid on around the corner of the school building and made long legs for the old horse shed out back. There, pending more permanent quarters, he had set up open-front housekeeping with three bales of moldy hay, a sheep-herder's stove, a penny candle in a tin cup, half a case of canned milk (dented cans), his straw suitcase and two good Rafter G bunkhouse blankets supplied against the chill of the mountain nights, in the first flush of her infatuation, by Miss Abigail Kate Louise Gresham.

Lazarus was not quite so agile.

Not familiar with the threadbare borrowing from J. Ray's *History of the Rebellion*, and confused by his companion's sudden decampment, the illiterate sheep-dog hesitated uncertainly. While so doing, he took a first-degree chill at the rasp of Clebe McSween's remembered bellow breaking out some furbearing ribaldry from inside the schoolhouse.

"Aaarrowww!" he said, and beat Able John to the horse shed by six blue merle lengths.

XI

The entire valley knew about Able John's last stand before sunrise Saturday morning.

Some few felt a twinge of regret—he was a likable galoot for all his gun-shy ways—but most accepted his backing off as more or less inevitable. A handful of unregenerate bunch-quitters like Euph Smith, Windy Red Horse, Hardpan Halloran, yes, and even old Mordecai Gresham himself, still dared hope the lanky parson would somehow manage, through inspiration of Abbie's pure, true love, to rise up and smite the Philistine.

It was time for a change in Upper Valley.

The rude spate of rustling and rowdyism that had marked the reign of King Clebe, was wearing mighty thin. Eagle Nest was long overdo for a good stiff dose of book learning and Bible preaching. The likes of Cleburne McSween and his dark-skinned crew of cross-river cattle importers were twenty years out of date. And the whole valley knew that most of the wild bunch would be glad to lay down the running iron and take up the bull-tongue plow. Given a third of a chance, the band would go out of business and bog down into decent citizens overnight. Even two of Clebe's own brothers, Clyde, the baby McSween, and Cyril Charley, the family smoothhead, had been coming to services regular and letting on, out loud, that for three cents (and two companies of Texas Rangers to guarantee live delivery) they would quit Clebe and join up with the normal folks in Eagle Nest.

But nobody quit Clebe McSween. Not against his will, they didn't. And Clebe hadn't made out any wills lately.

Saturday thus dawned and wore away without hopeful sign of revolt from any quarter. The diehard wishful thinkers for an Upper Valley miracle of courage returned to the cloth, gave up their vigil and turned to drowning their violated faith in vintage Taos Lightning at the Soledad.

This was understandable.

Marie was standing house treat and every ambulatory cow person from Jackpine Pass to the Rafter G was in town to see that her largess was not insulted by being ignored; and to get sufficiently embalmed in the process of this natural courtesy to be able to abide the sight of poor little old Miss Abbie being drug down the aisle on the substitute arm of Euph Smith—Old Man Gresham being bedded with a horse-kicked hip—and given over in front of the altar to that no-good, gun-toting cowthief, Clebe McSween.

Out at the other end of the valley, in the sanctity of her tear-splashed boudoir, Abbie herself grew alternately pale and flushed at the prospect of becoming a legalized McSween. She was a good loser but she hated to be beat on what ought to have been a pat hand. It looked now, though, as if she were going to lose the cussed sky pilot for certain sure. There was no question but what she loved the pistol-whippy string bean, yet, come a showdown, she was not going to give up a good man for a downright, dehorned coward.

She had had it straight from Euph how Able John had taken out on a grass-cutting run for the schoolhouse to lay out Clebe and the boys for dasting to defacify his altar into looking like a Juarez cantina. And then how he had folded his cards and snuck off to hide out in the horse shed with that agate-eyed Apache sheepdog when Clebe had slapped leather and told him to dust out.

No sir, by Jehosephat, love or no love, she wouldn't marry up with the Reverend Arkwright, now, if he was the final man this side of Cyril Charley McSween.

That, by all that was sacred to the oldest maid in Mescalero County, was foreverlastingly that! And amen to it.

Direct vision into the doings of the fainthearted Reverend at that moment would have brought her nothing but further shame. Bent flat on his kneebones in front of the bottleclad Sunday end of the Upper Valley schoolhouse, Able John was saying his farewell to the little building he had so prayed would bring both the three R's and a lacing of Bible instruction to the unlettered lambs of Eagle Nest.

Beside him, as he sought guidance from above, was his old suitcase packed with his few equipments and fond hopes for missionary success in New Mexico. Beside him, too, of course, was his limping shadow, Lazarus.

"Lord God of Hosts," concluded Able John aloud, inclining his steady brown eyes upward, "this flock truly needs a loving shepherd and fearless. The wolf is without the fold, the gentle wether dares not stir beyond the gates. Forgive me this weakness of spirit which hath unfitted me for guardian of Thy word in this far valley, and provide me the strength to go forth from my failure in dignity, as befits Thy servant.

"If Thou hast it in Thy sweet charity that Thine apostle should do otherwise than this, send me some sign, O Lord. Send it, now, I implore Thee, if Thou willst send it at all. The sun grows low and the hour of Thy servant's final shame is at hand. "If Thou willst but point me the way, I shall follow it, yea, though it leadeth me verily into the Valley of the Shadow: in Thy name I ask it—amen."

Able John waited, his gaze fastened on the ragged hole Clebe's shotgun had torn through the roof above. It was as though it were through this sinful entrance the requested portent might momentarily descend.

Nothing came through the hole, however, save the pertly cocked head and bright, beady eyes of a curious mountain jay, called by Able John's voice from his pecking into the outer shingle cracks for his breakfast of small red wood spiders.

"Aaarrroww," growled Lazarus, a lifelong critic of bluejays.

"Sssccrrawwkkk!" answered the jay rustily, and hopped from one side to the other of the hole, just as nature called.

Able John, dodging instinctively beneath the school desk pulpit to avoid this increment of animal insult to his existing burden of human injury, struck his head violently against the underside of the drawer. The impact knocked out the drawer's thin bottom panel and scattered its longheld schoolboy contents down about his hunched shoulders. When the deluge had slacked, Able John's glance fell upon that instrument of ancient warfare with which Providence had seen fit to answer his plea.

It had landed directly in his waiting hand, and it lay now to his remembering grasp with a feel of dear boyhood familiarity which excited him beyond measure. The years rolled back like dark clouds before a chain of summer lightning, and in the receding flash he saw again the hard-fought finals of the Peoria County Fair, and the unerring skill of the river-bottom farm boy who that afternoon went home with the slingshot championship of the entire state of Illinois, and a twenty-pound pickled ham to prove it.

A strength and calmness came into him which was as the strength and calmness of ten.

His long fingers wound more tightly yet about the never-forgotten feel of the gnarled grip. He raised his eyes again to the shotgun hole in the roof of the Upper Valley schoolhouse and, after a suitable silence of humble gratitude, bespoke himself with quiet fervor.

"Ask and ye shall receive, saith the Lord," said Able John Arkwright.

And got up and strode outside to put the suitcase back in the horse shed.

XII

Sundown. Menacing and monolithic as the westward rearing hulk of Dead Man Mountain, Cleburne McSween came stalking down the Upper Valley road. Dressed in old Wiley McSween's black burying suit, gun-belted, high-booted and spur-chained even on this, his wedding day, he approached the schoolhouse-church on foot and leading two saddled mounts. One was his own tall black, the other a milk-white mare no man in the valley had seen before. Behind him, at a distance befitting their lower rank, Winchester carbines or sawed-off shotguns barred across their saddlehorns, his four brothers rode in chop-walking escort of the clan leader.

The overflow crowd of uninvited guests, outnumbering the school's standing-room capacity by a noisy score, grew hushed and fell back away from the door as someone on the outskirts whispered hoarsely, "*Pssstt!* Yonder they come!"

Inside, where, custom be hung up and quartered out, Abbie already waited on the arm of Euphemistic Smith, the chill of the outside hush swept down the aisle to the remodeled pulpit—the teacher's desk was draped to the floor in a lovely pale white wagon canvas—and seized the Reverend Able John Arkwright about the Adam's apple with fingers of icy steel.

In that endless sixty seconds while Clebe made the door and paused to sweep the assembled host, all the prayer-sent sphizzerinctum and last-ditch gizzard which had come to Able John by way of the careless bluejay and the broken desk drawer, now vanished as though by some evil exhortation of the lower realm. Indeed, the quality of the fear crawling unspoken through the silence inside that tiny sometime church of Upper Valley would have shut off the windpipe of the Dark Prince himself.

Able John fought for breath and sought for some new sign that the previous signal sent through the shotgun hole had not been misinterpreted by him.

Again his belief on the Lord went not unrewarded.

From beneath the folds of wagon canvas enshrouding the teacher's desk came a sturdy, "aaarrroww!" of support. Heartened by this reassurance that everything was moving on schedule, Able John felt beneath the strangely bulging right-hand tail of his claw-hammer coat for further moral assist. Ah, that was better. His other hand, the left one, tightened at the same time about the companion object it held hidden in its closed grasp. Now, indeed, he felt restored.

"Steady, boy," he said guardedly to his invisible accomplice.

"Aaarrroww," replied the latter, and thumped the pineboard floor with a right good will.

Windy Red Horse, chosen head usher by the bride's faction because he was the only Rafter G man big enough to look a McSween in the eye without a stump to stand on, looked suspiciously toward the Reverend as the growl stole out from under the wagon canvas.

Able John put a quick hand to his middle, managed a puny smile, said hastily.

"Excuse me, brother. My nervous stomach, you know. It always acts up at weddings."

Windy nodded.

"You no worry, friend," he said. "Injun on your side. Look out window."

Able John walled an anxious glance toward the indicated south window. He saw the press of impassive dark faces crowded outside the dirty pane. He noted in particular the prunelike countenance of one matriarchal old crone who must have been Methuselah's twin sister.

"Susie Doklinny," informed Windy. "She headwoman Mescalero Apache. She you big friend."

"My what?" gasped Able John. "Why, that's the ancient heathen who shot at me aboard the Silver Mesa train."

"Sure," said Windy. "But that before you fixum up leg on little dog."

"Lazarus?" said Able John.

"Sure. Him sheepdog belong old Susie. She tell her

son Del Norte—him chief Mescalero tribe—come help you. She say, you want make fight on Big McSween, Apache on you side.''

''But I don't understand. Why should the Indians be on my side, against Cleburne McSween?''

''Del Norte him track dog after hurt. Him know Big McSween shoot dog. Him tell Susie you help dog, Susie tell him Apache help you. Apache always pay back favor.''

''No! No!'' objected Able John. ''A servant of the Lord cannot be responsible for an Indian War. You must tell your friends there can be no fighting.''

''Him up to you,'' said Windy Red Horse. ''You fight, Apache fight.''

''Dear Lord,'' said Able John, ''I am undone.''

''You sure as shooting are,'' rasped a familiar bear's growl. ''If you don't leave off palavering with that redskin and get on with the ceremony, I'll th'ow down on you. Me and the gal are plumb ready.'' Clebe broke off the warning to swing around and yell up the aisle, ''Get a move on, Abbie! I been waiting six years and I don't aim to put up with no last-minute fighting the bridle!''

His hand dropped to his thigh, came up filled with .45 Colt revolver. Waving the big weapon, he shouted at his four brothers.

''Spread out boys. Cover the congregation. Anybody moves to interfere, center him. I mean for me and Missus McSween to be harnessed and hitting it on a high lope for the honeymoon inside five minutes.''

He swung back on Able John.

''Start preaching, preacher. And don't take a breath till the cinch buckle's pulled up tight.''

Able John gulped and got out the Book.

Abbie came down the aisle with Euph and stood beside Clebe. She cast Able John a look that would have melted the heart of a quartz outcrop. But Able John would not meet the pleading of the tear-brimmed pools, and the last appeal appeared lost.

Painfully, he cleared his throat.

And the sullen crowd moved unconsciously forward to hear the yellow-backed circuit rider marry up the girl who loved him true, with the uncurried curly wolf from the Bar-K.

But for some reason Able John straightened and stood tall in the final second. His voice, while quiet and kind as always, was also clear and unflinching. His gentle face, in that stilled moment, grew firm set as the rock which Moses smote in the desert.

"For what is about to happen here," he said, "may the Lord have mercy on my soul."

There was a sound of sucked-in breath, all around, and Clebe McSween got pale and wicked-looking.

"It ain't funny, Parson," he snarled. "Get on with it."

Able John nodded, dropped his voice into the professional monotone, began the service.

"Dearly beloved we are gathered here . . ."

On and on droned the familiar voice. Able John's voice was the voice of a morally beaten man, a man left without pride or spiritual possession of any stripe. In the congregation there was no sound. Only Clebe's notably alcoholic breathing disturbed the shameful tension. At last Able John reached the end.

"Do you, Cleburne," he said, "take this woman to be your lawfully wedded wife?"

Clebe's mouth worked spasmodically.

"I do, dang you. Keep going."

Able John's calmness had by now, in the later words of a completely enraptured Euph Smith, "growed to a thing of purely beatitudinous remark."

"And do you, Abigail," he inquired with the equanimity of a muley-cow side-jawing a cud of sweet clover, "take this man to be your lawfully wedded husband?"

White as a creek-scrubbed bedsheet, Abbie turned her wide, wet eyes full upon the Reverend Arkwright. All the limpid schoolgirl love in the world was mirrored in their splashy depths. But Parson Arkwright seemed not to see. His eyes were still upraised upon the Lord.

Finally he lowered his gaze from the shotgun hole in the roof and cast them outward upon the restive multitude. In the ensuing pause not a bootheel scraped, not a spur rowel jingled.

Able John bobbed his Adam's apple, made the next-to-final statement.

"If there be any man present who knows why these two should not be man and wife, let him now come forward or forever hold his peace."

Again the pall of silence descended. It seemed to stretch from then until next Thursday night. To the marinated nerves of Clebe McSween the suspense became unendurable. Away to the rear of the audience, some nameless hero snickered.

Whirling in the jam-packed pews, Clebe let out the bellow of a punch-shot buffalo.

"Infernal funny, ain't it?" he yelled. "Pistolneck Idjut said it precisely like he expected some one of you non compost mentalists to acherally step out'n the ranks and speak up agin me and Abbie clinching it."

He took a lurching stride toward the crowd, his hand grabbing the butt of the .45.

"Well, hang it all, is there anybody?"

He got no answer beyond a general shifting of boots toward the exit. His roar became a howl.

"What ails the lot of you? You deef or something? Or just yellar like this here milksop sky pilot? Or mebbe you didn't hear what the parson said. All right, I'll say it for you agin."

Here, the swaying flower of the McSweens, half pulled the Colt from its holster.

"Is there anybody going to come forward, or ain't there?"

In the echoing stillness which followed, the Reverend Arkwright's soft voice sounded sharp and startling as Gabriel's horn.

"There is, Mr. McSween, indeed there is."

Clebe spun around, droop-jawed.

There, long legs spread, bony knees bent, left hand closed as though about some small round object, right hand reached rearward under the tail of his claw-hammer coat, stood the Peoria sky pilot.

As Clebe's jaws refused to come back together, and the audience waited spellbound for the execution, Able John smiled his first real smile in Upper Valley.

"I myself come forward to say you nay on this wedlock, Mr. McSween," he said. "Which, I believe, in the parlance of the time and place, 'makes it your move.' "

Clebe at last got his teeth together.

It was, for sure, his move, and he made it like the man he was.

It was a pretty good move too.

But it just wasn't good enough.

His .45 had not yet cleared leather when Able John cried out "sic 'em!" and a blue merle streak flashed from beneath the wagon-tarp pulpit cloth, taking dead aim on Clebe's leg just above where the boot top ended. As Lazarus charged, Able John's right hand came out from under his coattails with an old-fashioned elm crotch slingshot, and the other hand flicked fast as a snake's head to fit into the sling's worn leather a lumpy hardclay marble the general size and heft of a cast-iron horse chestnut.

Clebe yelled bloody murder as Lazarus clamped down

on him but Able John never really needed the diversionary tactic.

Long before Lazarus cleared canvas, his farm boy's skilled hands had loaded the sling leather, hauled it to full, earlobe, stretch, released it with a wicked, whirring "wwhhhrrraang!"

The glazed "clayie" took Clebe squarely between the eyes. His dog-bit yell blended with the thunderous report of the .45, as his trigger finger spasmed to send his shot crashing harmlessly into the floor in front of the pulpit. While the blast of the blackpowder load was still bouncing back and forth inside the tiny building, Clebe straightened up, quivered, went slumpy at the knees. He fell like a giant pine; proud and slow and with an ending, terrible crash. When he struck, he lay cold as the clay of the marble which had cut him down.

With some awkwardness, Able John turned to his awestricken parishioners.

"I believe," he announced apologetically, "that if you will examine brother McSween, you will find he is merely unconscious, not suffering any permanent impairment."

Then, making a funny, stiff little bow.

"It has been quite a number of years since I have enjoyed precise work of this nature, but it was a fairly simple shot. I doubt, really, that it was even of semifinals quality. Certainly it was nothing which would have won the "Land o' Lincoln" shoot-off. Not, at least, in my time."

Thus, modestly, did the 1878 Peoria County and Illinois State Junior Freehand Slingshot Champion, acknowledge the secret of his amazing victory and accept, after one last unbelieving pause, the thundering plaudits of the crowd.

He was, from that day, master as well as minister of all he surveyed in Upper Valley. He had, according to

Euph Smith, his prime admirer next only to Abbie Gresham, "Veenee Vicky Vidi-ed the valley to a fare-thee-well," vanquishing the powers of evil with the one weapon they cannot defend against—ridicule. It was a triumph as complete as Wellington's at Waterloo.

Oh, there was some piddling residual nastiness when Collis and Chauncey, the bad McSween brothers, made a move to pull their irons and throw down on Able John for dropping Clebe. But this threat flew off on the wings of an Apache warcry from the doorway and front windows of the schoolhouse. When the two miscreants stared up the aisle and saw old Susie Doklinny and her murderous-looking Mescalero sheepherders standing between them and the front exit, they abandoned their artillery in the field and retreated out the north windows, glass and all. They lit running and were not again seen in Upper Valley.

Nor, indeed, was Clebe.

Once Clyde and Cyril Charley had hauled him up the aisle, sacked him across his spooky black, got him home, cleaned up and brought around decent, he lit off down the hill for lower altitudes. His parting gesture was a rather sad one for a fallen monarch. As a wedding gift, when she and the parson should decide to get the job done, he left Abbie the pure-white mare which he had brought to bear her away from the church. The fact the mare turned out to be in foal to a jackass and ultimately delivered herself of twin muckle-dun mules, was in no way Clebe's fault. He had bought her off a sideshow spieler in a busted-down carnival in El Paso, and had the spieler's own word for it that she had been hand bred to the King of Zanzibar's personal coal-black Arabian stallion, a gift, in turn, of the Sultan of Inner Baluchistan.

Besides, the mules grew into a tolerable plow team and Able John and Abbie used them to put in and cultivate the first planting of Illinois corn in New Mexico.

As for the two good McSween brothers, Cyril Charley took up horse doctoring and made two hundred dollars before he was thirty-eight years old. And Clyde went to multiplying cows by natural means, a miracle he couldn't get over, not having heard about it under Clebe's management.

Estaban Sanchez married Mestizo Marie, which took them both out of bad trades and turned the Soledad into what Able John had thought it was in the first place. Marie gave the red lantern to the Arkwrights by way of a belated wedding present, and Abbie put a ruffled petticoat eyelet trim to it and reckoned it was the prettiest setting room lamp short of Albuquerque and Santa Fe, or anyways Ruidoso and Mesilla.

Susie Doklinny refused to take back the blue merle sheepdog, insisting Able John keep him as a token of the treaty she would sign and send in by Del Norte, ending the war between the Mescalero Apache and the United States Army.

Old Man Gresham got what Euph diagnosed as the "bronical asmatics" but what Mord swore were the "high mountain heaves," and moved down to live on the flatlands near Alamogordo, leaving the Rafter G to Abbie and Able John and to Little John, when he came along. Which was the same week the white mare dropped the muckle-dun mules. Which, turnwise, was taken to be a mighty fine omen and one guaranteed to get the boy off to just the right start in life.

At least that was the opinion of Euph Smith and Windy Red Horse, who stayed on at the Rafter G to make sure the pilgrim sky pilot stood by his word to Miss Abbie.

This, he did. And so, finally, all the bits and pieces of the Able John Arkwright story fitted where they went best, making the whole picture come out rosy as a chapped papoose. But that was long, long afterward. The story really ended about an hour after Collis and Chauncey dove through the schoolhouse windows and Clyde and Cyril Charley packed Clebe up the aisle and outside to his horse. It was then all the folks pulled out and went back to town to take up where they had left off on the free *tequila*, and to lay odds on what chance Elfego Baca or Billy the Kid might have had to beat the Reverend in a fair draw.

Abbie and Able John were left sitting out on the doorstep of the school with the dusk coming down hushed and cricketchirpy all around them. The purple shadows turned to black in the valley meadows and a loppy fourth-quarter moon came riding up, big and loomy as a ripe-cut canteloupe, from behind the eastern ridgetops.

In the tilted belfry above them, the waking owl fluffed his shoulder feathers and called down a fraternal "tahoo, tahoo?" to his lanky friend on the schoolhouse stoop. But Able John didn't answer the greeting. He only tightened the shelter of his long arm about the willing waist of his slim companion. From their home behind the broken baseboard of the front wall, the two tenant pack rats crept out to peer over the doorjamb at the human couple on the top step. First one, then the other, inquired of Able John as to who his pretty friend might be. Yet the tall quiet preacher replied to them not, nor even acknowledged their neighborly squeaks. Presently, the remaining few users of the bat roost beneath the schoolhouse ridgepole, streamed out through the shotgun hole in the roof to flit curiously around the wordless pair. Their sociable chitterings went likewise unrewarded. Even the demanding tail of Lazarus, hopefully bumping the porch boards, to augment his whine of suggestment that some progress be made immediately down the Upper Valley road toward Eagle Nest, and a nice hot supper, pounded on sans honor or acclaim.

Able John just pulled the perfumy form of Mord Gresham's daughter closer yet and buried his blue-shaven chin still more sinfully deep into the ash-blond fluff of hair which rested, soft as stardust, against his bony shoulder. When, at last, Abbie sighed and batted open the biggest, blackest-lashed, gray eyes in New Mexico and whispered huskily, "Able John, you aim to make a honest woman of me?" it was all over but the legal details.

Able John just sighed right back.

"Hallelujah," he said, and "Amen" murmured Abbie Gresham.

Left with the last word, Lazarus, the sometime Apache sheepdog and quondam canine philosopher, got up, scowled at his two companions, shook his head disgustedly.

"Aaarrowww," he said, and trotted off down the road toward Eagle Nest.

King Fisher's Road

I came into Kearney on the afternoon stage. It was four hours late, pretty bad even for the American Mail company. When I got down in front of the division office it was ten minutes of six P.M. Even so, no one had gone home yet. American Mail paid for twelve hours work and got it.

I stood a moment, unwrapping a fresh cigar and wondering anew why they had sent for me. The assignment was to open a new stage route between San Antonio and Uvalde, Texas, that I knew. But opening new routes was not exactly the way in which I earned my company keep, and so my curiosity mounted.

Going into the office I nodded at two clerks I knew but they kept their eyes to their accounts. Aha, I thought, I've been let out at last. The poor fellows are embarrassed by what they know and what I am about to find out. Well, no man lasts forever. The hand is quicker than the eye, they say, and in my business it had better be. Apparently, though, some diligent employee had reported to the division super that I was coming down with a hard case of slowing up. How this rumor had taken wing interested me. To my knowledge I hadn't turned down any private invitation to compete, nor come out second in any public performance of my work. This should have reassured me, but it did not. The truth was that of a given cold morning or after too many hours in the saddle I was a whisper less quick than an eye wink these latter days. But who had found me out, and how? That was the matter of interest.

Giving the cowardly clerks a good eyeing, I went on past their desks and stopped at the one to the rear of the office. This one bore a sign which read, "EVERETT D. STONE, SUPERINTENDENT," an accurate statement, if superfluous. Anyone would know Stone was a superintendent. He was too fat for a working man, and not worried enough. Presently he was frowning, though, and I took it he was not happy with the report he was studying. That seemed reasonable. It was a thick report and had a telegram pinned to it, and telegrams are always trouble. I stood by a polite bit, then scuffed my boots.

"Hello," I said, "somebody here send for a road opener?"

Stone looked up sort of flustered. He put the report quickly under some other papers, taking off his glasses and then acting real surprised to see me there.

"Harry, boy! Harry Roebuck!" he said, getting up and placing me a chair. "Sit down, sit down—"

I gave him a pretty well wrung-out nod, took the seat and said, "Well, Mr. Stone, who turned me in?"

He just looked at me, beaming.

"Harry, you old coyote," he said, "how have you been?"

"I've been right fine," I said, "but I got an idea I'm not going to stay that way."

He gave me the eye and said, "Um, yes, let's see here now," and began ruffling through some old waybills on his desk. "Cuss it all, I had that file right in front of me."

I gave him the eye back and reached over and pulled the report out from under the other papers.

"Yes, sir," I said. "Could this possibly be it, Mr. Stone?"

He took the report, looking it over as though it had just come off the key.

"Why so it is! I tell you, Harry, my eyesight is going bad."

"Mine isn't," I told him. "Mind reading me that telegram you got pinned on top? It looks to bear the same date as the one you sent me."

He gave me one more look and surrendered.

"First let me go back a ways," he said. "Do you remember Bunker Johnson?"

"Why don't you ask me if I remember my mother? You know I remember Bunk. He broke me in on this job." I watched him close now. "Don't tell me," I said, "that anything has happened to old Bunk."

Stone put up his hands.

"Now wait, get the whole story. We called you in here to go down to Texas and supervise the opening of a new stage route into Uvalde. Am I right?"

"As summer rain. And that brings up another point. Why me?"

"That," nodded Stone, "brings us right back to Bunk Johnson. We put him on the job and he couldn't handle it."

"Bunk couldn't handle a route opening? Must be some route. He's one of the best men you've got."

"He was one of the best," Stone said, handing over the telegram. "Read this."

I held the telegram up to the sunset light. It read:

JOHNSON KILLED GUNFIGHT J. K. FISHER
UVALDE THIS DATE. SIGNED. WESTCOTT.

I gave it back to Stone.

"Who's Westcott?" I asked.

"Our Uvalde office manager."

"That leaves us with J. K. Fisher."

"Yes. Ever hear of him, Harry?"

"Not till now. Should I have?"

Stone nodded grimly, voice tight.

"Try 'King Fisher,' " he said.

"Him," I answered, "I've heard of. Go ahead."

Stone laid it out for me then. Fisher had announced to all Texas that he was closing the Uvalde road to through traffic. Specifically he had warned American Mail they were not going to run their new stage line over it. Moreover, he had run the Uvalde manager out of town and back to San Antonio. He had then planted a sign squarely in the middle of the road proclaiming it was his road and that the rest of the world could take the other. When the company sent Bunk Johnson, their senior shotgun guard over from the Dallas office to make certain the first stage went through to Uvalde on schedule, Fisher ambushed the stage at his sign in the road, forced Bunk, and older man no longer in his prime as a gunman, to draw, then shot him off the seat box of the stage and left him dying in the dirt of the Uvalde road. It was here that they had sent for Harry Roebuck and the question now was, would Roebuck take the job or wouldn't he? Roebuck being me, and me seeing no place to hide in the division office, I threw in.

I still had a question or two of my own, however.

"I don't get it," I frowned. "Why would Fisher want that road closed? What's he got against American Mail? It don't make sense."

Stone wagged his head, held up his hands again.

"It makes sense, Harry," he said. "Hard, dirty sense. By now, most folks know the law has a habit of following American Mail west. We move into a town and trouble moves out. Fisher knows that, too, and trouble is his business. He's a hell-raiser and a rustler and is making money with his left hand faster than his right can spend it. Uvalde's his town and unless we get that new run through, it's going to stay his town. If he can buffalo American Mail, who's going to stop him?"

"Well, for one thing, what's holding up the Texas Rangers?"

"They're not on our payroll, Harry. You are."

"That's a handy way of looking at it—for the Texas Rangers," I said. "But it suits me. I'll take the job. When do I leave?"

Fool questions never go long begging for blunt answers and this one was no more than decently out of my mouth than a train whistled sharply down at the depot. Stone pulled out his watch.

"That's the 6:05 for San Antone," he said. "How soon you want to leave?"

I wasn't going to let him run any cold bluffs on me. I pulled out my own watch.

"6:01," I said. "Good a time as any to go to Texas and kill a man."

Stone looked at me a little hard.

"How's that, Harry?" he said.

"It's what you want done isn't it, Mr. Stone?" I answered him.

"Now, Harry, I didn't say that!"

"No, we never do *say it*, Mr. Stone. But somehow it always manages to come out that way, doesn't it?"

I started for the door but Stone caught up to me.

"I know it's a rough job, Harry," he said. "You don't have to take it."

"No," I said, "and I don't have to take the company's money, either, but I've developed some soft habits doing so all these years, and eating is one of the worst."

"Now see here, Harry," he came back at me, "there's no call for you to take such a hard-nose attitude. American Mail will always have some kind of a job for you."

"Thank you," I said, "but some kind of a job is not my kind of a job." The train tooted again just then and I started out the door once more.

"Harry," said Stone anxiously, "be careful!"

"Thank you," I repeated, "I never got hurt running for a train yet," and that is the way we left it.

It was seven hundred miles from the division office to San Antonio. The 6:05 was a makeup train of two mail cars, one chair car and thirty-three cattle car empties to be dropped at Fort Worth. Naturally we did not establish any new line records. I had plenty of time to think, which I didn't need at all. I had known when I left the office why American Mail had sent for me, and what my job was—or rather what it was meant to be—to go down to Texas and kill King Fisher, one of the two fastest guns alive. I didn't blame the company for the order, as a man with a reputation like King's doesn't leave either the law, or legitimate business folks, much of any other approach. But I had a hunch about young King Fisher and I intended to play it through. Providing, that is, I could get somebody to play it with me. In that direction my first move was almost straight across the street from the depot in San Antonio, and I made it as soon as I lighted down there the next evening.

Angling through the dust away from the depot, I squinted through the twilight to make sure my friends were still doing business in Bexar County and sure enough they were. The oil lamp hung from the front roof eave had just been lit and its rays showed me the sign hadn't changed a dot or a comma. "HDQTRS. TEXAS RANGERS, CO. A," it read, which was a good thing, for I required—required?—I had to have—the approval of my hunch by the Rangers before trying it on King Fisher. Also I might need their active backing, and they were pretty fair country gunfighters or, for that matter, city gutter-fighters, and what I had in mind for King was a sort of combination of John Wesley Hardin and the Marquis of Queensbury set to Texas rules.

Luckily, I caught Captain Randolph in a sinking spell and he not only approved my idea for dealing with the one-man war in Uvalde County but said that any further aid the Rangers could furnish me, I had only to name it. They had tried several of their own hunches on King Fisher and his Uvalde crowd without what you might call a crowning success anywhere along the line. My underhanded approach sounded just right to them and they graciously gave me the green light to go ahead and run its track into Uvalde—if I could.

My first need was for a good night's sleep, which I got for a dollar and a half at the Unicorn Hotel. I had quite a few visitors during the night but it takes more than a couple of hundred playful bites to keep a really tired man awake. Besides, everybody has to make his living the best way he can in this life, and I never did grudge an honest bedbug his pint of my blood.

Sunrise next morning I was hitting along the main road west out of San Antonio in a two-horse rig rented from the Alamo Livery & Prairie Hay Company, across from the firehouse and down the street from the Ranger headquarters building. That's the old firehouse, on the corner of the square, not the one they have now.

It was a fine morning, my team full of ginger and

even me feeling like I might live. My purpose, of course, was not to study the Texas daybreak but to feel out the party of the second part. When you go up against a gunfighter of King Fisher's reputation you have got to call it a war. And in a war the first thing you do is scout the enemy lines. For me, I had to see that reported sign of King Fisher's with my own eyes and, if possible, get a close-up look at the famous young man who had put it there, before deciding precisely how to open my campaign to get American Mail's first stage into Uvalde on time and as advertised.

Presently, I struck a county road coming in from the side. The turn-off sign read, "UVALDE, 55 MI.," and I set myself for the long drive. About four that afternoon, coming around a sharp bend made blind by heavy mesquite, oak and catclaw thorn trees, I very nearly had to burn off the hide on my team's hocks, hauling them up. The rig slid sideways, decided not to tip over, settled down in a cloud of red Texas real estate. I dug the grit out of my eyes and shook my head three to five times, but it would not go away. There it stood planted right square in the middle of the wagon ruts of the Uvalde road, and what it said was as to-the-point as a sat-on pin.

THIS IS KING FISHER'S ROAD
TAKE THE OTHER

I got down from the rig, still shaking my head, and walked over for a closer study of the sign. Looking at it, I had to grin.

There it was sure enough, the sign which was to become a legend, along with the wild youngster who put it there. How could you help grinning at that kind of brass? Planting a split-board sign in the middle of a public thoroughfare and expecting folks to take it seriously?

It was one too many for an old hand like me, and I stepped up to work it loose and throw it aside, still chuckling over the pure gall it had taken to put it there. But that was what fooled so many people about King Fisher. And what made him different. Deadly different. He did have that lighthearted sense of humor and playful good clean fun.

I had no more than put my hands to the sign, than a string of gunshots set in from immediately up-road. The first one took off my hat and knocked it skittering through the air. The following ones kept it going on the same jumpy course. I froze right where I was, hands still on the sign. But I did move my eyes enough to see who was working the artillery.

What I saw would have made a darkie break his gin bottle.

He was a young fellow, twenty-odd. Tall, dark-skinned, soot-black hair, Mexican handlebar mustache, eyes like obsidian chips, and dressed as no gunman of reputation before him, or since.

Starting at the top he wore a Chihuahua sombrero, snow-white, with a gold Aztec snake for a hatband. Next came a gold-embroidered soft buckskin jacket, a red silk waist-sash and—it's hard to believe even retelling it—chaps made out of Bengal tiger skins! After the chaps, the fact his boots were grass green leather with yellow dragons sewed in eight rows of pale petunia stitching couldn't shine. Neither could his spurs being hung with little silver bells which actually chimed when he walked. Nothing could hope to touch those cat-hair pants, not even the brace of ivory-handled Colts with which he was chasing my hat. But the way he was using those Colts was two other things again. He didn't miss that hat with a one of the twelve shots he threw at it, and he fired right-and left-handed, alternately, from horseback! He jumped that hat around like it was a tin can and him firing a .22 pumpkin roller from the shoulder. And he was only getting started.

When the hat hit the ground following his last shot, the gunman got down off his horse and walked slowly past me. Reaching the fallen hat, he reloaded one shell into his right-hand gun and pointed the gun at the hat. Then, turning away as though he couldn't bear to watch himself do it, he shot that poor wounded hat. Having put it out of its misery, he removed his own sombrero and held it to his chest while he bowed his head in respect. Then he turned to me and said with genuine commisery, "It's done for, poor thing. I'll give it a proper burying for you, mister."

Well, I looked him over and answered back: "Thank you. I reckon you would do as much for me, too, providing I asked for it."

"Let's say, providing you keep on asking for it, Mr. Roebuck," he said with a nice smile.

I looked at him sideways.

"You seem pretty well acquainted with me, friend," I said. "Who are you?"

The young fellow stepped back and looked down at himself as though to see if maybe he had forgotten to put on his pants, or something. But seeing the tiger skin chaps, red silk bellyband and all the rest of it was in place, he glanced back up at me sort of hurt like and said in a most gentle and courteous voice, "Now, Mr. Roebuck that wasn't too kindly of you. Take another careful look and see if you can't do better. Squint hard, now, it's bound to come to you."

I nodded, more to myself than to him.

I knew who he was all right and he knew that I did. There just weren't that many gunfighters wearing tiger chaps and white Mexican sombreros running loose in West Texas that spring. I was looking at the one and only, the original and no substitute—Mr. J. K. Fisher, of Uvalde.

The latter, waiting politely, said at last.

"Well, Mr. Roebuck?"

"Well, Mr. Fisher," I countered.

He shrugged.

"I'd say it was your move. What would you say?"

"I'd agree."

"What do you aim to do with it?"

"Go buy me a new hat."

He liked that. He broke into his sudden, sunny smile.

"You know, Mr. Roebuck, it's too bad you're working for American Mail. I got an idea we could get along right fine riding for the same side. What you think?"

"I got that idea, too, King," I told him carefully. "Otherwise, I wouldn't have taken on this job of opening up your road for the company."

Now the smile turned frostbit, chilling the voice along with it.

"Nobody's opening up my road, Mr. Roebuck. Not you, not American Mail, not nobody." He frowned in honest dismay, pointing to his sign. "Can't you *read?*"

"Sure," I said quickly. "But can you?"

That worried him. He knew I wasn't getting smart with him, and his frown deepened.

"What you mean?" he said.

For answer I gave him the paper which I had had the Rangers draw up for me.

"Open it up, King," I urged him, "and read it."

He hesitated, wanting to look inside and see what it said. He sensed it was something out of the ordinary, something to do with him and with why I was there for American Mail. But in the end his natural outlaw suspicion was too strong for him. He shoved the paper back at me, shaking his head.

"You read it," he said. "On your way back to San

Antone. You'll have lots of time for you're getting started right now.''

''Don't be a fool, Fisher,'' I said, taking the paper. ''At least read it—see what it says.''

''Mr. Roebuck,'' he replied, ''you get back in that rig and you wheel it around and you light out and don't you slow down till you're shut of Uvalde County, hear?''

''That your final offer, King?''

''It is unless you want to wind up where that other American Mail fellow did.''

''You mean Bunker Johnson?''

''Whatever his name was.''

''Whatever his name was, eh?'' He had said it offhandedly and now caught the anger in my slow repeat of his words. At once his attitude changed.

''Listen, Mr. Roebuck,'' he said, ''there wasn't time for getting any names. I asked this fellow to turn around and go back easy and nice as you can ask a man to do anything. He drew on me, left me no choice.''

I shook my head, still seething inside.

''No choice, King?'' I asked. ''You sure you wanted a choice? I just tried to give you one all wrote up in black and white.'' I tapped the paper in my hand. ''You wouldn't even look at it. No, you didn't want my choice and I don't think you wanted Bunk Johnson's. Now you listen to me, boy, and you listen good. You're going to get another kind of a choice now—from me personally. I'm ordering that stage you shot Bunk Johnson off of sent back through to Uvalde. When she comes, she'll be bringing you that other choice, *sabe?*''

''No *sabe*,'' he said. ''Try it again.''

''I'll be on that stage,'' I told him, ''right where Bunk Johnson was.''

''Then you'll wind up in the dirt right where he did.''

''That's the chance I'm taking, King. The one you're taking is something else again.''

"Such as?"

"Such as the difference between me and Bunk Johnson."

I had turned and headed for the rig with the statement, but he called softly after me.

"What difference is that, Mr. Roebuck?"

I wheeled on him, flashing the draw. The old Colt bucked and roared to the thunder of five shots blending. King Fisher's white hat jumped off his head and kept right on jumping through the air behind him, exactly as had mine earlier. As it landed in a chaparral thicket, I holstered the .44 Special and said just as quietly as I could.

"That difference, Mr. Fisher. Good day, sir."

I gave him a nod as short as a bobcat's tail and climbed into the rig. Backing the horses, I swung them about, heading them for San Antonio. King Fisher had to jump to avoid being run down. The last I saw of him he was standing in the dust peering off after me and shaking his head as though to say what a damned shame it was American Mail didn't know when it was licked.

Personally, I sort of agreed with him.

That night I spent in Castroville, a cowtown halfway between San Antonio and Uvalde. My idea was to spare myself the extra miles on the stage out of San Antonio next morning, while at the same time hoping to pick up some interim information on the enemy in the Castroville cantinas. I caught a mail rider going east and gave him a note for Captain Randolph and one for Charley Mertens in our San Antonio office requesting that he roll the Uvalde stage as planned, seeing that it picked me up here in Castroville not later than high noon. That done, I waited for midnight, time for the native telegraph to start clicking in from Uvalde and for local tongues to get sloshy enough to repeat what came off the key from King Fisher's town.

I had my news by one A.M.

Word was that another damnfool American Mail agent had collared King and challenged him on his own terms and trade—as a gunfighter. Over in Uvalde the populace was waiting and wagering on the outcome. Or rather waiting and looking for wagers on the outcome. For American Mail money was mighty scarce. King was swaggering the main stem of his hometown good-naturedly offering to lay ten for one on himself and getting no takers. The synthesis of opinion in Uvalde was that if the Texas Rangers couldn't pin back King Fisher's ears no mealy-nose American Mail detective was going to do it. As for King, he was telling his fellow Uvaldans that if they wanted to see how fast a four-horse stagecoach could get turned around in the middle of a thirty-foot county road, they need only show up out by his sign late next afternoon. Last I heard, going to bed, was that Uvalde was planning to take King up on his invitation, wholesale. It figured to be the biggest turnout in West Texas since Captain Jack Coffee Hays whipped the Mexicans at Salado.

Next morning the stage rolled in Castroville at 11:36 A.M. After a twenty-minute rest to water the teams, I took over on the box, relieving the regular driver. I noticed that on my way out of town several of the locals took off their hats and held them to their left breasts as I passed by. It gave me a nice feeling to know I wasn't without friends, even though a stranger.

I wasn't fooling myself any about King Fisher, however. His hand wasn't going to be holding a hat. But where I wasn't fooling myself about him, I was hoping I had fooled him about me. I had led him to think he had me in the same corner he had old Bunk Johnson, making me come at him with a gun in my hand. Yet I had no intention of playing the game to those rules. A man doesn't get old in this business giving away advantages to young gunfighters. I didn't mean to give one ounce of edge to King Fisher. All's fair in love and war, I figured, and what young King and I had to settle between us wasn't precisely a love affair. And I didn't let my conscience slow me up any, either. I wasn't five minutes off regular schedule—four P.M.—rounding that mesquite bend just shy of King's sign.

Well, I don't think Grant got a bigger cheer for taking Vicksburg than I did for taking that last turn on two wheels. That crowd was happier to see me than Sitting Bull was to see Custer, and for the same reasons. Still a man had to admit it was a thrill seeing that many good folks collected in one piece so far out in the sagebrush, and in such a high, fine humor, too.

The atmosphere at that road sign of King Fisher's was that of a small-time Manassas. As the citizens of our national Capitol turned out to watch the boys in blue rout Johnny Reb at the Battle of Bull Run, so the voting populace of Uvalde had come along to watch King Fisher and the American Mail detective shoot it out. I could tell with one look, coming around that bend, that I was being given less chance than Lee at Cemetery Ridge. That piebald collection of saddle horses, buggies, buckboards, surreys, Studebakers and Conestogas coagulated there in the boondocks was 110 percent in favor of their man. When they sighted me down the road and let out that yell, I don't think you could have sold a chance on American Mail for six hundred dollars, Union.

And King didn't keep them waiting.

Mounting up immediately, he swung his flashy paint into a high lope, skidded him up, short, ten feet the Uvalde side of his sign. On my side of the sign, maybe fifty feet—no, closer to seventy—I was doing the same with my four-horse hitch and big old highside Abbott & Downing coach. It got that quiet you couldn't hear a baby cry nor an old man hawk to spit. I mean that multitude didn't let out a peep.

In the stillness, King slid from his saddle, stepped clear of his horse. I wrapped my lines, set the brake, eased down off the driver's box, moved out to one side of the coach. There we were, the two champions, one of the law and the other of disorder, come to a halt facing each other at a distance of maybe sixty feet—just a deliberate shade outside good gunfighting range. The crowd sucked in and took a tighter hold on its breath. All eyes were on King Fisher and he knew it. He took one step toward me and spoke up frosty.

"All right, Mr. Roebuck, let's start the walk-up. You make it as close as you want. Cut loose when you're ready."

He started toward me again but I held up both hands real quick.

"Hold it, King," I said. "That's close enough."

He grinned and made a little bow.

"Age before youth and beauty, Mr. Roebuck. Make your move."

I returned the grin as best I could.

"I'm going to, King," I told him, "but not the way you think."

His grin was well gone now.

"Pull your gun, Mr. Roebuck—"

I shook my head, still holding up my hands.

"The only thing I'm going to pull, King, is the buckle on my gun belt. You shoot me while I'm doing that and you got a whole townful of readymade witnesses right behind you."

"Yeah," he said, "but you're forgetting one thing, Mr. Roebuck. They're friendly witnesses."

"All right," I answered him, "let's try it this way: you cut down on me while I'm dropping my buscadero rig and you'll get your own belt punched six extra holes before your gun clears leather. You don't believe it, *you* take a look behind *me*. Maybe you can't read but you can damn sure count. So count."

The crowd got pin-still as King looked past me to the stagecoach. I saw his eyes go wide, and knew why.

The old Abbott & Downing had sprouted riflesnouts. She was bristling steel barrels like a stirred-up quill pig. From beneath the canvas luggage cover of the roof decking two hard-looking riflemen held their Winchesters on a line with King Fisher's belt buckle. From the two forward and two rear window curtains of each side, below, peered four more earnest marksmen, their carbines pinned to the same target. Their total number was six, their reputations certain, their identity undeniable. They were the gentlemen in the white hats—the Texas Rangers.

King Fisher gave them, and me, a look of black disgust. He showed no fear of the Rangers but did include an expression of great disappointment in Harry Roebuck.

"It's a pretty lowdown trick, Mr. Roebuck," he said. "But what does it prove?"

"It proves you've got a lot to learn about life, King," I told him. "And, personally, I think you're man enough to learn your first lesson right here."

"What have you got to teach me, Mr. Roebuck? How to be a liar like you?"

"I didn't lie to you, boy," I said. "But maybe you did to me."

"Now what you mean by that?"

"I said I'd come back alone on the driver's box of that stage, just like Bunk Johnson came. I did it."

"Yeah, with six Rangers hid out behind your back!"

"Well, King, it looks like you brought along a few friends too."

"It isn't the same. You know it isn't. You lied to me, Mr. Roebuck."

I looked him in the eye, answering quietly.

"Well, boy, if I didn't keep my word, let's see if you can keep yours."

I unbuckled my gun belt and let it slide to the ground. The crowd from Uvalde pulled in behind King, the Rangers got out of the stage and moved up behind me. I armed out of my coat, started unbuttoning my shirt.

"You said," I went on, "that if I came back on that driver's box where Bunk Johnson was, you would put me right where you put him, in the dirt of this road."

I dropped my shirt and my voice with it.

"Let's see you do it, King. Like a man, without your guns."

He studied me through the longest five seconds on record, then slipped off his gun belt, slid his vacquero shirt off over his head and put up his hands. Soundlessly, under that hot Texas sun, we began circling.

What followed was the wildest bare-knuckle fight ever staged south of Chicago, with the six referees wearing white hats and Winchesters and the audience all armed and ready to cut loose with anything from a .22 derringer to a sawed-off shotgun if it didn't like the decision. But it would be unkind to detail that battle. King Fisher didn't have a chance. I beat him very nearly blind and when it was all over he was down in the dirt and all done. I was about as bad off but I was still on my feet. The cheering of the crowd had fallen off as though somebody had stuck its collective head in a bucket of swamp water. The Rangers moved silently in on King Fisher and the folks from his hometown moved silently away from him. Within five minutes the last of them was started back toward Uvalde. Groggily, King watched them go, leaving him alone with his enemies, a chastened, humbled man. When two of the Rangers had helped him to his feet, he turned to me.

"Well, Mr. Roebuck," he acknowledged unhappily,

"it looks as though you were right. Your word is better than mine. What is the next stage of the ambush? Back to San Antone with the Rangers?"

I shook my head soberly.

"No, King, the Rangers didn't come along to arrest you. They were just here to see we had a fair fight and to make sure, to their own satisfaction, that you couldn't read. I told them you acted like you couldn't, but I reckon they'd feel better about it if you showed them your ownself. Here."

I handed him the same paper I had tried to get him to read before, and this time he took it. After a puzzled look at all of us, he unfolded it and began frowning his way through what it said. Pretty quick, he looked back up.

"Why, I don't believe it," he said. "This here is a deputy sheriff's appointment for Uvalde County in my name. It's writ right there, 'J. K. Fisher,' plain as fresh paint."

"That's right, King," I smiled. "She's all yours, courtesy of the Texas Rangers. You see, they agreed with me that you'd make a better live deputy than a dead outlaw. They got Governor Marvin to go along with them on my idea and he added one of his own. There's a full executive amnesty for the state of Texas goes with that star Captain Randolph, yonder, is fishing out of his vest pocket."

I bobbed my head toward the Ranger captain standing off to our left. King looked over at him and Randolph stepped toward him holding out the emblem. King kind of straightened up.

"I guess that makes it my move, don't it?" he said.

"I'd say it did," I replied. "What you aim to do with it?"

He looked at me dead serious and said, "Same thing you did when I asked you that question, Mr. Roebuck."

I returned his look, puzzled.

"How's that, King?" I said.

"Go get me a new hat," he grinned. "Care to come along?"

"Oh, I dunno. What kind you going to get?" I played it sobersided now but it didn't slow him a wink.

"Well, something appropriate to my new standing in the community, I should think," he said. He moved to Randolph and took the star from him, pinning it carelessly upside down on his Mexican shirt, which he had gotten back into while we talked. Then, easing back over to me, he went on as though nothing had interrupted his statement. "Whatever kind of a hat they're recommending for wet-eared deputy sheriffs in West Texas this spring."

I had to hand him back his grin now, and something else as well. Reaching down, I got his gun belt out of the road and reached it over to him.

"Hang it on, Sheriff," I said. "I got an American Mail Company passenger run needs guarding into Uvalde."

King belted on his gun and, while I was getting into my shirt, picked mine up from the dirt and handed it to me with a bow and a sweep of his arm toward the coach.

"After you, sir—"

Straightening up he put his hand over his heart.

"The welfare of American Mail is the civic responsibility of every decent law-abiding resident of Uvalde County. I am deeply affected by this opportunity to make sure the sons of bitches understand it."

He watched me pass him by, headed for the stage, then gave his gun belt a determined hitch and started after me. The Rangers caught up his horse, tied him to the luggage boot, climbed aboard and waved the "all set" sign. I swung up to the box, followed by King Fisher. Reaching under the seat, King pulled out the regular guard's shotgun, barred it across his knees.

"All right," he said, "let's go."

I whistled up the teams. Slapping them smartly with the lines, I kicked off the brake and yelled, "Hee-yahh! Hee-yahh!" They hit into their collars and the stage began to roll. The minute it did, King made an excited motion toward the road in front of us and hollered out, "Hold on!"

I slammed the brakes back on and hauled up the teams. King jumped down and ran off up the road. Pretty soon he was back lugging his uprooted sign. Climbing back up with me, he stowed it under the roof-deck tarp, picked the shotgun up again and nodded to me.

"You never can tell, Mr. Roebuck. I might want to go back in business for myself some day."

I gave him the eye, shook up the teams, got the coach to rolling again. Half an hour later she was parked in front of American Mail's new office in Uvalde and the adventure of King Fisher's road was closed.

As for King, he did go back in business for himself some years later, and was killed in an ambush with Ben Thompson in the Vaudeville, a theater-saloon in San Antonio, in March of 1884.

They say King Fisher never had a chance, but I know better. I gave him one and it was a good one. Yet he didn't end any different from all the other wild guns before and after him. When the bullet with his name on it came along, he was there.

The Redeeming of Fate Rachel

The rider, following the stage road west, came to the last rise before the town somewhere nearing eight o'clock. Warily, he turned his mount from the road. Shortly, hidden by the wither-high sage, he swung down from the horse and walked to a spot where the brush thinned to give an unobstructed view of the flat below. He squinted through the early darkness, studying the distant wink of the settlement's oil lamps.

Shaking his head, he stirred uneasily.

How many times outside how many towns had he gotten down in the sage to stand thus and stare through the dusty starlight while his mind weighed the excuse of sworn and salaried duty against the dark excitement of the hunt which no money could explain and no oath of office justify? He did not know. He could not remember.

They had called him bounty hunter, although he was not that.

A deputy United States marshal on special service, yes, that he had been. And the special part of the service meaning that the Federal Government paid him to work through its catalog file of warrants of first-degree murder marked ''returned unserved,'' yes, that also was true. But that he had been the common scalphunting pariah, which the anonymity of his employment demanded he appear to be, was not true. Still the people, good and bad, of those other times and other towns could not know this and so called him what they did.

It was because of this calling and because of his inability to defend himself against its charges that he had given up his marshal's shield and the long rides and lonely starlight waits which were the other badges of his thankless trade.

Yet now he wondered anew at the validity of his long-ago decision.

Ten years, he thought. A long, a very long time ago. But apparently not long enough. The habits of a man's past did not forsake him. It was only the years themselves that fled. The years that dimmed but could not destroy an acquired pattern of life and death. The years that slowed the hand but only sharpened the memory of its lost speed. Nothing else changed.

Until this moment he had believed the years of exile following his last job in this same settlement had cured him forever of the excitement sickness that formerly seized him with such a final mile's scanning, yet here he stood as tightly drawn as ever in the old dangerous days.

Rachel shook off the thought, but could not shake off its incubus. It was still sitting his shoulders when he checked his mount at town's edge to glance at the sign which had replaced the one he remembered.

Welcome to
MOBEETIE
Cultural Capital of
the Panhandle
Pop. 697

He crowfooted his eye corners in the wry grimace that was his trademark way of reflecting an inside, accepting grin to go with the outside, dubious headshake. He rode slowly on. What had the population been that other time? Fifty? Seventy-five, perhaps? A hundred on Saturday nights? And where had the culture been hiding then? The same place it most likely was hiding now? In the bottom of a brown bottle at the Cattleman's Bar, or the Boar's Nest Saloon? One thing certain. Wherever it was, it wasn't hiding any more. It was standing up on its hind legs waving its paws to be recognized.

Culture with a capital K. Mobeetie had changed. She had come of age. No longer could she be called by the affectionate bawdyism of Fate's day, "the Cowboy Outhouse of the Plains." She had class now. She was a city. The cultural center of the entire, unadulterated Staked Plains, and no less. It wasn't a few swift years since Fate had been here. It was a whole lifetime. Fate felt sad about that. He spoke to his horse and the animal picked up to a shuffle walk, moving his rider more quickly past the tinpan blare of the numberless saloon pianos, on down the street to the darkened quarter of the few commercial houses flanking the entertainment district.

The maneuver was not in time.

Abreast the Pink Lady, obviously Mobeetie's answer to the prayers of the two-dollar trade, a blast of gunfire kicked open the establishment's batwing doors and a man, gun in hand, staggered backward into the street. He was followed by two toughs returning his fire. They cut him down squarely in front of Rachel's horse, in mid-street, then shifted their Colts to cover any play the passing horseman might have in mind. But Rachel had been there before.

Checking his horse only enough to prevent trampling the fallen gunman he touched his hat brim soberly to the two killers on the boardwalk, directed his mount around the body, held him on a steady, slow course down the street. The men from the Pink Lady watched him a bit, then turned and went back to their bourbon.

Down along the dark part of the main thoroughfare, Rachel pulled into the hitching rail in front of the Anderson Express Company. Tying up, he stepped quickly into the shadows of the roofed boardwalk. Nothing moved, or made noise in his vicinity. He put his hand to the office door latch.

Inside, a lone Rochester hand lamp burned on a wall base behind the door. Rachel, easing the dusted panels open, stepped through from the street. As he did, a figure moved out from the wall behind him. Another figure reached swiftly to blow out the wall lamp. Rachel set himself, but did not turn.

"I suppose," he said quietly, "that you have something in my back."

"Shotguns," answered one of the men. "Sawed-offs."

"It will do," said Rachel.

Now, from behind the shipping counter directly in front of him, a third man rose up and asked softly, "Rachel?"

The latter, unseen in the darkness, spread his arid grin. "With one 'l,' " he said. "Who are you?"

"T. C. Barnes," answered the other. "Criminal Division, Anderson Express."

"You're the one sent for me."

"Yes." Barnes turned to his henchmen. "All right, you men, wait outside. Light the lamp as you leave."

The men did as told, departed, careful to adjust the drawn shade on the door in going out. Barnes turned back to Fate Rachel.

"It's been a term of years, Rachel," he said, "but we've got a real nasty one on our hands this time."

"What do you mean, 'we'?" asked Rachel. "You got a midget in your pocket, Mr. Barnes? I haven't worked a law job for a long time. I'm not about to start in again either."

"Circumstances, Rachel," said the other, "alter cases. Like I said, we're in trouble. You, me, the express company."

"And who else?" asked Rachel quietly.

Barnes eyed him. "You're pretty quick, aren't you?" he said.

"I used to be. Go ahead, Mr. Barnes. Me, you, the express company—who else?"

Barnes quit circling, closed in.

"Does the name Ransom Briscoe mean anything to you?" he asked.

"Should it?" shrugged Rachel.

"He seems to think so."

"Oh?"

"You put him in Yuma for ten years."

"Butcher Briscoe, yes!" Rachel's eyes narrowed belatedly. "I'd forgotten he had a human name. But good Lord, Mr. Barnes, that was—" he broke off, as the significance of it dawned on him, then finished softly, "—that was ten years ago."

Barnes nodded. "He served every day of the ten, Rachel. Got out last month, showed up here in Mobeetie last week.''

''He would do that,'' said Rachel. ''He was sentenced from here. This is where he stood trial, and where I brought him in, and where I had to give the testimony that convicted him. He had a wife here, too. Pretty little thing, and nice. I never forgot her, and she never forgave me.'' He paused, looking at the Anderson agent. ''That was my last job, Mr. Barnes. You must know that. It was killing an Anderson clerk that put me on his track.''

''Of course I know it, Rachel. It's why the company had me come out here to meet you. They felt they owed you that much.''

''Let's get on with it,'' suggested Rachel. ''I don't take to mystery stories.''

''I'm not going to tell you one,'' said Barnes. ''This is a murder yarn, out-and-out. Briscoe took this local office for the day's receipts on Tuesday last. Got maybe two hundred dollars. And left two messages with the clerk. One was that he meant to take Anderson Express for every nickel they had, west of Wichita, that he intended to set up a raiding operation out here in the Staked Plains that would make the James boys look like sneak thieves.''

''Mr. Barnes,'' said Rachel irritably, ''did you bring me all the way down here to Mobeetie to tell me Briscoe had a big mouth?''

''No, I brought you down here to give you the other message—the one he left for you.''

''A message for me? From Rance Brisco?''

''No less. He told the clerk to tell the bounty hunter he was going to get him if it took ten years and ten thousand dollars. The company figured he had to mean you, Rachel. You worked the job alone.''

''I always worked my jobs alone, but it was decent of the Anderson folks to look me up and call me in.

Briscoe's a bad lot. He might try it.'' Rachel scratched his chin with the side of his thumb, shook his head frowningly. ''Now, the ten years I can figure. What's the ten thousand dollars supposed to mean, though? That throws me.''

Barnes bobbed his head abruptly.

''Briscoe told the clerk that, too. He's put a price on your head, Rachel. Literally. He's offering ten thousand dollars for your ears—with your head between them.''

Rachel returned the nod embellished with his quirky, dry grin. ''Well,'' he said, ''that's ten times what I got paid for him.''

''Yes, he mentioned that also.''

''Oh? Well, one thing sure. It's a wise move on his part giving himself ten years to do the job. It's apt to take him that long to get up the price at the rate he's going.''

''That's where you're wrong, Rachel. And it's why you ought to be interested in taking on this assignment—or at least the company thought you ought to be.''

''*Assignment?* What assignment, Mr. Barnes?''

''To get back Anderson's money.''

Rachel's warm gray eyes took on a puzzled cast.

''Didn't you just tell me he got only a couple of hundred in this Mobeetie haul, Mr. Barnes?''

''I did. But like Briscoe said, that was only the beginning.''

Rachel spread his hands helplessly.

''I wish you would quit cat-and-mousing me, Mr. Barnes,'' he pleaded. ''That is, unless you are just personally feeling mousey. I have ridden three hundred miles to find out what this thing is all about and so far you have been trying to pull me in with nothing but a wide circle of teasy bait drops. Now please lay off sprinkling the cheese, Mr. Barnes, and spring the trap.''

The Anderson agent scowled, made uneasy by the other's diffident courtesy.

"All right, Rachel," he said, "here's the whole chunk. Briscoe and his bunch took the Texas and Pacific's Colorado Flyer at Red Rock station the day after he hit our office here in Mobeetie. Shot our messenger and cleaned out the express car, including our shipment of cash."

"Like what shipment of your cash, Mr. Barnes?"

"Like the Fort Bliss army payroll. Going from Denver down to El Paso. Rance Briscoe's got it now and the Army is howling."

"How hard would you say they were howling, Mr. Barnes?"

"You're not going to like 'how hard,' Rachel." The Anderson man paused, jaw outthrust. "Ten thousand dollars to the decimal point!" he snapped.

"Thank you, that's about hard enough," nodded Fate Rachel, and put thoughtful thumb to chin-side.

"I guess you can read the rest of the trail," said Barnes.

"Yes," said Rachel, "I reckon that's so. But how does she size to you?"

Barnes watched him, to make sure he was not smarting off with him. Seeing that he was not, he laid it out as he saw it, and as the company had instructed him to.

"It means," he said, "that every cheap and high-priced hungry gun in the territory will be out for you. Every floater with a Colt, from here to Red River, will know that Rance Briscoe has come by the cash to back up his boast of buying your ears for ten thousand dollars. It means, exactly, that from the time you walk out of this office tonight, every armed stranger you pass on the street may be the one who has Briscoe's ten thousand already spent. Rachel, you're up against odds you can't buck alone. The company sent me here to tell you that

Anderson Express will back you with every means at its disposal, if you are willing, and ready, to put on your gun again and go after this man."

"You mean, don't you," said Rachel, "if I will agree to go after the company's money?"

"You find the man, you'll find the money. He hasn't had time to fence it, and wouldn't dare pass it yet."

"That's so."

"Well, Rachel? It's your life and our money. Have we got a deal?"

Fate Rachel stood thinking it over. The years rolled back, and with them he could hear and taste again all the wickedness and hate that hunting men for money had earned him in those former times. At last he raised his eyes and said quietly to Barnes: "No thank you. I was there once. I didn't like it."

"We'll pay 10 percent," said Barnes. "That's a thousand dollars on total recovery. A lot of money, Rachel. Especially, for saving your own life."

Rachel shook his head slowly.

"I want you to thank the company for warning me, Mr. Barnes. But I have earned my last dime as a 'dollar deputy.' I'll do my best against Rance Briscoe and his bunch, but I'll not take a dollar to go after his head."

"You're a fool, man. You won't have a chance."

"No, but I have a choice. And I made it ten years ago."

"There's nothing I can do to persuade you?"

"Nothing, Mr. Barnes. But there is something you could do to pleasure me. Is Mrs. Briscoe still living here?"

"Why do you ask that?" The Anderson agent pounced on the question with quick suspicion, but his companion only shrugged, soft-voiced.

"I thought you might have located her in your investigation," he said. "I'd like to look her up, if she's here in Mobeetie. Maybe she would listen after all these years. She was a fine girl, Mr. Barnes. I'd like to see her and try to set things straight.''

Barnes suddenly felt sorry for the gray-haired rider before him. He felt, too, a little foolish for having made him the company offer, after seeing him. He had not himself known Fate Rachel. But that this slow-talking old fellow could be the legend of ten years ago, he found more than he could accept.

''Sure,'' he said, ''Mrs. Briscoe's still in town, old-timer. She's working the Pink Lady.''

His listener nodded. ''I remember,'' he said, ''that she sang in those days, too. It's how she met Briscoe.''

''She's not singing any more,'' said Barnes.

''Well, a voice will go with the years. That's only natural. Thank you, Mr. Barnes. The Pink Lady, you said?''

''First one back up the street. You can't miss it.''

''I know. Met a fellow coming out of there tonight.'' Rachel touched his hat brim. ''Thanks, again.''

T. C. Barnes didn't answer him. He only stood and watched him go out into the street and untie his horse. Then he watched him go, leading the horse, walking up the middle of the street with that bent-kneed crouch and little rolling limp which never leaves the man who has worn the gun for a living, no matter the number of his years beyond the wearing. When Rachel had disappeared, Barnes blew out the wall lamp and muttered angrily to the smoky darkness, ''Damn, it's hell to grow old!''

Rachel found it hard to think of Eileen Briscoe working in a place like the Pink Lady. But investigation established that she was, and was doing so at the rock-bottom level. She attempted to solicit Rachel at his table almost before he could get his chair under him. He only knew it was she by the remembered throaty sound of her voice, and when he touched his hat and said, "Evening, Mrs. Briscoe," she only stared at him blurrily and answered, "Well, you must be from somewhere far back in the better days, but I can't say how far back, nor how much better."

"Don't try," Rachel told her gently. "Just put me down for an old friend."

"You must be pretty old, all right. I haven't been Mrs. Briscoe for—for—" She let it trail off, staring into her glass, and Rachel finished it softly for her.

"For ten years," he said. "Isn't that it, Eileen?"

The woman rolled her head, trying to focus on him.

"Say," she managed, "who are you? You seem to know an awful lot about me, and maybe about my troubles, eh? That's it. Rance sent you. He's out now, I heard."

"Yes, he's out, but I'm not here from him. Excepting by a long trail around."

"Well, it can't be long enough for me. Not from Rance."

"Eileen—Mrs. Briscoe, ma'am—I got nothing to do with Ransom Briscoe. I'm only here to talk to you. I got but a little time, and I thought you might remember me and we could maybe even up the old days. You sure you don't know me? I was mighty close to your husband, once. I remember you."

She frowned, trying to steady her gaze long enough to trace his sunburned features. But the effort was beyond her, and Rachel let it remain so.

"We'll have another drink," he said, "and let things work along natural."

The woman weaved her head, accepting the offer. It was on the fifth round that the floodgates of memory broke loose, letting the long-dammed waters through. As she talked, Fate Rachel felt the old, iron-fingered squeeze start within him.

Briscoe had left his young wife six months pregnant when he went to Yuma. He had never replied to her letters, never admitted paternity, never sent any money. He had money, for members of his gang in Mobeetie spent big for two years after Rance had gone away. Eileen, her figure and courage returned after the baby girl was born, had started singing in the better places. But beauty and music were fragile items on the frontier. Before long she was dancing in the not-so-good places, then not even dancing in the places which were too low to have names, good or bad.

The reason for the fall was not moral, but economic. The baby, never well, had taken a nameless chronic ill and ten years of paying incessant medical bills had brought Eileen Briscoe to the level where Fate Rachel found her.

Just recently, a new doctor from St. Louis had passed through the Panhandle studying frontier medicine. He had seen the girl and given a name to her malady. A name and a hope. There was a treatment for the disease, and a clinic in Kansas City where the treatment was practiced regularly and successfully. Otherwise, the end was as certain as tomorrow's sunset. But Eileen Briscoe had sold herself as far as she could. There were no more customers and the small hoard of money hidden in the old dresser at her town-edge shack did not begin to approach the amount mentioned by the St. Louis specialist.

When the story reached this point, Rachel's companion put her head down on her arms and began to cry. He let her sob until she slowed of her own accord, then asked softly, "How much did this doctor say is needed, Mrs. Briscoe?"

Eileen Briscoe shrugged hopelessly, head down, voice low.

"A thousand dollars, to start treatment. It might as well be ten thousand—"

Fate Rachel's gray eyes narrowed. The iron fingers around his belly made a final closing. He got up quietly and put his hand on the woman's rounded shoulder.

"Yes, ma'am," he said, looking toward the door, and thinking, beyond it, up the street, to the darkened office of the Anderson Express Company. "It might as well be."

Back outside, however, he paid no heed to Anderson Express.

Eileen Briscoe, in her wanderings, had given Rachel one clue. A girl working the Satin Slipper, a winter-thin version of Tombstone's Bird Cage Theater, had boasted of seeing Rance Briscoe since the Red Rock robbery. To an old manhunter this meant two possibilities: Briscoe was holed up locally and not on the run; the girl, having seen him once, might see him again.

How, then, to bring the one possibility to bear immediately upon the other? That, too, had an old lawman's answer: to find the man, flush the woman.

Rachel tied his horse well down the street from the garishly lit Slipper. It was eight-thirty, the evening performance not yet begun. He had half an hour to plant his poison with Edna Darcy, Briscoe's boastful—maybe—paramour. Going toward the cut-glass doors of the theater, he grinned his inward grin. With his total capital vested in the five dollars clinking in the lonely roominess of the side pocket of his faded corduroy riding coat, a half hour was ample. In a place like the Slipper he would be lucky to last ten minutes with that kind of money.

The foyer bar was not yet crowded. Most of the house girls were unemployed and his request for Edna Darcy was replied to promptly. The latter proved to be young, quick-eyed, curvaceous. Rachel didn't like her and the feeling was returned. He bought two drinks and dropped his bait abruptly.

"I am looking for Rance Briscoe," he said, "and was told to see you."

"By who?" asked the girl.

"A friend of yours—and Rance's."

"That will buy you exactly nothing, mister. You had better hit the rusty-dusty. Your cows must be lonesome for you and I don't like the taste of your whiskey."

She poured the remains of her glass into the heavy silver cigar tray on the table, and started to rise. Rachel put a hand lightly to her powdered arm.

"Ma'am, listen, I've got to find Rance. It's about that money he's offering for that bounty hunter which put him away for all them years."

The girl paused, watching him.

"What the devil are you talking about?" she said. "You want me to call the boss?"

"No thank you," said Rachel. "If you don't know what I'm talking about, then there's no way for me to warn Rance. If I can't find him, I can't tell him."

Edna Darcy sat down again. "Tell him what?" she asked.

"I'd better go," said Rachel. "The boss is looking this way. I don't want any trouble."

The head houseman was indeed eyeing them, but the Darcy girl said, "Don't pay him any mind; he won't open his yap unless I throw him the high sign. What do you want told to Rance Briscoe?"

Rachel glanced nervously around. Lowering his voice, he said quickly, "The Andersons are after him."

"My God," said the girl, "don't you think he knows that? Where you been, mister?"

"Places," answered Rachel.

"Such as which?"

"The Mobeetie office—tonight."

"And?"

"They've hired a bounty hunter to get Rance."

"That will hardly surprise him. He's been bounty-hunted before."

"Yes, ma'am. It's why I figured he'd be interested to know who they hired to do the job this time. It's the same one did the dirty work ten years ago."

Edna Darcy's face shadowed over. "That," she said, "will surprise him."

"Not if we work fast, ma'am. Will you see he gets the word? It's powerful important."

"Yes, I'll see. Who'll I say sent it?"

Rachel shifted restlessly.

"I went to jail with him on that ten-year stretch," he said, not adding he had gone only as far as the prison gates with Briscoe. "Just tell him that. He'll know who it is."

"I'd rather have a name," insisted the girl.

"And I'd rather not give one. Aiding and abetting is worth five to fifteen years where the main charge is murder."

"Murder?"

"Yes, ma'am. That express messenger Rance winged in the Red Rock job, he died this afternoon. Word came in on the telegraph just as I was locking up the office."

"The Anderson office?"

Rachel again flicked a glance around the barroom, now filling with thirsty early birds. "I took a job down there, swamping out. Thought I might hear something that'd let me get in on that ten thousand Rance is offering around. Money comes tough for us old coots, Miss. Any part of that ten thous—"

The girl got up, interrupting him.

"Get out," she said, "and keep your mouth shut. I'll get your message to Rance. He'll pay you something for it."

"Yes, ma'am, I know he will," said Rachel, backing for the doors. "Providing you get it to him, he's bound to."

Outside, he found a dark spot, disappeared into it.

Edna Darcy left the Slipper within minutes. She went across the street to her hotel room, a second floor front. Rachel saw the room lamp light up, then passed an anxious five minutes watching the drawn shade for shadows. None showed. Untying his horse, he led him across the street and to the far corner of the hotel, where he knew a second floor, outside stairway led down to the rear of the building. The stairway was also empty. Now it was guess and gamble.

The hotel backed on Third Street, and on Hartman's Livery Barn. A man could guess that Edna Darcy did not mean to walk to Rance Briscoe's hideout. Or did she? Might Briscoe have the cold nerve to be laying up, right here in Mobeetie? Rachel, remembering the fish-eyed outlaw, decided he would not. Briscoe was murderous, but not imaginative. He would be out in the brush someplace.

Mounting up, Rachel rode around to Third. Holding in at the corner, he was in time to see a two-horse light surrey swing out of the livery and head off down Third. No light showed in the barn, none burned on Third Street. It was impossible to say whether the driver was a man or a woman. But the gamble was less this time. Rachel took it without the five-minute wait. When the surrey left the last shack huddled on Mobeetie's southern flank there was less than thirty seconds, and a hundred yards of murky starlight, separating it from its mounted shadow.

Five miles south on the main road, the driver swung off on the Wolf Creek Ranch road and Rachel knew that it was Edna Darcy and that she was going to meet Rance Briscoe in the last place the law would think to look for him—in the abandoned Anderson Express stage depot at Faber's Crossing.

The idea made a man uneasy.

Faber's Crossing was the place he had taken Rance ten years ago. There had been three killings made that night in the shootout with Rance, all listed to Fate Rachel's gun, and Anderson had closed the station fearing its bad name would spoil it as an overnight stop. It had stood a decade with no tenants other than field mice, pack rats, brown bats and gopher snakes. Now it held another, deadlier resident—or residents—if Rachel's guess were correct; and his uneasiness grew deeper with each fall of his horse's hooves in the disused dust of the Wolf Creek road.

When he came up to the place, trailing the surrey more closely now so that he would not miss the location of whatever guards might challenge its driver, memory, black and fearful, reared out of the darkness with the hipshot roof and leaning wall timbers of the station.

"My God," breathed Rachel, "what am I doing here again?"

He held up his mount at the edge of the station house clearing, wanting, suddenly, to turn him back into the brush, to give the horse his head and let him run as far and fast away from Faber's Crossing as his limbs might carry him. But he did not. He had tried escaping the past by putting his back to it. He had tried ten long weary years of it. Yet that other night still lay as dark and dusty and no different in his mind from this present one. His hesitation in the sage outside Mobeetie had not been a false one. The years changed nothing but the hunger for the hunt. The thing which had to be done, which could not be faced away from, that didn't change. Rance Briscoe had waited in that darkened stage depot ten years ago; he waited in it still.

Rachel slid out from its worn, black holster, the obsolescent Cap-and-Ball .44 Remington. It felt like the handshake of an old friend, one once loved above all others but absent for too long. It felt strange, awkward, stiff and a little embarrassed. He put it back in the holster, shaking his head.

Across the clearing only one trace of light shown from the station house; a tiny, faint streak paint-brushing the sage out behind the relay-stock corrals. It fell, Rachel knew, from the kitchen window. It had to. There were no other windows in the rear wall of the rotting building. Edna Darcy guided her team to the beacon, halted the surrey just beyond it, in the weed-grown corral. No guards challenged her. No signs of life arose within the station. When she disappeared behind the corner of the rear wall, Rachel shadowed forward across the clearing, slid around the corner and up to the near frame of the lone rear window. He was in time to see nothing. The Darcy girl had vanished, and he had to assume she had already gone inside. That could mean the kitchen door was unbolted upon her arrival, and was unbolted still.

Rachel felt for the walnut handle of the old Remington. It gave him no reassurance. He set his jaw, craned to see what he might through the two-inch aperture of lamplight where the horse blanket hung on the inside failed of meeting the warped framing of the window. The effort yielded frustratingly to a decade's collection of spiderwebs, dead flies and Staked Plains dust. The door, then. Perhaps the ear might succeed where the eye had not. Again, frustration. He could hear the hum of voices but could not separate them either as to nearness, or number. One was a woman's voice, that was all he knew.

Good Lord! had the parallel of the past come down to this fineness, this last chanceful irony? Was he going to have to kick in the door and blind-jump a roomful of blurred voices exactly as he had done ten years ago.

Would the guns do all the talking once more? Giving neither side the time to surrender, to parley, to make any kind of sense at all? He made his mind quit marching the fearful circle. It was no good milling around the truth. The situation had come down to where it must; he was here, the wanted man was there. Only a door stood between him and his past.

Leave it, Rachel, leave it! the stillness around him shouted. Ride out, ride out! No one knows you came here, no one will know you have gone. Turn away, turn away. . . .

The crack of the door latch splitting out from its rusted socket beneath the drive of his boot broke into the stale-aired kitchen with the sudden, rapping sharpness of a rifleshot. Rachel, following it in, threw his first round at the lamp. Some segment of the old skill favored him. The heavy .44 bullet caught the base of the glass chimney, bursting out the light as though with a deft, blown breath, and breaking free none of the oil in the reservoir beneath the chimney, until the wick was lifeless of fire. Then, in the point-blank gloom of the plunge into darkness, the overly loud *drip, drip, drip* of the leaking fluid, spreading over the tabletop from the ruptured reservoir to fall upon the greasy floor beneath, was the only sound punctuating the blind dark of the Faber's Crossing stationhouse.

"Briscoe," said Rachel, from his position prone before the boarded-up door leading to the front of the abandoned building, "get the lady out of here."

There were no answering bursts of gunfire attracted by his voice, nor had he expected any. Total darkness confused the senses. A man is put out of element when he literally, and suddenly, cannot see. "Get the light," was not by accident the first law of the lawless—or of the lawful, who pursued them. Plunging, blinding darkness had disarmed more desperate gunmen than all the daylight drops on record.

"Just the lady, Briscoe."

If a man kept his word-strings short, and could force his play before all eyes grew accustomed to the pitch dark, he had some chance. Even when he had seen what Rachel had seen in the half second before his bullet crashed out the light.

There had been four of them, the same as the other night so long gone. Three riffraff hirelings, probably from the Red Rock job, and Briscoe. Briscoe seated at the table, the trio of gunmen bent behind him, listening to Edna Darcy. The dancehall girl talking swiftly. The four men watching her as wolves watch a buffalo calf when the snow is deep.

The singular identicality of place and number compounded the whipsawing of memories that went on, now, in Rachel's mind. But the problem remaining was no longer one of decisions; it was one of commitments already made, against those yet to be made. And no reply, either of voice or revolver, came from across the room to direct Rachel in the making. He waited, counting the seconds of silence like drops of life's blood, knowing they could become that if Briscoe and his men had the intellect, and the intestines, to outwait him, to hold motionless where they were until nature inevitably adjusted their confused vision. But Briscoe had a problem in this regard, a handicap beyond his chosing. He had Edna Darcy over there. And Edna might not want to wait for ten shades of black to become seven of gray.

"*Run, lady!*" hissed Rachel, cupping his hands to throw the sound to his left, falsely.

The sibilant warning was the trigger. There was a bumping scuffle, a curse, a rustle of satin. The rear door banged open, framed the dancehall dress and surrey-blown blond curls, hinged rattingly shut on the return throw of the tension-spring which alone held it closed with the latch-socket destroyed.

"You son of a bitch," said Rance Briscoe, into the echoing stillness. And that was all. From then, Rachel heard only a lip-rustle of cross-room whispering, quickly stilled.

After what seemed like fifteen minutes and was perhaps ten seconds, he caught a bump to his left. Then a scrape of rough cloth to his right. They were coming to him, working around the kitchen walls, both ways from the table, to converge on the shuttered door into the front, most likely. It was a good plan. It was second nature for an outnumbered man to put his back to a wall. Briscoe and his pack had figured that move. Now if they kept coming with their counter to it, they had him.

Rachel shook off the chill of the thought. He set his teeth to hold back his suspended breathing. In the intense quiet, the steady dripping of the coal oil from the broken lamp on the table was the moment's only sound. But, suddenly, to Rachel, its insistent thinness had the sweetness of a cavalry bugle calling the charge from over the hill. That damned lamp! Maybe, just maybe—

He pulled himself together, tensing for the leap. Fixing his target from memory, and from the oil's steady, small splash, he leaped out and away from the wall, rolled across the room, felt his back strike a table leg on the third roll, and froze dead still, on the contact.

The stink of the oil was in his nose, hand-close. As he crouched, motionless, he felt the splash of the next drip hit the back of his left hand. Feeling forward, he came to the wet slick on the floor. It went as prayed-for from there. He got the match from his vest pocket with the left hand, sent it on a long scrape and following-through drop into the center of the pooled oil. There was a hiss and flutter, a spurt of tiny, sulfuric fire. Then the oil caught and flared, orange and smoky, and the guns from cross-room thundered into its greasy bloom, even as it roiled upward. They splintered nothing but the grimy planking of the floor behind. Rachel, a full roll to the right of his tossed match, and clear of both fire and table, shot from the floor.

The range was no more than twenty feet, his targets set up like gallery ducks by the leap of the fire's light against the wall upon which they crouched. He dropped the first two with a round each. His third shot was a miss and he needed a fourth to anchor the third of Briscoe's gunmen. Swinging on Briscoe himself with the last round, he was too late. The outlaw chief had sprung through the rear door and was gone running through the starlight across the tumbleweeded stock corral. At the door, Rachel took a brace against its frame, brought the long barrel of the Remington in line, squeezed off the sixth shot with no sight picture save the instincts of ten years gone, guiding his unhurried aim.

He heard the sound of the bullet strike. It was like the slap of a wet bar rag upon dense, sour wood. Rance Briscoe didn't stumble, didn't fall. He was driven forward, face-flat, into the sunbaked adobe. And he lay there in a way that Fate Rachel had seen many times. A way that needed no walk-up to confirm the quality of eternal stillness shrouding the huddled posture.

At the house it was different. Two of the men, Kagel and Stillwell, proved lightly wounded. Both were local cowboys, young, ignorant, drawn into the Red Rock affair when wiser men had refused it. Arbecker, the third man, was an old hand, and tough. But he had taken his .44 slug high in the hip, a crippling if not dangerous wound, and it must appear his days along the owlhoot trail were ended, given the best of recoveries.

The gang had a buckboard hidden out in the corral hay barn, toward which Rance had been running, and in the jumping light of the now-burning station house Rachel made a little speech to its remaining members, concerning some possible use of this vehicle. His essential suggestion was that if the two young cowboys could get their aging outlaw mate into the buckboard and be gone across Faber's Crossing inside of the next deep breath, he would be inclined to forget he had met any of them. Providing, of course, that, prior to departure, the Red Rock loot might be accounted for, give or take say fourteen dollars and fifty cents.

This offer produced five seconds of hard-frowned, sober consideration, to which Rachel added encouragingly.

"Arbecker," he said, "you are no yearling and this is no strange pasture to you. You have told me that it was Rance who shot the Anderson messenger and since this agrees with the company's report I am ready to accept your claims. But you are well aware what 'accessory after' will bring you in a murder case and if you wish to earn that ten thousand of Anderson's at the rate of five hundred a year, why you have only to keep your mouth shut. For my part I will take no further action against you, save to place you in social contact with T. C. Barnes of the Anderson Express people, and that's a sacred promise."

The wounded outlaw eyed him, greed yielding finally to pain.

"I believe you would do it," he said between gritted teeth, "and I think I will take your word for it, as you seem to me a man who would not sell watered whiskey. Boys, bring out the box and help me to the buggy."

It was seven minutes before midnight when Fate Rachel rode up to the Longhorn Hotel in Mobeetie with the body of Ransom Briscoe sacked across the latter's led-horse. It was five minutes later that he roused T. C. Barnes from sound slumber to trade him the outlaw's remains for an Anderson Express Company sight draft, made out in blank, for $1,000. When the wall clock in the lobby began counting off the hour, Rachel was counting out the last of the company's $10,000 upon Barnes' rumpled bed, and Barnes was still in his long-handled drawers yelling for a quill pen and sanding pot to sign over the bounty money.

With the sight draft undried in his vest pocket, Rachel departed the Longhorn. Out front, the crowd of curious night crawlers attracted from the Pink Lady to analyze the burden hung across Rance Briscoe's horse, parted politely, even admiringly, to let his slayer through.

"That's him," he heard a man say. "That's Fate Rachel, right there!" It didn't dim the patent respect in the first man's tone when his companion replied, "That old geezer? You're drunk. He couldn't bounty-hunt a bobcat."

"What the hell," demanded the first man, "has being drunk got to do with it? You want to talk to somebody sober, go down to the jail and talk to that Darcy girl."

"And what the hell," inquired his companion, "has she got to do with it?"

"She was in with Briscoe's bunch. Come adriving hell for San Antone into town about half an hour gone. Wanted to turn herself in. State's evidence. Wanted the sheriff to get up a posse and go out and bury poor old Rachel, decent. She blabbed the whole thing. Said she never seen such guts. One old man kicking in a door and jumping four of the top guns in the Panhandle? And him with nothing but an old wood-handled .44 Cap-and-Ball? Huh! And you with the gall to stand there and—"

The words, and the crowd around Briscoe's horse, faded out for Rachel. True to the temper of street gatherings, this one was more interested in resolving its own arguments of ignorance than in gaining information bounded by the facts. They let Rachel ride out with neither hail nor farewell, so busy in describing to one another precisely the manner in which he shot down the four top guns of the Texas Panhandle, that none thought to inquire of him if he might have a word to say for himself in the matter.

For the record, however, he did not.

If two itinerant young cowhands and one rheumatic old train robber, along with Rance Briscoe, made up the four most feared gunfighters on the Staked Plains, that was no more than fair. For he knew, by the evidence of his own ears in guiding his old horse away from the din in front of the Longhorn Hotel, that before he put the last light of Mobeetie behind him, the history makers milling the dirt of Main Street would have the number of outlaws built to regimental strength and the artillery with which Fate Rachel destroyed them reduced to a .41 Short Colt derringer, or a single-shot caplock pistol, Model 1812.

Moreover, he was not interested in what Mobeetie made of the killing of Rance Briscoe. It was what he, Rachel, now made from it which counted.

He found Eileen Briscoe's shack on the north edge of the settlement. It was gray-board, unpainted. The two windows were broken out, patched with butcher paper and tacks. Over the door, on a trellis which must have been the only one in Mobeetie, grew a rambler rose.

Rachel got down from his horse, but did not need to knock. The woman came out, stood confronting him, a pale, pretty youngster of ten peering uncertainly from the doorway behind her.

"Who is it, Ma?" asked the child, and Eileen Briscoe said, "Hush, honey—it's a friend who knew your father."

Rachel took her hands and put in them the Anderson draft.

"What is it?" she said.

"A sight draft, Mrs. Briscoe, ma'am. On Anderson Express, for a thousand dollars."

"A thousand dollars—"

"Yes, ma'am. All you need do is fill in your name where the blank is, and they will pay you the money. It's for Rance, ma'am."

The woman was sober now, long sober. She looked up at Rachel and said tonelessly, "They got him."

"Yes," said Rachel.

"You got him," she said. And, "Yes," said Fate Rachel again.

She stood a moment. He could almost see each year pass across the emptiness of her eyes. Then she shook her head.

"I can't take it," she said. "It's yours."

"No, ma'am," said Rachel, inclining his head toward the nightgowned youngster, "it's hers."

She studied him, the lines of thought smoothing at last.

"It's like you," she said. "I remember you now. The trial. The sentencing. All of it. Do you think a thousand dollars—"

"A thousand dollars won't do anything for you nor me, ma'am," Rachel cut her off gently. "But it will do a lot for her." He kept his voice down, so that the child would not hear. "You remember what you told me about that clinic in Kansas City?"

"Yes, oh yes." The woman spoke quickly, then looked down at the draft in her hand. "A thousand dollars. In one night. Dear God, dear God—"

Rachel nodded, wrinkled his eye corners.

"I never did work cheap, Mrs. Briscoe," he said. "Sentiment doesn't pay in my business." He paused, warming the last words with his inside grin. "But sometimes express companies do."

He turned for his horse, putting foot to stirrup and

swinging up. Eileen Briscoe stepped haltingly forward. She started to speak but he leaned down quickly.

"The Anderson people will take care of your bill in Kansas City—anything past this advance."

Eileen Briscoe looked down at the Anderson draft once more, the tears beginning to run now. She dropped her gaze, lips compressed, gestured helplessly with the draft.

"But this—it's still yours—I can't—"

She had started forward impulsively, but Rachel heeled the horse a sidestep away. She halted and he checked his mount, looking back and down at her and at the little girl who had come out of the house to stand beside her in the puddled dust of the street. His words came very softly, very seriously.

"I'm happy, if you are, ma'am. It comes out even the way I figure it. A thousand dollars to end one life and begin another. You can't beat a trade like that in my line of work."

He checked the nervous horse for the final time, tipping his hat to the woman and child, voice rising happily.

"Fate Rachel, ma'am. A little old, a little tired, and an awful lot lucky."

He wheeled the horse, put him on a high lope. Eileen Briscoe and the girl stood watching after him. Both took a wordless step forward, waving hesitantly. In the uncertain sweep of the starlight they thought they saw him turn in the saddle and wave back to them. It was the way they told it later and a good way to tell it in any case. But it was not the true way.

Fate Rachel did not return their wave. When he swung his horse away from Mobeetie that long-ago night, he had done more than buy a new life for Eileen Briscoe and her daughter—he had sold an old life for himself. He never looked back on Mobeetie, never rode that way again.

Pretty Face

Hurd Clinton was twenty-eight, homeless as a poker chip, hard as a Sioux smile, lonely as a Wyoming winter sky. He was, as well, and for the moment, worried as a snowbound buffalo in wolf country.

To begin with it had been a lean year along the traplines. Fur had been difficult to come by, very poor in quality. His and Piute Montera's had been the only good catch brought into Jackson's Hole rendezvous that spring of 1838. Accordingly, with the price sent sky-high, he and Montera had decided not to sell at the rendezvous but to carry their catch on down to Fort St. Vrain, where a man could shade the rendezvous prices by 40 percent and make a real strike on the fur market. That much of Hurd's worrying brought him to his partner, Piute Montera.

The latter, as his forename would indicate, was a Piute Indian breed. A lean, muscle-jawed devil, his slant eyes and brick-dust skin aroused natural wonder as to where he had gotten the Montera part of the name. He looked all Indian, acted twice as red as he looked. Yet what was a man to do when the trapping was so bad and a fellow like this Montera sidled up to him with the hint that he knew a lake drainage basin up across the Canadian border where sable and mink were so thick they would fight to get first bite at the bait?

Hurd, for one, had gone along with him. And it had proved to be all the breed had said it was. They had gotten in and out of the country with their peltries fleshed, stretched, baled and loaded upon the pack horses in less time than it ordinarily took to put out and bait a line of sets. As a result they were going to be rich when old Ceran St. Vrain checked the last of their Canadian catch over the pelting counter at his private fort and fur post down south along the Rockies. To this point, Hurd had to admit, all credit had to be given Piute Montera. But they were still many long rides from dividing St. Vrain's money. And meanwhile a man had reason to worry.

The first thing learned in the mountains was that if the ears were bent more often than the mouth was opened, the health of the scalp was highly improved.

Montera had talked too much at Jackson's Hole. He had first been too easy about suggesting the St. Vrain trip, then too hard about insisting upon it. The disparity had put Hurd on the watch as they left the Hole and now, three days out of it, his wariness had brought reward. They were being trailed. The trailers were six in number, and riding barefoot ponies.

There had been no Indian trouble that year and it did not make sense that a small bunch like these would be thinking of jumping two trappers. Not for a few packs of furs. The pelts didn't mean that much to the purebloods. And that brought a man full circle in his fretting.

If not the trailing Indians, who might profit from the ambush? Someone say like a half-blood cousin? Like say Piute Montera? Eight thousand dollars—perhaps ten—all his own? Sixteen packs of prime Canadian fur with no partner's share to pay? Ah, that could make sense. Hard and dirty sense. It could mean that Montera was planning to kill him, or rather to have him killed. The breed was smart. Too many of the bunch at the rendezvous would remember he had started for Fort St. Vrain with Hurd Clinton, alone. But it would be nothing worse than expected mountain luck to run into a hostile ambush. That would fix everything. Next spring at the rendezvous the boys would shrug and say, "Hard doings; I hear old Hurd went under down toward the fort last year," and that would be the beginning and the end of the inquiry into his death.

Hurd broke his mind off the bleak trail of that thought to cluck softly in Sioux to his small Hunkpapa pony.

"*Ubagan, Wahiki*," he said, then added in English. "Push along, Bonehead. We've an alder grove to find for good old Piute."

Wahiki lifted his jughead, picked up the easy rhythm of his trot. His name in Sioux meant "the Bone," but the wiry animal understood well enough to whom the big white man referred when he called for more speed from Bonehead. Shortly his increased gait brought into view the certain grove of alders which Montera had described to Hurd and which he had suggested the latter ride ahead and scout as the coming night's camp spot.

Hurd had not taken the suggestion enthusiastically. With the six hostiles dogging them it was no country in which to split up. But Montera had brassed it out, laughing at his concern over the trailing braves, saying that Hurd was getting jumpier than a belled sheep and that the Indians were most likely tagging along for company. It was true they would do that upon occasion and Hurd, not daring to tip his suspicions of Montera, had complied with the breed's proposal.

But the long hot afternoon's ride had taken the edge off his caution. For the moment, coming down on the grove, he was thinking more of whether its trees might shelter a good spring of water, than if they might harbor half a dozen unfriendly Indians. Scouting the perimeter of the alders carelessly, he rode on into their shade to discover that they did, indeed, house a fine spring. Following a deep, slow drink, he dragged the saddle off Wahiki, crotched his Hawken rifle in a nearby sapling, loaded his pipe, stretched out to rest on the soft curl of the buffalo grass. Ah! this was more like it. Nothing like a stone pipe bowl of shag-cut Burley and a brief afternoon doze to lessen a man's troubles. Or perhaps to lift his scalp.

The first hint Hurd had that all was not well in the alder grove was when a drowsing glance showed him Wahiki flaring his nostrils toward the far edge of the small clearing surrounding the spring. He came rolling to his feet, the short hairs of his neck lifting.

This was fine. Here he was in the middle of a prairie grove, his gun cached twenty feet away and his Indian gelding whipping his ears and blowing out as though he had winded a hundred hostiles around the near bend. What the hell did a man do now? Sprint for his gun? Stand there with his arms folded, hoping the red prowlers would take him for the second coming of Anpetuwi, the white Sun God? Or should he go diving into the nearest brush where possibly he might gain ten seconds to think of something smarter? It had to be Indians Wahiki had winded. Hurd had circled the open grass butting that grove. Any white outfit approaching it would have been seen, or any already camped there, heard. However, there could have been a small party of red men laid up in the heavy cover just west of the spring clearing. Say like the six shadowy braves who had been trailing Montera and him, and whom Hurd had been looking for all the way in to the grove. Only now a man got the late-in-the-afternoon idea that he had not been looking for them nearly as hard as they had been looking for him.

Hurd's choice being simple, he did not hesitate in taking it. He went diving into the closest brush unashamed as any other arrant coward. The shade inside the new cover was as cool as the low laugh which came with it. He whirled, long body in a fighting crouch. The laugh came again, this time accompanied by a single soft word in a language which was second tongue to Hurd Clinton. By now his pupils were adjusted sufficiently to the deeper shade to make out the source of the low-voiced greeting. The discovery cut his breath short.

She was the creamiest one Indian girl who had ever stared straight back at a susceptible mountain man.

A little thing less than shoulder high to the towering Hurd, she was very light copper in color, with level, unslanted eyes and that rare mahogany-red hair sometimes encountered in the Hunkpapa and Oglala peoples. Her features were regular, the startling lines of her figure scarcely damaged by the cling of her doeskin camp dress. Hurd continued to hold his breath.

"*Hohahe*," she said, repeating the Hunkpapa greetingword. "Welcome to my tipi."

"*Ha ho*, thank you," replied Hurd with awkward politeness. "How are you called? What is your name?"

"*Wastewin*," she said, the dazzle of her sudden smile doing nothing to harm the claim. Hurd shivered to the realization. Wastewin in Sioux came out Pretty Face in English, and this Hunkpapa child was many pony journeys from uncomely. "*Wowicake*," he nodded in open admiration. "It's a true thing. Your tongue is straight."

It was now her turn to hesitate and grow uncertain.

"*Ha ho*," she blushed. "The *Wasicun* is pretty too. *Pte hcaka!*"

Hurd's blush paled hers. To be standing in front of a beautiful young girl no matter she was only a red Indian, and to have her running her big eyes up from your toes to your scalplock, not missing anything in between, was addling enough. Add to that that she looked you right in the eye and told you that for a white man you were a "real bull buffalo," and any human male was heading for a stampede. Hurd made his out of the brush clump in two jumps, had retrieved and shouldered his rifle in two more.

"Come on out of there," he ordered sternly, sweeping the thicket with the Hawken's muzzle.

Getting no response to the command, he repeated it in Sioux. At this, Wastewin came out into the clearing, letting the sunlight show Hurd his eyes had not deceived him inside the tangle.

"Listen," he said, rattling the Sioux at her, "I am in a bad country. There is great danger for me here. You are not of this country, I believe. Nor are you of the Piute people. I think you are Hunkpapa, one of my own foster-people. I think you will help me."

She frowned, then smiled suddenly.

"I know who you are and what you fear," she said.

Hurd's pale eyes narrowed.

"Go on," he said, restless glance roving the trees beyond her, "and keep this in your mind. If your tongue is not straight, the barrel of this Holy Iron is. Remember it is watching you."

Again the girl smiled.

"My tongue is straight, *Wasicun*," she told him. "There is no danger for you here. The Piutes are three days west, hunting buffalo."

"What Piutes?" rasped Hurd. "I said nothing about any Piutes."

"The ones you seek, Uncle Pte."

"Goddamit!" Hurd let the English blasphemy slip out. "My name is not Buffalo Bull. It is Milawangi."

"Milawangi, the Rusty Knife," repeated the girl innocently. "A fine name. I like it."

Hurd nodded without pleasure.

"Tell me your story, *Shacun*," he said, "and tell it swiftly. I don't trust you and I fear to stay here."

"A Hunkpapa name," continued the girl, ignoring him. "Do you know I am Hunkpapa, too, Rusty Knife?"

"I have already told you I thought so. Tell your story."

"Who is it that you know well among them?" persisted his companion. "Do you know the old chief, Iron Horse, and his young son, Flying Bird?"

The names struck hard at Hurd's memories of his boyhood among the Milk River Hunkpapa. But he only tightened his gaze, giving no sign of the disturbance.

"I am not saying who I know among my foster-people," he said, "but you are going to say who you are, and what you are doing here, six hundred miles from the homeland of the Hunkpapa."

He was beside her before she could move, his fingers seizing her arm in a wolf-trap grip.

"Now you talk quickly Pretty Face. I think you are playing with me. I think you may be the bait in a fine *wickmunke*, a nice Indian trap. I don't like traps, Hunkpapa, do you hear? I am twenty winters sick of them!"

She tried to pull away from him, eyes wide.

"I am hiding nothing from you, Rusty Knife—"

He drew her in close, bringing her soft face within inches of his.

"*Wasin'te!*" he snapped. "That's a pile of pure fat. You have no business here, so far from your true home. I think your words lie crooked in your mouth. Your story smells bad, like *pizi*, the gall of a dead animal."

"No, no, Milawangi!" The luring smile was gone now, the small face deadly serious. "My heart is good for you. I will speak the truth, I swear it."

"All right, then, Sioux girl, speak the truth. And while you do remember that the Holy Iron is stiff watching you." He punched the Hawken at her suggestively, and she recoiled, pushing the weapon's muzzle aside with her slim hand. "Let the *mazawakan* watch something else," she said. "His eye in my navel makes me nervous."

Hurd had to grin.

"All right," he nodded, dropping the Hawken's muzzle, "keep your words straight. My ears are uncovered."

They heeled down in the short grass after the Indian custom, and she began her story. Its details, delivered in the softly grunted Hunkpapa style, had the big trapper's attention from the first syllable.

"As a little girl," she said, "the *Kangi Wicasi*, the cursed Crows, stole me from my father's people. When I had sixteen summers, the Crows traded me to an old Piute chief, Cow Runner, for twelve spotted horses." She paused proudly. "No mares, *Wasicun*, all geldings!"

"You must have been a virgin," said Hurd. "Or else the price of squaws has gone up."

"I was a virgin." The pride was still in the words. "And a chief's daughter as well."

"Go on," ordered Hurd. "Be quick."

"Well, at first I was a willing wife," continued the Sioux girl. "Cow Runner was a chief of reputation and it was something to live in his tipi. But soon there was trouble. Cow Runner had a first wife, one who was there before me. She was a tall woman, a pure Ute, stately and strong as a mountain sheep but not pretty. Her name was Broken Face and she achieved it in this way: when she was in her younger years she was a great rider; then one day she was trampled by a newly captured wild stud that she was trying to gentle when it was her time of the moon; of course the horse got wild and that is how she received her poor scarred face.''

''Fool women,'' growled Hurd. ''Will they never learn to stay away from a stallion when it is their time?''

''This one did,'' nodded the girl. ''From that day when her face bones were broken she talked with a smile like a scalp-dance mask. No one would have her to wife until Cow Runner came to her father's lodge and—''

''Enough!'' Hurd's interruption snapped like a dry twig underfoot. ''I don't want the history of Cow Runner's first wife and her twisted face. Only this I want: where are the Piutes who are trailing me? What are they doing down in this country? Why does the half-breed white man from my camp come secretly into the camp of Cow Runner to talk about me? And I mean the half-breed white man who is called Montera, the one whose small name is 'Piute.' '' Taking the shot at Montera in the dark, Hurd concluded roughly. ''And lastly I want to know what you are doing in this grove of trees spying on me. *Nohetto*, do you hear me? That is *all* I want!''

''Of course,'' smiled the girl. ''Only give me time to tell it to you. It is really very simple. It is just that Broken Face hates me so deep that I have determined to run away and take the long trail back to my own people. That is why I am hiding here.''

Hurd knew she was lying. He shrugged, feigning indifference.

''Let's talk of something else,'' he said. ''Forget the Piutes. What is Cow Runner doing following my pack horses?''

''Cow Runner is following your pack horses?''

''You know damned well he is, you lying red slut!''

Hurd blazed the answer in English before thinking. When he had calmed himself enough to repeat the charge in Sioux, he was given another of the dazzling smiles for his reply. He was given even a little more than that. The girl made a sinuous movement, curling down into the fragrant nap of the buffalo grass. Her bare arm came across the tenseness of Hurd's thigh, her hard, lifting breast pushing after it.

"Wastewin is tired of talking," she murmured. "Let us now rest our bodies the one beside the other."

She had the doeskin campdress off over her head before Hurd could move to forestall her. His breath caught raspingly. He had seen women unclad more than twice before now. And he would have thought some of them had been passable. Yet he had never seen arms so round and sweet as these. Nor a back and belly so prime. Nor a set of breasts with the curve and wicked uplift of nipple to match this pair.

"Whoa up!" he ordered hoarsely, feeling the blood surge thick and bad within him. But her hand, quick and cool as creek moss, slipped inside his shirt and ran the corded muscles of his belly soft as a trout's shadow across pebbly stones, and he was in the grass beside her with no thought for any Indian in Wyoming save this slender one with the body of copper fire. . . .

They rested side by side, limbs carelessly outflung, the low angle of the sun shooting the grasses of the clearing with the last of the day's warmth. Presently Hurd spoke, his tones gentle with the hour's restfulness.

"I am far from my pack ponies, Wastewin," he said. "The day is going fast; I must travel soon." He thought a moment, trying to shape the words so that she would not get a wrong idea from them. These *Shacun* women had to be watched like a lost dog. One pat on the head and they would follow a man home. "I will remember you," he finished lamely, knowing that was not what he had wanted to say at all.

There was a long pause before she replied.

"To remember is nothing," she said at last. "To forget, though, that is something."

"I won't forget you either, *Shacun*—"

Hurd stopped abruptly, not having meant it the way it sounded. Damn, why couldn't a man just get up and out of there as he ought to? What was so different about this little Sioux?

"*Wasicun*," the girl's voice blocked his thoughts, "when I spoke the names of Iron Horse and Flying Bird a shadow of truth passed behind your eye. You know these names. You have heard them before."

"Yes, it's true."

"How so, then?"

"Iron Horse is chief of the Milk River Hunkpapa. As a boy I lived some winters with his band."

A look of consternation spread upon the girl's face. Her voice grew small, the lethargy gone from it.

"And Flying Bird, what of him?"

Hurd shrugged, still lolling on his back looking up at the sky.

"He was the son of Iron Horse. The first son. I took the Fox Lodge ordeal with him; we shared the declaration of blood brothers."

The girl leaned above him on one elbow, a feeling of urgency crowding her words.

"This Iron Horse," she said, "did he not also have a daughter?"

"No, only Flying Bird, no other children. Say, wait: there was a girl—older—gone before I came. I heard the old women talk of her. She was stolen by the—"

"By the Crows," his companion finished for him. Then, softly. "And her name, even then—Wastewin."

"Wakan Tanka be praised!" laughed Hurd. "We're sister and brother, you and I."

"Yes," said the girl, "and may Wakan Tanka forgive me. My father and his people never will."

The intensity of her low cry brought Hurd belatedly to his elbow. "What do you mean?" he said, the hackles of fear up in him, now, stiff as the hair on a cornered dog's back.

"Lie down, Milawangi, here by me—"

The Sioux girl dropped languidly back onto the grass but her following words leaped with urgency. "Do as I tell you, or you are a dead warrior. Take me in your arms as you did before. Make the moves of love again. *Hopo*, hurry!"

"No, never! I was a fool."

"You are a fool now! Get down here, as I say! Do it, *heyoka*, as you love your life!"

Hurd dropped then and fast. The girl sped on.

"I have lied, but listen to me now that you may know my tongue was straight at the last. I am all I have said but there is no Cow Runner and no peaceful buffalo hunt. The chief of the Piutes whose wife I was is no toothless old one—he is Mad Bull."

"*Mad Bull!*" The name burst through Hurd's lips. "You mean the one that's wanted by the Pony Soldiers? That's being hunted by every cavalry patrol south of the Shining Mountains? The murderer of white women and children? That scum of the prairies?"

"The same, yes. He and five other white-haters. They are after your pack ponies, and will kill you. That half-breed, Montera, he offered them all new guns that load many times to do it for him; to trap you here and take your hair in this grove."

Hurd groaned helplessly.

"Go on," he said, forcing his voice to hold low and his coiled muscles unmoving. "What of yourself?"

"Hearing of the plan," she answered haltingly, "I thought the honor of counting coup on you would put me above Broken Face. Knowing the Wasicun men think all Shacun women are female dogs to be serviced at will, I also hated you for myself. I stole down here ahead of the warriors to play you with my body, to make it easy for them to come up on you and to kill you."

"Lord God," said Hurd, "what a chucklehead I been!"

"Shhh!" The girl pursed her lips sharply. "All this I planned but I had not then had your hands upon me, nor your face in my eyes, nor known that you were blood brother to Flying Bird. I would die now for my treachery, but it is already too late. Mad Bull is around you!"

Hurd started to let his eyes move to check her warning, but she said to him fiercely, "Don't look! I can see them for you. They are back of you, to the west. They are waiting only for you to rise from my side, believe it!"

Hurd nodded imperceptibly.

"Move your right arm," he said. "I am going to steal a glance beneath it." As he spoke, he slid out of its scabbard his Hunkpapa skinning knife, lay the point of its eight-inch blade against the girl's naked belly. "If you cry out," he said, "I will let your boudins out upon this grass." Then, scathingly. "Believe it!"

She returned the nod, shifted the arm, gave him his view across the clearing. It was amply clear.

Sitting their unshod ponies at the edge of the alders were the six missing Piutes. Hurd had seen his share of unfriendliness. From Wind River in Wyoming to the Bear Paws in Montana, he had matched wits with the worst the horseback tribes had to offer. Yet never had he seen an Indian face to match any in that still-eyed Piute group.

The bastards. Their expressions were, every one, as hard and rough as rimrock. And they were, every one again, so heavily hung with war harness their potbellied mounts stood swaybacked with the weight of it. Lances, hand axes, bows, rifles, bullhide shields, cartridge belts, every possible tool of war, trimmed both horse and rider from hock to eagle-feather headdress. And where any knowing mountain man could easily see the first five of the waiting hostiles rated salt-tailed with scarcely a look, he could see the sixth earned the honor without any look at all.

Mad Bull was short, pale-colored, pockmarked. A nose the size and shape of a squashed melon smeared itself above the loose-lipped vacancy of his enormous mouth. He was shouldered, heavy-necked and paunched to suggest the animal for which he had been named, and from the glare he was presently bending upon Hurd Clinton, ugly-tempered to match.

Breaking his glance from the motionless hostiles, Hurd estimated his chances as an actor. The estimate fell short. The Piutes would get the idea he was shamming with the girl any second now. Then, the natural fun of their peep-tomming spoiled, they would come for him. Well, there was one sure way he could die useful. That was to roll away from the girl, grabbing up his rifle on the roll, and snapshooting the chief. Doing this, no matter the other Indians put him down the next minute, he would have doubled-up Mad Bull. Too bad it couldn't be good old Piute Montera in the chief's place, but a mountain jackass like Hurd had to take his chances where he blundered into them. Besides, he owed the girl something for her services. A dead husband seemed suitable, all circumstances considered.

He gathered himself for the roll-up, still keeping the knife in his companion's soft belly. But before he could release his coiled body a knock-kneed roan reply to a cornered trapper's prayer wandered out of the encircling alders. Muzzling the choicer saplings for their tender spring suckers, his trail horse, Wahiki, browsed unconcernedly along the near edge of the clearing.

The intrigued Piutes noted but paid no further heed to

the ugly Sioux pony. The dramatics being furnished by his tall white master were too absorbing, not to mention the part being played in his performance by Mad Bull's young wife. *Hunhunhe!* By the Gods, that Sioux vixen, that Wastewin, was clever! What a remarkable way to catch a white man. *Hau, hau*, this was one time a stinking *Wasicun* man was going to be rightly paid for shaming a *Shacun* woman. *Waste, waste*, good, good. But don't shoot him just yet. He is doing well. Hold the guns for another minute. In fact, don't even use them at all. Use only arrows. They hurt far more.

While his red hosts waited, Hurd did not. He leaped to his feet and went aboard the wandering Wahiki with a Hunkpapa yell that was still echoing when the wiry roan had him out of the trees and skimming the open grassland beyond. The startled Piute ponies hadn't even gotten their scrawny haunches gathered beneath them, before Wahiki had Hurd out of arrow-shot. The latter, however, did not trouble looking back to ponder his tactical success. Rifle balls were whistling if arrowshafts were not, and if that wasn't hot pony breath beginning to blow on the small of his back, it would do for a reasonable imitation. About here in the race a man got the idea, without examining it, that Mad Bull and his band had their mounts that close to Wahiki's rump they could have bitten off the roan's rat-tail simply by reaching for it.

In accordant response to his rider's honest Sioux shouts for more speed, Wahiki flattened out and opened up the twilight between Hurd and the hard-firing Piutes. To be realistic, the mountain man was a long, chanceful way from home free. But the cat-fast roan gelding had gotten him off and running in the right direction. The rest was up to Hurd.

It had to be put down to pure luck, the way in which he finally got rid of the hostiles. They ran him five miles up to the base of the foothills and got to crowding him pretty fine when a friendly black stormcloud came rolling down from the north rim of the prairie, shutting off the long green twilight as plungingly as a blown-out lamp. After that, it was only a matter of walking soft and circling wide.

Now, an hour later, trotting Wahiki along in the first starlight, Hurd was thinking the better of his original idea of hitting for Montera and the pack string camp—at least, of riding into that camp.

The breed would have his supper fire going by this time and if Hurd came into its light with his story of the alder grove ambush, Montera would be spooked. He would call off whatever plans he had made with Mad Bull, would be left free to make others which Hurd might not get wind of, as he had this one. On the other hand, if he rode into the fire with no story at all to cover his long absence, the breed would get equally jumpy. Again, if he stayed out of camp altogether, Montera would turn edgy wondering what had gone wrong with the alder grove trap. However, in the latter case he would be almost certain to try another of his moondark sneak-outs to contact Mad Bull for news. In the end this last chance seemed the best one to Hurd. He shook his shaggy blond head and tightened his knees on Wahiki's ribs.

"*Hookahey*, Bonehead," he said. "Put a little ginger under your tail. We got long tracks to make, providing we aim to pull camp in time to catch old Piute taking his next pasear."

The homely roan whickered, stretched into a mile-eating Indian canter. Behind them, far down in the valley, the timber clot of the alder grove faded swiftly. But within Hurd Clinton's last vision of its leafy shadow was that which would not dim so quickly. In Hurd's mind the Sioux girl's features persisted. And not in his mind alone, either. As the gaunt trapper swung to the rhythm of the roan's gait, the haunting face of Wastewin was in his heart as well.

The pack string camp went dark as Hurd had thought it might, the breed's small Indian fire dying to a needle-point of coals about seven-thirty. Minutes later, Montera moved toward the silhouette of his picketed mare. He was as loud about it as a buzzard's shadow scraping mesa rock. Still it was probably one of the few times when a shadow cast a shadow in moondark. Behind the breed, Hurd glided in a pair of Hunkpapa moccasins that had learned their craft where a noise as big as a cricket's cough could cost a man his hair.

Hurd gave Montera time to mount-up and move away from the still-loaded pack string, hidden in a nearby motte of poplar scrub, then closed on him, working swiftly in to where he was but twenty paces behind him. Five minutes, west, a rise in ground gave a twenty-mile view across open prairie. Crouching at skyline of this crest, Hurd squinted through the starlight. Below him Montera, putting his mare in a fast rack, was heading straight down the St. Vrain Trail. From the direction and gait he rode, a man was left with one reasonable guess as to his destination—the alder grove.

Hurd got back to Wahiki where he had left him in a gully south of Montera's fire. He swung up, turning the gelding toward the abandoned camp. What he had to do now would slow him up, but no man in his right mind would leave eight to ten thousand dollars in prime fur standing pack-loaded for the return of a partner who had arranged to pay him his split of the catch with a Piute bullet in the back of his head. There proved little trouble getting the pack string wrangled into line and moving behind the eager Wahiki. Once started, Hurd held the laboring pack line on a hard lope for the next half hour, kept pushing them at a good shuffle-walk for another hour after that, bringing them in long sight of the alder grove just short of moonrise. He nodded his satisfaction with the feat. He had not paralleled the St. Vrain Trail, taking advantage rather of the shortcut he had learned in his flight from Mad Bull's band. He was, in consequence, as convinced he had beaten Montera to the grove as he was that the latter had not seen him doing it.

Half a mile south of the grove, safely out of scent range of the Piute ponies, he hid the pack string in a shallow wash. Returning uptrail, he tethered Wahiki in a stray clump of sage a quarter mile north of the grove, retraced his way on foot. A hundred paces from the outer trees, the St. Vrain Trail topped a low boulder-crowned rise, then dropped into the little swale that held the spring and its tenant alders. Behind these friendly stones, Hurd now set up his watch.

He had no longer than convenient to wait.

Piute Montera came pounding in from the north, his lathered mare passing so close to Hurd's hiding place the latter could hear the saddle's girth-squeaks and the complaining break of the tiring mare's flatus.

Approaching the trees, Montera slowed his mount. Presently, he stopped her in mid-trail, sitting her there motionless. In his rocky nest, Hurd winced. Damn! had the breed heard or seen him? But he had not. Montera was waiting for another friend than Hurd Clinton. Directly, the crouching mountain man picked up the familiar vibrations of unshod ponies walking in deep dust. In another moment the shadows of the animals emerged from the grove, bore down on the silent breed. A lone shadow detached itself from the others, floated on toward Montera. In the first light of the rising moon, there was no mistaking its identity. It was Mad Bull.

Montera and the renegade chief began at once to talk

in Sioux, the lingua franca of the Wyoming plains.

"Now I want to know what happened this afternoon," the breed said. "I mean about the trap for the big *Wasicun* with the pale eyes and yellow hair. The one I told you to *wickmunke* for me. He did not come back to the camp I share with him. Do I understand you have killed him?"

Montera's closing query went a little anxious, but Mad Bull only said, "No, it is not sure that we did. Perhaps we did and perhaps we did not."

"What do you mean?" demanded Montera, anxiety shading now to anger.

"I mean nothing more than I say," replied Mad Bull, showing some of his own uncertain temper. "My young wife found him in the grove before we came up. Thinking to have him helpless for us, she lay her body down beside him. But he got away from us all the same."

"All right, my brother," said Montera carefully. "Tell me, how did he get away?"

"It was a strange thing. One moment he was lying there making the love moves with my woman. One moment he was on his ugly roan horse riding faster than a village dog fleeing his time in the boiling pot."

Montera scowled. "You think he saw you waiting behind him?" he asked.

"No, he didn't look around even one time."

"How do you suppose he knew you were there, then? Do you suppose the girl saw you and warned him?"

"Who knows about a woman?" shrugged Mad Bull. "In particular a young one. She looked up and saw us, all right. But then she continued the love moves and all of a sudden the tall one jumped up and ran for his pony. *Sat-kan!* I don't know. That Hunkpapa blood is thicker than buffalo wallow mud. That tall *Wasicun* was Hunkpapa-raised, you know. Perhaps the girl did tell him."

"Have you asked her? What did she say? Did she admit anything yet?"

"No, but I think she will pretty soon."

"How so?"

"Broken Face, my other wife, is asking her about it right now."

Behind his boulders, Hurd shuddered. Thinking back to his own Indian boyhood with its certain knowledge of how the Hunkpapa would have questioned a squaw suspected of having betrayed the tribe for a white man, he felt his insides draw in like green rawhide. Montera, fortunately, gave him no time to dwell on the grim prospect.

"He got clearly away, then, the tall *Wasicun?*" he said to Mad Bull.

The latter blew out through his nose disgustedly.

"I told you," he replied, "that it was not sure. As we ran him, the darkness of a big storm closed in. He swayed in the saddle as though one of our bullets had found him two different times, but we found no blood. Then the rain blew everything dark and we lost him."

"Well, don't worry, my brother," said Montera shortly. "I have another plan for killing him. I mean to have those furs, Mad Bull. By one killing or the other."

"All right," answered Mad Bull, watching him. "And I mean to have those new rifles you promised us, too, my brother. Also by one killing or the other."

The Indian's meaning was not lost on Montera but before he could think of a mollifying phrase, Mad Bull grunted and spoke again.

"What is your new plan for killing the *Wasicun?*"

Hurd strained to hear what came then. This was the moment. Piute Montera's answer had to pay off the long gamble he had taken in following him from the pack string camp. But the trail to disaster is white with the bones of gambles that had to pay off and did not. The breed's reply to Mad Bull was clearly audible, and precisely worthless.

"Let us go into your tipi, my brother," he suggested. "I could do with some humpribs and cold spring water before we talk."

"*He-hau*," rumbled the chief. "That's a good idea. I, too, am hungry. Let us go."

Huddled in the gully which backed upon his boulder pile, and led from it into the swale and, thus, into the grove, Hurd suddenly quit humbugging himself about what he was doing there. His trailing of the half-breed had nothing to do with finding out what new ideas Piute Montera had for putting him under. Hells little blue bells, he hadn't tracked the breed into Mad Bull's camp for a single honest reason other than to see that pretty-faced Sioux girl again. To see her and to make sure she was all right. Then, providing she was, and the wind lay just so, to make a try at getting her out of the Piute camp. A man could do no less by his boyhood debt to old Iron Horse and the Milk River Hunkpapa. As to Montera he could have fixed the breed's wagon simply by keeping going with the stolen pack string, leaving Montera to explain to Mad Bull how it was he could no longer afford the fine new rifles he had promised him.

No, it was the girl. Admit it, and get a move on.

After that, it was easy. He drifted down the gully into the grove, having no trouble finding the half-dozen Piute tipis which had been pitched since his afternoon adventure. He was in special luck, too. Since only so few squaws had come up to join the war party, no dogs or children were along. If he watched himself and took no unreasonable chances—He broke off the thought with a wry grin. That was a mighty big "if" when you were dealing with horseback Indians. A man had best forget it and take his chances as they came, reasonable or otherwise. The resolve had no more than formed in Hurd's mind, than the evidence to support it confronted his eyes.

Mad Bull's lodge was not set in the trees with the others, but out in the center of the clearing where he had lain with the Sioux girl. There wasn't a brush clump big enough to cover a chipmunk within thirty feet of it. Further, the night was a warm one and the lodge's sideskins were rolled up to provide ventilation, incidentally flooding the clearing with the light of the cook fire within. Still further, the braves in the war party were squatted in front of the lodge waiting for their chief to finish talking with Montera, their view commanding the entire clearing. Hurd set his teeth, shook his head.

From inside the firelight lodge he could catch only a jumble of voices. He could not tell from this if the Sioux girl were in there, or not. He knew, also, that he could lie and listen where he was until God grew old and died, before he learned. The wind was away from him and there was no chance of hearing the words clearly unless it shifted full-about. The probability of its doing that in the time Hurd had to spend, was about equal to the odds against an army mule being agreeable. Or a woman showing good sense. Damn! this could get skimpier than tracking bees in a blizzard.

He saw no sign either of Broken Face or the Sioux girl, wondered, with sinking heart, if the older wife were still working on the younger. Presently, hearing a deep female voice-tone added to those coming from the lodge, he breathed more easily. That figured to be Broken Face in there with Mad Bull and Montera. But then, perhaps, the Sioux girl was also in there. If not, where would she be? If, by God, she still *was* at all!

Arguing thus with himself, Hurd had talked himself into easing back around the clearing to scout the other tipis deeper in the trees, when the seated shadows inside

Mad Bull's lodge suddenly stood tall. The council was breaking up. Montera came out first, followed by Mad Bull. The third figure remained motionless within the tipi—Broken Face was not coming out. Before Hurd could make anything of that, Montera was talking loud and clear.

"You understand now?" he said to the Piute chief. "Is the whole thing strong in your mind?"

"Yes."

"It is a good plan, you think?"

"Yes, good enough."

"All right, I will go now."

"Wait a little," said Mad Bull, showing the Indian genius for apparent pointless thought. "We will ride some of the trail with you."

"How much of the trail?" Montera was quick with it, giving away his anxiety.

"Oh, enough. That's a fat moon up there. It is always a good idea for warriors to ride a little way with good friends when the traveling light is so tempting."

"What do you mean?" said Montera carefully.

"Nothing much." The braves were getting up, now, going for their tethered ponies. "My warriors say they would like to see your many furs which you will use to buy us the new guns when we have killed the tall *Wasicun* for you."

"You don't trust me?" Montera made no move toward his mare. "You think I would cheat *you*, a blood brother?"

"You would cut your own mother's throat for a sick weasel skin," said Mad Bull, matter-of-factly. "Get your horse."

"But you have seen the pack animals of the big *Wasicun* and myself!" protested the breed. "You have followed them for many days."

Mad Bull shrugged.

"The eye of a man is not the eye of an eagle. How do we know what you have in those packs? We have seen them only from afar. We want to see them as close as I am looking at you, that's all. My warriors have taken a small liking to this yellow-haired *Wasicun*. They don't want to kill him for nothing."

"All right," agreed Montera uneasily. "I have the furs and they are well hidden. You are welcome to ride with me and see them. I hesitated only because I did not want to risk the big *Wasicun* seeing me with you."

Mad Bull moved his huge shoulders once more.

"Why should you care what he sees tonight, when tomorrow his eyes will be looking up only at the sky above him? Get your horse. You make my tongue tired."

Montera made the agreement sign with his left hand, turned to get his mare. He knew the talk had reached its end, that further argument would be useless, even dangerous. Hurd, silently watching him ride away with Mad Bull and the five braves, knew something else: when the sun came up tomorrow morning it would not be Hurd Clinton's eyes staring up at the sky above, unseeing. The pack string and its precious furs was two miles south, not twelve miles north of Mad Bull's tipi in the alder grove. The difference, for Hurd, was ten miles. For Piute Montera it would be eternity.

Hurd backed away from the clearing, went drifting around its perimeter, toward the spring. It was there he found the Sioux girl, or what was left of her.

The Piutes did it a little more crudely than the Hunkpapa, lacking the latter's talent for details. But the main idea was the same. There was a cottonwood sapling spar four feet long laced at right angles to a second hastily trimmed limb of the same diameter, this one six feet long and planted in the ground to form a makeshift cross. From this crucifix, hung by the wrists, sagged the young

Hunkpapa squaw. She was conscious but not clear of mind. The low whimpering sounds coming from her raised the short hairs of Hurd's nape, reminding him of the mewing of a she-otter he had once seen Flying Bird beat to death with a throwing stick.

The ground between him and the girl was hard and dry, making it possible for him to reach her without leaving tracks. Starting to slash her loose, he had another thought, untying her instead. But the moment he touched her, to support her so that she would not fall, she tried to twist away from him and to cry out. He barred one arm across her face, holding her against him with the other. She had been beaten crazy, wouldn't know him if he gave her all night to remember, would yell hysterically the instant he let up on his arm-bar.

But there was no time for long thoughts. Hurd dropped his right arm free, spun the girl around with his left, whipped his balled right fist across the point of her slender jaw. Her head jumped back, fell forward, slack-jawed. Hurd had the quiet he needed in which to work.

His thought was to make it appear as though the prisoner had gotten herself free. The braves had started away with Mad Bull and Montera, but Broken Face was still in the camp. If she decided to resume work upon what remained of her young rival, only to find she had been cut loose, she would immediately raise the war cry and bring the braves racing back to the grove. But if she returned to find the girl had apparently escaped, unaided, then she would most likely undertake to trail her herself. That much brought a man up to the boudins of the matter.

The hard ground around the cross would show nothing. But the soft ground of the spring marsh, over which Hurd must move to reach Wahiki, would show a beautiful set of footprints for both the Sioux girl and himself. It would unless Hurd's idea worked.

Keeping a watch toward the clearing, he removed his and the girl's moccasins, hiding his own inside his shirt. Forcing the balls of his feet into the girl's small footgear, he lifted her unconscious form, started toward the spring. He scuffed and weaved his way along, making the sort of a trail an injured person would make and, in doing so, obscuring the fact his own feet were but partly encased in the mocassins of the Hunkpapa squaw. Past the pool of the spring, he hurried, coming to and crossing the tiny stream which drained from its basin away toward the outer prairie. Reentering the stream some distance below, he waded its cress-choked course out of the grove. He did not forget, as he left the alders, to send a grateful look up to old Wakan Tanka, the Sioux Great Spirit, for the fine cover of willow scrub which continued out into the prairie grass.

Arrived at a moonlit sandspit safely away from the Piute camp, he placed the Sioux girl gently down, cupping cold spring water into her face. She stirred, opening her eyes. Hurd, watching anxiously, was relieved to see that the look she gave him was quiet, not crazy, and that she plainly recognized him.

"How do you feel?" he said.

She nodded weakly, pain shooting her eyes with the effort.

"Listen," said Hurd, "you are going away from here with me. Do you understand?"

She shook her head, turned away from him.

He seized her roughly, shaking her.

"Come on, Pretty Face," he rasped. "Don't play Indian with me. Answer me. I command it!"

She rolled her head again, staring up at him. The moonlight struck her full in the face, glinting on the hot tears like quicksilver. Her hand gestured toward her mouth and as Hurd leaned forward she moved her lips, making her first sound since starting. The nameless muttering of those sounds sent Hurd's mind leaping back to the blood he had smelled upon his forearm from barring it across her face. He bent lower still.

The bastards, the mangy, lousy, murdering bastards. If they had taken her tongue—

But his inspection of her tortured mouth showed him the Piutes had not gotten that far. Broken Face's interrogation had apparently been interrupted by Montera's arrival. And to judge from the look of that poor mouth, the interruption had come about one knife-cut short of leaving Wastewin mewing like a blind kitten for the rest of her life. As it was, she was very badly hurt, would not talk tonight, nor for many nights. But she would heal, given the chance, and for the second time in ten minutes Hurd sent a grateful look toward the overhead stars.

"All right, Pretty Face," he said, "speak to me with your hands."

She nodded, and he went on.

"I am taking you down to Fort St. Vrain. We will go on my pony riding double. The moon is old and will make poor light for trailing. We have a good start. They won't catch us, if we move quickly. *Hookahey*, let's go."

Again, the Sioux girl shook her head, again turned her tear-streaked face away and would not look at him.

Hurd took her gently by the upper arms.

"Listen, girl," he said, "I have those pack horses and many rich furs hidden two miles from here. We can pick them up on our way. It is but a long pony ride to the fort, and we will be there tomorrow. I am asking you to go with me; I want you to do it."

Her answer, given in the handsign language, would not have made sense to anyone but another Indian—or to someone raised with the Indians. She refused his offer, she said. She thanked him for it but she would not burden him in his escape. He must not think of her, for she was no longer pretty, with her mouth all cut the way it was. He must go on alone. Perhaps, though, he would see her father, Iron Horse, and would say to the old man some brave lies about his Hunkpapa daughter who loved him still.

Hurd agreed quickly. "I will tell Iron Horse his daughter had a Sioux heart; that rather than betray a blood brother of the tribe, she took the Piute knife cuts inside the mouth," he said. "But why not tell him yourself? Why not come with me now?"

She dropped her eyes, hands moving swiftly in the signs. Please, Rusty Knife must hurry. The time was grown very short. Any moment now Broken Face would find her gone and raise the wolf cry of the Piute people. It was no matter about Pretty Face who was no longer Pretty Face. Let the Piutes find her there; they would find only Iron Horse's ugly daughter waiting for them.

Hurd made his decision. When Yunke Lo was breathing close behind him, a man moved. Yunke Lo was the Sioux God of Death. No man waited willingly for him. Crouching with Wastewin on a sand point in the prairie ten minutes from the Piute camp and sixty miles from Fort St. Vrain, Hurd felt the cold whistle of Yunke's breath very plainly. If this squaw would not come, he still must go.

He stepped away from her, pausing for a last swift look to place her in his memory. Doing so, he knew how a man must feel to leave a crippled pony for the buffalo wolves—one he could not take with him yet still didn't have the innards to either stay with and fight to save, or put a bullet through its suffering head before turning tail to run for his own miserable life.

It was then he knew he could not do it, and could never have done it, not for a dozen Yunke Los, nor a hundred broken-faced Piute squaws wolf-crying their braves upon his trail.

"Wastewin," he said, low-voiced, "these are my last words. I am saying that I love you and that I take you for my woman." He held up her small mocassins, tossing them to her in the traditional Hunkpapa man's betrothal gesture. "*Ohan*," he ordered her, "wear them!"

The change in her was as that of night to morning. She took up the mocassins, slipped them on, came to stand in front of him, head bowed, slim fingers moving nervously to trace the promise sign.

"*Canto'hnaka*," the slender hands said. "I come to you with all my love."

Awkwardly, Hurd kissed her, swept her lightly as a child into his arms.

"Now I will go to tell Iron Horse those brave things for you," he said, the long-empty lodge of his heart full with the feel of her soft against his breast. "And you shall hear me say them to him, *Shacun*, for you will be there at my side to listen."

She looked up, nodding shyly.

"Let us go, Milawangi," she gestured obediently in the sign language. "We have a far journey before us."

Hurd released her, took her slim hand in his.

"A very far journey, Pretty Face," he answered her, and together they went away from that place of danger, walking very quickly and quietly, side by side, through the waiting moonlight.

The Chugwater Run

The Chugwater run was rolling. The way station of Fort C. S. Shifter lay behind, the division point of Fort Phil Harney, ahead. Veteran driver Monk Gurley was applying the leather for keeps, the big Abbott & Downing coach wallowing bad-mannered as a square-hulled ship in troughy seas. Clearly there was a need for hurry beyond the ordinary in this morning's run of the Chugwater & Cheyenne stage line down to the lower fort.

With Monk upon the bucking seat clung an anxious-eyed young shotgun rider. If the old man, weathered, unwashed, shatteringly profane, was the prototype of the professional Western stager, the tense attitude of his youthful companion shouted "first run" at every pitch and sway of the battered Concord. Directly, this impression was borne out in oral affidavit.

"Well leastways, Monk," said the boy, forcing a

tooth-set grin, "we haven't seen hide nor hair of them so far."

Monk spat to windward, bobbed his ragged beard.

"Hang on, kid," he said, "we ain't halfways yet."

The youngster nodded, losing his grin.

"All the same," he insisted, "I'm still glad we haven't seen any sign of them."

Monk tensed, looking off, faded blue eyes narrowing.

"Trouble is, kid," he said, "you ain't been looking in the right places. Try straight ahead."

As he said it, he took a tight wrap on the lines of the four-horse hitch and the boy, glancing ahead, grew pale. A hundred yards away a line of mounted Indians in full war paint blocked the stage road, their leader holding up his hand, palm out, in the halting-sign.

"Like I said, kid," muttered Monk Gurley, *"hang on."*

With the low-voiced warning the old man yelled at his horses and drove them straight at the warriors, crashing the heavy stage into, and on through, their squealing ponies before they could react to get them out of the way. The rest of it went swiftly worse.

Recovering, the Indians raced their mounts after the stage. Strangely, they did not fire a shot, nor even unboot their rifles. Looking back, Monk grunted.

"That's bad, they mean to feather us. Low on powder I reckon. Hold your fire till they're hand-close, kid."

The Indians—they were Wind River Cheyenne—came on, whipping out and notching arrows to their squat war bows, their yelping wolf cries standing the cold sweat out on the young shotgun rider's forehead.

"All right, kid, *now,*" said Monk. "Get the chief."

The boy steadied his wet hands on the rusted ten-gauge double, swung up its stubby barrels. As they came to bear on the chief an arrow whistled past the boy's face and struck Monk Gurley low in the back. The old driver uttered only a soft, "ahhh," but slumped instantly and let the reins slide. Dropping his gun the boy dove for the lines, caught them, held in the horses, kept them on the road. But his cocked shotgun, bouncing down over the seat into the dashboard, dislodged both outside hammers. The charges exploded harmlessly skyward and the next moment the Cheyennes were running their ponies up even with the stage. Another three jumps had them grabbing the headstalls of the lead team, slowing the stage horses from full gallop to breaking trot to dead halt before the boy shotgun rider could think to retrieve, much less reload, his fallen weapon.

When he did make belated motion to do so, it was much too late. The Cheyennes had swarmed up to the top of the coach, seized him, thrown him bodily to the ground.

The shock of such a fall would have killed or crippled an older man and was still enough to stun the boy. For a number of seconds his vision was black then, returning, swam drunkenly. Before he could clear it, the Indians had ripped open the coach doors, dragged out its occupants—two soldiers from Fort C. S. Shifter and the disheveled young lady they had been detailed to accompany to the lower fort. As the girl and the young shotgun rider now looked on in sickening awe, the Cheyenne disarmed the white-faced troopers, held them helpless, beat them to death with their own riflebutts.

The boy, thinking the same fate near for himself and his companion, struggled to break free of the two braves standing guard over him. His object appeared to be to reach the standing Indian ponies, go aboard one of them and run for his own life. If so, he was not permitted to prove the cowardly intention. The two braves were after him like ferrets on a rabbit. One seized him, whirling him around, arm-pinned, as had been done with the soldiers, while his companion drew a murderous-looking butcher knife from his waistband, clearly meaning to plunge it into the desperate youth's abdomen. At the same time the warriors who had killed the soldiers were turning toward the girl and her guards, the foremost of their number flourishing an eight-inch blade which the boy, knowing Indians, and particularly Cheyenne Indians, literally from the cradle, recognized as a scalping knife. Impulsively he called out to the girl.

"Don't show no fear, ma'am. Likely they're bluffing."

She had only time to shoot him a look, but it was an eloquent one. In it he read, "You mean don't show any fear like you just did?" and he was immediately sorry he had blurted out the words. For two reasons. One, his own embarrassment and two, the girl's obvious lack of need for the advice. She was standing straight as a statue, looking the red devils in the eye proud and high-nerved as a thoroughbred horse. Seeming to take his example from her display, the young shotgun rider also straightened and stood tall. But neither determination was tested. Before the Indian knifemen could harm them, the Cheyenne chief shouted an angry order promising his own knife in the intestines to the brave who so much as scratched either of the youthful captives. At this, the warriors put up an instant, equally angry demand to know why they were stopped, by what reason the giving of such unheard-of mercy, such charity, such outright softheaded suffrance to white people?

The boy, who for reasons of his own had spent his brief life studying these Wind River renegades, was one of the rare whites on the frontier who both spoke and understood Cheyenne, by all odds the most difficult of the High Plains Indian languages. His own interest in the present conversation was thereby intensified, his attention riveted upon the challenged chief. The latter, an older, craggy-faced giant of a man, now wheeled upon his questioners.

"Fools! Empty-heads!" he cried out. "Don't you know this girl? You have eyes to see with, you have brains to think with—use them! *Look at this girl!*"

Scowling, the warriors crowded forward. One of them, peering more closely than the rest, widened his slant eyes.

"It's her!" he said. "He Dog is right. I know her now. It's the girl from the fort, the daughter of the Soldier Chief at Fort Shifter. *Oatōs!*"

"*Oatōs*, indeed!" snapped He Dog. "Didn't I tell you this stage was carrying something of great value? Why do you think I went to all the trouble to catch it? Eh? Answer me that, you bone-skulls."

A second sheepish warrior, still scowling to preserve face but nonetheless apologizing as far as a High Plains horseback Indian can go in that direction, now stepped out to face his chief.

"Well," he said, "we thought you meant the stage would be carrying some gunpowder. We must have powder for our guns, or we cannot make our war on the soldiers at Fort Shifter. Why did you deceive us? I remember distinctly that you said this stage was carrying more gunpowder than we had seen in our entire lives. Eh, how about that? Now you answer that."

He Dog strode over to the group now holding the girl and the young shotgun rider side by side. He struck a pose, throwing out an arm to indicate the girl.

"You are still fools," he sneered, "all of you! You speak of powder—that we must have powder to begin our great war on the white man in Wyoming—yet you cannot see a whole stagecoach full of it standing before your very eyes! *Mashanēs!* Idiots! Bah!"

A third puzzled warrior now came forward to protest.

"But we searched the stagecoach," he said. "There

wasn't a grain of powder in it. Not one small flake."

He Dog took hold of the girl roughly, dragging her away from the boy's side as one might drag a puppy by the scruff.

"No," he told the brave, "and there isn't one small grain nor flake of sense in your empty head either."

He straightened his arm, forcing the girl to stumble forward.

"Look at this girl!" he repeated.

He held her there, glaring at his warriors while they complied with his order. When he was satisfied he had them thinking at last, he went on.

"Say she was your own daughter and you were a powerful soldier chief. Say that, and think hard now."

He paused, eying them, then lowered his voice dramatically.

"How many cans of gunpowder would you pay to get her away from He Dog and the Wind River Cheyenne?"

The boy, listening throughout with white-faced intensity, made a second lunge to escape, his voice high with thoughtless anger.

"Why, you dirty, murdering red—"

He got no further than that with his English cursing of He Dog. The Cheyenne chief stepped to meet his clumsy leap, back-handing him with a single tremendous blow with the flattened back of his open hand, knocking him backward into the arms of the braves from whom he had escaped. The latter pinioned his arms at an order from He Dog, holding him as they had held the two dead soldiers.

He Dog went to his pony's side, took down from his saddlehorn a five-thonged, split-lash Indian quirt, returned with it to confront the young shotgun rider. Nodding to him almost cordially, he shook out the quirt, began, with merciless, methodical precision, the flaying, inch-by-inch, of the youth's face and chest.

In the staff and command room, departmental headquarters inside the stockade at Fort Phil Harney, Wyoming Territory, Major Ira Akers was addressing his officers. His tone suggested the terminal seriousness of the situation.

"Gentlemen," he led off, "the war between the States is over, but the war in Wyoming may be only beginning. It may, in fact, burst forth at any moment. Every post out here is still under-manned and what troops we do have are not first line. The Indians know of our condition."

He stepped to an adjacent wall map, pointing out upon it the position of Fort C. S. Shifter to the north.

"The difficulty up here at Shifter is patent. I don't care to sound melodramatic but I think you must all agree that the fate of this post may well be the fate of our own and, indeed, of all the others out here."

Again he paused, while a silent ripple of affirmative nods spread around the staff table. Akers receipted the nods with one of his own, continued tersely.

"Now your very careful attention, please. I have to hand a dispatch by courier from Captain MacClean dated Shifter yesterday. He reports a rumor that He Dog, the Cheyenne trouble-maker, has finally succeeded in his efforts to induce Red Cloud and American Horse to join him in his war to drive the white man out of Wyoming. And MacClean's scouts tell him that the Sioux have already started down from the Big Horn country; will, indeed, be around Fort Shifter no later than tomorrow evening. I do not need to tell you what this joining of the Oglala Sioux with the Cheyenne, if effected, will mean to the garrison up there."

He shook his head, a look of defeat in the glance he gave his silent staff.

"MacClean added that he was sending his daughter

down on today's Chugwater stage and consigning her to my official care. He put the reason for this act in a personal postscript, which I shall now read you."

He looked at them another moment, finished softly.

"... 'Ira, if you cannot get through to me within twenty-four hours the promised shipment of powder, now ten days overdue, I cannot hold Shifter. I have simply not got enough powder remaining to fight my troops longer than two days. With that limit in mind, I commend myself and my men to your mercy, but do not expect the impossible of you. Had I thought you could get the powder through, you would not now have the privilege of Betty's bright company. If the time should arrive you will explain to her the necessity for the falsehood I told her about the headquarters order recalling all dependents to Laramie. As you know, Ira, I am her whole family. You may become a father for the first time at forty-seven! If so, congratulations. . . .' "

As his voice faded, a junior lieutenant, thirty days fresh from Fort Lincoln and the social safety of Nebraska, burst out heatedly.

"It's a damned disgrace about that powder! I still don't see why—"

Akers held up his hand, cutting him off. He did not rebuke him, as he should have, but accepted the onus of his intemperate charge.

"You are all well aware," he said, "of the reason I have ordered that shipment of Shifter powder held here at Harney. But since the matter has been causing some evident rancor, I shall submit it to you once again."

During the slight hesitation he looked at his staff members as though appealing for tacit approval, but the latter would issue nothing but frowns of half-accusation, seeming thereby to support the young lieutenant. Akers set his jaw, continued wearily.

"It is my considered opinion—it remains my considered opinion—that we cannot risk the hostiles, in particular He Dog and his Wind River renegades, getting their hands on this gunpowder which we understand them to need desperately. If they are going to start a major uprising they cannot do it without a major supply of powder, and the only way, short of reducing a fort, for them to get such a supply is to seize it in transit. I maintain they know this and that they have been watching Shifter since early spring, expecting just such an opportunity to come to them from Harney. I further maintain that there is no reasonable way in which we may undertake, with safety, a delivery of this particular gunpowder to MacClean's garrison. We cannot, certainly, even dream of attempting it in face of his report of the Oglala coming down to join the Cheyenne."

"But," objected the brash lieutenant, thinking perhaps to enlarge an imagined advantage over his superior, "this He Dog has no more than fifty or sixty warriors, and he seems to be the key factor in this entire matter. Why have we not—why do we not—go out and put an end to him and his damned conniving. It would seem to me, sir, an elemental situation."

"It would be an elemental situation, Lieutenant," said Akers patiently, "if it were as simple as you suggest. To put He Dog out of business might very well dissolve the entire threat. But in connection with that end, it is not his fifty or sixty braves who will, eventually, put *us* out of business in the event of a successful uprising. May I remind you, sir, that Red Cloud and American Horse can put a thousand Sioux around any post west of Laramie and do it within days. Destroying He Dog and his few braves would scarcely diminish this prospect, and diminish it we must if Shifter is to be saved and He Dog's uprising aborted."

"Well, sir," insisted the young officer, "it is all very easy to say this Sioux threat should be diminished but if we are not to diminish it by striking at its head, which is certainly the Cheyenne, He Dog, how then are we to accomplish the deed? *How*, sir? That is what frustrates me.''

''It is what frustrates all of us, Lieutenant,'' said Akers. ''And it is precisely what I am talking about.'' He looked for a final time at his staff. ''Now if any of you in this room have any least, or last, notion of a way in which we may safely get that gunpowder from Harney to Shifter—*safely*, remember I said—then will that man please speak his mind. I am asking you in the hope that we may disregard rank and command for the moment. I want and need your help. Gentlemen?''

He waited. The officers exchanged their accusing looks for those of sympathy. They shook their heads in awkward response. In the end they had no more idea of a safe way in which to deliver fifteen giant canisters of Du Pont #1 Black Rifle Powder to Fort C. S. Shifter than did their harried commander. The latter read their silence accurately. He dropped his shoulders in defeat, turned from his officers to stand and stare out the north window across the deserted parade ground. When he spoke his voice was little more than a murmur, yet it echoed ominously as the dead march drum roll.

''God help the poor devils, then,'' he said, ''for we cannot.''

But as his words fell on the staff-room quiet, another sound obtruded; the bark and counterbark of military orders being issued from the guard post out front of Akers' headquarters and, following them, commingling with them, really, the crunch of a heavy vehicle's wheels on the gravel of the stockade street, the jingle of team harness and the shouting of a driver bringing his horses to a halt directly outside. Akers wheeled from the parade-ground window.

''Captain Martin,'' he said to his aide, ''will you

kindly see if that is the Chugwater stage? They are running three hours late.''

Martin stepped to the door, swung it open, flinched at what he saw outside.

''Yes sir,'' he replied, ''it's the Chugwater stage, sir. What's left of it.''

Akers was at the door in three strides, outside giving orders to the guard detail in three more.

In the moment it took the soldiers to catch up and hold in the lead team it was evident this was no ordinary arrival of the Chugwater run. Inside the coach were two dead soldiers propped up and tied in opposite seats. On top, on the driver's box, sat a youth of no more than seventeen. Shirtless, he was a welter of blood and blowflies. His eyes, swollen nearly shut, stared straight ahead. Of the regular driver, Monk Gurley, there was no sign whatever.

A guard corporal, moving to Akers' order, swung open the coach door. He had to leap back to avoid the body that spilled out to land at Akers' feet. The latter noted briefly the cause of death—a Cheyenne arrow driven to the feathers through the spine at kidney level—then turned away, white-faced, at what the Cheyenne had added to the body, or rather taken away from it, in the custom of their tribe.

''Monk Gurley, sir,'' said the corporal. ''The regular driver.''

Akers nodded, stepping forward to peer in at the dead soldiers. ''Second Infantry,'' he said over his shoulder, and the corporal said, ''Yes, sir, they're from Shifter, sir, I know them both.''

Akers went toward the head of the coach, where the dazed driver was being helped down by the rest of the guard detail. In the background the officers of the staff hung like witnesses unwilling to be drawn into the affair yet determined to miss nothing of its morbid details.

Stopping in front of the young stage driver Akers peered at him suspiciously, said quickly to Captain Martin who by now had caught up to him, "Who's this? I don't recall seeing him before."

"No, sir, nor I," said Martin, joining him in the stare.

"Johnny D, sir," answered the young driver for himself. "New shotgun rider for the Chugwater and Cheyenne folks."

"What's happened here?" rasped Akers. "Is this the regular Chugwater run? What Indians hit you? Well, boy?"

"Well, sir, yes, it's the regular run, and we was hit by a renegade bunch of—of—of Wind Riv—Ch—"

The boy had gone as far as he was going. He slumped, unconscious, in the arms of the soldiers supporting him. Captain Martin shook his head and said quickly to Akers.

"He doesn't look old enough to water the horses, let alone ride shotgun. Thank God MacClean changed his mind about sending Betty out on this run, sir."

Akers nodded abruptly.

"Yes. He must have decided against it when he saw this youngster. Get Doctor Farish up here. I want this boy brought around immediately. This whole thing looks wrong to me. Tell Farish we'll be in the staff room. Here, you men. Get this lad inside. On the double!"

Martin, saluting, turned away to shout at the guard corporal to go run up the post surgeon. The guard corporal, receipting the order and starting off, looked back at his two silent friends sitting in the Chugwater coach, and shivered.

"Jesus Gawd," he said. "What a way to die."

In the staff room half an hour later Johnny D, cleaned up, bandaged, brought hastily around, sat at the foot of the long table doing his best to answer Akers' questions.

"All right, boy," the latter began, "you're sure you feel up to talking?"

"Yes, sir. Knowing what I know, I got to feel up to it."

"Go ahead, then, we're listening."

"Well, sir," nodded the boy, "first off I heard what you and the captain was saying when you thought I'd passed out, out front. You were some right and some wrong. This is my first run and it's true I'm greener than park-bench paint, but you were wrong about the girl, sir; she was aboard our run."

The officers tensed, leaning forward. Akers held up a hand, restraining their questions.

"Go ahead, boy," he said low-voiced. "Tell it your own way, but hurry it along."

"Yes, sir, thank you, sir. Well, they hit us in that little meadow up at Point of Rocks. That's about midway 'twixt here and Shifter."

"Yes, yes, we know where Point of Rocks is. Keep going, boy."

"Thank you, Major, I will if you will give me the chance." Akers grimaced, his staff grinned, the boy continued without seeming to note either reaction. "Now it wasn't a big bunch that hit us, but there was a pretty big chief along with them. You all have heard of him maybe—He Dog?"

"That Cheyenne devil!" said Martin. "He's more of a white-hater than Red Cloud and American Horse put together."

"Yes, sir," nodded Johnny D. "And Monk Gurley, he said with Crazy Horse thrown in for bad measure."

Akers gestured impatiently.

"What about the girl, Captain MacClean's daughter? If they've—"

"Oh no, sir," interrupted Johnny D, "they never even laid a rough hand to her, excepting to hold on to her.

But that's just the trouble, them holding on to her."

"Exactly what do you mean?"

"Well, speaking *exactly*, sir, they're going to kill her if you don't do *exactly* what He Dogs says."

"Yes? And what does He Dog say?"

"Well, I'll try to remember it just as he give it to me, Major, but he hit me pretty good with that whip."

"Yes, we know. Take your time, boy."

The boy nodded, set his jaw, spoke carefully.

"He Dog said to tell you that he is going to burn out Fort Shifter as well as cutting up the girl if you do not send him some gun powder."

"Preposterous!"

"Yes, sir. On tomorrow's return run of this here same Chugwater stage."

"The fellow is insane!"

"Yes, sir, I know that to my own personal account. Tomorrow he said, sir. A whole coachful of it, Major. Loaded right up to the doorsills in the original cans. To be delivered to him at Point of Rocks before the sun stands straight up."

Akers got up from the table, strode to the parade-ground window, face working in a torment of doubt. Behind him Captain Martin spoke quietly.

"He does have Betty MacClean, sir."

Akers wheeled about, voice rising excitedly.

"He's bluffing! He can't take Fort Shifter without the Sioux and he can't interest them in a war without the powder to keep it going. He's using the girl in a last-ditch effort at blackmail. I believe he's heard from the Sioux and they've turned him down!"

"Oh no, sir," said Johnny D quickly. "That ain't so."

Akers whirled upon him irately.

"How do you know it isn't?" he snapped.

"I don't really *know* it ain't," said the boy soberly.

"All I can tell you is what Captain MacClean told me and Monk when he called us in to see him just before we pulled out this morning."

"Go on, go on."

"Yes sir; his last scout had come in at five A.M. Feller told him the Sioux was thicker than bottleflies at a buffalo shoot, one ride north. Said by daybreak tomorrow they'd have Fort Shifter sealed off tighter than a sun-shrunk hide. The captain, he claimed all that He Dog would have to do, then, would make one move toward taking the fort and the whole thing would blow up like a dynamited bridge."

"Nonsense! Why would he impart such military information to a stage crew? Why didn't he send it down by courier?"

The boy looked at him, frowning.

"He did send a rider, Major. Didn't he get through?"

Akers and his officers glanced at one another and Akers said hopefully. "There was a courier last night." But the boy only shook his head and said, "No, sir, it was one this morning I'm talking about. The captain he only give the message to Monk and me for extra insurance that it got here."

Akers turned away, gray-faced.

"They've done it," he said. "They've got Shifter cut off."

"Yes, sir," said Johnny D, "but that ain't the most important thing they've got, Major."

"Boy," said Akers, "you don't have to remind me about Betty MacClean. But I still can't risk sending that gunpowder. I dare not!"

At once the impetuous lieutenant from Fort Lincoln was on his feet.

"Major, it's *Betty MacClean* we're talking about, not some wagon-train woman or settlement trash! There isn't a man on this post who would not volunteer—"

''Impossible!'' Akers broke in on him. ''You will please be quiet, Lieutenant, and refrain from offering any further advice in this matter.''

He paused, then added with heavy deliberation.

''I will not send more men to certain death. Betty MacClean and the troops with her father in Fort Shifter are lost. There is nothing in this world we can do for any of them.''

In the ensuing stillness a lone voice raised objection.

''Excuse me, Major,'' said Johnny D, ''but I think there is something we can do for them.''

''*We*, boy?'' asked Akers. ''Do you mean yourself and the United States Army?''

''No sir, I mean you and me and them fifteen cans of gunpowder Captain MacClean was expecting.''

Akers stared at him, then turned to his aide, temper frayed by the fatigues of the long day.

''Get him out of here, Martin. See that he's well fed and better have him check with Farish again before he goes on to Cheyenne.''

Martin, however, had been studying the young shotgun rider.

''Begging your pardon, sir,'' he said, ''but I believe the boy has some definite idea in mind and with your permission I would like to hear what it is. Perhaps we owe him the opportunity. It would seem none of us are up to the problem, anyway. Let's hear what he has to say.''

Akers, who had started to rise, sat back down.

''All right,'' he said resignedly. ''At least the boy has *seen* the enemy. That's more than we have managed. Go ahead, young man, what's your idea?''

''Well, sir,'' said Johnny D, ''old He Dog he give me his Injun word he wouldn't touch a hair of that girl's head if you would do what he told you—send that gunpowder back to him on tomorrow's stage. Now not having any other choice in the matter, I give him my word back that I'd bring him the powder."

"You didn't!"

"Well, it was that or see the girl scalped."

"Yes, yes, I suppose. But good Lord, boy, how do you think—how do you think—you could ever actually go through with it? Bringing him back the gunpowder, that is? Of course you didn't mean it literally."

"Major, you can bet your life I meant it literally, I've already bet mine. As for you, you've got nothing to lose but a little gun powder. Or maybe so a fort. Or a whole war with the Wyoming Indians. What do you say, sir? You want to take a chance on winning instead?"

"Go ahead," said Akers. "I've been crazy enough to listen this far, I may as well go the whole way and get cashiered."

"Major, sir," said the young driver, "you ain't going to get cashiered. You just let me and the Chugwater stage line take them fifteen powder cans up to old He Dog and I'll personally guarantee to deliver them to the customer's satisfaction."

"Boy," said Akers acridly, "if we had wanted to *give* the gunpowder to the Cheyenne, I assure you we could have managed it without the aid of either you or the Chugwater stage line. Now you have taken enough of our time, young man, and I suggest you—"

"Major," said Johnny D, "I didn't say nothing about no gunpowder being in them cans, at least not very much. I will need a little. But mostly what I'll need is some rolled oats and coal oil."

Akers looked at him in a way which left no doubt as to his opinion of the mental competence of sixteen-year-old shotgun riders.

"*Rolled oats and coal oil*," he repeated softly. "Now, then, boy, are you absolutely sure there's nothing else you'll be needing?'' Johnny D ducked his head and grinned awkwardly.

''Well, yes, sir, there is,'' he said. ''About fifteen feet of fast burning fuse, and an awful lot of luck.''

''I see,'' said Major Ira Akers, although he did not see a thing at all except that this boy with the shock of sandy hair and outsize crop of orange freckles was either very daft, or very dumb, or very bright indeed—if not, in fact, a touch of all three.

''Johnny D,'' he said slowly, ''that's your name, eh, boy? Just a 'D' and nothing more, is that it?''

''Yes sir,'' said Johnny D, ''that's it. It's all my folks had time to name me, Major. My mother hid me in a feedbox when the Indians came. When they left, she lived just long enough to write in the dirt alongside the box that I was in there and that my name was Johnny D—'' He broke off, blue eyes clouding over. ''That's me, Major,'' he finished. ''Just a 'D' and nothing more.''

Akers nodded, his own eyes darkening.

''And those Indians were the Cheyenne?''

''Yes sir, this same Wind River bunch. It's how I come to know He Dog. I was only four, but there was a crack in the side of that feedbox. I could see out.''

Akers nodded again, feeling the tightening of the long chain of coincidence that tied this shaggy-haired frontier youth to his own fate, and feeling, too, the impelling urge to take the long chance which his story suggested.

''Johnny D,'' he said, ''if I were to take you at your word—the one you gave He Dog about the powder—how would you propose to carry it out?''

''Well, sir,'' said Johnny D, ''if you and the others will listen close, I will lay it out for you. . . .''

Johnny D, alone on the driver's box of the old Abbott & Downing coach, guided his fresh teams of army horses northward along the dim set of wagon tracks which was the route of the Chugwater Run between forts Phil Harney and C. S. Shifter. The Wyoming plain stretched endlessly away east, west and south. To the north a jumble of barn-sized boulders, lavender with distance, lay due ahead and low on the rim of the prairie. Johnny D glanced up at the angle of the morning sun, whistled and yelled at the horses. They responded but soon slowed again. The young shotgun rider talked to them like a mother instructing a venturesome toddler how to get back down off the barn roof by the same woodpile route he took to gain it. His tone was low, careful, full of concern—with a hidden edge of "just you wait till I get you down here." That sun stood only an hour off straight up. These army horses were fat, soft with grain and stockade living. Even with the black-of-dawn start Johnny D had given them, knowing they could not match gaits with his own tough mustangs, they were running late. That was Point of Rocks, yonder, and if he could not get these Fort Harney hacks up there in time, that brave little army girl—

He shook off the thought, yelled at the horses again.

They tried hard to respond and Johnny D called out to them, "Good boys! Good boys!" and let the lines lay loose on their rumps to show them he trusted them and appreciated their spirit.

After all, you couldn't blame it all on their lack of hard work. Fourteen giant canisters full of rolled oats soaked in coal oil did weigh something. The fact the fifteenth canister weighed a little light and contained no oats or oil didn't help any right now. Later, it would lift the load considerably but by that time the stout bays wouldn't be caring.

"*Hee-yahh*, boys!" yelled Johnny D. "*Hi-yupp! Hi-yupp!*"

As the laboring animals responded, the old coach

slewed around a bending turn in the road and for the moment the dust plume trailing it cleared away to reveal that the four in front were not the only army horses galloping northward on the return leg of the Chugwater Run. Behind the battered stage, tied with lead ropes to the baggage boot, in full rig of flat saddles, light bridles and wispy iron English stirrups, strode two lean, fit cavalry officers' thoroughbreds—running horses to the last trim line of slender fetlock and belling, blue-veined nostril.

Point of Rocks was very near now. Just ahead the stage road disappeared in the jumble of huge boulders that marked the historic outcrop. Johnny D cast an anxious eye at the sun. Calling to the horses, he brought them through the rocks and out into the sunken meadow that marked their center. The next moment he was hauling back on the reins, stomping the foot brake, skidding the big coach around, broadside, to its teams and to the roadbed. Ahead, blocking the way, waited some old friends of his. He had not expected them on this side of the meadow and their wordless, watchful presence moved thus out of the promised position on the far side, disturbed him mightily. A look at He Dog in his all-black outfit—black blanket, leggins, black eagle-feather war bonnet—did little to reassure him. And there was more than mere hunchy feelings to go on. The girl, Betty MacClean, was nowhere in sight. The thought jumped up in him, instantly, that they had taken her hair when he did not arrive at high noon. Dear Lord, if he had been responsible for that—but no—he must not weaken himself with such guilts now. He had a bargain to keep with He Dog, and he meant to keep it. He would think, and weep, about Miss Betty when his debt to the Wind River Cheyenne had been paid. He was, perhaps fortunately, given no more time to consider his position. He Dog was pushing his mount toward the coach. He halted the scrubby brute ten feet away, sat him staring up at Johnny D.

"Where is the powder, white boy?" he said.

Johnny D wrapped the lines, swung down from the seat box, stood away from the coach, facing the chief.

"We spoke of a trade. I had your word as a Cheyenne on it. So where is the girl?"

He Dog stared at him another long interval, then signaled his followers. Two of them dismounted, stepped behind the nearest boulders, returned dragging a bound and dirty-faced Betty MacClean. The warriors, bringing her forward, pulled the gag away from her mouth, slashed her bonds. He Dog, seizing her, shoved her stumblingly toward Johnny D.

"A Cheyenne keeps his word," he said. "There is the girl. Where is the gunpowder?"

Johnny D, catching and supporting the numbed army girl, helped her over to a low rock. Leaving her, he returned to the stage, dramatically threw open its near door. A deep sound rolled through the Indian ranks. In the sudden, deep silence the hissing of their indrawn breaths could be heard distinctly. The old Abbott & Downing was loaded to the seat level, and above, with sinister black canisters of a kind used to transport but one substance in the Western frontier world—gunpowder. And this was the best that money could buy, or blackmail bring. The vivid yellow-stenciled markings of the U.S. Army ordnance depot at St. Louis guaranteed that. In the stillness, He Dog exchanged narrowed glances with his warriors. *Emasóhevō!* By Maheo, there was enough powder there to fight a full year! Now the cursed Sioux would come into the war. Now He Dog could go to that arrogant Red Cloud and get some answers! *Nitasheema!* let things begin to move from here!

"There you are," said Johnny D, after letting them

look a good long time. "You keep your word, I keep mine. Come. Look at it. Open a keg. See how you like the quality. Don't take my word for it. I didn't make it, I only brought it out here for you."

The Cheyenne, led by He Dog, left their ponies and came over to inspect the powder. They pulled the first canister out of the coach, pried open its pouring lid. As they began their examination, fully intent upon it, Johnny D slipped away and joined the girl. He found her still brave but weak and shaky from her nightlong wait without food or water. She managed a wan grin as he came up.

"Well I sure am glad to see you again," she said. "How far behind are the soldiers?"

"There ain't any soldiers, Miss Betty," he answered. "There's just me and them two horses tied on the boot."

She looked at him, losing even the shadow of the smile.

"Do you think the Cheyenne will keep their word and let me go?" she said. "Let us go, I mean."

"I dunno, ma'am, you can never tell with Injuns. One thing I do know, though. We're going to find out in an awful hurry."

He glanced over at the Indians. They had the canister open now and were dipping their wetted fingers in it and tasting the adhering black grains. As they began to purse their lips and nod to one another in satisfaction, Johnny D turned quickly back to his companion.

"Are you a good rider, Miss Betty?" he asked. "Those are powerful jumpy horses. They'll take some handling in case we get the chance to use them."

The girl looked briefly at the tied thoroughbreds pulling and flinging their heads and walling their eyes at the smell of the Indians and their wild ponies.

"I'm army," she smiled. "If we get that chance, I'll take it with you."

"It ain't mine to take," corrected Johnny D uneasily. "It's theirs to give."

"I know. What do you think will happen?"

Johnny D started to move quickly away.

"The next thirty seconds will give you your answer to that," he muttered. "Hold tight, don't wrinkle a dimple. Stand there and pray. I got a little something to take care of."

"But, wait—" the girl began, and he stepped back to her side, dropping his voice and speaking side-mouthed.

"Listen, Miss," he said, "you do what I tell you. We ain't any time to be discussing the details. I got maybe half a minute left to take a chance that would turn a ghost pale. So you start praying and shut up!"

He was gone with the warning, starting past the Indian group, moving toward the far side of the coach. He did not make it.

"Boy!" called He Dog suddenly. "Where do you think to go? Come over here."

Johnny D fought down his fear, walked up to him with a smile. Or what he hoped was a smile.

"What is wrong?" he asked. "Is something wrong with the powder?"

Waiting for the chief's reply, his heart grew small. There were fifteen canisters in that coach. The one He Dog and his fellows were inspecting was three-quarters full of dry rolled oats and topped with one-quarter of pure Du Pont #1 Black Rifle Powder. One other canister, set on the bottom inside the far door, contained the original depot packing of pure powder. The other thirteen canisters, sealed with wax to prevent their odor leaking forth, contained not a grain of gunpowder. They held rolled horsemix oats soaked in coal-oil lamp-fuel drawn from the quartermaster's supply bins and drums at Fort Phil Harney. If the Indians had dug past the powder level in the bait canister, or if they now were going to open another of the canisters in the coach, Johnny D and Captain MacClean's pretty daughter were done for.

From He Dog's expression it was impossible to judge what had happened, or was about to happen. But when Johnny D stopped in front of him, he only grinned like a hungry wolf and said, "No, the powder is very good—tastes just right. We will take it."

The white boy shrugged, using all his knowledge of the Indian mind in his reply.

"Very well," he said. "I suppose that if you are going to be spitting that powder at the soldiers, one test will do as well as another."

He Dog glared at him suspiciously.

"Now what do you mean by that?" he said.

"Oh, nothing. But what good does it do to taste the powder? If I were trading a perfectly good white girl for it, I would want to see how it burned in a gunbarrel."

He Dog squinted at him. His warriors nodded and muttered a round of approving grunts. The chief showed his wolf grin once more. Reaching out, he patted Johnny D on the shoulder.

"You are a smart boy," he said, "and honest. Too bad your skin is the wrong color. You, Gray Bull," he directed a brave carrying an old-fashioned smoothbore flintlock, "try it in that grandfather of all guns. If it works there it will work anywhere. Hurry it up."

The warrior took a charge from the canister, began pouring it down the four-foot octagon barrel of his musket. Johnny D, seeing He Dog and the others move in on Gray Bull, took a deep breath and slid once more toward the far side of the coach. This time he made it. Bending, he took a look at the Indians through the spokes of the wheels, straightened, went to work.

Easing open the coach door, he removed the lid from the pouring bung of the bottom canister. His hand, slipping inside his buckskin shirt, brought forth a tightly coiled length of shiny black fuse. One end of this he inserted in the canister, replacing the lid and wedging it tight against the crimped fuse. Breathing shallowly, he dug in his pocket, found the big sulfur match he sought. Putting it to the scarred hickory veneer of the coach's door, he set his teeth and gave it a lighting scrape. The head dragged, crumbled, broke off and did not ignite. He froze, letting out his held breath. The snapping of the matchhead had sounded like the clap of doom. The Cheyenne must have heard it.

After a long moment, he forced another look beneath the coach's lowslung belly. Over on the far side Gray Bull was just waving back his comrades, shouldering his long-stocked piece, letting off its big outside hammer. As the rolling boom of the black powder discharged echoingly, Johnny D reset his teeth and went back to work.

The second match lit beautifully. But the fuse, after running fitfully for half an inch, died. Johnny D whipped out his knife, slashed a fresh cut a foot shorter. The third match scraped, flared, was applied to the clean fuse. Now it caught, sputtered, steadied, began to run quietly and quick, only a thin, traveling streamer of blue smoke bearing witness to its burning. Johnny D shut the door, stepped back, breathed again. As he did a remembered rough red hand fell on his shoulder and a familiar heavy voice was at his ear.

"What are you doing over here on this side of the high wagon, white boy? What are you up to?"

Johnny D, who could not know whether or not he had been seen, or if He Dog were playing cat and mouse with him or only asking a natural and direct question, brazened it out the best way he could.

"Why surely you can see for yourself," he said. "I was counting the cans. Making sure that you got all that was coming to you, all that I owe to you." He struck his palms together then held up the left hand in the Cheyenne gesture of friendship. "Is that all right with you?"

He Dog looked at him, not too friendly, as though perhaps he had seen him light the fuse to the genuine powder canister, then he broke out his evil grin for the third time.

"*Hēhe,*" he said, "yes, it is all right. You're a good boy. I like you. You tell your father and mother He Dog liked you. You tell them he let you go when he could have killed you. Especially the mother."

Johnny D looked at him, a strange light in his pale blue eyes.

"I will tell them," he said softly. "Especially the mother."

He Dog said no more. Yelling to his braves, he leaped up to the seatbox of the coach, unwrapped the lines, began kicking at the footbrake. His warriors, returning his eager shout, ran for their ponies. It was time, too, for Johnny D to be moving.

Driving around the rear of the coach he was met by Betty MacClean who, unordered, had gotten the two race-rigged running horses untied. Taking one of them he told her to get aboard the other. She did her best to obey but the highstrung animals were spooked by now and she could not find the stirrup. Johnny D leaped down to help her up and, as he did, he heard He Dog bellowing happily to the stage horses, "*Nonotov! nonotov!* be quick, hurry up, let's go!" and he saw the old coach begin to settle on her thorobraces for the starting lurch.

"That's Cheyenne for 'let's get out of here,' " he told the girl, literally flinging her up on the horse. "And it's a better idea for us than for them. Come on, I don't want to be within a country mile of that coach, or those Indians, come about three minutes from now!"

"Well, neither do I!" cried the girl. "Let's go!"

But as she spoke, Johnny D seized her bridle and held in her horse.

"No," he said, "just a minute. I can't miss this now. It wouldn't be honest."

"What ever are you talking about?" said his excited companion. "Come on!"

"No," said Johnny D. "I got to see that old He Dog gets what he bargained for—all fifteen cans of it."

He raised in his stirrups, peering across the meadow.

The coach was now nearly across the open ground, approaching an "S" turn the road made in passing through the last outcrop of rock before the limitless prairie resumed on the Fort Shifter side. He Dog, beating the tired army horses, was putting on quite a show for his admiring braves. The latter were racing their shaggy ponies in a pell-mell guard of honor before, after and alongside the careening coach. Neither driver nor escort took pause to notice the thin wispings of blue-white smoke trailing away to the rear from the doorcrack on the right side of the Chugwater & Cheyenne stage. Nor could Johnny D see it from his distant vantage; he could only pray that it was there. Pray, and wince in anticipation as the coach and the last of the Cheyenne ponies disappeared into the rocks.

After what seemed eternity and was in the order of five seconds, a tremendous upheaval burst above the tops of the cross-meadow rocks. Recognizable parts of stage coach and sundered black powder canisters mingled in the exploding column with the dust and rock of the shattered roadway. There was one ragged item, rising and falling like a great dark wounded bird, which was surely a black eagle feather war bonnet spun wildly upward on the wings of thirteen canisters of oil-soaked oats blowing up to the trigger of one full canister of Du Pont #1 Black Rifle Powder. As the delayed roar of the explosion rolled across the meadow, the nervous racing mounts of Johnny D and Betty MacClean reared and squealed in sudden fright. Had the boy not had hold of the lathered cheekstrap of the girl's mount, she would have been thrown, but he controlled the animal in time to hear her cry out, "Look, look!" and to follow her pointing finger to the far side rocks just as the unharmed army teams, still in harness and dragging the bodyless undercarriage of the coach, dashed neighing out into the open prarie and on away up the road to Fort Shifter. They were followed immediately by the bucking, squalling Indian ponies carrying the surviving members of He Dog's war party. These singed braves now gathered in a loose knot to stare back across the meadow at the white boy and girl, apparently undecided on the question of pursuit and punishment for the Trojan gift of the Chugwater stage. As they hesitated, a strangely forlorn figure trooped on foot out from the rocks, leading a powder-blackened pony. At the distance and from the broken-spirited bearing, it was difficult to recognize He Dog, war chief of the Wind River Cheyenne, yet he it was.

"Now," said Johnny D to his companion, "we will see how much I know about Indians—especially Cheyennes."

"What do you mean?" asked Betty MacClean nervously.

"If it's done right," answered Johnny D, "you can shame them into worse defeat than ever you could manage with shot and shell. The way I figured it from the beginning, if I could humble that old rascal in front of his top warriors, he would be done for as a war leader. It's worked better than I hoped. Staying alive, he's got to face the laughs of his people, and believe me when those Oglala Sioux hear how a white boy—and a girl, too, by jings!—put the kibosh on the biggest war-talker west of Laramie, or maybe even Fort Lincoln, why He Dog won't have no chance. He couldn't get up enough braves to play a good game of sticks after what's happened to him out yonder just now. Of course, that's all assuming that I know my Indians, like I said."

"What if you don't?" said Betty MacClean.

"If I don't," answered Johnny D, "then you and me are going to find out whether or not these jumpy devils we're on can outrun a pack of Cheyenne potbellies from here to Fort Phil Harney."

Across meadow, He Dog had now limped up to his followers. Johnny D and Betty could see his gestures and the former said quickly, "He's trying to get them to go after us. Get set to dig out." Five seconds passed. Then ten. At the end of what must have been nearly half a minute of motionless sitting and watching their lamed chief, the Cheyenne warriors began turning their ponies away from him. Within another half minute He Dog stood alone upon the prairie beyond Point of Rocks. He looked once across the sunken meadow toward Johnny D and Betty MacClean, then turned and limped off after his departed tribesmen. His spotted pony hesitated, whinnied anxiously, decided to stay with its outcast owner, trotted faithfully off in his uneven footsteps, the only true Indian friend He Dog was to know for all the remainder of his lonely days.

The honor guard was drawn up at the base of the flagpole on the Fort Harney parade ground. In front of it stood Major Akers facing Johnny D, drawn up rigidly at attention. At their sides, flanked to them and the squad, stood Captain Martin reading from a prepared vellum scroll. His voice carried loud and clear in the keen air of the early morning sunlight.

"For courageous action in the face of extreme danger and for the rescue and safe-guarding of Government property of great value, as well as the resulting relief of a military post in dire threat of destruction, and this relief per the following dispersion of large and militant forces of unfriendly Sioux and Cheyenne Indians, the Governor of the Territory of Wyoming in company with the commanding officer, United States Army, Fort Laramie, Wyoming Territory, is pleased to confer upon Johnny D this citation for outstanding contribution to the welfare and peace of the frontier community. Signed G. S. B. Hostetter, Governor, July 19, 1866. . . .''

Captain Martin stepped forward, presented the scroll to Johnny D, saluted the youngster and stepped back.

The latter grinned, blushed, scuffed his feet, stood fumbling the scroll. Mercifully, Major Akers smiled and put an arm informally about his shoulders.

''Dismiss the company,'' he told Martin, and walked Johnny D off to one side a ways.

''Now, boy,'' he said, ''I want you to think seriously about our talk last night. You've been on the post two weeks today, and you have some little notion of the life here. If you think you might abide it, and me, you're to remember I made my proposal only after hard thought and due consideration. A man gets lonely at my age and you and I, both being orphans, might find a great deal to bond us together.'' He paused, putting a hand to the youth's shoulder.

''Forty-seven's a little old to be a father for the first time,'' he concluded, ''but if you're game to try I think we might do worse than join forces, as it were.''

He threw Johnny D an awkward small grin, and concluded quickly.

''I mean to adopt you legally, Johnny D, if you will have me for a foster father. I know it's too soon right now, but you think about it. I've got six months more in this Fort Harney tour, and you'll have lots of time on your new job. What do you say?''

Johnny D hung his head, the idea of being anyone's son after all the orphaned years being more than he could look straight at and answer.

"Well, sir," he said, "I say that it sounds fine and that I will surely think very hard about it and I want to thank you for all you've done, so far." He hesitated, bringing up his glance. "You know, Major, sir, it gets a little lonesome out there on the prairie, too."

"All right, boy, we'll leave it right there," nodded Akers, stepping back and straightening to official formality once more. "Now, then, there's no time to be standing here talking about tomorrow, lad. On the double now. Look smart. Squad's right. You don't want to be late your first day on the new job!"

"Holy smoke!" grinned Johnny D. "I forgot all about that!"

Akers returned the grin, throwing a little salute of dismissal with it.

"Get along, son. It's not every boy your age gets a Government citation and a contract to drive the Chugwater stage all on the same summer morning." He paused for a knowing wink and a wave toward the waiting coach. "Especially with such a high-class cargo aboard!"

Johnny D brightened, peering toward the coach. He started out on the run, skidded to a halt, returned and pumped Major Akers' hand.

"Gee, thanks, Major." He waved the vellum scroll. "I mean for the paper and the parade squad and everything." Again he started out, again slid to a halt. " 'Specially the 'cargo'!" he called back, then ran on to the new stagecoach drawn up in front of the headquarters building. Leaping up on the wheelhub, he scrambled on up to the seat box. Up there, an older man sitting shotgun tipped his hat respectfully to him. Johnny D unwrapped the lines and settled in the driver's side. He waved to the two troopers holding the bridles of the lead team, the latter stepping clear as he leaned down and called toward the coach window, "All set inside?"

In reply to his query, Betty MacClean, seated within beside her father, leaned out the window smiling and waving up to him.

"All set inside, Johnny D! And remember there's a lady present. Don't talk like old Monk Gurley!"

Johnny D returned her wave, straightened ten feet tall upon the driver's box. Turning stiffly, he called to the cavalry escort waiting behind the coach.

"All right, sergeant, let's go. *Hee-yahhh*, there!"

With his yell, he kicked off the foot brake, laid the leather to the wheelers and the popper of the long whip about the ears of the leaders and was off in a shower of thrown-back dust and gravel. From the screen of this debris the grinning cavalry sergeant barked his "forward ho!" and the full-dress, eight-horse escort squadron galloped smartly away in the wake of the rocking coach. The last thing to loom through the clearing dust, as Johnny D and his honor guard of horse soldiers swung out of the stockade onto the northward-bending wagon tracks of the Chugwater & Cheyenne stage road, was the way sign which, for the youngest mainline driver in Wyoming Territory, summed up the full story.

"FORT C. S. SHIFTER," it read, "57 MILES."

Sundown Smith

It was utterly still upon the mountainside, as befitted a Sierra sunrise. Beside the lovely little mountain stream in a forest glade seemingly as remote as the moon from human evil, stood a ragged, one-man tent. Before the tent the coals of last night's campfire drifted a lazy wisp of scented pine smoke. The scolding of bluejays and the cheery small talk of the rushing creeklet provided the only important sounds.

Presently the tent flaps stirred and a man came out.

He stood yawning and stretching and scratching, clearly a man in no hurry to rush on toward his destiny. He was dressed in his customary nightclothes—which were also his dayclothes—a combination of worn, but very clean, blue jeans, and threadbare long-handled underwear. His faded gray flannel shirt he bore in the crook of his left arm; his run-over workboots he carried dangling in his right hand. The manner in which he accomplished his yawning and stretching and scratching while still retaining possession of these items was not a thing—not an art—lightly come by. It had taken years of patient practice.

Directly, the man had satisfied the morning's demand to ease the body ache of ground-sleeping and the minor epidermal disturbances set up by pine needles, small rocks, sand fleas and the other habitués of his mountain couch.

Taking pause, he contemplated his campsite. He was, in the act, surveying the new day, and his entire worldly wealth with it.

He did not see much. A weary, wise old saddlehorse. An ax with a broken haft stuck in a cedar stump. A battered black coffeepot beside the fire. A shard of shaving mirror hung on a branchlet of a nearby pine. A mug, a brush, a bar of soap and a granite washpan seated upon a stump beside the pine. Little things, of little value.

Back at the tent flaps the man pursed his lips, shook his graying head in a dolefully philosophic way at what he saw.

Everything that met his eye was much like himself: a little old, a little worn, a little worthless. Yes, he told himself musingly, he was a poor man. A very poor man, and, in the ordinary sense, homeless. Yet he knew that, somehow, he was rich. And, somehow, more at home in the world than most.

He nodded to himself with the thought, then looked over toward the fire. It was not twenty feet away, still the decision to cross over to it was not to be made hastily. After a suitable bit he nodded again and set out upon the journey. Arrived at the fire, he reached to pick up the coffeepot and set it upon the hook above the coals. But the moment that he bent forward, the old horse whickered petulantly.

The man stopped and looked off at the old horse. His

glance, if testy, was alight also with some inner warmth, for this was a very old, a very dear friend.

"Mordecai," he announced severely, "how many times I got to tell you not to talk to me till I've had my morning coffee?"

The question put, and going unanswered by Mordecai, he huffed on about the business of putting the coffee to boil—measuring and grinding the precious handful of beans—pouring the cold creek water—setting the pot on the hook over the coals—throwing onto the coals the exactly three chunks of bone-dry cedar required to roll the water, just so, wasting neither the man's time—which was worth nothing—nor the forest's firewood—which existed in an abundance of supply sufficient to stoke all the coffee fires of his lifetime ten million times compounded.

As he worked, he talked continually to himself in a lively two-sided conversation; this in the manner of the Western man who is much alone and who, perforce, enjoys his own company, or none at all. The man did not mind this for it reduced argument to the minimum and guaranteed victory in any debate to the party of the first part.

At the moment he was discussing Mordecai's future.

"Dawgone horse," he grumped. "Acts like he'd been took off his maw two weeks ago, 'stead of twelve years. I'm gonna get me another pony soon's I find work." He paused, glaring off, or trying to glare off, at Mordecai.

"You cain't stop and spin decent no more. You cain't cut, nor change leads without stumbling. You cain't head a critter worth a Indian-head nickel, and you cain't catch up to nothing over three months old, and you—"

He broke off, stomping his foot and whistling sharply.

"You hear me?" he demanded grumpily.

Mordecai heard him and whickered politely in reply.

"Dawgone right you do!" said the man. "And I mean

what I say, too. I'm a'going to do it. Someday—''

''Someday'' meant another ten or twelve years from then, or twenty. The old horse knew it, if the man did not. He had heard the identical threat more times, already, than there were pine needles on the floor of the little mountain glade. He whickered once more, the sound coming as closely as a dumb brute might come, to saying, ''huh!'' and then subsided wisely.

At the fire, the man gave him a ferocious look and returned his attention to the coffeepot.

A wisping stringer of aromatic steam was issuing from the ancient vessel, now, and the man removed the lid to inspect the cause thereof. Poking a tentative forefinger down into the pot, he winced and withdrew the member in considerable haste, flipping it and putting it tenderly to his lips to demonstrate that, as usual, he had burned himself in the line of duty.

But he was a man of some character, not to be deterred by the mundane frustrations of life.

Straightening from the fire, he moved over to the pine tree which bore the shard of shaving mirror. He peered into the glass, examining the quality of his five-day beard. In the marvelous mountain stillness the sound of his calloused fingers scraping over the wiry stubble was clearly audible. The man grimaced and shook his head at what he saw in the mirror.

He was looking at the reflection of advancing middle years and was not encouraged thereby. But the mirror showed more than that. It showed the crowsfeet at the eye corners deeply cut from the many years of smiling more often than weeping when the river failed to wash his way. It showed a tenderness of mouth and eye which knew no age, a love of the world and all within it, which could no more grow old than the rocks of the mountain around him. Yet all that the man saw was Sundown Smith, graying cowhand, itinerant ranch worker, saddle tramp, drifter, failure; a creature of the long-viewed, lonely places; a man without friends, family, or known next-of-kin.

Still, there was a certain light behind that aging eye.

Sundown tilted his jaw. He angled it here and there, judging the condition and harvesting readiness of his beard with the eye of a wilderness expert.

"I dunno, I dunno—" he said to the face in the mirror. "A man should truly ought to keep hisself slick-jawed in case of company."

He picked up the old-fashioned straight-edged razor, which lay upon the stump among the other shaving tools. He held it out from him, eying it askance and at arm's length, as though it might bite him, if provoked. Then, warily bringing it closer, he ran a testing thumb over its honed bevel. At once, he cried out sharply, wincing and sucking his thumb and shaking it to show, undeniably, that he had cut himself.

The performance was as predictable and invariable as that of burning himself to see if the coffee was hot. Sundown Smith was an inept man. A man who, in his entire life, had never learned a solitary thing—except how to be happy.

He now cocked a rueful eye at the injured thumb, then looked back at his reflection in the mirror. His grin, when it came, was as optimistic as the morning sun.

"Naw, shucks," he decided, touching the beard again and shaking his head. "I won't do it. I ain't 'specting no callers. Leastways, not this year." He refolded the razor, returned it to the stump, adding in explanation to the man in the mirror. "Besides, I got to pack up and move on this morning." He nodded to both his selves and stumped off toward the fire, mumbling to the original. "Yes, sir, got to be moving along. But I'll just have my coffee before I think about it. As for reaping that there stubblefield, I can shave any time. Maybe next

February. Say, March at the earliest. Yes, sir, April, anyway. Or May. . . ."

In such deceiving ways are ordered the lives of us all. Sundown Smith had just made a decision which could cost him his life. He did not know that, of course, and believed that he had handled the situation with great firmness and determination—qualities he admired vastly and knew very well that he did not possess.

Returned to the fire, he pulled up a convenient rock and seated himself. He poured a cup of the asphaltic brew from the tarred pot and sampled it cautiously. With an effort he swallowed the preliminary taste, his reaction indicating that it had the zest of liquid carbolic. Yet, with the brew once down, he widened his pale blue eyes and exclaimed to the mountainside, "Wonderful!"

When he took a second, exploratory sip, however, he shook his head critically. "Might need just a touch of sweetening," he allowed, doubtfully, and reached into one of his many pockets—he had donned the tattered shirt now—and brought forth an ancient leather poke of the variety used to carry nuggets and gold dust.

Peering around to make sure he was not observed, he loosened the drawstrings and extracted one lump of cane sugar.

The moment he did this, the old horse whickered aggressively from his picket pin on the grassy creek bank. Sundown glared over at him resentfully. Closing the poke, he restored it to its hiding place and complained his way over to the old horse. His mien was one of outright menace, but once at Mordecai's side, he again searched the clearing to make certain there were no spies about, then growlingly fed the sugar to the bony gelding.

Starting back to the fire, he stopped, wheeled around and said defiantly to the horse, "One of these days I'm going to find out what it tastes like with sugar in it! You see if I don't! Dawgone horse—"

At the fire, he seated himself, upon the ground this time, his back to a friendly, windfallen log. Reaching, he retrieved his coffee cup from the rock upon which he had left it. As he started it toward his lips a mountain jay scolded him with sudden sauciness from above.

Sundown scowled up at the jay and scolded him right back in a whistle-perfect imitation of the bird's rusty-throated comment. Then, winking broadly at the offender, he turned back to his coffee. Retasting it, he smiled as though it were the veritable nectar of the gods. He leaned back against the log, raised the cup on high, drank steadily.

All was right in the small, lonely world of Sundown Smith.

The little campsite beside the talkative stream was now as nature had made it. It was a rule of Sundown's existence that man was not created to improve upon the other works of the Lord. When he left a place, he tried to see that no stone lay differently from the way it had when he had come upon that place. It was, perhaps, his way of acknowledging, without presuming upon the relationship, that there was a Creator and that he, Sundown Smith, was mightily beholden to Him for such gifts of sunshine, pine smell, bluejay argumentation and creek-water small talk, which made of Sundown's life the blessing he considered it to be.

But now Sundown was tightening the last strap upon the ill-shaped bedroll behind Mordecai's saddle. Then, standing back to scan the campsite, he nodded, finally satisfied he had left no scar upon the sweet land.

For some reason he sighed. He always felt a little sad when he left a place which he knew he would never see again. It was like saying farewell to an old friend even though he had known that friend a mere brief night.

But it was time to go. Where, or why, Sundown Smith

did not know. It was just time. Time, maybe, to look for that job that never got found. Time to seek out a new set of bluejays with which to argue. Time to climb a new mountain. To see a new sunrise. To hear a new stream laugh in some different, lonely place. It was just time to travel on.

Sundown waved his hand to the little glade and turned to mount up. As he did so, he stood, poised, one foot in the nearside stirrup, head cocked, listening intently.

Far and faint and thin with distance, he heard the baying of a pack of hounds. It was not a musical baying but a fierce and savage and an eager sound, and it made Sundown fearful. The least shadow of a frown crossed his face.

Leaving the old horse, he went up on a rocky ridge, nearby, which overlooked the entire slope of the mountain. It was the first time that morning he had moved faster than a contemplative amble, or muttering stomp, and it was evident he sensed some impending trouble.

His instincts had not betrayed him: he was about to learn that the question "to shave, or not to shave," could be a deadly one.

The previous night, down in the valley mining community of Carbide Wells, an unknown killer had struck at an isolated ranch-house outside the main settlement. He had gotten away into the hills without being identified, save that he was a "kind of rough-looking, trampy man; a stranger with a 'stubbly' beard"—and that dangerous identification had been made by a small boy at the ranch.

The nature of the killer's crime had no bearing upon Sundown Smith's story, and, moreover, decent words could not be found to describe it for anyone's story. Suffice to say that when the townfolk and rough miners of Carbide Wells found the young widow Bromley, they voted the killer the rope—*whoever* he was, and *wherever* they should find him.

Now, having reached the rocky bridge, Sundown crouched poised atop it, peering down upon the slope below. The sight which met his anxious gaze fulfilled the fears put up in him by the angry baying of the hounds. Far down along the rocky shoulder of the mountain, a mounted posse was moving upward, single file. Ahead of this grim string of manhunters, held in leash by a man on foot, three cross-bred airedale-and-bloodhound trail dogs bawled fiercely, as they followed upon the track of their demented quarry.

That was the manner in which Sundown Smith became aware of the presense of evil upon his mountainside; with the sighting of three vicious cross-bred hounds and a hanging posse five minutes behind the human brute who would come to have, in later years of mountain lore, a name remembered to this day on the eastern slope of the Sierra—the Beast of Carbide Wells. And it was the manner in which, seconds later, Sundown came to learn that there was nothing but himself, and his wise, weary old horse, standing between that shadow of human evil and certain death at the end of the posse's rope.

As Sundown now straightened from his frightened look below and would turn to go back to Mordecai and remove both the old horse and himself from this climbing danger, a noiseless figure rose up from out the rocks behind him and felled Sundown with a single blow from the gnarled treelimb club which he bore in his hairy fist.

Sundown fell heavily and his assailant seized from his frayed belt-holster the old cap-and-ball Colt's Revolver, which had been Sundown's camp mate for perhaps longer than even old Mordecai. He turned its muzzle upon Sundown, as the latter now rolled over and made groggy effort to sit up. Succeeding in the effort, he squinted painfully up into the face of the man bending over him with the rusted gun.

When Sundown saw him, he knew that his first fearful feeling at hearing the hounds crying upon the mountainside had been a true premonition.

The face above him was the face of a madman. It peered at him from the form of a Neanderthal brute who cowered and crouched and snarled like the hunted beast he was. There was no similarity between the Beast and Sundown Smith save that both were born of woman. But, wait. There was one small sameness about them. No, two small samenesses. Both wore poor and rough and ragged clothing, and both wore a five-day bristle of heavy, graying beard. It was a singular similarity. And, swiftly, a lethal one.

"Get up!" ordered the Beast, jamming the Colt's muzzle into Sundown's temple. "Make one sound and I'll blow your head off." His voice was a rasping, throat-deep growl, and he certainly meant his command literally. But Sundown was compelled to advise him otherwise, out of all honesty.

"Not with that old cannon, you won't, mister," he grinned painfully. "Shucks, firing pin's been broke most fifteen year. I use her for hammering tent-pegs."

Instantly, the Beast slashed Sundown across the forehead with the long barrel of the weapon. The blow smashed him down onto the rock of the ledge.

"It will kill you all the same," snarled the fugitive. "You had better believe it!"

Sundown nodded his head with difficulty.

"I believe it, mister," he said. Then, with a jerk of the thumb which indicated the slope below, he added.

"They after you?"

The other's lips writhed in what was intended to be smile, but came out a silent snarl. "They *were* after me," he said. Then, savagely. "Get out of them clothes!

Boots and all! We're gonna switch duds, complete."

Sundown's blue eyes widened apprehensively.

"Now wait just a minute, fella," he protested. "That posse don't know me from Adam's off-ox!"

"Don't worry," leered his companion. "They don't know me either."

Sundown at first nodded, as though that were an information of some relief. Then, belatedly, he realized what had gotten past him. "That's what I meant!" he gasped. "If they don't know you and they don't know me, and they was to catch up to me in your clothes, they might—"

"Percisely," said his threatener. "Not only they might, I'm betting my life they will. Now you get out of them clothes. Boots, first!" He broke off, cackling in a wild sort of demon's laugh which put the goose bumps up Sundown's spine from chine to clavicle bone. "Them hounds don't know me, personal, no more than the posse does. It's these here old workboots they're trailing—" As he talked, he was toeing off his low-heeled brogans and kicking them toward Sundown Smith. "They'll foller whoever's in them!"

He interrupted himself for another of the demoniacal laughs, then let Sundown in on the secret of the joke.

"I never did want to die with my boots on," he chortled, "so I'll just let you do it for me!"

As instantly as the crazy laugh had broken, it stopped. Sundown had been standing still, listening to the demented fugitive, forgetting to continue with the disrobing which the latter had ordered. Like a bolt, the long revolver barrel struck again. It caught Sundown across the bridge of the nose, driving him to his knees on the rock ledge and spinning the forested world about him. When he could hear again, it was to recognize the snarl of the Beast in his ringing ears. The words were, "*Hop to it, you hear me? I'll lay your skull wide open next time!*'' and Sundown nodded that he understood, and began pulling and tugging to get his boots off, so that he might exchange them for his life—and the foul footgear of the killer.

The two men stood by Sundown's wise old horse, down at the abandoned campsite. They had now completed the transfer of clothing and the time, for both of them, was growing short. Upon the mountainside, beyond, the baying of the hounds was hoarsely near, and the voice of their handler could be heard shouting them on.

Staring off toward the renewed clamor of his pursuers the Beast growled like a cornered animal, then swung up on Sundown's old horse. He pulled Sundown's old Model '73 Winchester from the saddle scabbard and snarled down at its owner, ''You use this for driving tent-pegs, too?''

Sundown put up his hands as though to ward off a possible shot, and answered hurriedly. ''Oh, no—that's my camp meat gun. Be careful. She works.''

''She better work!'' rasped the Beast, and levered the Winchester in a sharp, hard way which showed that he knew the gun and how to use it for something deadlier than getting in camp meat. He stood in his stirrups, twisting to look off in the direction of the mountain slope.

''Listen to them hongry-bellied devils a'bawling for their breakfast,'' he muttered. ''Ain't that sweet music to a man's ears? Especially, when he's got a good horse under him and a center-shooting gun in his hand?'' He laughed the weird laugh again, then snapped at Sundown, ''Get going. Walk toward them yonder trees. And walk nice and deep and straight. Stomp hard. Leave them hounds a sharp-edged set of prints to sniff out. March!''

Sundown threw up his hands, appealing to the other's human mercy.

"Listen, mister. This is cold-blood murder. That posse won't give me two seconds to explain. They won't even let me open my mouth." He paused, then concluded fearfully. "Mister, they won't give me a chance!"

The brutish rider leaned down, hissing the words at him.

"They won't give *you* a chance? Listen, you no-good saddlebum, I killed a woman down there last night. She played the lady with me and I killed her for it. She called me an animal, you hear? *Me!* An *animal!* Well, she won't call nobody an animal now—not ever . . ."

He paused, a fiercely angry expression passing over his face. There was a sudden sort of fear in it, too, as though he had just remembered something about his crime. Something he had forgotten, and which was dangerous to him. He shook his head, talking now to himself.

"Nor that kid neither; the dirty, sniveling, little sneak!" He tailed it off, then went on. "Not by the time I get back down there, he won't. I'd ought to have got him before. I knowed there was something I forgot. If only them three cowboys hadn't of rode in on me just when they did. But the kid won't tell. Oh, no, he won't tell. He'll be just like his maw. Nice and quiet and with that funny, vacant-eyed look—" He uttered the cracked laugh once more, sat in the saddle staring off emptily. Recovering with a jerk, he whirled back to Sundown Smith.

"They won't give *you* a chance," he repeated hoarsely. "Mister, what chance you think they'd give *me?*"

Sundown looked up at him with quiet dignity, answering with a courage that neither of them recognized.

"Mister," he said, "what chance you think they ought to give you?"

The Beast kicked the old horse into Sundown and drove the steelshod butt of the rifle down into the cup of his shoulder, caving him to the ground.

"Now you get up, mister," he told Sundown in a dead level growl, "and you walk like you was told to walk."

This time Sundown obeyed him. He crossed the open ground of the glade, his enemy herding him from horseback, and behind. At the timbered edge of the clearing the latter hauled up the old horse and snarled down at Sundown, "That's far enough."

He hesitated, twisting in the saddle, again, to listen to an excited burst of yelping from the dogs. Then he turned back to Sundown Smith.

"Good luck, 'killer,' " he told him, uttering the crazy laugh in appreciation of his own grisly joke. "You oughtn't to have no trouble with that posse. Just tell them who you are. They'll understand." Then, wanderingly, and with the vacant look in his eyes once more. "We're all just strangers passing on the long, long trail. So long, 'stranger.' "

He broke forth into his wild laughter for the last time, and rode out, driving the old horse into the timber. They had disappeared in a matter of seconds.

Sundown stood stock-still for a long, held breath, staring after them. Then he wheeled and ran back toward the rocky ledge. There, he fell upon his stomach and peered over, tense and fearful of his pursuers as the true killer had been before him. What he saw below turned his saddle-tanned face pale as a clean-washed bedsheet, brought the beat of his frightened heart high and suffocating into his throat.

The hounds and the posse were nearly upon him. They were, in chilling fact, coursing the very ledge beneath the one where Sundown crouched—not thirty feet from his whitened face. They had one more switchback of the trail to negotiate and they would be upon the ledge with him.

Now the prospect of death was very near, and very clear, to Sundown Smith. Also the prospect of life.

On foot, unarmed, a man who had never raised either hand or voice in anger against a fellow man, he had, somehow, to run down and seize the real murderer for the Carbide posse, before the Carbide posse ran down and seized him for the real murderer. The odds against him were eleven to one—the number of men in the posse—plus three savage, cross-bred hounds and thirty feet of hemp rope.

Sundown wheeled blindly to flee, instinct his only guide.

He began sliding and slipping down the rocks toward his former campsite, and toward the cheery little mountain streamlet which formed its frothy skirt. At water's edge, he plunged in to his knees, and began stumbling and fighting his way up the green-foaming current. He made it to an upper bend of the small raceway, got around the bend and up and over a four-foot falls above it. There, he held up to regain his breath, looking back and downward upon his late camp, as he panted desperately, and thought, in the same vein, of some way in which he might extend his momentary advantage over the hounds and their hard-eyed masters.

As he watched, the dogs came bawling into the clearing below. At mid-clearing they went into a mill, straightened out, ran Sundown's track to the streambank, milled again where he had entered the water. Their handler pulled them off the scent and returned, with them, to mid-clearing. The posse now came up on the gallop. Swinging down from their lathered mounts, its members went into gesturing discussion with the houndman. The delay, Sundown knew, would be brief.

He was now at the bend of another stream than the icy small one in which he presently crouched.

He had been lucky, had gotten a start on the dogs, had borrowed ten minutes on his life's saving account. He could, possibly, get away now if he thought only of himself. But in his entire life, Sundown Smith had never thought only of himself. And the habits of a lifetime do not alter, even in the face of death.

Sundown's mind was not on the hounds or the possemen. It was on the words of the Beast—the words he had snarled about that little boy left on the lonely ranch somewhere down in the valley—a very young, very innocent, very much alive little boy who would now be the only witness in the world who could identify the *real* killer. It was suddenly in the desperately reaching mind of Sundown Smith that the brute who had brought down the mother, would not hesitate to stalk the son; as, indeed, he had threatened to do.

The criminal will always return to the scene of the crime, was the thought which now framed itself in Sundown's mind. Well, Sundown did not know about that. But he did know about something else. He had spent a lifetime in the wild and he knew this: *that an animal will frequently return to its last night's kill*—and the man who had taken his old horse, Mordecai, and left him afoot in his murderer's filthy rags, was not a man but an animal.

Sundown's face mirrored the terror that thought brought up in him. He reached, again, to seize the pine root which would pull him out of the stream. Once upon the rocky bank, above, he resumed his flight, following the faint trail along the stream's edge. Soon he was out of the heavy timber, into a more open, boulder-dotted country on the very flank of the mountain that loomed above Carbide Valley. As he reached this exposed terrain, the baying of the hounds was renewed with a bursting clamor. Sundown knew what the change in the baying meant. They had found his exit-point above the waterfall and their handler, sensing the nearness of chase's end, had unleashed them.

With the speed of life urgency, but not panic, he wheeled and ran once more. He knew where he was going, now, and he ran with a strength he had not possessed before. He was running for two lives, now, and somehow that idea lent him the will to outdistance the dogs to the objective that could mean the second, far more important, of those two lives.

He remembered, from the previous day's journey around this same mountain flank, an old logging flume standing stark and rickety upon the crest above the trail. From its vantage above the trail, it plunged down the mountain's side straightaway toward the valley so far below. If a man could reach that flume ahead of the hounds, and if it still ran with water, and if he still had the strength to climb up its underpinnings and plunge into its precipitous race—

The three questions drove Sundown onward. They drove him well. He did beat the hounds to the flume, he did clamber up its sun-bleached timbers, he did find water in its weathered flume and he did summon the will to leap into that water and to be whirled away down the mountainside.

The hounds had come so close they had torn a strip of cloth from his trouser leg. The posse had galloped up so swiftly that they had seen him poised to plunge into the flume, and had fired at him from horseback, one of the ricochetting bullets striking him across the bunched muscles of his right shoulder and staggering him almost off the high dizziness of the flume's trestle.

He was thus marked for the killing, should they ever

come up to him, but Sundown did not care about that. He cared only about the one other question which still remained unanswered in his race to reach the valley: who would come first to the secluded ranch house outside Carbide Wells?

Would it be Sundown Smith, or the Beast who struck by night?

The sun went, twilight came, lingered briefly and was gone. Full dark fell and still Sundown had not come to the ranchhouse. But as the moon rose far out across the misting fields of the long valley, he saw, close at hand, and hidden until now by some bouldered brush lands lying before him, the lamplight of a cheery kitchen window winking at him with warm hope. Gathering his tired limbs, he set out on the last of the hours-long trail.

The Rochester lamp on the red-checked tablecloth in the kitchen of the Bromley ranch house guttered to a sudden draft stirring through the room. Both the small boy and the old woman seated over their supper in the kitchen, glanced up at the one window. But the window was closed, and so was the one door into the room from the front of the house, and the one door out of it to the back of the house; and Bobbie Bromley and his Aunt Martha Sonnenberg nodded to each other and matched pale smiles and bent again to their eating.

Outside the house, along the kitchen wall, a shadow rose up from the high grass and brown weeds ten feet past the window, toward the front porch of the house. The shadow moved along the wall, to the window, and stopped. Then it moved again, and its maker slid in beneath the window and stood up beside it to peer in side-glancingly, and swift.

It was Sundown Smith.

When he looked in, his first thought was to sigh and to smile, for the boy was all right, and he was in time.

But the second thought came in on the heels of the first, and he glanced nervously toward the front porch.

Was he in time?

He had just sneaked past that front porch and seen, there, the shotgun guard posted by the posse. The guard had been propped up against the closed and bolted front door, tilted in his chair as though naturally dozed off at his post of duty. But now it seemed to Sundown that he had never seen a man sit so still—a breathing man—and, of a sudden, the chilling thought re-took him: *was he in time?*

He had feared to stop and alert that guard. The man, in the startlement of being awakened, and seeing him so roughly clad and unshaven, might fire before he asked any questions, or before Sundown could answer him any. The sawed-off 10-gauge L. C. Smith in his lap had loomed awfully blunt and deadly-looking to Sundown, and he had not dared to move over the rail and announce himself, at the time. Now, that second chilling thought was telling him that perhaps he was not in time, that perhaps it was now too late to awaken the guard. A man had to know, however. He could not simply stand there beneath that window waiting for the killer to make himself known—if he *was* there ahead of Sundown.

The drifter shrank closer to the wall, returned again to the tall weeds, crawled swiftly to the front porch rail and over it to approach the guard on tiptoe and to touch him lightly on the shoulder and whisper aloud, "It's a friend—please don't move or make a sound."

The guard obeyed Sundown. He neither moved, nor made a sound. And it was then Sundown noticed something. The shotgun which had been in the guard's lap only moments before, was no longer there. The shotgun was gone. And around the guard's neck, as Sundown leaned fearfully forward to see, was a short piece of broken halter rope, tied and rove in a perfect imitation of a tiny hangman's noose.

The guard was dead. Sundown did not touch him and did not need to. A man senses these things when he has lived long alone among the wild creatures, learning their ways, acquiring their instincts. The guard was dead and the small boy and the old woman were alone in the Bromley ranch house.

Alone, except for Sundown Smith.

Sundown was at yet another bend of the stream.

He could flee, now, and save himself. The posse man's horse stood saddled and ready in the outer yard. Life lay only that short distance away, and life was still sweet to Sundown Smith. But he looked at the shadow of the horse under the cottonwoods in the outer yard, and shook his head.

There had been something in the little boy's face, a look of loneliness and longing, all too familiar to Sundown Smith. Sundown knew how it felt to be alone—and lonely.

He shook his head again, and turned and went back over the porch rail and toward the kitchen window and toward seven-year-old Bobbie Bromley. Sundown was terribly afraid but would not turn away now. He understood the terminal quality of his decision. It was Sundown Smith against the Beast of Carbide Wells.

The kitchen window glass shattered with an inward, nerve-wrenching crash. The boy gasped and the old woman cried out. By then Sundown was through the window, had leaped to the table, seized and blown out the smoking lamp. The inrush of total blackness was blinked away by all three in the handful of seconds which followed. In this stillness, Sundown's soft voice pleaded with the two at the table. "Boy," he said, "and you, lady, you must believe me. I am your friend. There is not time, now, to tell you who I am—but the other one, the one you may think I am—is outside the house. He is yonder, there, in the night, somewheres, and he has come back down off the mountain to kill the boy—"

He stopped, and he could hear their breathing, close and tense in the thinning darkness of the room.

"But, mister—"

"No, boy, don't talk. Listen."

Sundown stopped, again, taking his own advice and listening for a sound outside the house. He heard only silence, and the stir of the wind wandering up the valley.

"Lady, are you kin of the boy?"

"No, not bloodkin. He ain't any of that left."

"It makes him and me even," said Sundown softly. "Boy, do you think I killed your mother?"

"You look like the man—your clothes and all—but you don't sound like him."

"Believe yours ears, boy. Will you do that for old Sundown? Lady, will you believe in me? And tell the boy to listen? A woman knows. A woman's not like a man. She feels. She senses things. I mean past her eyes and ears. You know what I mean, lady? You believe me?"

"Yes," said Aunt Martha Sonnenberg. "I believe you. We will do as he says, Bobbie. If that man who killed your poor dear mother is out there—"

Outside the broken window a dry weed scraped against the cracked sideboards of the house's wall. There was no wind moving at the moment, and Sundown finished quietly for her, "That man *is* out there, lady. Come on. Into the parlor. Go first, boy. Take my hand. Here, lady, you take my other one."

They went soundlessly, Bobbie leading the way, feeling the excitement and fear of the deadly game rise up within him. Sundown held up, listening at the door into the kitchen. Then he came away, quickly, and whispered to Aunt Martha. "He is out there in the kitchen. Just came through the broken window. Now, there is that horse of the shotgun guard's out under them cottonwoods. Can you ride?"

"Of course I can ride!"

Sundown eased open the front door, took her by the arm, forcing her out upon the porch.

"Then, lady," he said, "you get on that horse and you ride for Carbide Wells and you pray every jump of the way!"

Aunt Martha Sonnenberg was sixty-seven years old. She had been in that valley when the Piutes were bad and when a woman took orders from her menfolk without talking back. "Lord bless you, cowboy!" she murmured. "I'll be back with help soon's the horse will let me." She was gone then, scurrying across the dust of the moonlit yard like an old hen running from a hawk shadow. She got the horse free, and made it up onto him and got him safely away in a snorting gallop.

But it had all taken time, and made noise, and now the door into the kitchen slammed open and banged back against the parlor wall, and Sundown could hear the brute breathing in the blackness. He had not let go of Bobbie Bromley's hand the whole while, and now he squeezed it hard. Bobbie squeezed back, firm and quick, and Sundown thanked the Lord above that the boy had gumption and innards enough to go around.

Sundown felt in the dark for the chair back near his left hand. Finding it, he changed the set of his feet, let go of the boy, swept up the chair and hurled it across the room toward the breathing of the Beast.

It was the luck of the innocent, then. The chair struck thuddingly and, as it did, Sundown seized up the boy and ran out the front door and dove, with him, over the porch rail into the tangled, windblown weeds. Behind him, he heard the Beast growl deep in his throat. He put his hand over Bobbie's mouth and whispered, "Lie quiet, boy. I don't think he seen us go over the rail. The chair must of took him, full-on, and that's God's luck, as ever was."

Presently, they saw the silhouette of the killer come out and move around the porch. Then it disappeared back into the house and they saw the flare of the match spurt up in the kitchen, as the Beast found and lit the lamp. His figure, black and hulking against the lamplight, the guard's shotgun dangling from one long arm, the deepset eyes shining like a varmint's in the yellow glare of the coal oil put the shivers to the bone in Bobbie Bromley's thin body.

Sundown tightened his arm about him and said, "Boy, we cain't stay here, now. He means to come out and tromp us out with the light and the scattergun. He knows I ain't got no weapon. And less'n we can find one—"

He stopped, listening hard again.

A new sound—or, rather, an old one—had come to his straining ears. Just up the valley, near the rock-girt rise over which he had come to drop down on the Bromley ranch house, the baying of hounds in full tongue burst into sudden, startling clamor. Sundown shivered now. The odds in the game were going up. Now he had not alone the deadly stealth of the killer against him, but the lethal creep of the clock, as well. For if the posse should come up soon, with the men finding the murdered shotgun guard and the dogs finding him, Sundown Smith, then he would still hang. And hang so swiftly he would be given not even the chance to state his true name, let alone the nature of his defense, or state of innocence.

"Mister Sundown—" the boy had been thinking, and now whispered tensely to the old cowboy holding him. "You said something about us finding a weapon. I know where there's a turrible weapon. I seen Paw use it onct, when I was little, to near kill a proddy range bull that had wandered into the yard and cornered Maw 'twixt the barn and the house.''

''Boy,'' said Sundown Smith, ''what are you talking about?''

The killer was moving through the house again, now, coming from the kitchen, through the parlor, with the lamp and the shotgun.

''The old hayfork,'' answered the boy, watching the killer, with Sundown, and keeping his voice down to a field-mouse rustle. ''It's in the barn, where Paw left it. He broke it on the bull and bought hisself a new one next trip to town. Maw sold the new one when we auctioned off the equipment after Paw was took.''

''You sure it's there where your Paw left it? You seen it lately, boy?'' muttered Sundown.

''No, I ain't certain. But I know where he left it.''

''Can you find it, you reckon?''

The boy was still watching the house. The killer had come out on the porch now and was standing holding up the lamp, throwing its light this way and that.

''I reckon I'd better *try*,'' he said to Sundown, and Sundown nodded and felt a lump come up in this throat. He patted the boy on the shoulder and whispered back, ''me, too,'' and reached around in the grass until he found a rock the general size and heft of a Rocky Ford muskmelon. ''When I pitch this rock over to the far side of the house, you be ready to evaporate like a broom-swatted cat, you hear?'' he asked the boy. ''I hear,'' replied the latter, and Sundown rose up and pitched the rock over the house.

The rock fell, just so, on the far side of the house. It made a good crackling noise in the matted-dry weeds over there and the killer was off the porch and crouching toward the sound like a big, dark-bearded cat walking down a covey of fledgling quail. He moved so quickly that Sundown had to remind the boy to run, before he might smell out the decoy rock and come for them, full tilt.

They made it to the barn, slipping in the rear through a broken wallboard the boy knew of. The doors were hasped and locked, and the killer had not heard them across the barn lot. They had, perhaps, five minutes to find the old hayfork, and to figure out what to do with it when—and if—they did find it.

"Boy," said Sundown Smith, "he'll be here soon. There ain't but just so many places he'll look afore he *knows* where we are. Two sides, and back and front of the house, and that's it. He's been front and one side. We ain't no world of time."

"You wait here, Mister Sundown."

"No, we dassn't separate for a minute. Here's my hand."

The boy took his hand and, together, they went through the musty gloom of the empty barn to the stall head where the lad remembered his father putting the rusted head of the old hayfork. The fork was there; the fork and about two feet of the broken, spear-pointed, hickory haft which was all that remained of its once five-foot handle.

"She'll do," said Sundown Smith, taking the wicked tines from the boy, and feeling them, and the remnant of handle, in the darkness. Then, softly. "Boy, is there nothing else you can think of? Anything at all, we might use for—well, you know."

"No," said the boy, "nothing."

"She'll *have to do*, then," said Sundown, hefting the fork. "Let's go, boy."

"Mister Sundown, I got a name. It's Bobbie. Bobbie Bromley. Junior."

"All right, Bobbie. We still got to go. Fast."

"You going to stab him with the fork? Hide behind the door, maybe, and get him when he comes in?"

"I wouldn't dast risk it. Not with his kind. He's like a wild critter, boy. He'd smell me out."

"Well, what you aim to do then? If you're afraid to use the fork on him, how's it to do us any good?"

"We got one chance, boy. Is that a loft ladder yonder?"

"Yes, sir."

"Is there a hay trap in the loft?"

"Yes, sir; over this here front stall, right where we're at. Paw used this stall for hay storage."

"All right, boy. You skin up that ladder and you keep an eye peeled on the house. When you see him coming you knock twicst on the loft floor. You hear?"

"Sure. But we can see him coming from here. Them wallboard cracks is half an inch wide. They'll let that lamp shine through, easy."

"Boy," said Sundown, "when he figgers we're out here in the barn, he ain't going to be coming after us with no lamplight to let us lay for him by. He'll be coming in the pitch dark, and all you'll see of him is his shadow floating 'crost the barn lot. Now you get!"

"Yes, sir!" gulped Bobbie Bromley, and got.

The earth in the bed of the stall was loamy and soft and deep with the working of many an unshod hayrig pony's hooves. Sundown was able to get the sharp-pointed stub of the handle well down into it. Almost, in fact, halfway down to the iron of the fork head itself. He set it as precisely beneath the frame of the trapdoor in the loft floor directly above, as he was able to guess at in the nearly blind gloom of the barn. He had only the slightly less black square of the opening to work by, but that had to suffice. And to suffice fast.

Above him, now, he heard the two sharp raps on the

floor, and his heart came up against the base of his throat, cutting off his breath.

More than one sound came to him in the ensuing silence.

Up-valley, the hounds were drawing nearer, their belling taking on a fierceness it had not held before. Sundown recognized it as the same change in their cry he had heard upon the mountainside, just before reaching the logging flume. They had been unleashed again, and were running.

Time again: time was trying to kill him and the Bromley lad as surely as was that black shadow floating toward them across the barn lot. If that posse took him, Sundown, now, the true murderer would need only to shy off and hide out until the Carbide men had gone on. He would then be free to continue his stalk of the boy. For whether the men took Bobbie along with them or not, they would leave the ranch convinced they had destroyed his mother's killer, and that he was thus removed from danger. True, the lad might try to defend him. But no convincing he had forced on the latter by knocking in that kitchen window and blowing out the lamp would hold up with those tight-jawed men who had been running his track since early dawn and who, certainly, when they now came up to him, would be in no mood to listen to the thin stories of either a homeless drifter, or a big-eyed, weanling ranch boy. The old woman, now, Aunt Martha, she would have been a different pot of pepper. Her word would have held off the rope long enough for the men to fan out and put the dogs on the real killer's track. And had her word been not enough, she likely would have taken up a whiffletree or a churn handle and impressed the Carbide committee directly. But Aunt Martha was long gone, and the chances of her getting back from town in time to take a stand in favor of Sundown Smith were about equal to an Apache Indian's winning a popularity contest in Yavapai County, Arizona.

No. It was still Sundown Smith against the Beast.

And soon.

Outside the locked barn doors, now, he heard the scrape of a boot. Then the snuffling, exactly like that of an animal, at the three-inch crack between the sun-warped doors. The Beast was trying to smell him out.

The quality of the outer night's darkness was now being thinned by the climb of the moon. When the killer left the doors to slide around the barn wall, pausing every few steps to sniff anew at some new separation of the sliding boards, Sundown could clearly follow the blot of his shadow. In this way, he knew when he had reached, and glided through, the missing board at the back of the barn. Now it was up to Sundown.

Deliberately, he ran for the foot of the loft ladder. Having the jump on the killer, he beat him to the rickety steps, and up them, into the loft. At the foot of the ladder, the Beast stopped, staring upward into the absolute pitch-dark blackness of the haymow.

When Sundown heard the creak of the first rung, he moved two steps away from the ladder's head. And only two steps.

From then, he counted each rung creak until there was utter stillness again. The Beast was in the loft, at the ladder's head—holding his breath, waiting for his eyes to adjust to the greater darkness. Sundown held his own breath, praying he could outlast the other. He could. Presently, he heard the labored indrawing of the killer's heavy breath begin again. Instantly, he spun about and leaped away from the ladder head, toward the loft hay trap and Bobbie Bromley. As instantly, the Beast snarled and lunged after him.

Sundown counted his steps away from the ladder, as he had counted them running toward it in the barn below. When he had taken the same number, he jumped as hard as he could to clear the yawning hay trap. He alighted safely on the far side, colliding in the soft mat of hay beyond with the hidden boy. In the same instant he heard behind him the killer's startled gasp, as his reaching feet found, and treaded wildly, the empty air of the open trap.

There followed a silence that seemed interminable but could not, in fact, have lasted more than fractions of a second. The period to this dread pause was a single wrenching cry from below. After that, there was no sound at all in the old barn. None, that is, save for the whisper made by the lips of Sundown Smith moving in fervant thanks to Providence for a delivery from evil which could not, surely, or solely, be explained by his own small, desperate craft.

The hounds came up to Sundown, with the posse at their bawling heels, just as he and the boy emerged from the darkened barn. The exhausted posse men would not listen to any protest, either of Sundown's or Bobbie Bromley's. They had the evidence of their own eyes, and that of the hounds' noses. It was enough. They had the rope shaken out and flung up over the hay-winch beam almost before the drifter or his new friend could utter an intelligible word, and certainly before the ranch boy could comprehend that they truly meant to hang the gentle man who had saved his life. When they had rove the coarse noose about Sundown's neck and tightened it testingly over the hayloft beam, he understood, and then he rushed forward crying his outrage between choking sobs and blows of his small fists at the braced legs of the rope men.

Still, the leader of the posse would not listen. Signaling one of the men to subdue the boy, he brought from his saddlebag the piece of trouser-leg torn from Sundown's faded Levi's upon the mountainside above. He fitted it into place on the drifter's leg and said to the boy, "Bobbie, this is the man who hurt your mother. He has lied to you but you must not believe him. You must believe us. We know what we are doing."

"You don't! you don't!" cried the boy, but the leader made a grim sign to his men, and they stood back to make room for their fellows on the rope's end.

"Take the boy around the corner of the barn," ordered the leader, and the man who had Bobbie nodded and dragged him out of sight, as instructed.

But the boy would not quit; not any more than the drifter had quit when he had the opportunity. Once the barn's corner hid him and his captor from the other men, he kicked hard and sure through the darkness, and his sharp boot toe did not miss the mark. The posse man yelled out a curse and let go of the boy to grab his injured shin.

Bobbie shot away from him like a stomped-on cottontail. Scooting on around the barn, he found the broken board at the rear, slid in and dashed through the darkness toward the front stall. The shadow man had still had the shotgun when he had fallen through Sundown's trap. If Bobbie could find that weapon, now, maybe he could use it to make the posse men understand that seven years old and all stirred up, did not disqualify a boy from knowing what he knew, and being able to testify to it. Yes sir, if they wouldn't listen to a little boy, maybe they would listen to a big gun.

It took a great deal of courage to go near that stall, and near what lay within it, impaled upon the broken hay fork. But Bobbie Bromley went into the stall, and found the guard's double-barreled, full-choke, Ithica 10-gauge shotgun. And, with the weapon, he returned to the barnfront scene, just as the ropemen lay back on the rough strand, and Sundown's boot toes lifted free of the ground.

With no time to do anything else, the boy shouldered the huge double and triggered the left barrel blasting upward into the night, and into the barn's winch beam and the Carbide posse's tautened rope.

The charge of Number 4 buckshot dissolved the rope and a foot and a half of the end of the winch beam. Sundown fell to earth, unharmed save for a chafing of his five-day beard, and the Carbide posse men swung about to face a seven-year-old ranch boy who still had one shell to go, and didn't hesitate to let them know it.

He devoted the gape of the 10-gauge's bores to the general vicinity of the posse leader's belt buckle, and directed his remarks to the latter in no uncertain terms.

"*The other tube's for you, Mr. Hannigan—*" he broke off the threat to cock the big outside hammer of the remaining barrel, and in the silence which ensued, he added tearfully, "*—less'n you 'gree to look in the barn like Mister Sundown asked you to. Now you git!*"

Mr. Hannigan was no fool. He did not care to argue points of proper procedure with a small boy and a very big shotgun on full cock. He got.

The rest of the posse men went with him. When they had pried off the hasp of the doors and had flung them wide and stomped inside, holding high the Rochester lamp fetched from where the killer had left it in the house, they all stopped, stark-staring, at what they saw in the first stall.

The leader quickly blew out the lamp and said to his men, "Boys, get out of here; we can come back in the morning with tools and a wagon."

Outside the barn, he put his heavy arm around Bobbie Bromley's shoulders and muttered, "Bobbie, I reckon you know we're sorry. You done a brave thing, boy, and we're all mightily proud of you. Yes," he said, looking up to nod at Sundown Smith, "and of your friend, yonder, too."

He stepped to Sundown's side and said in a low voice, "We mean it, mister. You got a home in Carbide Valley long as you want."

Sundown just smiled in his sad, slow way, and shook his head.

"Thank you, Mr. Hannigan," he said. "But when the boy is rightly settled, I reckon I'll just be drifting on."

In Carbide Wells, it was just a little after sunrise. It was a day shot full of sunshine and good cheer. In front of the local office of the Inter-Pacific Stagelines, a Concord coach was drawn up and a small crowd gathered.

Here assembled were the good folk of Carbide Wells, town and countryside, gathered to say goodbye to little Bobbie Bromley. It ought to have been a happy time, but it was not. Like Sundown Smith, Bobbie Bromley was now without kith or kin in the whole broad world, and he was being sent on the morning stage to San Francisco, where the state authorities would find a home for him.

To one side of the crowd stood Sundown Smith and his wise old horse, Mordecai. Upon the seat box of the stage Bobbie Bromley was perched beside the grizzled driver, trying to be far braver than he was. Neither his heart nor his eyes was in the business. Both were bent across the heads of the crowd toward Sundown Smith. And it became suddenly very doubtful that Bobbie would ever get to San Francisco. Or, indeed, that he would ever start for San Francisco. That last look at Sundown and old Mordecai said more, in silence, than all the noisy wishes of the crowd could ever render in out-loud farewells.

In the final, fateful second before the stage driver kicked off his brake and yelled, "Hee-yahh!" at his waiting horses, Bobbie slid down off the seat box and ran waving, from that high, unhappy perch, toward Sundown Smith. As he reached him, the drifter got down from old Mordecai and gathered the boy up in his arms and held him there, defying the closing crowd like an aging gray wolf brought to bay, bewildered and confused, but determined somehow to defend what was his, and the boy's.

There was some hot talk, then, and loud. But Mr. Hannigan, who was the mayor of Carbide Wells, shut it off pretty prompt. "The question is," he said, "whether the boy goes our way, or his own. We'll put it to a vote." He paused, spreading his thick legs and jutting his big jaw. "Hannigan," he said, "votes for the boy."

Sundown and the boy stood high upon the mountainside looking back and down upon Carbide Wells for the last time.

They were leaving the valley to go over the mountain and look for that job of Sundown's, which it was to be hoped they would never find. On the way, they would seek some new bluejays with which to argue. They would search for another sunlit glade on another lofty slope. They would listen for the laughter of some new, small stream, in some different and distant place. But this time it would not be a lonely place.

With this thought, Sundown nodded to himself, and plodded on up the trail, the boy coming gladly behind him.

On the last rise before the trail bent to hide the town, Sundown paused to wait for the boy, and for the old horse the boy was leading. When they came up, the three of them stood looking back, just for the least, grace note of time. Straightening, Sundown nodded for the final time.

"Indeed," he said softly to himself, and through force

of life time habit, "the question comes naturally to a man's mind, if there will ever be another lonely place for Mordecai and me. . . ."

When he spoke, the boy smiled up at him and put his hand in Sundown's hand and the two friends turned and went over the last rise, the old horse following them like a faithful dog.

The Hunting of Tom Horn

Sometimes a man has to lie to save his own neck, and sometimes to save somebody else's. I had to lie once to save another man's life, and I don't know to this day whether I did right or wrong.

It was on the old Jim Birch stage road about halfway between Lordsburg and Tucson. I was Tucson-bound, coming back from having trailed a bunch of rustled stock for the Association over into New Mexico. In those days we could do that, the cattlemen's associations in both territories being glad to see a cow thief caught, no matter whether by an Arizona detective, or a New Mexican one. I will say, though, strictly as an item of professional pride, that we boys from the Arizona side had a little better record for arrests and convictions. Maybe that's why I hadn't gotten too much cooperation from the Lordsburg sheriff, just now, and why I was riding back to Tucson empty-handed. Anyway, I was over a week late in getting back, and in no need whatever of further delay. But on a lonely stage line in Arizona Territory, trouble was always as close as the next bend in the road.

In this case, what lay around that next bend was a lynching bee, and when my pony snorted and put on the brakes and that hard-tailed bunch of range riders posed around the kid on the piebald gelding eased off on the rope around his neck and looked my way, mister, you could have heard a drop of sweat hit that roadside dust.

It was trouble, all right, the worst kind. Only question was, was it my trouble, or just the other fellow's?

I didn't know yet. But I got down off my horse nice and quiet and went walking toward the lynchers real easy. You see, the way I'm built, I couldn't help myself; I had to find out. I suppose that's the streak of cussedness that made me a stock detective. Anyway, it was the streak that put me to walking up on those flint-faced cowboys, when I ought to have been high-tailing it away from them as fast as old Shoofly could carry me. Which was somewhat.

But I was never known for good sense, only for inferior judgment. I picked out the foreman and braced him.

"What seems to be the difficulty?" I asked.

He jerked a thumb over his shoulder, his reply notably unloquacious. "Take a look for yourself," he advised.

I stepped around his horse and complied.

It was a tied-down, two-year-old beef, thrown alongside a small fire. The running, or single-iron was propped in the flames, still heating. The evidence, though simple, was ample: a brand blotter had been interrupted at his trade. I turned back to the foreman.

"You know a single-iron when you see one, mister?" he inquired, giving me a look as hard as gunhammer steel. "This particular one fits just perfect under this boy's stirrup fender. That satisfy you?"

I tried to trade tough looks with him.

"Not quite," I said. "You can't hang a man just for changing a brand. Not these days. It's eighteen-eighty, mister."

"*I* can hang him," he answered back, not flicking a lid. "I'm E. K. Carnady, managing foreman, Mescalero Land and Cattle Company. Now, how about you?"

"How about me?" I said, eying him back. "I'll tell you about me, Mr. Carnady. I'm against hanging a man without full and fair trial, for *any* reason."

This Mescalero Company foreman was a big man, running a big, notoriously hard-case cattle outfit. He wasn't of the breed to buy any offhand interference.

"Mister," he said, "you open your mouth once more, we'll run you up alongside this hot-iron artist. We been after him six months, and we mean to swing him. *Now*, how about *you*?"

"Do you even know who he is?" I stalled.

"Don't know, don't care. The kid was caught burning a Mescalero cow. We didn't wait for no formal introduction."

It was time for the lie. I had set it up. Now I had to carry it off like the cold-deck bluff it was.

"Well, I do know him," I said. "What's more, I want him, and I mean to take him."

The foreman nodded past me to two of the cowboys behind me. They moved up, flanking me, hands on their holsters.

"And who might you be?" he asked, real quiet.

"Charlie Shonto," I answered, just as quiet.

"From Gila Bend?"

"There's another Charlie Shonto?"

"Don't get smart," he said, "you're flanked. Your fast gun don't mean a thing to my boys. Moreover, we ain't sent for no help from the Arizona Cattlemen's Association. Time comes we can't catch our own cow thieves, we'll let you know."

I shook my head.

"You don't listen good, Mr. Carnady," I said. "This boy has been on our list since last July. That's a year ago, come next month. We're tired of chasing him."

"So?"

"So, he's our boy, and I'm taking him into Tucson. I got to earn my keep, Mr. Carnady, same as you and your boys, here." I eased one step to the side, half turning to get both him and the two hands in pulling view. The other riders were out of it and sitting quiet. "Now, I do hope you don't mean to make me earn it unpleasant," I finished up. "I prefer working friendly."

Carnady gave me a long looking over. Then he waved carefully to his hard-case flankers. He wasn't going to fight the Association—an outfit that had an unmatched reputation in the Southwest—but all the same he felt compelled to go on record, personally.

"All right, Shonto," he nodded. "But you know range law and you know you had no call to mix in here. We had this kid dead to rights."

It was my turn to nod. I took it on the acid side.

"You pretty near had him dead," I agreed, "but not to rights. Not to *his* rights, anyhow." I gave him three seconds to think about it, then went on. "Yes, I know range law, Mr. Carnady, and I know regular law, too. So I'll tell you, right out, what I mean to do. I'm turning this boy over to Sheriff Gates in Tucson. You want to come in and press cow-stealing charges against him, that will be the place to do it—not out here on the range, with you and your men as judge and jury." I threw him another pause, then nailed him down. "The day of the rope is done, Mr. Carnady. You know it, I know it. And we both know I'm only doing what's right and legal."

I bent my crouch a little more toward the two gunhands. "Now, you men get the noose off the boy and cut his hands loose. Hop it!"

They hesitated, looking to Carnady for their yes or no. He gave them another yes, and they cut the rustler free.

"All right, kid," I said, "rein your horse over here."

He did so, and Carnady watched him bitterly.

"You're only putting off the inevitable, Shonto," he told me. "The kid was born to hang. He'll make it without your help, *or* mine." I nodded to that, agreeing with the general idea, then started off with the boy. Carnady raised his voice. "And, Shonto," he warned, "you'd better have him in that Tucson Jail when we come after him!" I held up my horse, nettled by his tone.

"He'll be there," I said, flat-out, "safe and sound."

"He'll still hang," he persisted tartly. "Range law or regular, he'll end on a rope. Remember I said it."

"I'll remember," I promised. "See you in Tucson, Mr. Carnady."

He held me a minute with that hard look of his, then nodded and said very soft, almost to himself.

"It's a long ways, yet, Mr. Shonto. With that boy you may just never make it."

We were lucky at Cow Creek Station. The weekly stage from Lordsburg was there, hung up with a wheel-change. All I had to do was wait around until after supper, and ride on into Tucson with my prisoner in style. It was a prospect pleasing in more varieties than getting that kid rustler back of bars. I had been sitting on Shoofly the better part of two weeks and was good and touchy in the tailbone. Those old Concord seats were going to feel like feather beds. Overcome by the prospect, I offered to take the kid for a walk to sort of let him get the ache out of his own backside before we sat down to eat.

It was deep dusk, when we set out down the road below the station. I was preoccupied somewhat. I hadn't been able to get out of my mind the foreman's warning about the boy. There was something about it, and the kid, himself, that I kept thinking I ought to remember. I had seen him, or his face, somewhere before, I was certain. But I couldn't remember where for the life of me—and that fact was very nearly the death of me.

He was a big kid, curly-headed, handsome, good-natured as a hound pup. And smiling, always smiling. Polite, too. Polite as a colored preacher talking to the devil. Like right then, for instance, as we strolled along under a three-quarter moon, just smelling the sweet sage and hot sand cooling off after the daytime swelter.

"Mr. Shonto," he grinned sheepishly, "I wonder if it would trouble you too entirely much, sir, if I was to ask you—well, naw, you wouldn't—excuse me, sir."

"Well, come on, boy," I said. "Don't lead me to the altar like that and then leave me standing there. Speak up, I ain't the Sheriff."

"Well, sir, I was just thinking if you would have the trust in me to turn my hands loose for just one good stretch. I'd give you my bounden word, sir."

"You would, eh?" I eyed him good. "All right, I'll just take your word, then. For one stretch."

I undid him—took off the cuffs—and he flexed his hands, worked his shoulder muscles and the like.

"Oh, my," he said, "that certainly is some grand, Mr. Shonto. Thank you ever so kindly, sir."

He put his hands up and took the stretch, long and luxurious. Then lowered his reach and put out his hands toward me, shy-smiling like I'd commuted his sentence, or something. Unthinking, I went to put the cuffs back on him and he struck at me so fast I didn't know what had happened until I'd landed on my back in the dirt, and he'd grabbed my gun off me whilst I was shaking my head to get the cobwebs out of it.

"Indian wrestling trick," he said. "Learnt it from the San Carlos tribe, over to Fort Apache. Sorry, Mr. Shonto, but I only give you my word for one stretch. Now, ain't that so?"

I made it back to my feet, still groggy.

"You seem to be doing the talking, boy," I replied. "Just keep going."

He smiled, bright-faced enough to shame the moon.

"Yes sir, thank you, sir. Just what I intend doing, soon as we can get back to the station stock corral and pick up my pony. And please move steady and nice, Mr. Shonto. You know how I feel my debt to you."

I had started to edge away from him, to get a set at jumping him. Now, I nodded and gave it up.

"Yes, it seems I do, boy," I said, feeling the crick in my back where he had thrown me. "You don't need to fear for me turning on you."

"I reckon that's so, sir," he grinned. "Let's go."

I got his pony out of the corral for him, him directing me from behind the hayshed corner, my own Colt covering me every step of the way. He swung up on the paint back of the shed, stuck my revolver in his belt, told me goodbye and God bless me till I could find more rewarding work.

"Hold on, boy," I said. "I don't believe I caught your name."

"Don't believe you did, either, Mr. Shonto. Didn't toss it."

"Would you mind, son? A man sort of likes to know who his friends are."

"You mean his enemies, don't you, Mr. Shonto?"

"You know what I mean, kid. I'm bound to come after you. I give my word in the Association's name that

I'd turn you over to Sheriff Gates in Tucson. I'll do it, too, boy. One way or the other."

He shook his head, the smile still 100 percent uncut good will.

"Some other summer, maybe; not this one, Mr. Shonto—" He started his pony away, then held him up. Obviously, another impulse of charity had seized him. He yielded to it with charming grace. "However, sir," he said, "in case you want to send me a picture postal of that Tucson Jail, just mail it to General Delivery, Arizona Territory, care of Tom Horn. So long, Mr. Shonto."

This time when he turned the paint and flashed his happy smile, he was gone. All I could do was stand there scratching my thick head and talking to myself in terms of tenderness never meant for mother's ears—his, or mine.

Tom Horn! one of the most fantastic badmen the Southwest ever spawned. He didn't look a day over eighteen years old and already had a reputation for cold nerve second to nobody's in the outlaw business. I had seen his smiling likeness on enough wanted-flyers to paper a six-room house; and I would rather have gone blindfold into a gopher hole after a rattlesnake than to take out, alone, after that boy. But I had told a deliberate lie to save his life, and I had used the name of the Arizona Cattlemen's Association into the bargain. The fact it was a poor bargain didn't change a thing. It was still up to nobody but Mrs. Shonto's simple-minded boy, Charlie, to make good on its stated terms.

I would have that kid back in Tucson for that Mescalero Land & Cattle Company rustling trial, if it was the last ride-down ever I set foot into stirrup for.

The country down below was desolate, brooding, empty; full only of the glare of desert sun and big silence—

Apache country. I was bellied down on a high rock scanning it through a pair of field glasses. My nerves were balled up like a clenched fist.

Tom Horn had headed straight into that stillness down there, figuring I wouldn't follow. Odds were, he could have won his bet. That was bad country any time, and especially bad just then.

Broken Mouth, called "*Boca Roto*" by the local Indians, and, by any name, the poorest friend the white man ever had in Arizona, was making a last move to keep *Apacheria* for the Apaches. He and his mixed band of New Mexico Mescaleros and local "Cherry Cows," Chiricahuas, had been on the raid since early spring. The old chief had served notice on the U.S. Army at Fort Yavapai that any soldier, *or* civilian, caught in his hunting preserve would be given the full welcome. In Apache talk that meant they would entertain a man all night, then—well, you could put it this way; that man's first sunrise with Broken Mouth and his red wolf pack, would be his last. Still, I had to face the fun.

Tom Horn was down there, somewhere. That left me no choice. In my business a man has got to be ready to live by his word, or die by it.

It was late that afternoon when I saw the old dreaded Apache sign; black smoke rolling upward from some burning settler's home or barn. The track line I'd been running on Tom Horn led toward the smoke, and I spurred over the near rise in the wagon road he'd been following, to see if I might be in time to help the poor devils. I wasn't. I no more than topped the rise, than I hauled old Shoofly in.

Coming toward me, up the far side of the rise, was an old farm wagon loaded down with cheap furniture, torn mattresses, chicken crates, all the pitiful remnants of an Indian burn-out, including two red-eyed little kids.

On the seat with the kids, was a dismounted cavalry trooper, doing the driving. Behind the wagon rode seven other troopers, and, in front of it, came their sergeant. When he saw me, the sergeant threw up his hand and called the halt, and I rode down for the talk.

"You're a little late, mister," he opened. "And so were we."

I nodded, tight-mouthed.

"I can see that. Apaches, eh?"

"Some folks call them that."

"Yeah, I know what you mean." I looked past the sergeant, to the two kids. "Poor little things. I reckon their folks were both—"

"Yeah," said the sergeant, "they were."

"Which Apaches?" I asked. "Do you know for sure?"

"Bronco Mescalero. Some Cherry Cows mixed in. Broken Mouth's bunch. You ever hear of him?"

"Somewhat."

"Well, then, you've heard enough to turn around and follow us back to the fort."

"That depends, sergeant. You haven't by any chance seen a tall, curly-headed boy riding a red sorrel paint, have you?"

"Might be we have. Why so?"

"He's a wanted man."

"You a bounty hunter?"

"Nope. Stock detective for the Cattlemen's Association."

"Oh? Well, yes, we seen your boy. Not thirty minutes down the road." He jerked his thumb over his shoulder, toward the smoke, and I turned my horse.

"Thanks, sergeant. Good luck to you."

"Yeah. Sorry I can't say the same to you."

A little puzzled, I held up. "How's that, sergeant?"

"Just that I hope you never catch the kid," he said.

"He's the one saved these two little ones, here. Rode into the Apache surround, head-on. Broke through it, got into the house, held them off till we hove in sight. Then he lit out like we'd caught him sucking eggs."

"That's like him," I nodded. "Which way did he take?"

"A way I'd advise you not to follow, mister detective; smack-dab in the tracks of them Apaches."

"It's a poor way," I agreed, "but I'm bound to go it."

He shook his head scowlingly, turned his horse to signal the forward-ho to his men.

"Oh, sergeant," I added. "You're a soldier. You ever took on an order you'd rather get horsewhipped than to go through with?"

"Sure. What you getting at?"

"I'm only doing a job of work. It don't pleasure me at times. You buy that?"

"Yeah, I reckon. I dunno. So long, detective." He started to signal his men again, then melted a little. "Happen you get back with your hair in one piece, detective," he grudged, "might be you could still use some help to hold it together. If so, remember Fort Yavapai lies yonder, six miles down the road. They won't chase you past the front gates—I don't think."

"Thanks for the kind thought, sergeant," I grinned. "It'll likely keep me awake all night."

"It better," he answered, with no grin, and yelled at his troopers to move it out. They went over the rise, none of them looking back, and I was left alone with that job which didn't always pleasure me. I clucked to old Shoofly and we got on with it.

Along about sundown, I got too close to Tom Horn. I jumped him out of a dry wash just shy of some badland hills. Neither of us wanted to shoot, and so it settled into a horse race.

It soon became apparent to Tom that I had the better horse. He had to do something to lose me, and he did. He led me square through the middle of the Apache camp, and left me there to do my own explaining. In a physical way, it was simple. He had spotted the camp from a high point, and I hadn't. He was able to dash his horse right over their supper fire, so sudden did he come on them, and to get on away into the thickening twilight before they realized they'd just missed a certain chance to grab themselves a white man. Thus aroused, they were ready for me, and didn't miss their second chance. Old Shoofly ran right into them, but those devils feared no horse and could handle any that was ever foaled, running full tilt or standing. They had him halter-hung and sat on his haunches, and me knocked off his back, in about fifteen seconds. I was lying on the ground alongside their scattered fire, while the beat of Tom Horn's horse's hoofs was still drumming away into the desert dusk. When my head quit swimming and I could sit up and take a look, I found the ugliest one Indian in southeast Arizona bending over me. We didn't need any introductions.

"White man know me," he mumbled through his disfigured lips. It was a statement, not a question, but I felt bound to answer it, no matter.

"Yes," I said, "I know you. You're Boca Roto, the Mescalero chief. The one that's declared war on all the whites."

"Yes," he grunted, acid-bitter. "Me Broken Mouth." He pointed to the terrible scars and purple burn welts that twisted his face. "You know how me get sick mouth? Yes, from white man." He sat down by me, while, behind us, the other Indians rebuilt the fire. His face, though hideously marked, was not a cruel face. Hard, yes. And bitter as bear gall about something. But not outright vicious and mean, as a man would have expected from his reputation. Now, while I listened, Broken Mouth told me his brief story. And the bitterness and the flint-steel look of him fell into place.

"White man own store, right here, Apache Wells," he began. He pointed to the remains of the old adobe ruin in which his band had camped. I looked around. There were the still-standing walls of two buildings, some nearly complete, some weathered down to three or four feet high. A few cottonwood trees grew near the hand-dug white man's well, which the nomad Apache kept cleaned out for their own use, and which gave the place its evil name. I shivered and nodded. He returned the nod, resumed his tale. "White man store owner he say me steal from store. Me say I no steal. No Apache steal anything from white man when he give word he no do it, I tell him. But he say me lie. He say he teach me no lie any more. His friends hold me by arms. He take branding iron for cow, and heat in stove. Then he burn my mouth like you see. He say, 'There, you no lie no more, you no steal.' But white man wrong. I come back, steal one more time."

He paused to point again. My eyes, following his direction, came to a halt on a weathered wooden headboard surrounded by sagging, sun-warped pickets, just beyond the store.

"I have *my* friends hold *him.* Take out tongue, far back in throat. Then me tell him, 'There, now we even. You no lie no more either.' Next day soldiers come down when see buzzards in sky. Find him dead, all blood run out his body. Soldier Chief he say, '*Dah-eh-sah,*' death to Broken Mouth. Broken Mouth answer, '*Zas-te!*' kill Soldier Chief. So long time war now. No peace for Apache people until last soldier gone."

With this pause, he pointed to me, tapping me on the chest.

"Last soldier no go, until last white man gone. So me

say *zas-te!* all white man, then we have peace again."

He sat silent after that, and finally I asked him the big one, using all the control I could.

"Does that mean you're going to kill me, chief?"

"No can help it," he shrugged. "Apache law. Me no hate you. You look like brave man. Words good, eye steady. But Mescalero law say you die."

"All right. When?"

"When sun come, first light of day in morning."

"How about meanwhile, chief?"

"No, you no worry about meanwhile. We no hurt you. We treat you good. Put you against wall when sun come up, just like soldier do Apache warrior. You die honorable. Quick. Many bullets through head and belly. All right?"

As he saw it, this was high courtesy. I answered to it the best way I knew how.

"Yes, certainly. Thank you, chief. I salute you."

I looked around again, stalling in desperation, hoping for some miracle to develop, trying, the while, to tough it out, to "talk light" of my coming execution.

"You got any particular wall in mind, chief?" I asked, backing it with what I supposed was a tip-off grin.

But the Apache sense of humor wasn't this well developed, it seemed. Broken Mouth took me literally. He also took his sweet Mescalero time in the process of so doing, examining the available selection without prejudice, and mighty carefully. Finally, he nodded through the darkness, now fully down, toward a piece of standing wall with a gaping doorway in it.

"We use that one," he said.

Unconsciously, my eyes hung on the spot, while his didn't. And a good thing, too. I only saw the face peering around the edge of that doorframe for a split-tail second. But the firelight bouncing past the Apaches squatting around broiling their supper meat had lit up the happy grin and quick bob of curly brown hair just long enough.

That was Tom Horn over back of that doorway wall.

It was an hour later, the moon not yet up but coming any minute. Broken Mouth and I sat along the wall where he was planning to have me shot, he on one side of the empty doorway, I on the other. I was trussed up like a Thanksgiving turkey, he was almost asleep under his black felt hat. On the ground in front of us, scattered in blanketed lumps on the bare dirt, slept the other Apaches. One of them sat hunched upright, dozing on guard at the fire. Of the Horn kid, there had been no further sign and, by now, I had given up hope of his making a play to break me free.

I had no sooner nodded to myself in mute agreement with this dismal opinion, however, when I saw a white hand slide out past the doorframe, curl itself in my direction and throw me a sassy finger wave, before pulling back out of sight.

I straightened up both myself and my opinion.

Tom Horn was one of the greatest Indian scouts who ever lived. The Apaches admitted it, as well as the whites. To begin with, he apparently had circled back and snuck in to enjoy himself watching me squirm. But he had stayed a little too long for his own peculiar set of morals. Tom was against capital punishment in any form. You might say he was professionally opposed to it. When he heard what he had led me into, that old Boca Roto was meaning to cut me down come daybreak, it just wasn't in his character to set by and wait for sunup; or moonrise, either, for that matter.

As I watched, the hand came out of the doorway again.

This time, it crept around Broken Mouth's side of the

frame. Gentle and deft as a cardsharp palming a space ace, it lifted the chief's hat off his head and laid it on the ground beside him. Then it disappeared to return with a chunk of adobe brick in it. It raised the brick up and brought it down on Boca Roto's skull. Then it put down the brick, picked up the hat, put it back on the chief's head. With the old devil unconscious, the rest of Tom Horn slid out that doorway and stood sizing up the other Apaches out by the fire. Looking over at me, he nodded and touched the brim of his hat, sober as a circuit judge. Next thing, he floated out through the ground-sleepers and came up behind the one at the fire. Easing out his revolver, he took hold both edges of the guard's hatbrim, jammed the hat clean down over his ears, caved in the back of it, nice and quiet, with his pistol barrel. *Then*, he grinned over at me, and had the gall to tap himself on the forehead with the tip of one forefinger to indicate the overall braininess of the total operation.

When he drifted back to begin slashing me loose, he frowned at the tightness of my bonds, speaking under his breath.

"This here sort of thing is bad for the circulation, Mr. Shonto. A man your age has got to be more careful how he gets tied up."

I handed him a walleyed look and a likewise whisper.

"I'll be a damned sight more careful who I save from the rope, hereafter, I'll promise you that, boy," I told him.

"Shucks, now, Mr. Shonto," he said reprovingly, "if you hadn't of saved me, who'd be untying you now?"

"Well, that's one way of looking at it," I answered, standing up and working my limbs to get the numbness out of them. "But let's don't quibble it. We can continue auguring your noble unselfishness closer to Fort Yavapai. You any objections to that course?"

He bowed, sweeping off his hat.

"*Despues de Usted, Patron*," he said in Spanish. "After you. Age before beauty."

"Thank you," I said, "for nothing."

The rest went pretty good. We got over to the Apache picket line without any fuss being put up by the ponies. We cut them loose and hazed them out into the night with wild yells and arm waves, then ran through the rocks to where Tom had our two saddled horses stashed and waiting. We went aboard them and got long gone from there, as the first angry yelps of the horse-chasing hostiles began to burn the night behind us.

It was the second morning, real early. Tom and I were laid up in some high rocks, looking over the back trail. We were feeling edgy. The kid shook his head.

"Damn," he said, "I wish we had them field glasses of yours, Mr. Shonto."

"I'd rather have your eyes, boy," I told him. "They saved us from getting jumped twice yesterday. How about this morning? You figure we've lost them for good? Maybe they've quit and went home. Who knows?"

"I do, Mr. Shonto," he said. "They never quit and they ain't got no homes. How far we from the fort, you figure?"

"Eight miles maybe. But I don't like the looks of that meadow just ahead. Too many rocks, and too big ones."

He nodded, agreeing.

"It's that way, or none, though. Either we go through that meadow, or ride half a day around it. And we ain't got a half day, Mr. Shonto. Look down yonder."

I looked. Far down, looking like sow-bug dots crawling the trail we had just come up, were a dozen Apache.

"You're right, boy," I said. "It's more like half an hour. Let's use it."

Twenty minutes later we were into the first of the meadow rocks. Another few pony steps and we stopped dead. Ahead of us on a ridge closing off the far side of the meadow sat another dozen Apache. We were bottled.

"If you will excuse me, Mr. Shonto," grinned Tom Horn, "I think I will be riding along."

"Just a minute, boy," I said. "You by any chance going on toward Fort Yavapai?"

"Well," he scratched his jaw, "hadn't thought of it, but now you mention it, why not?"

"Why not, indeed?" I gritted, and jumped my horse, with his, into a hammering gallop toward the Indians ahead. We got up pretty close to them and might have broken through, just on brass alone, when of a sudden I took one through the meat of my right leg and was knocked clean out of the saddle. Horn saw me go, and slid his horse to his hocks, turning him to come back for me. He made an Indian-style pick-up of me, and we got going again, double-mounted, just as the Apaches came over the ridge behind us, to join those we'd tried to butt through in front.

Now, I'd have thought the cork was in, tight. But not Tom Horn.

"Hang on, Mr. Shonto!" he yelled. "Here we go, double or nothing!"

He was grinning as usual, the threat of death by Apache rifle lead no more impressive to him than that by Mescalero Land & Cattle Company hemp rope. But his high-spirited shout was wasted. Five jumps and his horse took a smoothbore musket ball through the shoulders. He went down hard, us getting free of him on the fall, but forting up behind him the next minute, Tom putting a Colt bullet through his head to quiet his thrashing, while I looked to my hurt leg and our general position.

The leg wasn't bad, only bad enough so that I couldn't run on it. Our setup was not so lucky, but we did have some reasonably good rocks to back us. We also had another little chance. Old Shoofly was grazing off about fifty paces, with good rocks and brush cover between him and us. I pointed him out to Horn.

"I reckon I can put up enough smoke to hold them off long enough for you to get to him," I said. "Good luck, Tom." It was the first and last time I called him by name, and I saw him react to it. "Fort's not far. I can stick it here, till you get back. Now beat it, kid. One hero's enough in the family."

I'd thought he was going to refuse, but he only grinned.

"All right, Mr. Shonto. A boy's bound to respect the wishes of older folks. Hold the thought—I'll be right back!" Which he was. He didn't head for the fort, at all, but only spurred Shoofly right back to our rocks, slid off of him with his big grin, and announced, "Like I said, Mr. Shonto; double or nothing."

Well, after that I could believe anything, and very nearly had to. That crazy kid talked me into another run at those Indians, claiming if I could put him up alongside of one of them, he would guarantee to knock him off his mustang and we'd ride out in style, each with our own horse. He did it, too. And we managed to get a lead on them, I suppose by the out-and-out shock of us having the guts to try anything so empty-headed. It was only a few pony lengths to begin with, but Horn had picked a good scrub and we soon opened it up to where they quit forcing, and firing. Other than lobbing an occasional rifle shot to keep us honest, and loping along about a half mile back, they seemed to have lost real heart for closing in. Especially, after the kid got two of them, and me, one, in the early hard running. They made a second go at us when we rounded the last butte and saw Fort Yavapai a mile off across the juniper flats, but we lasted them out. I think that next to seeing Tom Horn's hand reach out that doorway and crown Broken

Mouth, the next best sight of my life was watching that army sergeant friend of mine yelling down off the catwalk for the gate detail to, "Swing 'em, you bastards—riders coming in!"

Inside, I couldn't get out of the saddle and had to be helped down. Horn was there to do it with the troopers siding him. They got me onto the ground just as the sergeant puffed up.

"I just remembered your invitation," I told him. "Sorry we're a little late."

"Better late than never, which you almost was," he answered. Then, frowning it, "I see you brought the kid back."

I looked at Horn, smiling a little wearylike.

"You got that wrong-side-to, Sergeant," I said. "The kid brought me back." Horn ducked his head at this, and put on that shy grin of his. I moved over to him and laid my arm on him for support. "I mean what I just said, boy," I told him. "You saved my life." I straightened a little and caught his eye. "But I mean what I said before, too. Nothing can change that. Soon as I'm fit to sit leather, you're going to Tucson. I give my word to put you in that jail, kid, and you're going to be put in it. You hear?"

He'd been looking a mite worried, but now brightened.

"Oh, that!" he said, relieved. "Shucks, now, Mr. Shonto, don't you fret none about that. I understand your situation, sir." Here, he reached a hand to my shoulder, sincere as a Methodist minister. "Moreover, Mr. Shonto, sir, I agree with it wholeheartedly."

"What's that, boy?" I said, surprised.

"A man's got to stand by his word, that's what, sir!"

I studied him a minute, barely able to suppress my astonishment at this about-face. But he didn't crack one inch.

"Well," I finally said, "if that's the case, you won't mind giving me your word that you won't try anything on the way back to Tucson. How about that, boy? You game?"

"As a goufy rooster," he swore at once. "You've got my word, Mr. Shonto, and this time I mean it. You can trust me all the way."

I looked at him good and hard, then nodded.

"All right, remember that, kid. I'll be depending on you." I turned to the troopers. "Come on, boys," I said. "You better get me inside. I'm a shade used up."

We rode up the center of Old Tucson, heading in at the hitch-rack in front of the mud-walled jail. We'd come the last five miles on Shoofly, Horn's Apache mustang having suddenly gone lame as a kicked dog. I'd thought maybe it was some trick of the kid's to get me in front of him, mounted double, but he hadn't said boo, and was still grinning and saying "yes, sir" to every word, when we got down. I threw the reins over the rail and we marched in, me still watching him sharp as a hawk.

Jim Gates got up from his desk when we came through the door. He knew me, of course, but I could see the kid was a stranger to him. He just had that kind of a sweet face. No matter how many times you saw it on a wanted flyer, you couldn't remember it for a bad one.

"Sheriff," I said, "this here is Tom Horn. I'm turning him in on a cow-stealing complaint by the Mescalero outfit. They'll be in to press charges, if they haven't already."

"They have, Charlie," he nodded, then sized up the kid. "Tom Horn, eh?" he said. "Son of a bitch, he sure don't look it, does he?"

"Oh, I ain't really, Sheriff," claimed Horn, with his head-ducking grin. "You see, acherally, I was took at an early age by the Pima Apache, and never heard of Tom Horn till this here Association man come along and—''

I put a hand to his arm, and cut him short.

''Save it for the jury, son,'' I advised him. ''The Sheriff's got a dozen pictures of you right in his top drawer.'' I turned to Gates. ''Jim,'' I said, ''no matter this kid has got a poor start, he deserves better. He saved my life at a time—two times—when he could have got clean away, by himself. But he stuck, and then gave his word to come in to Tucson and surrender peaceful, and he's done it. I'm asking you to remember all that when his trial comes up.''

Gates took hold of young Horn.

''All right, Charlie,'' he agreed. ''I'll see he gets a total fair trial.'' He started over to the cell block with the prisoner. At the door into the block the Sheriff held up to fuss picking the key out of his ring, and I called to Horn, ''So long, boy, and good luck to you.'' He just looked at me in an odd, sidelong sort of a way, shook his head slightly, and said not a word. ''What's the matter with you, kid?'' I asked. ''Don't you believe in saying goodbye?'' Then, he grinned, but still wagged his head in that funny way, and said, real soft.

''Not till it's time, Mr. Shonto. Not till it's time—'' Then, just as soft but to the Sheriff. ''Let's go, Mr. Gates, sir. I don't want to keep you from your work.''

Jim and me traded looks, then he took the kid on into the cell block and I said, ''See you down the road, Jim,'' and walked back out in the street to see about some breakfast and a hot-towel shave. The hash house was half a block down, so naturally I went to ride it. I took a minute, maybe two, to tighten Shoofly's cinch, check my bedroll and the like, just as a matter of habit. Then I took hold his reins to mount up. That's when the voice hit me from behind.

"Wait along a bit, Mr. Shonto," it said.

Well, I knew that voice by now, and I made my turn slow and careful. It was Tom Horn, of course, just standing and grinning in the jailhouse door and jangling the Sheriff's keyring in his left hand, while his right balanced the office sawed-off in my general direction. As I stayed quiet, eyeing the shotgun, he called back over his shoulder cheerful as a jaybird.

"Now don't you fret in there, Mr. Gates. You told me yourself that it was your best cell."

He moved out onto the boardwalk, scanning the empty street before tossing the keyring into the dirt under the hitch rail. Then he sauntered up to me, ducking his head.

"Sorry, Mr. Shonto, but I need *our* horse."

"Boy," I charged him reproachfully, "you give me your word." He nodded soberly, then lit up his 100-carat grin.

"I sure did, Mr. Shonto," he admitted, "but I didn't make no similar promises to that Sheriff, did I, now?"

He looked at me pure as a choirboy. I couldn't help myself. I'd been taken again, and I hoped I was man enough to appreciate it. I stepped away from old Shoofly.

"Boy," I said, "he's all yours."

He got on the horse, keeping the shotgun my way. I put a hand on his near thigh, easy and light.

"And, boy," I added, "there's something I said in yonder, which I'll repeat out here, scattergun or no scattergun. Good luck to you."

I was sober with it, and it got to him. He looked down an awkward minute, then, impulsive as usual, reached down his hand.

"Mr. Shonto, sir," he said, "if you don't mind—"

He wasn't grinning any more, and I took his hand. We exchanged a quick, hard grip. Then I stepped back away from Shoofly and Horn was back to his quirky grin just as fast as he'd turned serious the minute before.

"Well, here goes nothing," he said, with the final, sunbright smile. "*Hee-yahhh!*"

With the yell, he spurred the old horse away from the rail and off down the Tucson main stem on the cowboy run, fanning him with his hat on every jump. I stood and watched him go, following him down all the long gallop which took him out of Old Tucson and into his dark future in far-off Johnson County, Wyoming.

They can say what they want about Tom Horn, and it is true that he did wind up at the end of a rope. But that was twenty years later, and for my part I will always think of Tom Horn as a boy with a grin crackly enough to warm your hands by on a cold day—yes, and more pure nerve to go with it than a train robber with a toy pistol.

I don't know for sure to this day whether I did right or wrong to save Tom Horn's life that time down in Arizona Territory, but I will tell you one thing.

I got a pretty good idea.

A Mighty Big Bandit

It was a real nice day. Early fall, woodsmoke hazing the air, nippy in the shade, dozing-warm in the sun, quiet as cotton both in and outside town. For me, I wasn't fighting it. A man doesn't get many vacations in my line and I was making the most of this one. It was up in Minnesota, a fairly decent piece from the Chicago office, my idea being to get as far away from my work as possible for a Pinkerton. Trouble was, some friends of mine from Missouri had the same idea—with trimmings. They not only wanted to get as far from their work as possible, but as fast. When that rattle and slap of gunfire broke loose in town, it brought me bolt upright in the old fishing skiff that was drifting me down the little Cannon River, just outside Northfield.

I stand something like six-four with my boots off, which they were right then. Stretching, I could see over the road bridge, down toward the square. There was a shoot-out going at the First National Bank, and it looked to me as if the local folks had ambushed themselves a couple of tinhorn bank robbers. I have been more wrong, but precious seldom.

Bank robbers, yes. Tinhorns, not quite.

I thought I recognized the last man out of the bank, even from the distance. Big fellow, rough-cut, burly, yet graceful and quick as a buck deer. Time he and his pals had cleared the doors and were mounted up, two, three of them had been knocked clear out of them saddles and the remaining six of them, the big man riding last, were hitting it on the flat gallop for the Cannon Bridge.

It occurred to me, along about that time, that this was the same bridge I was drifting toward. Now I had no sure way of knowing who they were, even though the burly one looked familiar. But I did know one thing; since I was in the same business—on the other side—they might know me. It took me rather strongly that it would be a profitable idea if I rowed like crazy and skinned in under that bridge until they had pounded across it. Pinkerton or not, I was on vacation. What's more, my gun was in the spare room out at the farmhouse where I was staying, and furthermore my mother had raised a cautious son. Not bright maybe, but outstandingly careful. I went under that bridge like a water skater looking back over his shoulder at a walleye pike.

I will say that I have done very few smarter things in my time.

The five lead bandits hauled up at the bridge not ten counts after I disappeared under it. They sat there reining and holding down their lathered horses, waiting for the big man to come up. He didn't keep them long, and I had, sure as sin sells high, recognized him right. It wasn't anybody but Thomas Coleman Younger, and what he had to say to the little squint-eyed fellow leading the bunch would have frozen the ambition even of

Horatio Alger. Cole had a voice like a he-bear with a bad cold, anyway. I will tell you that it surely came through to me clear and meaningful that fall day in Northfield, Minnesota.

"Dingus," he said, "no posse in sight yet, what's your hurry? Now you want we should split up, or stick together?"

Names are certainly interesting. It all depends where you hear them. In some places, like the boys' privy back of the old schoolhouse, a dingus was one thing. Here, in Northfield, right atop a shoot-out bank robbery, it was another. Like, say, a pet nickname for Jesse Woodson James.

Yes sir, that was it. The James gang. And the better part of seven, eight hundred miles from Missouri. I will tell you, mister, I was sweating like a 2:01 trotter in the third heat.

"Split up," whined Jesse, in that reedy, wild voice of his, which all us Pinkertons had heard described a hundred times. "We'll meet, like planned, back at the slough. Six o'clock, sunset. Come on, let's ride!"

They put the spurs in deep, going over that board floor bridge to beat Pickett's last charge. When the dust died back, they were gone and I crawled out from under the bridge shaking fit to shed my teeth.

Well, sure enough, six professional friends from the Show Me state, and any one of them would have struck me dead quicker than a cottonmouth water moccasin. I had to get into town pretty fast, then. Positive identification of its members within five or ten minutes of the robbery, could put the James-Younger gang out of business before nightfall. I knew only Cole personally, but the others were familiar to me from wanted flyers. Far as I knew, I would be the only man in Minnesota who could say for certain who had busted the Northfield Bank. Vacation or not, I had to put what I knew on the wire, or start looking for other work. Being a detective for twenty years sort of warps a man's morals. He gets to thinking he's got to do right.

The telegraph office was next to the bank. A pretty good crowd was already jamming up in front of it by the time I puffed in from the river. I used a few elbows and squeezed in the door, which, being held shut from the inside by two shotgun guards, wasn't easy. The guards were surprised enough that they let me get up to the telegrapher, who jumped up and had at me as if I'd insulted his wife's cooking.

"Hold on there, buster!" he yelled. "Just who the hell you think you are?"

"Special Investigator, Pinkerton, Chicago Office," said I. "Got something important I'd like to put on that wire of yours."

"Not a chance, mister," he growled. "We're holding the key open. Just had a bank robbery here. Gang's headed south."

I gave him my bone-dry look.

"So I noticed," I said.

That sharpened him up. "You notice anything else, mister?" he asks, mighty suspicious. The two shotgun guards moved in on me, right then, too. So I gave them all an innocent nod and straight, sober look.

"Seems I did, now you mention it," I answered.

"Yeah? Like what maybe?"

"Like who robbed your bank maybe."

"All right, Mr. Smart-alec Special Investigator: like who maybe robbed our bank?"

"Oh, like Jim, Bob, and Cole Younger maybe. And Frank and Jesse James. Maybe."

He walled his eyes and got a little desperate, at that.

"Mister," he said, "if you're trying to be funny—"

I gave him a bobtailed nod.

"You put it on that wire," I told him, "and see how funny it sounds."

Having said which, I excused myself and started for the door. There I had to hold up and add a PS.

"And when you've put it there," I said, "sign it 'Yancey Nye.' "

That put up all of their eyebrows, and gave me the chance to shoot them a proper sneer of superiority. But you can't trust those Scandanavian hayseeds.

"Well, by damn!" said the telegrapher. "*The 'Yankee* Nye'?"

"Naw," I soured up quick, "you're thinking of Yankee *Bligh*. He's another fellow. Works down to Kentucky and that way. Always playing up to the boss and getting his name in the papers. I said 'Nye,' N-Y-E, Yancey Nye, you got it?"

"Sure," he said. "Hell, we thought you was somebody."

Well, that's the way it goes. I huffed on out of there and up to the livery barn, where I had my rented rig. It was not over fifteen minutes after I'd climbed out from under the Cannon River Bridge that I was ambling that old buggy horse back out to the Nils Swenlund farm, where I was boarding. Past getting a little nap before the evening fishing, I hadn't a plan in the world. There wasn't any Pinkerton accounts in the bank losses, and I was still on vacation. That's what I thought. But I hadn't consulted with my six outlaw friends from Missouri. Nor with one little seven-year-old Swede farm girl from Minnesota; a little girl who had more pure nerve than any outlaw or gunman I ever went up against in my whole life.

Jenni Swenlund was her name, cute as a blond mouse with her taffy braids and peasant jumper. Half an hour later I was standing with her in the barn lot saying goodbye to Nils and Mrs. Swenlund, who were setting out to be with a neighbor woman whose time it was that day. The good folks were some worried about me and the kid getting on by ourselves, so I was easing them off about it.

"Now you all run on," I smiled. "Take all the time you need with that new baby over yonder. Me and Jenni will make out just dandy. Likely, she can show me where that big lunker is hiding out down by the bridge."

Mrs. Swenlund was still fretted, but gave in some.

"Well, if you're sure now, Mr. Nye."

"Sure, I'm sure," I waved. "Now you all get a move on. That baby'll be old enough to vote before you get started."

That got a smile out of her, and away they went, them waving back and the little girl throwing them kisses and goodbyes until they were lost down the county road. With that, she turned to me, all business.

"Come on, Mr. Nye," she tells me. "Thank goodness they're gone. Now maybe we can get some work done around here."

"Work?" I dug in my heels. "Now, whoa up, there, Princess. I didn't contract to farm this forty."

"All right, you want me to show you where that old lunker is down by the bridge, or don't you?" she demanded.

"Why, sure," I stalled, "but—"

"No buts, Mr. Nye. You just come along and help me hay the mules and get in the afternoon eggs—or else."

I threw her a quick grin and a surrender wave. "Yes, ma'am!" I said. "Show me the way. I'd rather pitch hay to mules than kiss a pretty schoolteacher."

Well, we got into the barn and went to work, me haying the mules, Jenni shagging the old hens around and looking for floor eggs. Hearing an extra loud squawk from one of the barred rocks, I looked around and saw Jenni trying to get it down off a high roost.

"What's the matter, Jenni?" I grinned. "That old biddy giving you more argument than you come prepared to handle?"

She stopped reaching and fetched me a disgusted look.

"Not if I get my hands on her, she isn't!" she told me. "She's broody and doesn't belong in here." She made another dive for the bird, which flopped off the roost and out the nearby front window of the barn. Jenni made a last grab for her as she sailed out the opening. Then she stopped short, threw a scared glance out the window, and ducked back down below its frame. "Mr. Nye," she says, low-voiced, but calm as custard, "come here and look out yonder."

Well, I started over to her grinning half foolish and wondering what little-girl something had gotten her all stirred up about that old chicken.

"What'd she do?" I said, coming up to the window. "Lay an egg on the jump?"

I hadn't any more than gotten this empty-headed remark past my grown-up's grin, than I took my own glance out the window. I pulled back from it as though somebody had jabbed me in the eye with a hayfork. I grabbed Jenni and clamped a hand across her mouth and plastered her and myself back against the barn wall. Then I whipped a second look out the corner of that window just to make sure I'd seen what I'd seen.

I had.

It was Cole and Bob Younger and the sixth man of the gang, the only one I didn't know, riding their sweated horses up the Swenlund lane, slow and watchful yet desperate and strung-up as wounded game. I could see they must have seen the Swenlunds take off, and figured the place was deserted. Since they were watching the house mostly and not the barn, I was sure they hadn't seen Jenni and me. But there was doubt enough to wring me wet before they pulled their horses to a halt in the barn lot, midway of us and the house.

Bob was real bad hit. Cole and the other man were siding him, holding him on his horse. Cole, that great bear of a man with his gray eyes, curly brown hair, pleasant look and friendly way, was showing blood in half a dozen places, but still sitting straight and bossing the retreat. The other fellow, swarthy as a foreigner, with a heavy black beard and forehead no higher than a razorback hog's, didn't look to be hit any place. Cole was first to speak, his voice, even though he was hurt so serious, gentle and soft as ever.

"All right, boys, looks like them folks did come from this here farm. We'd best look around to make sure, though, that there ain't nobody else to home."

"Well, let's not be all day over it," snarled the unwounded man. "We got to meet Frank and Jesse and your brother Jim come sundown. You heard Jess."

Cole clutched Bob closer.

"Pitts," he said, "Frank and Jesse will wait. That's why I sent Jim with them; to see that they did."

Charlie Pitts! I ought to have recognized him. I'd seen that mean-animal face on a dozen wanted flyers. I was slipping. But Pitts wasn't. Again, he snarled at Cole.

"Your brother Jim! Bushway! He ain't going to hold Jess and Frank up none. He's bad hurt as Bob, here. Maybe worse." He paused, then added with a sneer. "By the way, how come you Youngers took most of the lead back yonder?"

Cole withered him with a hard stare, and a soft reply.

"Could be, Pitts," he said, "that we waited for it a mite longer than you other boys."

Pitts scowled back stupidly. He was a human brute,

not up to the outlaw class of the Jameses and the Youngers.

"Go on," ordered Cole. "Check the house. Find what you can of bandages and medicine for Bob. I'll hold here with him and the horses till you get back. Hop it."

Pitts slid off his mount and went cat-footing it up to the house. Jenni pushed my hand away from her face, giving me a big-eyed look that made me cold inside.

"What's the matter, Mr. Nye," she whispered. "Are they real bad men."

"They're not men, honey," I murmured. "They're animals, hunted animals. You understand?"

"Yes, but they're hurt, Mr. Nye. They need help." She shook her head. "Can't you see they're wounded, Mr. Nye?"

"Sure, enough, honey," I said, desperate to get it through to her what danger we were in, "that's right. They're wounded, and a wounded animal will kill you. Now don't you argue with your Uncle Yancey, Jenni. You just show me where that hayloft ladder is. I don't see it, and we're going to need it, powerful bad."

"But, why—" she began, femalewise.

I grabbed her hard and talked the same way.

"Now you look out that window again and you tell me what that man looks like that's coming from the house. You're only a little girl but I want you to look at that man real good. Careful now; don't let them see you."

She nodded and peeked out. I could see Pitts coming toward Cole and the horses, and I could see Jenni watching him. He was walking with his bent-kneed crouch and his silent snarl. He came up to his horse and pulled his Winchester from its scabbard, putting his revolver back in his belt.

"All right," said Cole, "now the barn. And hurry it; Bob's bleeding terrible."

Pitts growled like a feeding dog, wheeled and came toward the barn doors, not ten feet from where we crouched at the window. Here came a killer. Even a child knew it.

"Come on, Mr. Nye," whispered Jenni. "The loft ladder is yonder back of the feed room."

We scrambled up that ladder and lay down in the deep hay on the loft floor just in time. There was a two-inch crack in the loft floorboards, through which we could watch below, and my eyes were as big as Jenni Swenlund's, as we both did so.

"Don't even breathe loud," I told her. She bobbed her braids and gave me a pale-small grin and a pat on the hand. I never knew a kid like that, before or since. She had more sense and spirit than any grownup I ever worked with.

Down in the barn, now, it had got so quiet you could hear the manure flies buzzing around the mules. Of a sudden there was a crash of splintering wood and the doors, hasp and all, flew apart. Charlie Pitts, who had kicked them in, came stalking forward levering the Winchester. He looked behind the feed room and into the mule stalls, turned to the door and called to Cole.

"All clear, bring him in; nobody here, neither."

Cole came in carrying his young brother, Bob, in his arms like a child. Behind him, the trained Missouri thoroughbreds walked in quick and close as hunting hounds.

"Shut the doors," said Cole, "and give me them things you got from the house." He put Bob down in the clean straw of the stall beyond the mules—the one square under where Jenni Swenlund and I lay in the loft. "Easy, now," he said to Bob, "we're going to get you cleaned up, now. Lie quiet, boy, it may hurt some."

Bob, barely conscious, groaned his reply, and Cole went to work on him. Pitts, having seen to the horses, came and stood over them, breathing hard and nervous.

Up above, Jenni and I lay flat as two mice with the cat walking past. The stillness got so deep there was no chance even to whisper any more, and I had to pray the little girl would know to go on keeping stone-still. That she finally couldn't, was no fault of hers. A short straw got under her nose, and it was either move a hand to brush it away, or give a loud sneeze. She made the right choice but in shifting her arm to use the hand, her elbow brushed a little streamer of hay dust down through the crack in the floor. I grabbed her and rolled sideways, just as Charlie Pitts flashed his .44 Colt and drove three shots through the boards where we had been.

I looked at Jenni. She was all right, but had both hands over her mouth to hold in her fright. This was all to the good; now she *knew* that death was standing down there below. I gave her a squeeze, a nod, a pat and the best grin I could manage under the circumstances. She returned the nod, her eyes bigger than a brace of china-blue milk saucers.

"All right!" snarled Pitts, "whoever's up there, come on down. And come mighty careful."

I didn't know what to do but put finger to lips, warning Jenni to make no answer.

"You coming down," asked Pitts, "or am I coming up?"

For me to reply, and to start down that ladder, would draw me certain death. Somehow, Jenni sensed that. Before I could clap a hand over her mouth, she called down.

"Just a minute, mister, I'm coming—"

I had to let her go, then, but I did it knowing that Cole Younger would never let harm come to a little child. But Cole was still bent over Bob. The minute Jenni appeared at the head of the ladder, Pitts, the crazy man, fired blind, just at the movement of her bright little dress. By grace of God it was a clean miss, and the next instant Cole had leaped across Bob and hit Pitts so hard it drove him clean across the stall and over a tool bin, flat-sprawled.

"You feebleminded idjut," he roared, "it's only a little bitty girl!"

Pitts got up, wiping the blood from his mouth.

"She ain't too little to talk," he snapped.

As he said it, he raised up his revolver to fire again. Cole near broke his arm taking the gun away from him.

"You'd shoot a *kid?*" he said incredulously.

Pitts bared his teeth.

"I'd shoot my own kid, were it come down to him or me. We ain't leaving no witnesses behind, Younger. You know Jess's orders on that."

Cole turned him loose, called up to Jenni real soft.

"Come on down, honey. Be tolerable cautious, now. Them ladder rungs look looser'n a old horse's teeth."

Jenni smiled sort of palelike, and started backing down. Pitts moved in, took hold the ladder, gave it a vicious shake.

"Get a move on, you little brat!" he rasped.

Jenni gave a low cry, lost hold of the ladder, fell clear to its foot. Cole jumped Pitts like a mad grizzly. He very nearly mauled and beat him to death before he was stopped from it by Jenni asking him to please not hit the man any more, as he likely hadn't meant to hurt her!

Cole dropped Pitts and crouched over her. He dug out his bandanna awkward and fumbling.

"Here, honey," he said, "leave me wipe away them great big tears."

Noticing an old piece of shaving mirror nailed to the stall partition, he reached it down and held it up for Jenni to see her face.

"Lookit, there, at what them streaks of salt water are a'doing to your dimples!" he grinned.

She grinned back, but Cole lost his smile the next

minute. He was seeing something else in that mirror, and it was me peering over the edge of the loft above. I could see his face, too, the way the angle of the glass was, and our eyes met for one dead-still second. Then, Cole just shook his head and muttered soft as ever.

"My, my, the things a person does see when he ain't got his pistol cocked."

Pitts, limping over just then, scowled black and ugly.

"What'd you say?" he demanded.

"Nothing," answered Cole, "to you."

Pitts glared.

"Well, then, I'm a'saying something to you. Same as I said before. We ain't leaving this kid here."

Cole got up from Jenni's side, his gunhand shifting.

"You're dead right we ain't, Pitts. Not bad hurt the way she is. I'm staying with her."

Pitts shook his shaggy head, small eyes glittering.

"All right, you're welcome to stay, Younger. Stay and get strung up by your lonesome. Me, I'm making it on to Frank and Jess while there's yet time. Stand aside."

Now it was Cole's head that shook slowly.

"Not without Bob, you ain't going no place. He's fixed good enough to ride, now, and you're taking him along."

Here, Bob raised up in protest, but Cole put him down.

"Hesh up, Bob. You're going. I'll meet you all at the slough come sundown, like planned. The little girl's my affair, though. You ain't putting your neck in no rope for me, nor her."

Bob knew the lateness of the hour, both his and the gang's.

"All right, Cole," he said. "We'll wait for you."

"Yeah," sneered Pitts, "at least five minutes."

Cole put hand to gun butt, gray eyes nailing Pitts.

"Get Bob on that horse and get him out of here," he said.

Pitts, too, knew the time of day by now. He only nodded and helped Bob up on his mount. Bob swayed, then steadied. He said, "I'm all right, Cole," to his brother, and Cole said, "Move out, Bob, and God bless you." The two outlaws walked their horses to the lane, then put them on the lope and were gone down the county road in seconds. Cole, turning away from the barn doors, looked up and said quietly.

"All right, mister Pinkerton man, come on down and come friendly—"

When I had got down, he looked at the empty place my pistol ought to be.

"Why, Yance," he said, "I'm surprised at you. You don't hardly look decent without your working tools on."

I winced and grinned. "I'm supposed to be on vacation."

"Oh. Well, now, I'm a heap relieved, Yance. I thought maybe you had retired."

"Looks like I ought," I answered, pretty dismal. "You mind if I have a look at the little girl, Cole?" He nodded it was all right, but I held up a minute. "One thing," I said. "You recognized me in that mirror just now. How come you didn't let on to Pitts?" He shrugged, embarrassed.

"Aw, now, Yance, you know we was in the same Missouri outfit. I cain't turn on a fellow Confed'rate soldier."

"Cole," I said, "you're in the wrong business for a man with normal sentiments like that."

"Now, shecks, you know what I mean, Yance. Cold-blood murder like that damn Pitts was a'talking for that pore little thing yonder. Why that's downright sinful!"

"It sure is," I agreed. "Let's look to her before you bust out bawling. She's passed out cold."

"Sure, Yance, sure." He went with me, and we both got down beside Jenni Swenlund. I gritted my teeth when I saw the leg. Cole looked at me, frightened.

"It's broke compound," I said. "That means when the bone shoves out through the skin like this. Give me your bandanna."

He border-shifted his Colt to his left hand, dug out the bandanna, passed it to me.

"You going to put a twist on her, Yance?"

"Got to. She'll bleed out, if we don't. First we got to get that bone back in if we can. Lay hold her ankle. She may twitch pretty sharp."

As Cole put his big hands on the little leg, Jenni opened her eyes and looked up at him.

"He won't really hurt me, will he, mister?" she asked.

Cole glared at me. I thought he'd drill me then and there.

"She heard you!" he accused. Then he patted her braids careful as though they were glass. "Now, now, honey, he was only funning," he said. "Why, if he was really to hurt you, Uncle Cole would blow his head off." He glanced up at me, nodding softly. "Go ahead, Yance. And, remember; 'Uncle Cole' ain't funning!"

It was maybe an hour later. We had her on the bed in her folks' room up to the house. She was unconscious again and looking pale as a ghost. Cole was patting and stroking her hair, scared half-sick. He still had his cocked Colt in his off-hand, keeping it on me while he fretted over Jenni. I knew I had him where the hair was short, no matter.

"Well, Cole," I challenged, "what you going to do?"

He just groaned with his helplessness.

"Yance," he confessed, "I purely don't know."

"Well, you better do something, and pretty quick."

"You mean about her, don't you, Yance?"

"And *you*, Cole," I answered. "Can I see you outside?"

Cole Younger was not a brainy man, but a gentle-humored big bear, simple in both mind and imagination. Decisions were beyond him, but he understood warnings. He got up.

"Rest easy, now, honey," he told Jenni. "I got to be gone a bit, but I ain't leaving you. Don't have no fears."

Outside the door, I looked at him hard as bedrock.

"You notice that fresh bandage?" I said. "It's all blood again. Soaked knee to ankle in thirty minutes. She don't have a doctor, Cole, she's going to die."

He was in a place where his own life was on the line, too, yet he didn't take two breaths with his answer.

"Yance," he said, "happen I let you ride inter Millersburg and fetch back a doctor, will you guarantee you won't tell I'm out here?"

I had to tell him, no, and he agreed.

"I reckon not," he said sadly. "It wouldn't be no different nor lying, and I never knowed you to lie in your life."

"It's not your life we're talking about, Cole," I reminded him. "You better think of something fast."

He cringed as if I'd hit him with a whip. Turning, he went back in the room, staring around it in desperation. I watched him and, of a sudden, saw his face light up when he spied an open wardrobe full of Mrs. Swenlund's things.

"Yance," he said, whirling on me, "you ever get married up? I disremember."

"Nope," I said warily, wondering what was in his slow mind. "Why you ask?"

He beamed happy as though he had proper sense.

"Well, then, your wife won't mind seeing you in the company of a strange woman, will she?" He jabbed the Colt toward the wardrobe closet. "Start handing me out them female unmentionables!"

I looked at him, then at the farmwife's clothes.

"My God," I said, "you really mean a *strange* woman, don't you?"

"Heavens to mercy, no!" he vowed, widening his catfish grin. "We'll make a mighty handsome couple, you'll see." He flicked his glance to the bed and saw that little Jenni had come awake. Swinging his herd bull's bulk between me and the girl, he growled with deadly coyness. "*Won't we*, Yancey dear?"

Since he had shoved the Colt three inches deep in my belly with the question, all I could do was grunt and give in. "Whatever you say, *dear*," I agreed, and started handing him the unmentionables.

Now it was the main stem, Millersburg, Minnesota; a typical dirt-street hick town. Up the center of the road, creaking in from the farm country, came the narrow, high-side corn wagon, canvas cover laced over its bed. I was driving. On the seat with me was Cole Younger, dressed in Mrs. Nils Swenlund's Sunday best. The outfit was complete with starched petticoats, overshawl, flowered print dress, poke sunbonnet. Yet despite the heat of the day, Cole had a buggy blanket over his knees and was snuggled up to me like young love with the lights turned off. Also snuggled up to me, under the blanket, was the snout of his Navy Colt. The two old mules plodded steadily. Ahead, the shingle we were looking for loomed up: I.V. BERQUIST, M.D. Cole gave me a delicate nudge with the Colt.

"Turn in," he cooed.

"Yes, ma'am," I said, and gee-ed the mules down the right-hand alley, to the doctor's rear yard. There was a backdoor to the office, and Cole slid down off the seat and knocked on the panels. Dr. Berquist opened the door a moment later and Cole put the long Colt barrel under his nose and asked,

"Can you sew up a thirty-six caliber hole through a man's head, Doc?"

That thick, hairy arm coming out of that print dress was more than Dr. Berquist had been ready to write a prescription for. "Why, no!" he gasped. "Of course not!"

Cole tapped him on the shoulder with the Colt barrel. "Then don't make a sound," he said, "and you won't have to try." He shoved him back into his office, following him in. In a moment he was back. "All clear, Yance; bring the little tyke in," he told me. I lifted Jenni out of the straw-filled wagon bed and carried her in. Inside, the doctor ordered me to put her on the table. I did and Cole and me bent over, with him, watching like hawks to see what news showed in his face. Right away we could tell it was bad. But still he didn't say anything.

Cole shot a nervous look at the clock on the wall. It was five P.M. He put his huge hand on the doctor's arm.

"We're short on time, Doc. How long will it take?"

Berquist shook his hand off, scowling.

"It can't be hurried. Not with a fracture like this."

Cole brought the Colt above the tabletop.

"How long, Doc?" he repeated softly.

Berquist stared at him defiantly.

"A half hour at least. Perhaps longer."

"Damn!" said Cole, still soft. "That's dismal!" Yet he never hesitated. Going to the front door he turned the "Doctor-Is-Out" sign to the street, pulled down the shade, came back to the table, looked again at the clock on the wall, said quiet as spider silk, "Go ahead, Doc; and don't make no mistakes."

When Berquist finally put down his instruments and

tied off the last bandage, it was five minutes till six P.M. Cole, long out of his woman's clothes, grabbed him and spun him around rough and hard. "She all right?" he growled.

"For now, yes," answered the doctor.

"What you mean, for *now?*"

"Precisely what I said. She will be all right if kept perfectly quiet. If she is moved suddenly, or handled in any way roughly—"

Cole shoved him aside.

"That's enough, Doc. Nobody's going to be rough with her. Thanks for your help. You'll get your reward in heaven, unless you want it sooner. One peep out of you that we've been here and—"

Berquist interrupted him, showing no fear at all.

"I doubt you need worry about me following you, Mr. Younger," he said. "Descriptions are out on all of you, and others will recognize you as easily as I. Further, every law officer and local posse in southern Minnesota is already in the field looking for you and the others. You will never get out of this state alive."

Cole scowled, tapped him with the Colt again.

"Just remember that if I don't, Doc, neither does the little girl. You savvy them sentiments?"

This Berquist had a heavy skull, like all those Scowegians. He wasn't going to buckle one inch to Cole, and I moved in quick.

"He means it, Doctor," I told him. "Don't give any alarm before we're well away. These Missourians are killers." I gave Cole a special look. "*All* of them," I added.

Cole admitted the compliment courteously.

"Regretful, sir," he said to the doctor, "but true." Then, to me. "Move, Yance. No more palaver."

I picked up Jenni Swenlund and went out the back door. Cole followed. He never looked back at Dr. I. V.

Berquist. Outside, Jenni safely stowed in the bed under the tarp, him and me back up on the seat, he poked me with the Colt.

"Mind what I told the Doc, Yance. Remember I'll be back here under the tarp with the little tyke." Saying which, he slid off the seat and beneath the canvas cover behind me. All I could see of him was the Colt's nose. "All right," he concluded, "let's go. You drive one mile south on the Madelia Road. Turn left at the Hanska Slough signpost. You got that straight?"

I took a look back at the doctor's office. I thought I saw the rear shade stir a bit. Taking the hairiest chance of my life, I repeated his directions in a too-loud voice.

"Yes sir! One mile south on the Madelia Road. Turn left at Hanska Slough sign!"

He very nearly put that Colt through my kidneys.

"Keep your big mouth shut, Yance," he rumbled, "and dig!"

"What's the great rush, Cole?" I said, mad at being poked so hard and knowing, anyway, he wouldn't dast shoot me just now. "Jesse said six o'clock. That still gives you five minutes."

"Which is four more than *you* got, Yance," he promised, "happen you don't light out, right quick."

I nodded meek enough, and whipped up the team.

So it was we set out from Madelia, my only hope the slim one that Dr. Berquist had heard those loud-repeated Hanska Slough directions and would figure out what they meant. It wasn't much of a hand to back against the likes of Cole Younger. Not to mention the James boys. I've bluffed bigger pots with a busted flush going into four aces. But my real bet was still on Cole, and on what he would do about that little girl under the wagon-tarp with him, when the chips were down. One thing sure. I was going to find out.

* * *

The country was desolate, heavily wooded. The slough was brackish, lonesome-looking. Through the ground brush I could see the crude wickiup the outlaws had made. I got only the one glimpse of it. I made out two wounded, much-bandaged men lying inside. Crouched over the fire outside was Charlie Pitts. In the brief look, I saw no sign of the others. If Frank and Jesse were there, they were out in the brush somewhere. As soon as Pitts heard the crunch of our wagon wheels on the slough road, he jumped for his rifle and dove out of sight.

At that time we were maybe a scant furlong from the camp. Coming to the wickiup moments later, we had to pass under a big, low-limbed hardwood. I never thought to look up. The next thing I knew, that crazy Pitts had jumped down off the overhang and hit me with his boots between the shoulder blades, sprawling me clean off the seat and onto the ground. He lit the seat and braced himself to finish me off with his rifle. He didn't get a fine sight drawn. From under the wagon tarp behind him, up reared Cole and laid his pistol barrel across the back of Pitts's hat. Pitts, he just caved in and slid off the seat. Cole slid onto the driver's box, picked up his rifle, stepped to the ground, covering both of us.

"All right, Yance," he said, "get up real careful. Pitts—throw a rope on him."

As the latter growled and went about tying my hands, Cole noticed the two men in the wickiup to be his brothers Jim and Bob, and that there was but three horses on the picket.

"Three horses!" he barked at Pitts. "Where's Frank and Jesse?"

"They've cut out on their own," mumbled the hang-dog Pitts. "Said to tell you they wasn't needing no more wounded Youngers to hold them back."

Cole nodded, as though to expect no more from his

famous friends. "How come you didn't turn tail with them?" he asked.

"Fat chance! They was gone when I got here. Left the message with your brothers. Real question is, what're *we* gonna do?"

"Light out after them, I reckon. Saving for one thing; I got the little girl in the wagon yonder."

"You ain't!" Pitts was absolutely bashed in by it. I took a hunch it was time for me to horn in, but Pitts recovered and reached for his belt gun before I could make up my opening speech. "Well," he said, "we're getting out of here right now and the kid ain't going with us. I'll see to that, and if you try to stop me I'll cut you in two."

He had the drop on Cole. Moreover, Cole was trapped another way. His own life was at stake and he knew Charlie Pitts was right. To fool around a minute longer with mother-henning Jenni Swenlund was to put them all, including his two wounded brothers, Bob and Jim, in the shadow of the noose. He watched Pitts head for the back of the wagon, that same dumb, desperate look on his face I had seen in the Swenlund bedroom. And in the same way as then, he got a happy light in his eyes at the last second.

"Hold it, Charlie!" he yelled. "We *got* to take her with us. She's our hostess!"

Pitts whirled around. "Our what?" he said, surprised, and giving me my chance to buy into the game.

"Your hostage," I translated for him. "You know, that's somebody you hold a gun on, so's the other side don't dast shoot. You remember, like in the war."

"Yeah, Charlie," Cole pushed it, "sort of like a pass through the enemy lines. Get the idea?"

Pitts grinned. "Sure," he said, "you bet I do." He shifted his Colt to cover Cole again. "And I'll be the one using that pass. Fetch her out'n the wagon."

With no choice, Cole did it. Meanwhile, I got the three horses off the picket, also given the same option. Pitts turned the third horse loose, hitting him viciously across the haunch with the revolved barrel. He galloped off into the timber. Pitts now mounted one of the remaining two.

"All right!" he snapped. "Tie the kid on this other horse, hard and fast."

"You wouldn't do that!" gasped Cole. "Not even you, Pitts!"

"Put her on that horse," said Pitts, "or I'll blow her brains all over your vest."

Cole and I looked at each other and knew we had to do it. We laced her on real careful, the splinted little leg sticking out straight. She was brave as ever, and smiled and told us not to be afraid, that Pitts wouldn't hurt her. Cole couldn't take that. He moved in close to Pitts's stirrup, starting to plead with him. Pitts lashed out with his spurred boot, catching Cole, full-face, and ripping him like a saber blade. But the act took his gun off me, and I went up onto the wagon seat and jumped from it, at him. He got the Colt on me in mid-air. The big .44 bullet took me across the meat of my shooting arm, turned me half around, slammed me into his horse's ribs and down onto the ground. He never looked down at me but only yelled, "*Hee-yahh!*" at his horse, and took off leading poor little Jenni's mount behind him on the flat gallop.

They didn't get five jumps on the way to the woods.

Out of that heavy cover came a blasting of posse gunfire that drove Pitts out of his saddle and cut his horse down like it was both done with a mowing scythe. Cole, quick as a cat, ran out and grabbed Jenni off her loose horse and got her back to the wagon and wickiup, the posse not daring to fire, of course. But while he was doing it, I thought I saw a chance, and reached for Pitts's rifle lying on the ground. Out of the brush beside me came a spurred boot I recognized, kicking the gun away. The boot was followed by what was still in it, and its mate; Pitts was again on his feet, only lightly wounded, and having got back to the wagon while the posse was watching Cole and Jenni.

Now there was double hell to pay.

With Jenni put in the wickiup and me ordered in there to look to her, Cole and Pitts overturned the Swenlund wagon and, with the wounded Bob and Jim Younger crawling out to fort up back of it with them, put up a hard return fire, pinning the posse down just about as tight as the posse had them pinned down. Pretty quick a white handkerchief waved from a shotgun barrel across the way. Cole rasped, ''*slack off!*'' to his comrades, and a silence thicker than swamp fog settled in.

''Mr. Nye,'' called a voice, ''are you and Jenni Swenlund all right? This is Sheriff Glispin of Madelia.''

''We're all right, Sheriff,'' I answered. ''How many men you got?''

''Fifteen. Plus Dr. Berquist from Millersburg. Who are the men with you, other than Younger?''

''His two brothers, Bob and Jim, and Charlie Pitts.''

''Will they surrender?''

I looked out at Cole, under the wagon. He shook his head.

''They say not,'' I replied.

''Well, will they permit you to bring out the Swenlund girl under a flag of truce?''

Again Cole shook his head, again I answered in negative.

''Do they mean to use the little girl as a hostage, then?''

''Yes, Sheriff, that's it I'm afraid.''

There was a long, ominous pause then before Glispin

spoke again. And when he did, the pause only got more ominous.

"All right, Mr. Nye," he said. "Do your best."

The last daylight was going. No sound came from the silent woods. Behind the overturned wagon, Bob and Jim Younger lay with their terrible wounds, but with rifles waiting for the posse to move. Out beyond the wagon a stride, Charlie Pitts lay up back of the dead horse. In the entrance of the wickiup, where he could watch everything, crouched Cole Younger. Darkness would be down in minutes. With it, they had a hairline chance to slip away. But Charlie Pitts, crazed and brutal as ever, could not wait. Leaving his dead horse, he got behind the wickiup without Cole seeing him. Next moment he had broken through its thin backwall of brush and had his Winchester aimed between Cole's shoulder blades.

"You move," he said to the big Missourian, "I'll drill your backbone. You!" he snapped at me, "get that kid up and bring her over to me." I did it, as I had to. Pitts got a brawny arm around her little waist, lifted her off the ground, back to him, as a shield. Backing out of the wickiup, he stepped clear of it and the wagon. "Sheriff!" he yelled across at the posse, "I'm coming through. Get me a good horse ready. One funny move and the kid dies. You got ten seconds."

As he held up, waiting for Glispin's reply, Cole looked at me, nodded quickly, drew and handed me his revolver.

"All right, Yance," he said. "I'll take his attention; you try to come at him from behind. Good luck, old soldier."

"Cole," I answered, dead straight, "the same to you."

We went out, then, me through the back wall, him by

the front opening. Pitts was through waiting for the Sheriff. He threw down his rifle, pulled his belt gun, put it to Jenni's head.

"All right, Sheriff!" he shouted, "I warned you!"

His yell was still echoing when Cole moved in on his left flank, stabbing just one word at him.

"Pitts!"

Charlie whirled to face him. Cole began walking slow toward him. Pitts fired into his big body, one, two, three shots, all plain hits. Cole kept coming. Pitts broke. He dropped Jenni and began to run blind. He picked the wrong way to go—straight into me. I came up from behind my bush and put five of the six slugs in Cole's gun into his belly. The jolt took him like sledge blows, driving him by steps clean back to the wagon, where he finally fell. It wasn't a shoot-out, it was an execution. When it was over, I walked up to where Cole was hunched down on the ground, cradling little Jenni in his arms. I stood there looking down at them.

After a minute, Cole glanced up and smiled tiredlike. His own wounds, later found to be eleven bullets lodged in that bear's body of his, finally had him anchored. He could not get up, and had to hand Jenni up to me. I took her from him and said quietly, "So long, Cole."

He made a funny awkward little wave in reply. When he did, Jenni smiled and called back to him.

"Goodbye 'Uncle Cole.' "

He winced like he'd been knifed. Then looked guilty to right and left, as though to make certain nobody had heard the kid, or was listening to him, or watching. Then he blew her a kiss with his huge paw and muttered roughly.

"Goodbye, little honey, goodbye."

He pulled out his old calico bandanna, the one he'd used to wipe the tears off Jenni's face in the Swenlund barn, and took a swipe at his powder-grimed eyes. He didn't even seem to realize he did it, but sat there staring off after us as we went toward the posse's line, as though he was seeing into another world, and a better one. Maybe he was, I never found out. When Jenni and me passed through the posse line, the firing began again, and I didn't wait to see the end of it.

Later, of course, my line of work being what it was, I did hear about it. It wasn't a good thing, any way you want to look at it, but I wonder just how bad it was, too.

Under Minnesota law of the day there couldn't be any death penalty. After weeks of suffering from their wounds, Jim, Bob and Cole were given life sentences in the state penitentiary at Stillwater. History will say they were outlaws, thieves and murderers. Well, maybe they were. It wasn't my job to say. But I know one little farm girl up near Millersburg who will give you a mighty big argument about one of those three condemned bandits. But, then, why not? He was a mighty big bandit. Thomas Coleman Younger. In my book, as in that little farm girl's, they don't come any bigger.

Isley's Stranger

He rode a mule. He was middling tall, middling spare, middling young. He wore a soft dark curly beard. His bedroll was one thready army blanket wound round a coffee can, tin cup, plate, razor, camp ax, Bible, copy of the *Rubáiyát*, a mouth harp, some other few treasures of like necessity in the wilderness.

Of course, Isley didn't see all those things when the drifter rode up to his fire that night on Wolf Mountain flats. They came out later, after Isley had asked him to light down and dig in, the same as any decent man would do with a stranger riding up on him out of the dark and thirty miles from the next shelter. Isley always denied that he was smote with Christian charity, sweet reason or unbounding brother love in issuing the invite. It was simply that nobody turns anybody away out on the Wyoming range in late fall. Not with a norther building over Tongue River at twilight and the wind beginning to snap like a trapped weasel come full dark. No, sir. Not, especially, when that somebody looks at you with eyes that would make a kicked hound seem happy, and asks only to warm his hands and hear a friendly voice before riding on.

Well, Isley had a snug place. Anyway, it was for a line rider working alone in that big country. Isley could tell you that holes were hard to find out there in the wide open. And this one he had was ample big for two, or so he figured.

It was a sort of outcrop of the base rock, making a three-sided room at the top of a long, rolling swell of ground about midway of the twenty-mile flats. It had been poled and sodded over by some riders before Isley, and was not the poorest place in that country to bed down by several. Oh, what the heck, it wasn't the Brown Hotel in Denver, nor even the Drover's in Cheyenne. Sure, the years had washed the roof sods. And, sure, in a hard rain you had to wear your hat tipped back to keep the drip from spiking you down the nape of your shirt collar. But the three rock sides were airtight and the open side was south-facing. Likewise, the old grass roof, seepy or not, still cut out ninety-and-nine percent of the wind. Besides, it wasn't raining that night, nor about to. Moreover, Isley was a man who would see the sun with his head in a charcoal sack during an eclipse. It wasn't any effort, then, for him to ease up off his hunkers, step around the fire, bat the smoke out of his eyes, grin shy and say:

"Warm your hands, hell, stranger; unrope your bedroll and move in!"

They hit it off from scratch.

While the wanderer ate the grub Isley insisted on fixing for him—eating wasn't exactly what he did with it, it was more like inhaling—the little K-Bar hand had a chance to study his company. Usually, Isley was pretty fair at sizing a man, but this one had him winging. Was he tall? No, he wasn't tall. Was he short, then? No, you wouldn't say he was exactly short either. Middling, that's what he was. What kind of a face, then? Long? Thin? Square? Horsey? Fine? Handsome? Ugly? No, none of these things, and all of them too. He just had a face. It was like his build, just middling. So it went; the longer Isley looked at him, the less he saw that he could hang a guess on. With one flicker of the fire he looked sissy as skim milk. Then, with the next, he looked gritty as fish eggs rolled in sand. Cock your head one way and the fellow seemed so helpless he couldn't drive nails in a snowbank. Cock it the other and he appeared like he might haul hell out of its shuck. Isley decided he wouldn't bet either way on him in a tight election. One thing was certain, though. And that thing Isley would take bets on all winter. This curly-bearded boy hadn't been raised on the short grass. He wouldn't know a whiffletree from a wagon tongue, or a whey-belly bull from a bred heifer. He was as out of place in Wyoming as a cow on a front porch.

Isley was somewhat startled, then, when his guest got down the final mouthful of beans, reached for a refill from the coffeepot and said quietly.

"There's bad trouble hereabouts, is there not, friend?"

Well, there was for a fact, but Isley couldn't see how this fellow, who looked like an out-of-work school-teacher riding a long ways between jobs, could know anything about *that* kind of trouble.

"How come you to know that?" he asked. "It sure don't look to me like trouble would be in your line. No offense, mind you, mister. But around here—well, put it this way—there ain't nobody looking up the trouble we got. Most of us does our best to peer over it, or around it. What's your stake in the Wolf Mountain War, pardner?''

''Is that what it's called'' the other said softly. Then, with that sweet-sad smile that lighted up his pale face like candle shine, ''Isn't it wonderful what pretty names men can think up for such ugly things? '*The Wolf Mountain War*.' It has alliteration, poetry, intrigue, beauty—''

Isley began to get a little edgy. This bearded one he had invited in out of the wind was not quite all he ought to be, he decided. He had best move careful. Sometimes these nutty ones were harmless, other times they would kill you quicker than anthrax juice.

He tried sending a return smile with his reply.

''Well, yes, whatever you say, friend. It's just another fight over grass and water, whatever you want to call it for a name. There's them as has the range, and them as wants the range. It don't change none.''

''Which side are you on, Isley?''

''Well, now, you might say that—'' Isley broke off to stare at him. ''*Isley?*'' he said. ''How'd you know my name?''

The stranger looked uncomfortable, just for a moment. He appeared to glance around as though stalling for a good answer. Then, he nodded and pointed to Isley's saddle propped against the rear wall.

''I read it on your stirrup fender, just now.''

Isley frowned. He looked over at the saddle. Even knowing where he had worked in that *T-o-m I-s-l-e-y* with copperhead rivets and a starnose punch, he couldn't see it. It lay up under the fender on the saddle skirt about an inch or so, purposely put there so he could reveal it to prove ownership in case somebody borrowed it without asking.

''Pretty good eyes,'' he said to the stranger. ''That's

mighty small print considering its got to be read through a quarter inch of skirting leather."

The stranger only smiled.

"The skirt is curled a little, Isley, and the rivets catch the firelight. Call it that, plus a blind-luck guess."

The small puncher was not to be put off.

"Well," he said, "if you're such a powerful good blind-luck guesser, answer me this: how'd you know to call me Isley, instead of Tom?"

"Does it matter? Would you prefer Tom?"

"No hell no, that ain't what I mean. Everybody calls me Isley. I ain't been called Tom in twenty years." His querulously knit brows drew in closer yet. "And by the way," he added, "while it ain't custom to ask handles in these parts, I never did cotton to being put to the social disadvantage. Makes a man feel he ain't been give his full and equal American rights. I mean, where the other feller knows who you are, but you ain't any idee who he might be. You foller me, friend?"

"You wish me to give you a name. Something you can call me. Something more tangible than friend."

"No, it don't have to be nothing more tangle-able than friend. Friend will do fine. I ain't trying to trap you."

"I know you aren't, Isley. I will tell you what. You call me Eben."

"Eben? That's an off-trail name. I never heard of it."

"It's an old Hebrew name, Isley."

"Oh? I ain't heard of them neither. Sounds like a southern tribe. Maybe Kioway or Comanche strain. Up here we got mostly Sioux and Cheyenne."

"The Hebrews weren't Indians exactly, though they were nomadic and fierce fighters. We call them Jews today."

"Oh, sure. Now, I knowed that."

"Of course you did."

They sat silent a spell, then Isley nodded.

"Well, Eben she is. Eben, what?"

"Just Eben."

"You mean like I'm just Isley?"

"Why not?"

"No good reason." Isley shrugged it off, while still bothered by it. "Well," he said, "that brings us back to where we started. How come you knowed about our trouble up here? And how come you got so far into the country without crossing trails with one side or the other? I would say this would be about the onhealthiest climate for strangers since the Grahams and Tewksburys had at it down in Arizony Territory. I don't see how you got ten miles past Casper, let alone clear up here into the Big Horn Country."

Eben laughed. It was a quiet laugh, soft and friendly.

"You've provided material to keep us up all night," he said. "Let's us just say that I go where trouble is, and that I know how to find my way to it."

Isley squinted at him, his own voice soft with seriousness.

"You're right; we'd best turn in. As for you and finding trouble, I got just this one say to say: I hope you're as good at sloping away from it as you are at stumbling onto it."

The other nodded thoughtfully, face sad again.

"Then, this Wolf Mountain War is as bad as I believed," he said.

"Mister," replied Isley, "when you have put your foot into this mess, you have not just stepped into *anybody's* cow chip; you have lit with both brogans square in the middle of the grand-daddy pasture flapjack of them all."

"Colorful," smiled Eben wryly, "but entirely accurate I fear. I hope I'm not too late."

"For what?" asked Isley. "It can't be stopped, for it's already started."

"I didn't mean too late to stop it, I meant too late to see justice done. That's the way I was in Pleasant Valley; too late, too late—"

He let it trail off, as Isley's eyes first widened, then narrowed, with suspicion.

"You was *there?*" he said, "in that Graham-Tewksbury feud?"

"I was there; I was not in the feud."

"Say!" said Isley enthusiastically, curiosity overcoming doubt, "who the hell won that thing, anyways; the sheepmen or the cattlemen? Naturally, we're some interested, seeing how we got the same breed of cat to skin up here."

"Neither side won," said Eben. "Neither side ever wins a war. The best that can be done is that some good comes out of the bad; that, in some small way, the rights of the innocent survive."

Isley, like most simple men of his time, had had the Bible read to him in his youth. Now he nodded again.

"You mean 'the meek shall inherit the earth'?" he asked.

"That's close," admitted his companion. "But they never inherit anything but the sins of the strong, unless they have help in time. That's what worries me. There's always so much trouble and so little time."

"That all you do, mister? Go around looking for trouble to mix into?"

"It's enough, Isley," smiled the other sadly. "Believe me it is enough."

The little cowboy shook his head.

"You know something, Eben," he said honestly. "I think you're a mite touched."

The pale youth sighed, his soft curls moving in assent.

"Do you know something, Isley?" he answered. "I

have never been to any place where the men did not say the same thing. . . ."

Next morning the early snow clouds were still lying heavy to the north, but the wind had quieted. Breakfast was a lot cheerier than last night's supper, and it turned out the newcomer wasn't such a nut as Isley had figured. He wasn't looking for trouble, at all, but for a job the same as everybody else. What he really wanted was some place to hole in for the winter. He asked Isley about employment prospects at the K-Bar, and was informed they were somewhat scanter than bee tracks in a blizzard. Especially, said Isley, for a boy who looked as though he had never been caught on the blister end of a shovel.

Eben assured the little rider that he could work and Isley, more to show him to the other hands than thinking Old Man Reston would put him on, agreed to let him ride along in with him to the homeplace. Once there, though, things took an odd turn and Isley was right back to being confused about his discovery.

As far as the other hands went, they didn't make much of the stranger. They thought he looked as though he had wintered pretty hard last year, hadn't come on with the spring grass. Most figured he wouldn't make it through another cold snap. To the man, they allowed that the Old Man would eat him alive. That is, providing he showed the gall to go on up to the big house and insult the old devil's intelligence by telling him to his bare face that he aimed to hit him for work. A cow ranch in October is no place to be looking for gainful employment. The fact this daunsy stray didn't know that, stamped him a real rare tinhorn. Naturally, the whole bunch traipsed up to the house and spied through the front room window to see the murder committed. Isley got so choused up over the roostering the boys were giving his protégé that, in a moment of sheer inspiration, he offered to cover all Reston money in the crowd. He was just talking, but his pals decided to charge him for the privilege. By the time he had taken the last bet, he was in hock for his wages up to the spring roundup. And, by the time he had gotten up to the house door with Eben in tow, he would have gladly given twice over that amount to be back out on the Wolf Mountain flats or, indeed, any other place as many miles from the K-Bar owner's notoriously lively temperament.

He was stuck, though, and would not squeal. With more courage than Custer's bugler blowing the second charge at the Little Big Horn, he raised his hand and rapped on the ranch-house door. He did bolster himself with an underbreath blasphemy, however, and Eben shook his head and said, "Take not the name of the Lord thy God in vain, Isley. Remember, your strength is as the strength of ten." Isley shot him a curdled look. Then he glanced up at the sky. "Lord, Lord," he said, "what have I done to deserve this?" He didn't get any answer from above, but did draw one from within. It suggested in sulfuric terms that they come in and close the door after them. As well, it promised corporal punishment for any corral-mud or shred of critter-matter stomped into the living-room rug, or any time consumed, past sixty seconds, in stating the grievance, taking no for an answer, and getting the hell back outside where they belonged.

Since the offer was delivered in the range bull's bellow generally associated with H. F. Reston, Senior, in one of his mellower states, Isley hastened to take it up.

"Mr. Reston," he said, once safe inside and the door heeled shut, "this here is Eben, and he's looking for work."

Henry Reston turned red, then white. He made a sound like a sow grizzly about to charge. Then, he strangled it, waited for his teeth to loosen their clamp on one another, waved toward the door and said, "Well, he couldn't be looking for it in better company, Isley. Good luck to the both of you."

"*What?*" said Isley in a smothered way.

"You heard me. And don't slam the door on your way out."

"But Mr. Reston, sir—"

"Isley." The older man got up from his desk. He was the size of an agey buffalo, and the sweetness too. "You remember damned well what I told you when you drug that last bum in here. Now you want to run a rest camp for all the drifters and sick stock that comes blowing into the barnyard with every first cold spell, you hop right on it. I'm trying to run a cow ranch, not a winter resort. Now you get that pilgrim out of here. You come back in twenty minutes, I'll have your check."

Isley was a man who would go so far. He wasn't a fighter but he didn't push too well. When he got his tail up and dropped his horns, he would stand his ground with most.

"I'll wait for it right here," he said.

"Why, you banty-legged little sparrowhawk, who the hell do you think you're telling what you'll do? *Out!*"

"*Mr. Reston—*" The stranger said it so quietly that it hit into the angry air louder than a yell. "Mr. Reston," he went on, "you're frightened. There is no call to take out your fears on Isley. Why not try me?"

"You?"

The Old Man just stared at him.

Isley wished he was far, far away. He felt very foolish right then. He couldn't agree more with the way the Old Man had said, "you." Here was this pale-faced, skinny drifter with the downy beard, soft eyes, quiet voice and sweet smile standing there in his rags and tatters and patches and, worst of all, his farmer's runover flat boots;

here he was standing there looking like something the cat would have drug in but didn't have the nerve to; and here he was standing there with all that going against him and still telling the biggest cattleman in Big Horn basin to wind up and have a try at *him!* Well, Isley thought, in just about two seconds the Old Man was going to tie into him with a list of words that would raise a blood blister on a rawhide boot. That is, if he didn't just reach in the desk drawer, fetch out his pistol and shoot him dead on the spot.

But Isley was only beginning to be wrong.

"Well," breathed Henry Reston at last, "try you, eh?" He rumbled across the room to come to a halt in front of the slight and silent mule rider. He loomed wide as a barn door, tall as a wagon tongue. But he didn't fall in on the poor devil the way Isley had feared. He just studied him with a very curious light in his faded blue eyes, and finally added, "And just what, in God's name, would you suggest I try you *at?*"

"Anything. Anything at all."

Reston nodded. "Pretty big order."

The other returned the nod. "Would a man like you take a small order?"

The owner of the K-Bar jutted his jaw. "You ain't what you let on to be," he challenged. "What do you want here?"

"What Isley told you—a job."

"What brought you here?"

"There's trouble here."

"You like trouble?"

"No."

"Maybe you're a troublemaker."

"No. I make peace when I can."

"And when you can't?"

"I still try."

"You think me giving you a winter's work is going to help you along that path?"

"Yes. Otherwise, I wouldn't be here."

Again Henry Reston studied him. Reston was not, like Tom Isley, a simple man. He was a very complicated and powerful and driving man, and a dangerous man, too.

"I make a lot of noise when I'm riled," he said to the drifter. "Don't let that fool you. I'm a thinking man."

"If you weren't," said the other, "I wouldn't be asking to work for you. I know what you are."

"But I don't know what you are, eh, is that it?"

"No, I'm just a man looking for work. I always pay my way. If there's no work for me, I travel on. I don't stay where there's no job to do."

"Well, there's no job for you here in Big Horn basin."

"You mean not that you know of."

"By God! don't try to tell me what I mean, you ragamuffin!"

"What we are afraid of, we abuse. Why do you fear me?"

Reston looked at him startled.

"I? Fear you? You're crazy. You're not right in the head. I'm Henry F. Reston. I own this damned country!"

"I know; that's why I'm here."

"Now, what the devil do you mean by that?"

"Would the men in the valley give me work? They're poor. They haven't enough for themselves."

"How the hell do you know about the men in the valley?"

"I told you, Mr. Reston. There's trouble here. It's why I came. Now will you give me work, so that I may stay?"

"No! I'm damned if I will. Get out. The both of you!"

Isley started to sneak for the door, but Eben reached out and touched him on the arm. "Wait," he said.

"By God!" roared Reston, and started for the desk drawer.

But Eben stopped him, too, as easily as he had Isley.

"Don't open the drawer," he said. "You don't need a pistol. A pistol won't help you."

Reston came around slowly. To Isley's amazement, he showed real concern. This white-faced tumbleweed had him winging.

"Won't help me what?" he asked, scowlingly.

"Decide about me."

"Oh? Well, now, you ain't told me yet what it is I've got to decide about you. Except maybe whether to kill you or have you horsewhipped or drug on a rope twice around the bunkhouse. Now you tell me what needs deciding, past that."

"I want work."

Henry Reston started to turn red again, and Isley thought he would go for the drawer after all. But he did not.

"So you want work?" he said. "And you claim you can do anything? And you got the cheek to hair up to me and say, slick and flip, 'try me.' Well, all right, by God, I'll do it. Isley—"

"Yes, sir, Mr. Reston?"

"Go put that Black Bean horse in the bronc chute. Hang the bucking rig on him and clear out the corral."

"Good Lord, Mr. Reston, that outlaw ain't been rode since he stomped Charlie Tackaberry. He's ruint three men and—"

"You want your job back, Isley, saddle him."

"But—"

"Right now."

"No sir," Isley began, hating to face the cold with no job, but knowing he couldn't be party to feeding the mule-rider to Black Bean, "I don't reckon I need your pay, Mr. Reston. Me and Eben will make out. Come on, Ebe."

He began to back out, but Eben shook his head.

"We need the work, Isley. Go saddle the horse."

"You don't know this devil! He's a killer."

"I've faced them before, Isley. Lots of them. Saddle him."

"You, a bronc stomper? Never. I bet you ain't been on a bucker in your whole life."

"I wasn't talking about horses, Isley, but about killers."

"No, sir," insisted the little cowboy stoutly, "I ain't a'going to do it. Black Bean will chew you up fine. It ain't worth it to do it for a miserable winter's keep. Let's go."

Eben took hold of his arm. Isley felt the grip. It took him like the talons of an eagle. Eben nodded.

"*Isley*," he said softly, "*saddle the horse*."

The K-Bar hands got the old horse in the chute and saddled without anybody getting crippled. He had been named Black Bean from the Texas Ranger story of Bigfoot Wallace, where the Mexican general made the captive rangers draw a bean, each, from a pottery jug of mixed black and white ones; and the boys who got white beans lived and the boys who got black ones got shot. It was a good name for that old horse.

Isley didn't know what to expect of his friend by now. But he knew from long experience what to expect of Black Bean. The poor drifter would have stood a better chance going against the Mexican firing squad.

The other K-Bar boys *thought* they knew what was bound to take place. This dude very plainly had never been far enough around the teacup to find the handle. He was scarce man enough to climb over the bronc chute to get on Black Bean, let alone to stay on him long enough for them to get the blindfold off and the gate swung open.

But Isley wasn't off the pace as far as that. He knew Eben had *something* in mind. And when the thin youth had scrambled over the chute poles and more fallen, than fitted, into the bucking saddle, the other hands sensed this too. They quit roostering and hoorawing the pilgrim and got downright quiet. One or two—Gant Callahan and Deece McKayne, first off—actually tried helping at the last. Gant said, "Listen, buddy, don't try to stay with him. Just flop off the minute he gets clear of the gates. We'll scoop you up 'fore he can turn on you." Deece hung over the chute bars and whispered his advice, but Isley, holding Black Bean's head, heard him. What he said was, "See that top bar crost the gateposts? Reach for it the minute Isley whips off the blind. Hoss will go right on out from under you, and all you got to do is skin on up over the pole and set tight. You'll get spurred some by the boys, but I don't want to be buryin' you in a feedsack, you hear?"

Fact was, that, between Gant and Deece giving him last-minute prayers, and the other boys getting quiet, the whole operation slowed down to where the Old Man yelled at Isley to pull the blind, and for Wil Henniger to jerk the gate pin, or get out of the way and leave somebody else do it—while they were on their way up to the big house to pick up their pay. Being October and with that early blizzard threatening, he had them where the hair was short. *Wil yelled out, "Powder River, let 'er buck!"* and flung wide the gate. Isley pulled the blind and jumped for his life.

Well, what followed was the biggest quiet since Giggles La Chance decided to show up for church on Easter

Sunday. And seeings that Giggles hadn't heard a preacher, wore a hat, or been seen abroad in daylight for six years, that was some quiet.

What Black Bean did, sure enough deserved the tribute, however. And every bit as much as Giggles La Chance.

Moreover, there was a connection between the two; the Devil seemed involved, somehow, with both decisions.

That old horse, which had stomped more good riders into the corral droppings than any sun-fisher since the Strawberry Roan, came out of that bucking chute on a side-saddle trot, mincy and simpery as an old maid bell mare. He went around the corral bowing his neck and blowing out through his nostrils and rolling back those wally-mean eyes of his soft and dewy as a cow elk with a new calf. He made the circuit once around and brought up in front of the chute gate and stopped and spread out and stood like a five-gaited Kentucky saddlebred on the show stand; and that big quiet got so deep-still that when Dutch Hafner let out his held wind and said, "*Great Gawd Amighty!*" you'd have thought he'd shot off a cannon in a cemetery four o'clock of Good Friday morning.

Isley jumped and said, "Here, don't teller in a man's ear trumpet thataway!" and then got down off the chute fence and wandered off across the ranch lot talking to himself.

The others weren't much better off, but it was Old Man Reston who took it hardest of all.

That horse had meant a lot to him. He'd always sort of looked up to him. He was a great deal the same temperament as Old Henry. Mean and tough and smart and fearing neither God nor Devil nor any likeness of either which walked on two legs. Now, there he was out there making moony-eyes at the seedy drifter, and damn fools out of Henry F. Reston and the whole K-Bar crew.

It never occurred to Old Henry, as it later did to Isley, that Eben had done about the same thing to him, Reston, in his living room up to the ranch house, as he'd done to Black Bean in the bucking chute: which was to buffalo him out of a full gallop right down to a dead walk, without raising either voice or hand to do it. But by the time Isley got this figured out, there wasn't much of a way to use the information. Old Henry, cast down by losing his outlaw horse and made powerful uneasy by the whole performance, had given Isley his pay, and Eben fifteen dollars for his ride—the normal fee for bronc breaking in those parts—and asked them both to be off the K-Bar by sunset. Eben had offered the fifteen dollars to the Old Man for Black Bean, when he had heard him order Deece and Gant to take the old horse out and shoot him for wolf bait. Old Henry had allowed it was a Pecos swap to take anything for such a shambles, by which he meant an outright steal. But he was always closer with a dollar than the satin over a can-can dancer's seat, and so he took the deal, throwing in the bucking saddle, a good split-ear bridle and a week's grub in a greasy sack, to boot. It was maybe an hour short of sundown when Isley riding Eben's mule, and Eben astride the denatured killer, Black Bean, came to the west line of the K-Bar, in company with their escort.

"Well," said Dutch Hafner, "yonder's Bull Pine. Good luck, but don't come back."

Isley looked down into the basin of the Big Horn, sweeping from the foot of the ridge upon which they sat their horses, as far as the eye might reach, westward to Cody, Pitchfork, Meeteetse and the backing sawteeth of the Absoroka Range. The little puncher shook his head, sad, like any man, to be leaving home at only age forty-four.

"I dunno, Dutch," he mourned, "what's to become

of us? There ain't no work in Bull Pine. Not for a cowhand. Not, especially, for a K-Bar cowhand.

"That's the gospel, Isley," said Deece McKayne, helpfully.

"Fact is, was I you, I wouldn't scarce dast go inter Bull Pine, let alone inquire after work."

Gant Callahan, the third member of the honor guard, nodded his full agreement. "You cain't argue them marbles, Isley. Bull Pine ain't hardly nothing but one big sheep camp. I wisht there was something I could add to what Dutch has said, but there ain't. So good luck, and ride wide around them woollies."

Isley nodded back in misery. "My craw's so shrunk it wouldn't chamber a piece of pea gravel," he said. "I feel yellow as mustard without the bite."

"Yellow, hell!" snapped big Dutch, glaring at Deece and Gant. "These two idjuts ain't to be took serious, Isley. Somebody poured their brains in with a teaspoon, and got his arm joggled at that. Ain't no sheepman going to go at a cowboy in broad day, and you'll find work over yonder in the Pitchfork country. Lots of ranches there."

"Sure," said Isley, "and every one of them on the sharp lookout for a broke-down line rider and a paleface mule wrangler to put on for the winter. Well, anyways, so long."

The three K-Bar hands raised their gloves in a mutually waved, "So long, Isley," and turned their horses back for the snug homeplace bunkhouse. Isley pushed up the collar of his worn blanket coat. The wind was beginning to spit a little sleet out of the north. It was hardly an hour's ride down the ridge and out over the flat to Bull Pine. Barring that, the next settlement—in cow country—was Greybull, on the river. That would take them till midnight to reach, and if this sleet turned to snow and came on thick—well, the hell with that, they had no choice. A K-Bar cowboy's chances in a blue norther were better than he could expect in a small-flock sheeptown like Bull Pine. Shivering, he turned to Eben.

"Come on," he said, "we got a six-hour ride."

The gentle drifter held back, shading his eyes and peering out across the basin. "Strange," he said, "it doesn't appear to be that far."

"Whoa up!" said Isley, suddenly alarmed. "What don't appear to be that far?"

"Why, Bull Pine, of course," replied the other, with his sad-soft smile. "Where else would we go?"

Isley could think of several places, one of them a sight warmer than the scraggly ridge they were sitting on. But he didn't want to be mean or small with the helpless pilgrim, no matter he had gotten him sacked and ordered off the K-Bar for good. So he didn't mention any of the options, but only shivered again and made a wry face and said edgily:

"I'd ought to know better than to ask, Ebe; but, why for we want to go to Bull Pine?"

"Because," said the bearded wanderer, "that's where the trouble is."

Eben was right. Bull Pine was where the trouble was.

All the past summer and preceding spring the cattlemen had harassed the flocks of the sheepmen in the lush pastures of the high country around the basin. Parts of flocks and whole flocks had been stampeded and run to death. Some had been put over cliffs. Some cascaded into the creeks. Others just plain chased till their hearts stopped. Nor had it been all sheep. A Basque herder had died and five Valley men had been hurt defending their flocks. So far no cattleman had died, nor even been hit, for it was they who always made the first jump and mostly at night. Now the sheepmen had had all they meant to take.

Those high country pastures were 90 percent government land, and the sheep had just as much right to them as the cattle. More right, really, because they were better suited to use by sheep than cattle. But the country, once so open and free and plenty for all, was filling up. Even in the twenty years since Isley was young, the Big Horn basin had grown six new towns and God alone knew how many upcreek, shoestring cattle ranches. The sheep had come in late, though, only about ten years back. Bull Pine was the first, and sole, sheep town in northwest Wyoming, and it wasn't yet five years old. The cattlemen, headed by Old Henry Reston, meant to see that it didn't get another five years older, too. And Isley knew what Eben couldn't possibly know: that the early blizzard threatening now by the hour, was all the cattlemen had been waiting for. Behind its cover they meant to sweep down on Bull Pine in a fierce raid of the haying pens and winter sheds along the river. These shelters had been built in a community effort of the valley sheep ranchers working together to accomplish what no two or three or ten of them could do working alone. They were a livestockmen's curiosity known about as far away as Colorado, Utah and Montana. They had proved unbelievably successful and if allowed to continue uncontested, it might just be that the concept of winter feeding sheep in that country would catch on. If it did, half the honest cattlemen in Wyoming could be out of business. On the opposite hand, if some natural disaster should strike the Bull Pine feedlots—say like the fences giving way in a bad snowstorm—why then the idea of winter-feeding sheep in the valley would suffer a setback like nothing since old Brigham Young's seagulls had sailed into those Mormon crickets down by Deseret.

Knowing what he knew of the cattlemen's plan to aid nature in this matter of blowing over the sheepmen's fences during the first hard blizzard, Isley followed Eben into Bull Pine with all ten fingers and his main toes crossed.

By good luck they took a wrong turn or two of the trail on the way down off the ridge. Well, it wasn't exactly luck, either. Isley had something to do with it. But, no matter, when they came into Bull Pine it was so dark a man needed both hands to find his nose. Isley was more than content to have it so. Also, he would have been well pleased to have been allowed to stay out in front of the General Store holding the mounts, while Eben went within to seek the loan of some kind soul's shearing shed to get in out of the wind and snow for the night. But Eben said, no, that what he had in mind would require Isley's presence. The latter would simply have to gird up his courage and come along.

Groaning, the little K-Bar puncher got down. From the number of horses standing humpback to the wind at the hitch rail, half the sheepmen in the basin must be inside. That they would be so, rather than home getting set to hay their sheep through the coming storm, worried Isley a great deal. Could it be that the Bull Piners had some warning of the cattlemen's advance? Was this a council of range war they were stepping into the middle of? Isley shivered.

"Ebe," he pleaded, "please leave me stay out here and keep our stock company. Me and them sheepmen ain't nothing in common saving for two legs and one head and maybeso a kind word for motherhood. Now, be a good feller and rustle on in there by your ownself and line us up a woodshed or sheep pen or hayrick to hole up in for the night."

Eben shook his head. "No," he insisted, "you must come in with me. You are essential to the entire situation."

Isley shivered again, but stood resolute. "Listen, Ebe," he warned, "this here blizzard is a'going to swarm down the valley like Grant through Cumberland Gap. We don't get under cover we're going to be froze as the back of a bronze statue's lap. Or like them poor sheep when Old Henry and his boys busts them loose in the dark of dawn tomorry."

"It's Old Henry and the others I'm thinking of," said Eben quietly. "We must be ready for them. Come along."

But Isley cowered back. "Ebe," he said, "I know that kicking never done nobody but a mule no good. Still, I got to plead self-defense, here. So don't crowd me. I'm all rared back, and I ain't a'going in there conscious."

He actually drew up one wrinkled boot as though he would take a swing at the drifter. But Eben only smiled and, for the second time, put his thin hand on Isley's arm. Isley felt the power of those slender fingers. They closed on his arm, and his will, like a Number 6 lynx trap.

"Come on, Isley," said the soft voice, "I need your testimony." And Isley groaned once more and put his head down into his collar as deep as it would go, and followed his ragged guide into the Bull Pine General Store.

"Friends," announced Eben, holding up his hands as the startled sheepmen looked up at him from their places around the possumbelly stove, "Brother Isley and I have come from afar to help you in your hour of need; please hear us out."

"That bent-legged little stray," dissented one member immediately, "never come from no place to help no sheepman. I smell cowboy! Fetch a rope, men."

Eben gestured hurriedly, but it did no good. A second valley man growled, "Ain't that Tom Isley as works for Henry Reston?" And a third gnarled herder rasped,

"You bet it is! Never mind the rope, boys; I'll knock his head open, barehanded."

The group surged forward, the hairy giant who had spoken last, in the lead. Eben said no more, but did not let them beyond him to the white-faced K-Bar cowboy.

As the burly leader drew abreast of him, the drifter reached out and took him gently by one shoulder. He turned him around, got a hip into his side, threw him hard and far across the floor and up against the drygoods counter, fifteen feet away. The frame building shook to its top scantling when the big man landed. He knocked a three-foot hole in the floor, ending up hip-deep in a splintered wedging of boards from which it took the combined efforts of three friends and the storekeeper's two-hundred-pound daughter to extract him.

By the time he was freed and being revived by a stimulant-restorative composed of equal parts of sheep-dip and spirits of camphorated oil, the rest of the assemblage was commencing to appreciate the length and strength of the drifter's throw. And, realizing these things, they were politely moving back to provide him the room he had requested in the first place. Eben made his address direct and nippy.

They had come down out of the hills, he said, bearing news of invading Philistines. They were not there to become a part of the Wolf Mountain War, but to serve in what small way they might, to bring that unpleasantness to a peaceful conclusion, with freedom and justice for all. Toward that end, he concluded, his bowlegged friend had something to say that would convince the sheep raisers that he came to them, not as a kine herder bearing false prophecies, but as a man of their own simple cloth, who wanted to help them as were too honest and God-fearing to help themselves at the cattlemen's price of killing and maiming their fellowmen by gunfire and in the dead of night when decent men were sleeping and their flocks on peaceful, unguarded graze.

This introduction served to interest the Bull Pine men and terrify Tom Isley. He was not up on kine herders, Philistines and false prophets, but he knew sheepmen pretty well. He reckoned he had maybe thirty seconds to fill the flush Eben had dealt him, before somebody thought of that rope again. Glancing over, he saw Big Sam Yawkey—the fallen leader of the meeting—beginning to snort and breathe heavy from the sheepdip fumes. Figuring Big Sam to be bright-eyed and bushy-tailed again in about ten of those thirty seconds, it cut things really fine.

Especially, when he didn't have the least, last notion what the heck topic it was that Eben expected him to take off on. "Ebe!" he got out in a strangulated whisper, "what in the name of Gawd you expect me to talk about?" But the Good Samaritan with the moth-eaten mule and the one thin army blanket wasn't worried a whit. He just put out his bony hand, touched his small companion on the shoulder and said, with his soft smile, as the sheepmen closed in:

"Never fear, Isley; you will think of something."

And, for a fact, Isley did.

"Hold off!" he yelled, backing to the hardware counter and picking himself a pick handle out of a barrel of assorted tool hafts. "I'll lay you out like Samson with that jackass jawbone!"

The sheepmen coagulated, came to a halt.

"Now, see here," Isley launched out, "Ebe's right. I'm down here to do what I can to settle this fight. There's been far too much blood spilt a'ready. And I got an idee, like Ebe says, how to stop this here war quicker'n you can spit and holler howdy. But it ain't going to be risk-free. Monkeying around with them cattlemen is about as safe as kicking a loaded polecat.

They're touchier than a teased snake, as I will allow you all know."

Several of the sheepmen nodded, and one said; "Yes, we know, all right. And so do you. You're one of them!"

"No!" denied Isley, "that ain't so. Mr. Reston thrun me off the K-Bar this very day. Ebe, here, made him look some small in front of the boys, and the Old Man ordered us both took to the west line and told to keep riding. I got included on account I drug Ebe in off the range, and Old Henry, he said I could keep him, seeing's I'd found him first."

His listeners scowled and looked at one another. This bow-legged little man had been punching cattle too long. He had clearly gone astray upstairs and been given his notice because of it. But they would hear him out, as none of them wanted to be flung against the dry-goods counter, or skulled with that pick handle.

"Go ahead," growled Big Sam Yawkee, coming up groggily to take his place in front of the Bull Piners. "But don't be overlong with your remarks. I done think you already stretched the blanket about as far as she will go. But, by damn, if there's a sick lamb's chance that you *do* have some way we can get back at them murderers, we ain't going to miss out on it. Fire away."

"Thank you, Mr. Yawkey," said Isley, and fired.

The idea he hit them with was as much a surprise to him as to them. He heard the words coming out of his mouth but it was as though somebody else was pulling the wires and making his lips flap. He found himself listening with equal interest to that of the Bull Pine sheepmen, to his own wild-eyed plan for ambushing the cattlemen in Red Rock Corral.

It was beautifully simple:

Red Rock Corral was a widened-out place in the middle of that squeezed-in center part of Shell Canyon called the Narrows. If you looked at the Narrows as a sort of rifle barrel of bedrock, then Red Rock Corral would be like a place midways of the barrel where a bullet with a weak charge had stuck, then been slammed into by the following, full-strength round, bulging the barrel at that spot. It made a fine place to catch range mustangs, for example. All you had to do was close off both ends of the Narrows, once you had them in the bulge. Then just leave them there to starve down to where they would lead out peaceful as muley cows.

Isley's idea was that what would work for tough horses would work for tough men.

The sheepmen knew for a fact, he said, that the hill trail came down to the basin through Shell Canyon. Now, if added to this, they also knew for a fact, as Isley did, that Old Henry and his boys were coming down that trail early tomorrow to knock over their winter feed pens and stampede their sheep into the blizzard's deep snow, why then, they would be catching up to the first part of the Isley Plan.

Pausing, the little cowboy offered them a moment to consider the possibilities. Big Sam was the first to recover.

"You meaning to suggest," he said, heavy voice scraping like a burro with a bad cold, "that we bottle them cattlemen up in Red Rock Corral and starve them into agreeing to leave us be? Why, I declare you're balmier than you look, cowboy. In fact, you're nervier than a busted tooth. You think we need you to tell us about ambushing? That's the cattlemen's speed. And you can't go it without people getting hurt, kilt likely. Boys," he said, turning to the others, "some deck is shy a joker, and this is him. Fetch the rope."

"No! Wait!" cried Isley, waving his pick handle feebly. "I ain't done yet."

"Oh, yes you are," rumbled Big Sam, moving forward.

Yet, as before, he did not reach Tom Isley.

Eben raised his thin, pale hand and Big Sam brought up as short as though he had walked into an invisible wall.

"What the hell?" he muttered, rubbing his face, frightened. "I must be losing my marbles. Something just clouted me acrost the nose solid as a low limb."

"It was your conscience," smiled Eben. "Isley has more to say. Haven't you, Isley?"

The little cowboy shook his head, bewildered.

"Hell, don't ask me, Ebe; you're the ventrillyquist."

"Speak on," nodded his friend, "and be not afraid."

"Well," said Isley, "I'll open my mouth and see what comes out. But I ain't guaranteeing nothing."

Big Sam Yawkey, still rubbing his nose, glared angrily.

"Something better come out," he promised, "or I'll guarantee you something a sight more substantial than nothing; and that's to send you out of town with your toes down. You've got me confuseder than a blind dog in a butcher shop, and I'm giving you one whole minute more to hand me the bone, or down comes your doghouse."

"Yeah!" snapped a burly herder behind him. "What you take us for, a flock of ninnies? Jest because we run sheep don't mean we got brains to match. And you suggesting that we set a wild hoss trap for them gunslingers and night riders of Old Man Reston's is next to saying we're idjuts. You think we're empty-headed enough to buy any such sow bosom as holding them cattlemen in that rock hole with a broomtail brush fence on both ends?"

"*No,*" said Isley calmly, and to his own amazement, "*but you might trying doing it with blasting powder.*"

"What!" shouted Yawkey.

"Yes, sir," said Isley meekly, "a half can of Du Pont #9 at each end, touched off by a signal from the bluff above. When all of them have rode into Red Rock Corral, down comes the canyon wall, above and below, and there they are shut off neat as a newborn calf, and nobody even scratched. I'd say that with this big snow that's coming, and with the thermometer dropping like a gut-shot elk, they'd sign the deed to their baby sister's virtue inside of forty-eight hours."

There was silence, then, as profound as the pit.

It was broken, presently, by Big Sam's awed nod, and by him clearing his throat shaky and overcome as though asked to orate in favor of the flag on Independence Day.

"Great Gawd A'mighty boys," he said, "it might work!"

And the rush for the front door and the horses standing back-humped at the hitch rail, was on.

As a matter of Big Horn basin record, it did work.

The Bull Piners got their powder planted by three A.M., and about four, down the trail came the deputation from the hills. The snow was already setting in stiff, and they were riding bunched tight. Big Sam Yawkey fired his Winchester three times when they were all in the middle of Red Rock Corral and Jase Threepersons, the storekeeper, and Little Ginger, his two-hundred-pound daughter, both lit off their respective batches of Du Pont #9 above and below the Corral so close together the cattlemen thought it was one explosion and Judgment Day come at last.

Well, it had, in a way.

And, as Isley had predicted, it came in less than forty-eight hours.

The sheepmen were mighty big about it. They lowered down ropes with all sorts of bedding and hot food and even whiskey for the freezing ranchers, as well as some of their good baled sheep hay for the horses. But they made it clear, through Big Sam's bellowed-down advice, that they meant to keep their friends and neighbors from the hills bottled up in that bare-rock bulge till the new grass came, if need be. They wouldn't let them starve, except slowly, or freeze, unless by accident. But they had come out from Bull Pine to get a truce, plus full indemnity for their summer's sheep losses, and they were prepared to camp up on that bluff—in the full comfort of their heated sheep wagons—from right then till Hell, or Red Rock Corral, froze over.

That did it.

There was some hollering back and forth between the two camps for most of that first day. Then it got quiet for the better part of the second. Then, along about sundown, Old Henry Reston yelled up and said: "What's the deal, Yawkey? We don't get back to our stock, right quick, we won't have beef enough left to hold a barbecue."

Big Sam read them the terms, which Isley wasn't close enough to hear. Reston accepted under profane duress and he and Big Sam shook on the matter. Naturally, such a grip had the force of law in the basin. Once Old Henry and Big Sam had put their hands to an agreement, the man on either side who broke that agreement might just as well spool his bed and never stop moving.

Realizing this, Isley modestly stayed out of the affair. There were other inducements toward laying low and keeping back from the rim while negotiations went forward and concluded. One of these was the little cowboy's certain knowledge of what his fellow K-Bar riders would think of a cowman who sold out to a bunch of sheepherders. Even more compelling was the cold thought as to what they would *do* to such a hero, should they ever catch up to the fact he had plotted the whole shameful thing. All elements, both of charming self-effacement and out-right cowardice, considered, Isley believed himself well advised to saddle up and keep traveling. This he planned to do at the first opportunity. Which would be with that night's darkness in about twenty minutes. It was in carrying out the first part of this strategy—rounding up Eben and their two mounts—that he ran into the entertainment committee from the Bull Pine camp; three gentlemen sheepherders delegated by their side to invite Isley to the victory celebration being staged in his honor at the Ram's Horn Saloon later that evening.

Isley, confronted with this opportunity, refused to be selfish. He bashfully declined the credit being so generously offered, claiming that it rightfully belonged to another. When pressed for the identity of this hidden champion, he said that of course he meant his good friend Eben. "You know," he concluded, "the skinny feller with the white face and curly whiskers. Ebe," he called into the gathering dusk past the hay wagon where they had tied Black Bean and the mule, "come on out here and take a bow!"

But Eben did not come out, and Jase Threepersons, the chairman of the committee, said to Isley, "What skinny feller with what white face and what curly whiskers?"

He said it in a somewhat uncompromising manner and Isley retorted testily, "The one that was with me in the store; the one what thrun Big Sam acrost the floor. Damn it, what you trying to come off on me, anyhow?"

Jase looked at him and the other two sheepmen looked at him and Jase said, in the same flat way as before, "*You* thrun Big Sam agin that counter. There wasn't nobody in that store with you. What *you* trying to come off on *us*, Tom Isley?"

"Blast it!" cried Isley, "I never laid a finger on Big

Sam. You think I'd be crazy enough to try that?''

The three shook their heads, looking sorrowful.

''Evidently so,'' said Jase Threepersons.

''No, now you all just hold up a minute,'' said Isley, seeing their pitying looks. ''Come on, I'll show you. Right over here ahint the hay wagon. Me and Ebe was bedded here last night and boilt our noon coffee here today. I ain't seen him the past hour, or so, and he may have lost his nerve and lit out, but, by damn, I can show you where his mule was tied and I'll fetch *him* for you, give time.''

They were all moving around the wagon, as he spoke, Isley in the lead. He stopped, dead. ''No!'' they heard him say. ''My God, it cain't be!'' But when they got up to him, it was. There was no sign of a double camp whatever. And no sign of the bearded stranger, nor of his moth-eaten mule. ''He was right here!'' yelled Isley desperately. ''Damn it, you saw him, you're just funning, just hoorawing me. You seen him and you seen that broke-down jackass he rides; who the hell you think I been talking to the past three days, *myself?*''

'' 'Pears as if,'' nodded Jase sympathetically. ''Too bad, too. Little Ginger had kind of took a shine to you. Wanted me to see you stuck around Bull Pine a spell. But, seeing the way things are with you, I reckon she'd best go back to waiting out Big Sam.''

''Yes sir, thank you very much, sir,'' said Isley gratefully, ''but I still aim to find Ebe and that damn mule for you.'' He bent forward with sudden excitement. ''Say, lookit here! Mule tracks leading off! See? What'd I tell you? Old Ebe, he's a shy cuss, and mightily humble. He didn't want no thanks. He'd done what he come for—stopped the trouble—and he just naturally snuck off when nobody was a'watching him. Come on! we can catch him easy on that stove-up old jack.''

The three men came forward, stooped to examine the

snow. There were some tracks there, all right, rapidly being filled by the fresh fall of snow coming on, but tracks all the same. They could have been mule tracks too. It was possible. But they could also have been smallish horse tracks. Like say left by Pettus Teague's blue-blood race mare. Or by that trim Sioux pony belonging to Charlie Bo-peep, the Basque half-breed. Or by Coony Simms's little bay. Or Nels Bofors' slim Kentucky-bred saddler. Or two, three others in the camp.

Straightening from its consideration of the evidence, the committee eyed Tom Isley.

"Isley," said Jase Threepersons, "I'll tell you what we'll do. All things took into account, you've been under considerable strain. Moreover, that strain ain't apt to get any less when word gets back up into the hill that you come down here and hatched this ambush idea. We owe you a'plenty, and we ain't going to argue with you about that there feller and his mule. But them cowboys of Old Henry's might take a bit more convincing. Now suppose you just don't be here when Big Sam and the others come up out of the corral with the K-Bar outfit. We'll say you was gone when we got here to the hay wagon, and that you didn't leave no address for sending on your mail. All right?"

Isley took a look at the weather.

It was turning off warmer, and this new snow wouldn't last more than enough to cover his tracks just nice. The wind was down, the sun twenty minutes gone and, from the rim of the bluff above the corral, sounds were floating which indicated the roping parties were pulling up the first of the K-Bar sheep raiders. To Isley, it looked like a fine night for far riding. And sudden.

He pulled his coat collar up, his hat brim down, and said to Jase Threepersons, "All right."

"We'll hold the boys at the rim to give you what start we can," said Jase. And Isley stared at him and answered, "No, don't bother; you've did more than enough for me a'ready. Goodbye, boys, and if I ever find any old ladies or dogs that need kicking, I will send them along to you."

Being sheepherders, they didn't take offense, but set off to stall the rescue party at the rim, true to their word.

Isley didn't linger to argue the morals of it. He got his blanket out from under the hay wagon, rolled it fast, hurried to tie it on behind old Black Bean's saddle. By this time he wasn't even sure who *he* was, but didn't care to take any chances on it. He just might turn out to be Tom Isley, and then it would be close work trying to explain to Dutch and Gant and Deece and the rest, what it was he was doing bedded down in the sheep camp.

He had the old black outlaw swung around and headed in the same direction as the fading mule tracks—or whatever they were—in something less than five minutes flat. The going was all downhill to the river, and he made good time. About eight o'clock he came to the Willow Creek Crossing of the Big Horn, meaning to strike the Pitchfork Trail there. He was hungry and cold and the old black needing a rest, so he began to look around for a good place to lie up for the night. Imagine his surprise and pleasure, then, to spy ahead, the winky gleam and glow of a campfire, set in a snug thicket of small timber off to the right of the crossing. Following its cheery guide, he broke through the screening bush and was greeted by a sight that had him bucked up quicker than a hatful of hot coffee.

"Ebe!" he cried delightedly. "I knowed you wouldn't run out on me! God bless it, I am that pleased to see you!"

"And I likewise, Isley," smiled the gentle-voiced drifter. "Alight and thrice welcome to my lowly board."

Well, he had a wind-tight place there. It was nearly as warm and shut in from the cold as the old rock house out on Wolf Mountain flat, and he had added to it with a neat lean-to of ax-cut branches, as pretty as anything Isley had ever seen done on the range. And the smell of the rack of lamb he had broiling over the flames of his fire was enough to bring tears to the eyes of a Kansas City cow buyer.

Isley could see no legitimate reason for declining the invitation.

Falling off Black Bean, he said, "You be a'saying Grace, Ebe, whilst I'm a'pulling this hull; I don't want to hold you up none when we set down—"

While they ate, things were somewhat quiet. It was very much the same as it had been when Eben came in cold and hungry to Isley's fire out on the flats. Afterward, though, with the blackened coffeepot going the rounds, Isley rolling his rice-paper smokes and Eben playing some of the lonesomest pretty tunes on his old mouth harp that the little cowboy had ever heard, the talk started flowing at a better rate.

There were several things Isley wanted to know, chief among them being the matter of the Bull Pine men letting on as if he had jumped his head hobbles. But he kept silent on this point, at first, leading off with some roundabout inquiries which wouldn't tip his hand to Eben. These were such things as how come he didn't recognize any of the tunes Eben was playing on the harp? Or how did Eben manage to evaporate from the sheep camp at Red Rock Corral without any of the Bull Piners seeing him. Or why didn't he let Isley know he was going? And how come him, Eben, to have lamb on the fire in October, when there wasn't any lamb?

To this tumble of questions, Eben only replied with his soft laugh and such put-offers as that the tunes were sheepherder songs from another land, that the fresh snowfall had hidden his departure from the hay wagon bed spot, that he knew the Bull Piners planned a party for Isley and didn't wish to stand in his way of enjoying the tribute due him, and that for him, Eben, lamb was always in season and he could put his hand to some just about as he pleased.

Well, Isley was a little mystified by this sort of round-the-barn business. But when Eben made the remark about the Bull Pine party being due him, Isley, he quit slanting his own talk, off-trail, and brought it right to the bait.

"Ebe," he said, "I'm going to ask you one question. And you mighten as well answer it, for I'm going to hang onto it like an Indian to a whiskey jug."

"Gently, gently," smiled the other. "You'll have your answer, but not tonight. In the morning, Isley, I promise you."

"Promise me what?" demanded the little cowboy. "I ain't even said what I wanted."

"But I know what you want, and you shall have it—in the morning."

Isley eyed him stubbornly.

"I'll have what in the morning?" he insisted.

Eben smiled that unsettling sad-sweet smile, and shrugged.

"*Proof that I was with you all the while*," he said.

Isley frowned, then nodded.

"All right, Ebe, you want to save her for sunup, that's fine with me. I'm a little wore down myself."

"You rest, then," said the drifter. "Lie back upon your saddle and your blanket, and I will read to you from a book I have." He reached in his own blanket, still curiously unrolled, and brought forth two volumes; one a regular-sized black leather Bible, the other a smallish red morocco-bound tome with some sort of outlandish foreign scripting on the cover. "The Book of the Gospel," he said, holding up the Bible; then, gesturing with the little red book, "the *Rubáiyát* of Omar Khayyám: which will you have, Isley?"

"Well," said the latter, "I can tell by some of your talk, Ebe, that you favor the Good Book, and I ain't denying that it's got some rattling-tall yarns in it. But if it's all the same to you, I'll have a shot of the other. I'm a man likes to see both sides of the billiard ball."

Eben nodded soberly, but without any hint of reproval.

"You have made your choice, Isley," he said, "and so be it. Listen. . . ."

He opened the small volume then and began to read selected lines for his raptly attentive companion. Lazing back on his blanket, head propped on his saddle, the warmth of the fire reflecting in under the lean-to warm and fragrant as fresh bread, Isley listened to the great rhymes of the ancient Persian:

". . . And as the Cock crew, those who stood before
The Tavern shouted—'Open then the Door!
'You know how little while we have to stay
'And once departed, may return no more! . . .' "

". . . Come, fill the Cup, and in the fire of Spring
Your winter-garment of Repentance fling:
The Bird of Time has but a little way
To flutter—and the Bird is on the Wing. . . ."

". . . A Book of Verses underneath the Bough,
A Jug of Wine, a Loaf of Bread—and Thou
Beside me singing in the Wilderness—
Oh, Wilderness were Paradise enow! . . ."

". . . Yesterday this Day's Madness did prepare,
Tomorrow's Silence, Triumph, or Despair:

Drink! for you know not whence you came, nor
why:
Drink! for you know not why you go, nor
where. . . ."

". . . The Moving Finger writes; and, having
writ,
Moves on: nor all your Piety nor Wit
Shall lure it back to cancel half a Line,
Nor all your Tears wash out a Word of it. . . ."

The poetry was done, then, and Eben was putting down the little red book to answer some drowsy questions from Isley as to the nature of the man who could write such wondrously true things about life as she is actually lived, just on a piece of ordinary paper and in such a shriveled little old leather book.

Eben reached over and adjusted Isley's blanket more closely about the dozing cowboy, then told him the story of Omar Khayyám. But Isley was tired, and his thoughts dimming. He remembered, later, some few shreds of the main idea; such as that Old Omar was a tentmaker by trade, that he didn't set much store by hard work, that he didn't know beans about horses, sheep or cattle, but he was a heller on women and grapejuice. Past that, he faded out and slept gentle as a dead calf. The sun was an hour high and shining square in his eye when he woke up.

He lay still a minute, not recalling where he was. Then it came to him and he sat up with a grin and a stretch and a "*Morning, Ebe*," that was warm and cheerful enough to light a candle from. But Eben didn't answer to it. And never would. For, when Tom Isley blinked to get the climbing sun out of his eyes, and took a second frowning look around the little campsite, all he saw was the unbroken stretch of the new snow which had fallen quiet as angel's wings during the night. There was no Eben, no mule, no threadbare army blanket bedroll. And, this time, there were not even any half-filled hoofprints leading away into the snow. This time there was only the snow. And the stillness. And the glistening beauty of the new day.

Oh, and there was one other small thing that neither Tom Isley, nor anybody else in Big Horn basin, was ever able to explain. It was a little red morocco book about four-by-six inches in size, which Isley found in his blanket when he went to spool it for riding on. Nobody in Northwest Wyoming had ever heard of it, including Tom Isley.

It was called the *Rubáiyát* of Omar Khayyám.

The Deputization of Walter Mendenhall

When Walter Mendenhall came into Eudora it was such a June morning to make a stone in the road seem beautiful and the quarreling of the sparrows in the manured dust of main street sound lovely. The stage ride up from Rock Springs and the railroad had been smooth, as well. No broken rims, no frozen axles, no sand dig-outs, nothing whatever of woe to mar the moonlight and sweet smells of the prairie hay ripening in the summer heat. Business had been good, too. More and more people out here were going to flat heels and laces and giving up on their cowboy boots that wore twenty years between half-solings. There had been healthy orders of both button and full-lace models in Laramie and Cheyenne, with no reason to suppose the same luck wouldn't obtain in Lander and Riverton and back to Casper. When he got home to Chicago, this trip, Walter Mendenhall could look forward at last to getting that raise to $18.75 per week, plus commissions and travel, of course.

Walter got off the stage at the Alhambra House, where he always stayed, and went in and registered. He took the best room in the place, the second-floor front which stood at the head of the outside stairs to the privy. It took some nerve to spend $1.35 for a room for one night, but that June morning and those good sales in Cheyenne and Laramie were heady stuff. And, indeed, success was only beginning to come to Walter Mendenhall. At the South Pass Emporium, just down the street, he made a call on Mr. Sam Eden, the proprietor, and was given an order for three dozen pairs of black shoes, a dozen of the new brown color, and half a dozen high buckskin beige ladies' buttoners! This was merchandising on the grand scale; an order of that magnitude came no oftener than Halley's comet or triplet calves. Even upon the part of the staid and stable Walter Mendenhall, and even at eleven o'clock in the bright Wyoming morning, the event called for drinks on the house—always providing there were not too many early risers in the house.

Going into the Antlers, the biggest and best of Eudora's three taverns, and the only one open before noon, Walter determined that there were but three customers in the place and forthwith made his call to drink upon him and the Officutt-Jepson Shoe Company.

He was handed a minor shock when four more old prairie rats got up out of a dark corner where, eyes blinded by the glorious outside sunshine, Walter had not seen them. But an offer was an offer. Swallowing his unease, the master salesman put forward his finest open and frank expression of pleasure, and dug for the four silver dollars with which he now determined to plunge all the way in.

"*Two* rounds on the house!" he announced, with emphasis precisely put to establish his generosity, and spun the dollars out upon the bar with a goodwill which could not be questioned, even though, for lack of practice, the pieces of silver fell flat after a wobbly turn or two.

The first round, striking bottom on fairly empty and receptive stomachs, was eminently a success. Walter felt within him the glow of an expansiveness not familiar but quite rewarding. The second round only extended the circulation aroused by the first and Officutt-Jepson's top Far Western representative became imbued with a completely revolutionary resolve. "Step up, boys!" he called heartily. "We'll have one more and go burn down the schoolhouse!" There were no arguments. By now, the word had spread and he was buying for eleven men and Packrat Annie, the old Gros Ventre squaw who swamped out the Antlers twice a month with her wet mop, whether it needed it or not. Half the crowd knew the little shoe salesmen to say good-day to, the other half had seen him in Eudora, or Lander, or Cheyenne or wherever, and knew that he was all right. Noon dinner was drunk under and no pause taken to diminish the fun, except to throw out the old squaw who had gotten obstreperous after the fashion of her people full of firewater, and attempted to scalp Doc Hindemyer without benefit of surgery, or even of permission. It was perhaps one P.M., the day outside grown fiercely hot and still, when the gunfire echoed from down main street and Slim Watrous, at the head of the bar, pulled his Colt and said, "Hell, come on; that's down to the bank!" and dashed out of the Antlers on the bow-legged and unsteady run. He was followed by all the drinkers except Walter Mendenhall, who had no business pending at the Bank of Eudora, and the four old saddlebums who had grabbed a quart from the bar and scuttled out the rear door into the alley at the first echoing shot. The barkeep, too, remained faithful to his trust, resisting the urge to join the rush. Indeed, he brought out a bottle of good whiskey—Old Crow—and put it on the mahogany and said to his remaining customer. "Have one on the house; this here's the first time the bank's been robbed this spring."

Walter took the drink but he was feeling a little out of place now. It had seemed so easy to drift into the friendly, drawling way of talking and thinking that these Wyoming men practiced. A few fingers of the old equalizer and even a shoe salesman from Chicago started using words like partner and yonder and howdy. Walter wasn't inebriated or insincere. It was good for business to mix in with the locals and let them know you had no eastern airs about you. Walter felt he ought to have done more of it sooner. But that wasn't what was making him hesitate, as he downed his Old Crow and watched the batwing doors of the Antlers and waited expectantly for the first returnees to bring the report on the shooting down at the bank.

The thing was, he decided, that those gunshots had put a change in the air. It was something intangible but strong. Something very definite and native to the parts. It was something that could turn a guffawing, crude Slim Watrous into a narrow-eyed, gun-handling, quick-reacting frontiersman. A man who, even half full of bad whiskey, could come to the surface immediately, and who knew what to do when he got there. It was something the menfolks of Eudora had that those of Chicago did not.

Walter Mendenhall decided that, hereafter, he would stick to selling shoes. A fellow in his position had no business getting mixed in where pistols were being fired off and where bullets were flying around in broad daylight. He found himself hoping, of a sudden, that none of his recent drinking companions had taken him at some value that he did not intend. He hoped they hadn't fallen literally for his friendly attempts to say howdy and yonder and partner the way that they did.

But he was a cautious man. He didn't believe in waiting on luck. "I think," he told the barkeep, "that I will go over to the hotel and see if I got any mail. Goodday." The barkeep flattened a black deerfly the size of a humming bird, and said, "Sure." He retrieved his wet bar towel and examined the anatomy of the spread-out insect. "You better shake a leg, I reckon, even though the mail ain't due for two hours. Ride easy."

At the doors, Walter stopped and turned. "Why do you say that?" he asked. "I mean about the mail and me?"

The barkeep had not been mean or critical in the way he said it. He had intended it as friendly. Any man who spent $27 in his place before noon dinner was entitled to the truth. "What I meant," he amplified, "is that if the galoot got away down there at the bank, and was toting any of the bank's cash, or if anybody got winged in the fracas, then all able-bodied occupants of Eudora had best get the hell indoors and slam up the shutters. Once old man McCullers starts down the main stem handing out them pewter posse tags of his, you got to be able to prove you're either dead or over 90 years old and ailing. Otherwise, you're stuck. See what I mean, partner? Last time there was a holdup hereabouts, McCullers deputized two U.P. Chinamen and the wooden Mohican down in front of the cigar stand next the barbershop. He'll hang a badge on anything that isn't moving or looks able to stand up, and don't duck when he stabs them. That's where you and the mail comes in. Even if the mail stage ain't due till 3 P.M., you'd best hole up in the hotel till about dark. Good luck."

Deputized? thought Walter Mendenhall. Me? The friendly shoe salesman from Chicago? Me, given a sheriff's star and put on a horse and sent out to catch a badman? A bank robber? Using real live ammunition in his revolvers?

"Thank you," he said to the barkeep. "Thank you very much. "I might stay, but I don't have my gun along and it's been quite a while since I've done much hard riding."

"I daresay," nodded the barkeep. "But you keep standing there in them batwing doors talking it up with me, and you'll find out Eudora hospitality ain't limited to free shots of Old Crow and big orders for high-button shoes."

"How's that?" asked Walter Mendenhall politely, wanting to be on his way to cover but not wanting, at the same time, to show any yellow stripe. That would be as bad for business as kicking a stray dog or insulting a prostitute. He couldn't act too cowardly in front of the Antlers barkeeper, no matter how wildly his feet were straining to carry him across the street and into the cool safety of the Alhambra House.

"I say," he repeated, "what was that?"

The barkeep stared at him. It was a divided look, struggling between irritation and admiration.

"You're either stupid or the greatest Lesbian since John Wilkes Barre," he said. "In either case, it's too late to retreat."

"Booth," said Walter, frowningly. "John Wilkes Booth."

"Yeah," said the barkeep, "that's the one."

"Thespian," said his informant, "and he wasn't really great. It was his brother, Edwin, that was so famous."

"Yeah," agreed the barkeep, "well, you have it your way and I'll have it mine." He was untying his apron and slipping off his rubber-band work cuffs. "I got an appointment with the dentist in Laramie, which I will make as soon as I get there." He reached for his derby hat, jammed it hastily on. "I'll go out the back way," he said. "It's closer to Laramie. Give my regards to Sheriff McCullers."

"To who?" said Walter, stepping back into the Antlers and cupping an ear. It was extremely noisy outside in the street, what with all the running about and shouting that had set in while he conversed with the barkeep.

"McCullers," answered the barkeep, sliding out the dim rear entrance. "He's the fat one headed in from the front hitch rail. The one with the brown-paper sack full of pewter badges. Just call him 'Sheriff.' He'll understand."

Too late, Walter Mendenhall wheeled to face the street doors. The slatted panels swung inward. A fat and perspiring man at least three feet wide and six and a half feet high, fixed him with a beetle-browed stare.

"*You!*" he roared in a voice any range bull would envy. "*Get a horse and a rifle; you're depootized!*"

Stunned, Walter tottered toward him.

"Me?" he croaked. "Walter Mendenhall?"

"Whatever your name is," boomed the sheriff. His thick fingers dived into the brown-paper sack, speared a badge, hooked it onto Walter's paisley vest with a strike and a snagging set of its rusted clasp pin that defied the ordinary eye to follow in its blinding speed. "You can ride a hoss, can't you? And carry a rope?"

"A rope?" groaned Walter. "You mean a rope to—"

He couldn't bring himself to say it, but Sheriff McCullers could. "You're damned tootin', I mean a rope to hoist a man with!" he bellowed. "What you think this is, Chicago? Get a move on; I'm short of men." He broke off to stare at Walter Mendenhall. "That's why I'm tagging you," he said, and went out to leave Walter wondering if he had meant he had been forced to start deputizing shoe salesmen because he had run out of real men, or if he had merely implied that he had run short of his regular supply of Eudora men and so was adding transient males to the honor roll for riding after whoever it was that had assaulted the bank.

"Hey!" he yelled, belatedly realizing the significance of a hanging posse, "did the robbers kill somebody?"

"Here," growled Sheriff McCullers, pulling Walter out of the Antlers by his shirtfront and lifting him free of the ground and depositing him in the first saddle on top of the first unpleasant-looking local bronco tied to the saloon hitch rail, "you use Slim's hoss. Slim got it down yonder to the bank. Bullet took him square in the head."

"You mean he's dead?" gasped Walter. "That fine young man who just ran out of the Antlers, so brave and quick with his gun?"

"That's the one," said the sheriff, "and he's deader than a dido bird."

"Dodo," said Walter diffidently.

"He's stone-cold, spell it any way you want. Come on, boys!" The sheriff wheeled to face the street. "Everybody mount up! We got to get a move on. Curly will be in the next county before we can come up to him."

"That's so!" a man shouted back excitedly. "With a killer like Curly Purcell you got to take every precaution; you can't waste no motion. Mount up, boys, mount up!"

There was a stir among the group now a'gathering at the Antlers hitch rail. Many a voice rose in spirited agreement but not one hand reached for rein, or boot, or oxbow stirrup. McCullers knew the signs of incipient desertion and was equal to the emergency.

"No use stampeding, either," he boomed reassuringly. "Everybody into the Antlers; we'll hold a meeting and elect the officers of the posse. First five rounds is on the city of Eudora. Inside, men! We've got to get the details ironed out." He reached up and plucked Walter

Mendenhall out of the saddle where he had placed him the moment before. "Come on, Dude," he said, "we'll run you for recording secretary. I reckon you're the only one of us can read what he writes. You'll be the first educated vigilante in Wyoming Territory."

Walter held back, thinking to fade away in the crowd during the general press to be first at the bar, but he was among warmer friends than he knew. Two tall cowboys took him under the arms and carried him across the threshold of the Antlers, placating his fears, the while, with positive assertions that he didn't have a thing to worry about and that, with Sheriff McCullers backing him, there was no chance that he would be defeated and that he could count on, right then and there, being elected unanimously.

The happenings now assumed another hue. After two or three rounds the men were getting sterner, not more mellow. Walter, noting this, believed that his first idea that the Eudorites were ghouls celebrating a man's demise in advance would have to be altered. These fellows were not drinking out of carnality, they were taking on courage for the hard work ahead. They were taking no chances. They might catch up to Curly Purcell and actually have to hang him. Walter could tell that this was the drift of their worries by listening to the fragments of talk being made at the bar. Some little of it was loud and rough but most of it was uneasy, and scarcely any of it was of the high good humor which had been present at the start of the invasion of the Antlers.

Twenty minutes, no more, was taken in this manner. Then Sheriff McCullers said it was time to go and all the men, including Walter and his two unappointed chaperones, headed outside and got on their horses and rode off down the main street toward the bank. Walter, on Slim Watrous' mean-eyed buckskin gelding, saw that there was still a considerable crowd of old men and boys around the front doors of the bank. Peering closely, as he rode by with the posse, he could make out the lank form of Slim sprawled on the boardwalk with Doc Hindemyer bending over working on him. This struck him as odd, since McCullers had said Slim was dead. One of his partners, the blond one with the nice grin, seemed to read his thoughts, for he drawled in ready explanation, "Old Doc, he don't believe in letting them go easy. He'll fool around with him fifteen minutes, or so, then get up and walk off and say 'to hell with it.' But he's wasting his time on this one. I seen the hole my ownself. It's square between the eyes. All black and blue and looking like the devil. Ugh! Old Slim, he never even gave a squawk. Just stiffened up and fell over."

Walter Mendenhall nodded and gulped. The horses were picking up a little speed now, leaving the town behind, heading into the empty sage. He squinted ahead. The sun glared frightfully. It was hot. Heat waves wriggled over everything. "It's wide open," said Walter to the blond young man. "You can see ten miles. How could the bandit have disappeared so fast?"

The cowboy grinned his nice grin and pointed ahead. "See that dust yonder? No, no, over to the right. Off the road. Yonder where the rocks start to rise?"

"Oh, yes," answered Walter, making out the tiny puff of dust. "Is that him?"

"Sure. He's heading for the high ground. They always do. He knows he can't shake us in this broad daylight. He will have to find a hole and bluff us off till dark, then he might ride out and break through us and get clear, still."

"What do you think will happen?" panted Walter, bouncing and jouncing painfully to the buckskin's rolling lope.

"You never know," smiled the blond youth. "Mostly nothing. I been out with old McCullers four times. We caught one of the fellers. He got six months in the Lander Jail.''

''Six months? For shooting someone?''

''Naw, he stole a heifer. Butchered it for meat, actually. He was a nester; you know, a squatter. Happens all the time. Some of the boys wanted to string him up, but McCullers ain't that crazy. It's long past the day when you can hang a cow thief. I mean, if there's more than a couple of witnesses.''

By now Walter was having all and more than he could do to stay with the buckskin. It was a notable achievement to nod and essay a return of the blond's pleasant smile. In any event, the other one of his two guides was neither light haired, nor hearted, and now growled, ''Shut up, Jess. This dude don't know nothing. Don't fill him with no ideas, you hear? This ain't a heifer-stealing posse.''

''Sure,'' said Jess, the affable one. ''Hell, I reckon he knows that, don't you, Dude?''

''What?'' managed Walter, wincing with the hurt of the saddle. ''You reckon I know what?''

''About this here posse. That it ain't no ordinary one.''

''How's that, Jess? I don't get you, I'm afraid. I've never been with a group such as this before.''

''Few have,'' vouchsafed Jess. ''Or would want to. This here's a hanging posse, mister. . . .''

It was sunset when they took Curly Purcell. The posse, elated at the bloodless entrapment of such a famed outlaw, voted to withhold the execution of judgment until dawn. Time was needed to consider the situation and decide if they would return Purcell to Eudora and a slower justice via jury trial at Cheyenne or Laramie. The long hot ride and the meekness with which the killer of Slim Watrous had surrendered when cornered in the South Pass rocks midway between Eudora and

Lander, had led some of the possemen to second thoughts. Perhaps, after all, the bandit's story was partway truthful. Maybe, as he so avidly claimed upon giving up, he had not fired a single shot in Eudora, and it had been the bullet of one of the townfolk that had felled the unfortunate Slim. There was some small case, at least, for waiting until Doc Hindemyer had dug out the slug from between Slim's eyes. If it did not fit the bore of Purcell's gun, then things would have to be reconsidered all the way around. The bandit would surely get ten years in the Territorial Prison, perhaps twenty years, but the rope would seem to be a poor risk right at the moment. So the hanging posse became a hanging-fire posse, and Walter Mendenhall, for one, was mightily pleased and relieved.

After a good supper of antelope steaks—one of the boys had taken a long lucky shot at a pronghorn on the gallop—the atmosphere eased even further. There was no longer much talk of stringing up the killer next day, but merely of taking him on into Lander where there was a decent jail and turning him over to the Fremont County sheriff, Harlow Willcott. The Eudorites would get all the credit for the chase and capture of "Killer Curly" Purcell, and the Lander folks could have the dubious privilege of transportation of the prisoner to trial.

The Eudora men settled in for a good night's rest on the prairie—always an occasion of some pleasure for townsmen caught up in the pressures of city life—and, short of dividing the watches over the tightly bound captive, little disturbance was made for a tougher verdict, once the antelope meat and strong-dog coffee had taken effect. Nothing will so bank the fires of vengeance in a Western man, Walter Mendenhall was forced to observe, as good meat, hot coffee, stout tobacco and the company of cowards of equal rank.

It was only eight hours after the brutal slaying of Slim

Watrous but already the air was cleared of lust and the sweet light of reason burned everywhere within the little high country pine flat where Curly Purcell's career of crime and violence had come to its inglorious end.

Walter was quite encouraged. Even the terrible suffering that was his from those hours bumping and clinging to the hard saddle and bony back of Slim's buckskin seemed now to be endurable, and indeed, worthwhile. This was law and order functioning as it should. It made a man proud to be a member of such a force in protection of the community. It was like no feeling Walter had experienced in his sheltered Chicago life. Out here, he decided, the real values were nearer the surface of everyday life. Civilization was a cleaner, more actual thing. It was a working word, and not just an expression of the effete and the weak and the untried of the big city. Even while he groaned aloud in the pain of his saddle wounds, Walter Mendenhall was happy. This was living. This was working. This was serving. It beat the daylights out of selling shoes.

He dozed. The night was balmy and beautifully still. Overhead the great white Wyoming stars stood guard in the blackness. Around about, the soft fragrant smells of the summer night spread their heated perfumes. Now and again a friendly, silly coyote yapped wildly from the ridge above. Far on up toward South Pass, a timber wolf howled lonesomely and long. It was wonderful. It made a man feel, for the first time in his life, that he was a male. It made him understand what "man" meant. Walter was amazed. He had never thought about it before, but he was a male animal. He had hair on his chest.

He came awake with a start. The huge form of Sheriff McCullers loomed over him. "Get up," the sheriff ordered. "I've sent Ed Jeeter on into Lander to have Sheriff Willcott alerted to our capturing of Purcell. That leaves you to stand his guard shift with young Jess Harper. Up.''

Walter stumbled to his feet, digging at his eyes, groping mentally and physically to come to grips with this latest extension of his newfound membership in the circle of malehood. ''Me?'' he croaked. ''Why me? I haven't even got a gun.''

''Jess has a gun,'' said McCullers. ''Move.''

He gave Walter a propelling shove up toward the gnarled cedar to which Purcell was pinioned. The friendly shoe salesman made no further resistance, but went on through the darkness to the cedar tree. Jess Harper was there waiting for him. ''How you feel?'' grinned the blond cowboy. ''Hope you ain't sleepy as me. Man alive, I can't get up the gumption to blink.''

''I'm fine,'' said Walter. ''I had a good nap.''

''Sure enough?'' queried the other. ''Say, maybe you'd keep an eye on both Purcell and McCullers for me.''

''What do you mean?''

''Oh, you know. Just let me get a little more sleep. Purcell ain't going no place. I tied him to that tree myself. Nothing but a knife will get him loose.''

''Why, I don't know,'' stammered Walter. ''That's quite a responsibility, but I guess I could handle it, if you say so. A man has to do his share.''

''That's so,'' nodded young Jess. ''And I might add that you're a pretty good man, too. I been watching you today.''

''Well, my word, thank you very much. It's hardly like selling shoes, but I rather like it. The air is so fresh and clean, and it's so quiet and all. I don't mind at all except that I'm awfully sore.''

''Shucks, you'll toughen to that in no time. Thanks for doing my shift. If you see McCullers coming up to check on us, give me a kick in the ribs. I'll be up bright-eyed and bushy-tailed quicker than you can say a dirty word."

"All right," said Walter Mendenhall, and the stillness resettled itself and for about ten minutes there was no sound up by the stunted cedar tree save the snoring of Jess Harper and the low, uneven breathing of the bound prisoner sitting at the foot of the tree. Then, softly, the doomed man spoke to his guard. "Mister," he said, "would you want to talk a little? It's mightily still up here, and there's only you and me. I won't be pleadful nor whimpery."

Walter leaned forward, looking at him closely for the first time that day. He saw a small, thin man, sunburned, blue-eyed, wispy-haired. He didn't look or sound or seem dangerous, but on the contrary was a quiet-voiced, twinkling-eyed man who appeared, and acted, as though he would be safe as sherry wine.

"Why, certainly," said Walter Mendenhall. "If you want to talk, talk. I'm not really a posseman, you know."

"What?" said the other, greatly surprised, "you're not? Why, I would have swored you was older at this game than McCullers hisself. And you say you ain't never rode out with a posse before? Well, I will be jiggered!"

Walter had not said that he had never ridden out with a posse before, and Curly Purcell did not look, truly, as if he were jiggered, or about to be jiggered, but Walter was highly pleased and Curly was not infinitely surprised to see him that way.

"Yes," said the Chicago shoeman, "it's true. This is my first manhunt. I must say that, so long as it has not come to—well, you know what I mean—it is a rather exciting thing as long as no one gets hurt."

"Sure," said the small pleasant outlaw, "that it is; I feel precisely the same way myself."

"I'm glad. I wouldn't want you to misunderstand me. It's not that I enjoy chasing a fellow like this. It's only that it is quite an adventure. You know, for a shoe salesman, that is."

"No!" said the other, amazed. "A shoe salesman? You? Why you set that buckskin like you was molded of straight cowboy clay. I never seed a man look any better in the saddle. I thought you was a rancher, or maybe a Texas Ranger in disguise. It's incredibelous. A shoe salesman! Imagine that? Why you seem born to the leather!"

Walter felt his chest enlarge. The terrible chafing redness of his inner thighs, the hot torment that burned the insides of his knees and ankles where the white skin was scraped down to the weeping flesh, disappeared to be replaced with a numbing throb that he would not have traded for the peace and serenity of kings.

"Well, I had a spotted Welsh pony when I was twelve. A man never forgets how to ride. It's like shooting a gun, or loving a woman. It just is a natural thing, *with a man.*"

"With *some* men," corrected Curly Purcell. "And I must say that you are one of them. You surely had me fooled. A shoe salesman. I can't get over it."

"It's true," admitted Walter. "I make almost seventeen dollars a week, plus commissions."

There was a pause during which the other shook his head regretfully, "I wish you hadn't told me that," he said at last, and softly. "It don't seem fair."

"I know," agreed Walter. "It is a great deal of money, but then I work very hard for it, and there is some element of risk involved."

"Oh, dear me, you mistook my meaning," said Curly Purcell. "I am so sorry. I hope you can find it in your heart to overlook it. I'm an uneducated man, and say things in a crude way. My heart, though, is sound. I wouldn't harm a housefly. Please say you understand."

Walter shook his head, puzzled.

"I would like to," he said, "but I can't. What is it that you've done?"

"Well, I said it's a shame about that money you make, and it is. Now that you force me to tell you, I must say that a man of your certain-sure ways and means ought to be making that much an hour, not a week."

"Seventeen dollars an hour?" said Walter Mendenhall. "Why, neither Mr. Jepson nor Mr. Officutt themselves draws that high a pay. You must be joking me because I'm a dude. That's all right, though; I expect that for a little while. A man has got to earn his way with other men. You don't just make it all in one day."

"No sir," said Curly Purcell, "you surely don't. My business, even, requires time to work up to the top. I do believe I was in it at least six months before I was making decent wages and had earned a name for myself in my profession."

"You mean," said Walter Mendenhall unbelievingly, "as a bank robber?"

"Oh, no," said the other quickly, "that's only a sideline; stage coaches are my main dish. You can lay out a better route and make your calls more often. Banks are too far apart and too few in number, really, to work out a good route on. Besides, there's more money in stages and the open air is healthier."

Walter waited a minute, gathering his thoughts.

Then he plunged bravely in.

"How many men have you killed, Mr. Purcell?" he demanded sternly.

Curly shrugged.

"Do you mean accidentally, or in the line of work?" he asked.

"Either," said Walter grimly.

"None," said the outlaw. "It's bad for business."

Walter frowned.

"But in Eudora they said you were a killer; that's what they called you. They said it as though you had done in plenty of men, say like Jesse James or Billy the Kid."

"That's ridiculous!" snapped the other. "You know how it is. They don't like to think they're chasing after a penny-ante thief. And they're not, either. But 'killer' sounds a lot wickeder and more noble to them when they tell about it at the saloon afterwards. Shucks, if I was really a gunman they wouldn't be within six miles of me this minute. McCullers has been a sheriff for twenty-six years and never drew a shot in anger from any outlaw, nor fired one hisself. It's all in the bandit business."

"How about Slim Watrous?" asked Walter accusingly.

"Was that the feller back in Eudora? Well, I done told the posse about him. I never even fired my gun back there. There wasn't no need. Nobody was shooting at me. They was all firing up in the air for show. One of them got a little low and plugged Slim, I suppose. It will happen now and again. Hazards of the trade." He was quiet for a moment, then said: "Friend, what did they tell you they meant to do with me? Was it take me into Lander and turn me over to Willcott?"

"Why, yes," answered Walter, "I believe that it was. Why do you ask?"

"Because," said Curly Purcell, "if Willcott gets me, I will never reach Laramie or Cheyenne alive."

"What!" said Walter. "What is that you say?"

"It's true," replied the meek outlaw, "and McCullers knows that it is. In Lander they are holding a warrant for me and have been for three years. I will never make it out of that town alive. They say I killed a man there, too. It is a black lie, but what good is the word of an ignorant, homeless man? They will hang me as surely as a skinned-out shoat in slaughter time."

"And you swear," asked Walter Mendenhall, "that you didn't do it?"

"Not alone that," said the sad bandit, "but I can prove I was in another territory at the time."

"Why," breathed Walter indignantly, "that's terrible!"

"It's worser than that," said Curly Purcell. "It's downright crooked."

A silence obtained, then, and for some two or three minutes neither man said anything. Finally, it was Walter Mendenhall who broke the stillness, as Curly Purcell had anticipated that he would.

"There must be some way," said the friendly Chicago shoe salesman, "to prevent a miscarriage of justice like that. . . ."

It was insane. Walter knew that later in his life he would look back and call it that. But he also knew that for this moment of that life he had risen to his true estate as a male of the species, and he was going to do what he had to do and let the consequences fall where they might.

The actual part of stealing the stock knife from the side trouser pocket of the heavily sleeping Jess Harper was nothing. To a Chicago boy skilled young in the art of lifting fruit from the peddler's cart, or sundries from the piled counters of the five-and-ten stores, the theft of the clasp knife was simple. Using it to sever Curly Purcell's bonds was another matter, and one requiring a strong shift of adult morals. But Walter made the transition. He did manage to cut Curly three or four times in the process, but he got him free and he did it without arousing Jess or any of the others in the sleeping camp farther down the flat. How Curly would escape from the point of his being freed of the ropes that bound him to the cedar tree, had not been arranged. Indeed, when Walter had hesitantly suggested that these later details might prove too many for solution, Curly had smiled his sad smile and said for Walter to leave the risk of such unknowns to him. He said that he had never had things easy in his whole life, and that it was no part of Walter's responsibility as a Samaritan to figure out every one of the angles of his new friend's getaway from the rank injustice awaiting him in Lander and the bogus murder warrant held there by Fremont County Sheriff Harlow Willcott.

It required ten minutes of chafing his limbs and walking and doing knee bends and suchlike exercises for Curly to get his circulation restored and to reckon that he was ready for the next part of it.

It was here that Walter Mendenhall was repaid for his Christian pity and good spirit.

Curly Purcell moved past him, bent over the sleeping Jess Harper and took carefully from its holster the long-barreled Colt's revolver the cowboy wore. He shoved the heavy weapon into the waistband of his trousers, but before he did that, he spun it up into the air in a road agent spin and caught it by the butt and, bending down again, put its steel barrel alongside Jess's blond head with sufficient skillful force to render unconscious the youth on the ground. Then, having holstered the gun in his pants' tops, he turned to Walter Mendenhall.

"My friend," he said in his soft, slow, and somehow sad tones, "we have come to the parting of the ways. Here we must take our separate roads toward what dark bourne of tomorrow no man knows. But I wish you well and I want to thank you once again for this opportunity to renew my career. Be assured that you will be well paid for this night's work, and that you will have good reason to remember Curly Purcell with some kindness."

He was talking strangely, Walter thought. All at once,

he was no longer the poor and uneducated, ignorant, itinerant victim of a vengeful society. His words had the ring of cynicism and certainly not of rude, untutored beginnings. ''Wait a moment,'' said Walter Mendenhall, and started forward. But Curly could not wait. And he did not.

He struck Walter very gently and very expertly with the pistol barrel, but he struck him all the same, and the big city salesman of Officutt-Jepson and Company, Chicago, went down soundlessly into the soft dust at the base of the cedar tree in the little pine flat at the foot of the high rocks leading upward to South Pass and to freedom for Curly Purcell. For a swift moment the slender outlaw, after retrieving something from beneath a nearby stone, worked over the body of the shoe drummer, then he stood up. He threw back his shoulders and stretched tall. Of a sudden he looked neither small nor insignificant, but rather lean and hard and glittering of light-blue eye. His jaw took on the hook of a fighting cutthroat trout, and his hand fondled the handle of the worn Colt as though it were the welcome grasp of an old friend, which it was, and then he glided off through the starlight down toward the sleeping camp as silently as a puff of smoke. For a man like that it was no trick at all to get Slim Watrous' tough buckskin gelding off the picket line and mount him and guide him away from the sleeping possemen. It was no more than ten minutes after Walter Mendenhall had pitched face-forward into the dust that the outlaw departed the pine flat on the best horse in the Eudora posse, and it was no less than three hours later before Jess Harper recovered consciousness and saw that the captive was gone. By that time, of course, Curly Purcell was far, far away, riding in what arcane direction and toward what next adventure of sudden gunfire no man might know. All that the disgruntled posse could do was to get up, relight the supper fire, boil up some more coffee and wait for daylight cursing the trailers' luck that had robbed them of the fame and possible reward-money fortune of bringing in William Tracy "Curly" Purcell.

As for his part, when fully recovered of consciousness and some degree of wits, as well, Walter Fargo Mendenhall took council with his inner soul and decided that the bandit had paid his debt and that for him, Walter, to reveal his insignificant role in the regeneration of Curly Purcell would be both vain and unwise. It might even be permanently disabling. Or at least damaging to his credit in Eudora and Lander. He doubted that Sheriff McCullers would understand. He was uncertain of Jess Harper and the others, too. After all, a man had been shot and $15,000 in currency was missing from the Bank of Eudora. You did not balance an account like that in southwestern Wyoming by cutting loose the overdrawn party. Even the fact that Curly had repaid the kindness with a pistol-barrel blow across the bony processes of the skull did not mitigate the circumstances of Walter Mendenhall's culpability.

Walter Mendenhall was the first to comprehend this legal technicality, as he was, or would be, the very last to violate it. His position was further guaranteed when, upon return to Eudora and his hotel room, he was reminded of Curly Purcell's final words to him. In going to empty out his pants pockets prior to packing the begrimed garments into his valise and donning his spare pair of pinstriped trousers, he was intrigued to find that Curly had left him a small legacy after the baronial manner of his outlaw kind. It was, in fact, the time-honored fifty-fifty split, and not one nickel missing of the sum.

In the bank's accounting of the loot there was an even $15,000 gone. In Walter Mendenhall's pants pockets, folded hastily but nonetheless neatly and with professional dispatch, was exactly $7,500 in $50 and $100 bills. Walter was aghast at the find, but not stricken stupid. In his limited legal opinion he was clearly accessory after the fact to the robbery of the Bank of Eudora, Wyoming. If he were to return the money it would be at clear threat to his freedom and his future. When, after careful investigation of the matter—including the news that Slim Watrous had been hit between the eyes by a stone fragment from the bank's granite facade and merely knocked out long enough for the posse to leave town—Walter made his final and irrevocable decision in the case of Curly Purcell.

He gave his remaining shoe samples to Packrat Annie, along with a quart of Old Crow and $5 cash of his own, that is to say, old wealth, and forthwith departed Eudora on the evening stage for a new start in life. With nothing in his heart but the inspiring example of William Tracy Purcell and no penny in his thread-bare pockets save the $7,500 of brand-new Government bills furnished on blind faith alone by the Bank of Eudora, he knew that it would not be easy. Yet somehow he believed that he would make it. If a man had confidence in himself, as a man, no obstacle could deter him. All it took was gullability and a sharp stock knife.

Sighing luxuriously, Walter Mendenhall lay back on the bone-hard cushions of the Rock Springs Stage.

His next conscious memory was of the coach making a tilting, skidding halt sideways in loose creek gravel, and of a thin, razor-edged voice ordering the driver to throw up his hands and for all passengers to pile out and elevate likewise. Terror seized him but did not have time to wrestle him for long. While he sought desperately about the confines of the Concord for a hiding place for his fattened purse, the door flew open and a tall slender outlaw took him by the coat lapels and literally threw him out of the Rock Springs Stage. Before he could recover himself, outside, the masked bandit had relieved him of his wallet, barked at the driver to wheel his teams on down the road, and was running off into the sagebrush beyond the creek crossing, toward his tethered mount.

Walter Mendenhall heard the ring of the horse's iron-shod hooves on the gravel of the creek bank briefly and in staccato measure. Then the robber was gone and he was alone with the darkness and the unruffled driver and the empty feeling in his inside coat pocket where recently had reposed the wages of his sin.

"Did you see his face?" asked the driver, swinging down to help him back into the coach.

"No," said Walter.

"How about the horse? Did you get a look at him?"

"No," said Walter, climbing aboard. "Why?"

"It was a buckskin," said the other man. "I would have swore it was Slim Watrous' old gelding, but it couldn't have been. That there wasn't Curly Purcell."

"No," said Walter Mendenhall. "Curly is short and skinny and stoop-shouldered."

The driver peered down at him. "You must mean some other Curly," he said. "Curly Purcell is wide and hefty and the size of a boar grizzly standing straight up."

Walter Mendenhall shook his head.

"Seven thousand five hundred dollars," he said.

"What's that?" called the driver, wheeling the teams and lurching the coach up out of the creek gravel.

"Seventy-five dollars," answered Walter Mendenhall; "I said I lost seventy-five dollars."

"Lucky it wasn't your life!" snorted the driver. "You sure you didn't see that horse?"

"Yes," said Walter wearily, "I saw him."

"Did you mark his color?"

Walter turned to the coach window, nodding slowly and sadly to the passing stars and the black Wyoming skies.

"Yes," he called back, "I did; he was a buckskin."

Ghost Town

Why was a town built there, at all? Who first stopped in that precise place and said, "this far will I go and no farther?" And when he had stopped and stayed, why did the others stop and stay, also? What was there in that time which is not there in this to excuse a settlement, to explain a small city, to attract a whole people?

The answer is somewhere in those silent winking panes of broken, dusty glass.

What was the original name of the crossroads hamlet? Not the name by which the weekending excursionists from the nearby big city call it today, but the name by which it was called when those windows were gleaming and new and unbroken, when that paint was bright and unpeeled, when those boards were green and alive with the honeyed sap of the sawmill, whose blue smoke arose from the mountains half a hundred miles to the west. What hopes, what dreams, what visions of a better tomorrow did they have, those people who came to this place, saying, "Here will I cast my lot and toil for my bread and make my home and rear my children and come at last to the dust that awaits us all"? And why did they think to dream these dreams on this sunbaked flat where now only lizards run and pack rats scuttle? What brought them to tarry here and seek to make true this mirage of a safe and abiding life where the only resident today is the stillness that hurts the ears and the only passerby the wind that edges the nerves and somehow makes the heart ache with loneliness and the soul reach yearningly across the echoing silence to the years of yesterday? Why here and not in another less lonely and alien place?

The answer is somewhere in the dust whorls that play down the white and red sand of the street, that lick at the tilting sills of the gray and umber houses, that pry at the banging doors and whisper among the silver weeds and brown grasses that lap, like sear and lifeless tides, at the shorings of these sinking hulls of the desert.

There is a ghost that stalks the stilled streets of this place. It never talks because no one will ever listen. The tourists only stare in vain at this paintless ruin of man's blood and toil and imagination, not seeing, with their ignorant and pitiless eyes the token and the toxin of their own tomorrow. They do not see the ghost. They do not want to listen to him. They want only to gape and to complain and to drink cold beer in the century-old tavern and to wander interminably sweating and grinning and arguing and talking very loudly, and looking earnestly into nothing but the prices of the trinkets on sale in the shabby stores and then, of course, for the whereabouts of the rest rooms and the slot machines.

But the ghost wanted to talk. He always came down into the town when the bus came out from the big city with its load of panting, red-faced sightseers. He wandered the streets waiting for someone to stop him and to say hello and to ask him to come and sit down over in the shade and to rest and perhaps talk a little, but no one ever did. Their gapes and stares and peerings went right past him. They looked but they did not see. It was a ghost town but they never thought to look for the ghost. The town was there. They could see its houses. They could touch them. When no one was looking they could steal some small piece of them to smuggle back aboard the bus and take back to the city and brag about to the neighbors who were not of the adventuring sort, or the nefarious. But the ghost they could not see, or would not see, and so he wandered in vain and wearily to find someone who would listen to his story and be made the custodian of those answers, those truths, which he had guarded the many, many years, and which had lain, and still lay, locked in the silent windowpanes and the whispering dust whorls.

Then the particular day and the particular busload of perspiring curious from the city arrived.

The ghost grew suddenly and at last alert, for one of the people getting down from the fuming, steaming vehicle looked down the long dusty street, saw him, smiled and waved and came toward him. . . .

They climbed up out of the town to a sunny bench of sandstone which looked out over the Pahquoc Valley. The boy, having studied the folder given out aboard the bus, could identify the Santilla Range across the valley, the desolate Cortege Mountains to the north, the treeless fangs of the Bay Rum Hills to the south. Where he and the old man sat, comfortable beneath an overhanging clump of red desert willow growing beside the spring of cold water that flowed from the rock and briefly down the tawny flank of the slope below, they were in the footstool hills of the Big Bernardinos. Above them lay pine trees and above the trees, mountain lakes and, in the winter, heavy snows. In the midst of so much space and silent grandeur the Pahquoc was not lost but indeed seemed the crown jewel in that ring of loneliness and awesome distance. The boy nodded, and waited for the old man to speak. The latter had told him that he knew of this view place where they might see the Pahquoc Valley as few since that first man had seen it these nearly one hundred years ago. The boy, he had said, might ride up on his old burro if he wished. Naturally, to a city lad, this was irresistible. So the old man had said for him to come along and look and listen. He had a story to tell, to pass on, really, he said, and it was always best in his opinion to put such responsibilities in the hands and hearts of the young people. Older folks didn't understand and wouldn't believe. Young folks, boys especially, were different. They wanted to learn and they made good listeners and they could remember what they were told, too. Girls were all right, the old man had admitted, except they were only small women and with all the faults of the big ones; especially not being able to remember things.

Now both the old man and the boy had gotten their wind back from the steep climb and the burro was chewing on the willow trees and the spring was gurgling with its wonderfully wet sound over among the shaded rocks and the time seemed about right for the beginning. It was. The old man was the one who nodded, now, and lit up his pipe.

"Bingham Springs," he said suddenly, "that's what they called it first. That's not what he called it, but what they called it, after him. The only name that he had for it was home. He never thought of it in terms of putting a name to it. Have you got a name for your house, boy?"

The boy shook his head.

"Of course not," said the old man. "For your dog you do, and for the kid down the street, or your teacher, but you don't call your house anything but home. That's the way Bingham was. He didn't have the vanity to attach his name to something God put there; he just moved in and was thankful to find such a fine place to hide and to rest up after his long journey across the desert."

"What was he hiding from?" asked the boy.

"From himself," said the old man, and sat smoking for several long seconds.

"You see," he went on, "Bingham had been hurt and he was afraid. He didn't dare settle near where there were other folks. He had tried that and had found only trouble and grief and pain. He didn't want any more of that. All he wanted was the quiet and the solace and the solitude that can be found only in the far places where other men are not, and don't want to be. You understand that, boy?"

The boy nodded soberly. "Sometimes I feel that way," he said. "Sometimes I get awful tired of trying to explain things to people. It's like about that old town down there. The way I feel about it isn't put in this book." He held up the tourist folder. "This book doesn't say anything that I wonder about. Like if there were boys like me playing down there in those streets long, long ago. And what games they played and if they had dogs and shinny sticks and all that. About girls too. Did they have any girls and what were they like and were they pretty like the girls today? and all like that. They don't tell you anything in this book."

"Sure," said the old man. "That's why you came up here with me, eh? I promised to tell you about the old town and you wanted to learn what you could; you climbed all the way up here with Mary Frances and me just so's you could learn something that wasn't in the book, isn't that so?"

"That's so," agreed the boy. "That, and also I felt you needed a friend, too. That you wanted to talk to somebody who would listen, just the same way I wanted to listen to somebody who would talk. You know how that is?"

"Yes," sighed the old man, "I surely do."

They sat silent again for a little time, allowing the warm sand-scented wind to waft up from the baking roofs below them and to stir the cool willows and lift the antelope flies off the burro's tough hide for a moment or two. Then the old man began again.

"Bingham came here," he said, "sometime in the fifties. That's the eighteen-fifties, boy; a long, long time back."

"Almost a hundred years," said the boy. "That's a century."

"You're a smart boy. I knew you were."

"Thank you. I liked you right off too. I always wanted to meet and talk with a real old desert prospector. Gold is great stuff. Did you ever find any? I mean, much?"

"I never did, no. I was lucky in different ways."

"But you are a sure enough prospector, aren't you?"

"Of a kind, of a kind. Don't you want to hear the story, boy? You changed your mind?"

"No sir," denied the boy vehemently. "Not an inch. I just get excited when I think about gold."

"I know, I know," said the old man. "Listen to this . . ."

Originally it was only the wasteland.

When Bingham came out of the desert following the Pahquoc wagon road which went on up through the Bernardinos to California and the sea, there was nothing to be seen of value at the place where the stunted cottonwoods, twisted sycamores and few scrub willows grew and where the road dipped down into and then up out of the great wide wash of parched sand, and where the good cold water came up out of the hot red and gray sandstone and made the overnight oasis for the few travelers to the promised land who came that southern, mercilessly torrid way across the barrens of the Colorado to Spanish California.

But Bingham looked about that place, and felt something.

It wasn't anything of worth, anything which might be harvested and sold. He found there only the cry of the wolf and the wind and the burn of the sun and the cool blessing of the night and the magic lantern of the desert moon and the wondrous lonely silence of the white stars.

Yet Bingham felt something, and he stayed.

He built himself a small house after some time had passed and his fright and weariness had gone and his pride begun to return. He cleared the artemesia and the greasewood and the juniper and joshua and made fences of cedar poles from the nearby foothills to show himself the nature and extent and the reassuring geometry of his fields lying about his house. Still, there was nothing there. When the fields had lain thus some time, he made a plowshare at his own crude forge and put his single toothless mule to it and broke the dry red crust of the desert land and made furrows in his fields so that they would look more like the fields where he had come from. But it was no help. There was still nothing there, and not even weeds. If he had some seed, then he would have no water to make them sprout and to keep them coming after they had sprouted. There had to be water. Otherwise the cottonwoods and sycamores that shaded his small house and the little vale where the travelers parked their wagons to rest and water their teams would not grow where they did. And neither would the willows which, thin and yellow-green, outlined the bed of the dry wash which came down from the hills, and behind them from the high Bernardinos. But that water was far underground and creeping in the crevices and fractures of the sedimentary rock under the hot sand, and no man could get it out of there in enough quantity even to bother digging a well. Oh, a deep well dug in among the largest of the sycamores—the sycamores always were the best water witches in a dry land—would yield, yes, that was true. Even a shallow well, if luckily dug to hit the right breaking and draining of the rock slanting down from the hills and mountains, would fill slowly and water a man's thirst and the thirst of his mule and that of his dog, if he had one, but that was all. It would not fill enough to use for watering a patch of greens, or of feed for the mule, even. Bingham knew that. He had learned much of this desert country, for he had lived in it since fleeing his farmland past and whatever it was that had driven him, years gone, into the wastelands of the west. And so, having the cool spring to water his thirst and the thirst of his mule and of the lean, ribby, blue merle sheepdog that trotted everywhere by his side or in the tracks of the old mule, he dug no well and wasted no yearning for better than he had. Yet still those empty fields and those brown furrows devoid of green life worried him and made him think.

Travelers continued to pass that way, for his springs were the only surface water for three days travel to the east and two to the west. These voyagers-through were glad to see the oasis and even the strange, little-spoken man who lived there, but they laughed at him, or at least shook their heads in doubt or superiority or, if they were kind, in pity. True, they drank from his watering place and even began, after a while, to call his camp Bingham Springs. They drank from the basin he had dug out and rocked up to catch the flow of the water, and their small children and their old people bathed in the overflow pool that Bingham had made with his shovel and his sweat into a pond thirty feet by fifteen feet and three to four feet in depth, the largest single show of fresh water west of Colorado's channels, or its overflows, and east of the snow-water lakes in the high California mountains fifty miles and four thousand feet upward from Bingham's oasis beside the great dry wash called the Pahquoc, and so named after the immense sun-blasted valley that it watered with its shifting sands and gray boulders borne down upon the melting freshets of spring and the sparsely scattered cloudbursts from the high peaks in midsummer. Flash floods they called them, the desert people, and the water they brought down in torrents was of no service to any man or any beast, but only moved the sand and boulders to different places and left them in varying patterns to simulate a great river and its tributaries but without one drop of permanent or of flowing, useful water to be seen. So the travelers laughed about Bingham and the "Pahquoc River" and the seedy old mule and cockle-burred ancient dog with the one blue and the one yellow eye, and only eight teeth remaining. Also, as they laughed and shook their heads at Bingham, they took his help in every way it was offered, which was in every way that Bingham could afford, and they went on with no thought of paying any money or leaving anything of value in payment for the water or the bathing place or the labor and advice that Bingham gladly gave them. Here was a grizzle-bearded fool of a desert rat living alone in the middle of nowhere and it was he who should be grateful to them for stopping, not they who might owe him some debt of survival, actually, or at very least goodhearted aid, comfort, information on the trails and waterholes ahead and on the spots where they could expect to encounter the Pahquoc Indians. But Bingham never complained. He took his pay in the laughter of the children playing in his rocked-up basin below the springs and in the grateful looks of the old people who knew they might not live to see the Pacific Ocean or, if they did, that they would not care too greatly for the view. The others, the middle-aging mothers and fathers, the ones who owned and drove the wagons, they, too, were looking for places to live, pieces of land to work, homes to call their own and peace and quiet and protection, the same as Bingham was. But this place of his here in the desert was nothing, it was a wasteland, nobody but a fool far off in his mind would want such land or could abide staying on it. As for anyone who would actually plow or fence it in, as Bingham had done, well, in a civilized community, they had names for such cases and they were put into county homes and kept locked up and safely away from normal folks and their innocent little kids. And so they hitched up and drove on and if they ever found what they were looking for Bingham never knew. None of them came back that way, or sent word, or by any act or thought remembered or paused to care about the man who gave them water and rest and bread, if he had it, at Bingham Springs in the Pahquoc Desert. . . .

It was a cold late winter day that Old Tap died. It was a sad day for Bingham and yet an exciting one, too. When he went down toward the dry riverbed to bury his old friend, Bingham had only his rusted shovel and the body of the old dog dragged behind him on a little sled made of cottonwood limbs lashed together. When, half an hour later, he had dug the grave for Old Tap two feet deep into the sand and silt of the wash's bottom, Bingham had a fortune which no man could assay—or he had an idea that he had such a fortune. He became extremely agitated at the condition of the sand in the bottom of the hole, and he put down his shovel and he left Old Tap lying on the cottonwood sled. Fetching the mule, he climbed upon it and rode away up the big dry wash into the low Ocatillo Hills and, through them, on toward the Big Bernardinos. When he had ridden all day and was at the foot of the big range, he saw before him a peculiar wall of dark rock. The wall was hundreds of feet high and the bed of the dry wash appeared to run blank up against the wall and to end there. But Bingham knew better. At the base of the towering stone buttress grew thick willows and giant sycamores and three-and four-hundred-year-old cottonwoods, and Bingham shouted to the mule, urging it upward across the forbidding face of the great dark dam of bedrock that seemed to cut off the bed of the waterless Pahquoc River.

Just at sunset and with the range above burning red and black in the last light, Bingham and the mule topped out on the cross ridge and saw what lay behind it. The mule stretched out its homely muzzle and brayed with pleasure at the scent coming to them. The man, Bingham, could not move, he was so struck with the sight of the gleaming green water and thick dark bands of trees and emerald grass that grew beside it and followed its sparkling channel upward through the narrow V-shaped canyon to disappear into high mountains beyond. The sight was enough to strike any man speechless, but more than most men would it render awed and silent a man of the desert. On the mountainside of the great stone dike the Pahquoc was a live stream of gorgeous clear green water, rushing and tumbling and swirling among the rocks and sandbars of its canyon-bottom course. On the desert side, mere thousands of feet through the base of the cross-flung dike of mother rock, it was a dusty-dry and lifeless channel of sand and random mountain debris of tree limbs and boulders washed into its course from its many side-channels spurring in from the other, adjacent flanks of the steep Big Bernardino Range. Bingham sat there on the old mule and took off his ragged felt hat and held it unconsciously at his breast, and felt very near to God and to things not understood by mortal man and brute beast.

The Pahquoc River, his river of rocks and parched silica and red silt, was not a dry wash and not a joke over which the travelers through his homeplace could shake their heads and feel sorry for that old fool Bingham. The Pahquoc was a live stream—it flowed and sparkled and smelled wondrously fresh; and by some miracle of nature and of the higher intelligence of Him, up there, it disappeared into the sands of the Pahquock Desert at the foot of the Bernardinos and flowed, from there, how many a hundred mile no man knew, out under that furnace heat and hell of blasted rock and sand to end in a place none would ever find. But what Bingham knew and what he understood at once was that he had discovered the legendary underground river of the Pahquoc, and he knew then, with a great and lifting joy, that this was the secret of the centuries-old cottonwoods and sycamores that flowered in the wasteland at his resting place on the Pahquoc wagon road. His home and his homestead stood upon the banks of a river of fresh and vital clear water—a river that flowed as surely and as life-givingly a few feet beneath the heartless sands, as any which swept and roiled its currents upon the surface of a richer and more verdant land.

Bingham realized that he was rich.

He knew that at last he had found not only peace but security, that shifting, uncertain and priceless thing for which all search their lives away, and mostly in vain.

He turned the old mule down toward the green channel and that night the moth-eaten animal grazed in such pastures as it had never known, nor would again. For his part, Bingham, too, was happy past reasonable measure. From his cheery campfire of driftwood, he listened far beyond midnight to the rushing music of the water going to its arcane grave at the foot of the great stone dike. It was a sound of angels to any desert wanderer, and when it was mingled with the friendly yapping of the coyotes upon the hills above, the querulous but not inimical yelps of the kit and gray foxes coming to water above his camp, and with the keening, long cry of the timber wolf in the dark pines far above, then a man knew heaven as closely as he would ever know it in terms of the earth.

Next morning Bingham went back along the bottom of the Bernardinos to the Ocatillo Trail that went to California from his crossing fifty miles westward in the desert. He followed the trail over the mountains and to the Pacific settlements, and there he filed in the U.S. Land Office upon the place where his springs were. When he was certain of this legal thing, he went home with the old mule and got to work.

First, he made a Fresno scraper from the iron back of an old wood-burning range abandoned in his grove by a party of Kansas folks. It was only a third or fourth the capacity of a real scraper, but Bingham had his whole life to spend and was not in haste. Beginning at the grave of Old Tap—the faithful brute lay now in the rocks of the sycamores above the springs—he scooped away the bed of the Pahquoc at a point well above his already plowed and furrowed fields. He worked for weeks and when he was done he had a deep pond, deeper than the withers were high on the bony old mule, or than his own dusted hat crown was high above his gray and pepper and stained yellow beard and his sun-scorched face. Toward the end he was working first in ankle-deep water, then in knee-deep water. When he finally quit and put aside the scraper the water lay green and clear and stirring with the current of life in an artificial lake a hundred feet long and half as wide. Then, never pausing, he set to work on the apparatus he would use to lift the water out of the riverbed and into the laterals, the irrigation ditches, that led to his various fields. He had seen the device in old books when he was a boy, and it was the same arrangements of a vertical wooden wheel with bucket scoops turned by a horizontal second wheel powered then, as in the Biblical times of the pictures he remembered from the book on Egyptian history of the Nile, by a plodding, fly-bitten and patient mule.

When, in earliest spring, all was ready, Bingham put the old animal into the wheel harness and started it upon its way around and around and around. With squeaking axles and groaning spokes, eased as they complained with huge daubs of antelope tallow, beginning to turn and to interlock and to work perfectly, the first of the bright green water came gurgling and splashing up out of the river-pool reservoir and spilled with a race and splash down the laterals and along them into the secondary and tertiary ditching rows that led its eager currents into the fields by the side of the dry and dust-bound Pahquoc River.

When, in several days of turning the two wheels and dipping the green water into the laterals above the reservoir, the earth in the fields had become wetted and dark sienna and burnt umber in color, rather than vermilion and seared yellow and dead gray, Bingham took the old mule out of the wheel harness and put him to the plow and turned the moistened furrows and put into them by a seeding device of his own fertile invention, the various cereals and leafy forage crops that he wanted to see flourish there in the desert by the glory of God and the strange wonder of the upside-down river that He had led Bingham to discover and to bring to yield.

In due time, with the water brought thus to his red fields, those fields became green and golden. Springtime was gone then and the travelers were coming through from the east, and when they saw what was going forward there in the desert at Bingham Springs, they no longer laughed, or shook their heads, or felt sorry for Bingham.

Indeed, they showed him respect and now, when they had gone on to the California settlements they did come back again and they did remember Bingham, and why not? The verdant jewel he had wrought from the sand of the wastelands could be seen from forty and fifty miles away, by the naked eye. It was the only greenery between the Colorado and the Big Bernardinos. It was a paradise in the wilderness, and now other men saw what Bingham had always seen there in that great sandy solitude. They, also, went into the U.S. Land Office on the other side of the mountains and filed on the rich land up and down the channel of the Pahquoc from Bingham's place. Soon there was a happy and a contented crossroads there. A store was built. And a forge. And the stageline routed its coaches through the place and the newcomers worked hard and were good people and meant to stay and live and die there, like Bingham before them. They built community irrigation systems, and community waterwheels and were very safe and rewarded there in the wasteland with their small farms and their few green trees and careful little fields and their upside-down river. Time passed quickly and well for all. Bingham found that his new neighbors were new friends and that now they did thank him for his work and his discovery and his faith, and that they were proud to live with him there and to be all of the same family. No inquiry was ever made of his past, except as it pertained to his life at the springs, and gradually he returned to something of his old confidence and courage and good heart. It was good to be among people again, and to find them depending upon you, and you upon them. That was God's plan, anyway, and Bingham was very happy to once more be a part of it.

More years slipped away and some changes came about.

The few who had first settled there grew to several and the several to enough. Windmills and water pumps of far superior force and flow were introduced into that country and came, soon, to the springs. The Pahquoc was still of adequate strength for these and even though the small fields grew large, and then huge, some of them, and the town went upward in size and number of inhabitants to match its renewed wealth of underground water and expanded boundaries of green crops, it was still a village of landowners and workers of the land. They gave it a new name, then, to be sure. It was Willow Springs. This sounded more like a town of importance than Bingham Springs, and besides, although much had been owed to Bingham in the beginning, the debt had long been paid. Now the town was in a new phase of its growth and needed a fresh name. Bingham thought this was as it should be, too. He had been somewhat forgotten and was not consulted in these rich years, as he had been in the beginning seasons long ago. But he held no hardness within him and was still happy to live at the springs, no matter which name they were given. In a way this was his town, these were his people. He had brought them there and they had built the place through the good years, and it had all started with him, Bingham.

Yet nothing truly good is left to endure in peace by the restless minds and reaching grasps of men. Willow or Bingham Springs was not built alone over a river of underground water; another treasure lay beneath the Pahquoc. . . .

When the other man came to Willow Springs in the 1860's he too, like Bingham in the beginning, was looking for something. It wasn't peace and safety. It wasn't plowed fields and irrigation water. But he was looking for something and he found it.

He came there and examined the dry bed of the Pahquoc and nodded to himself. He worked up the riverbed among the debris washed down from the mountains, and he continued to nod. Then he came back and he rented a pack mule and another mule to ride, from Bingham, who had lost the old mule by now, and he told Bingham that he wanted to ride up the river and follow it to its source and to see what Bingham had seen all those years ago behind that dark wall of rock that sent the Pahquoc underground up there at the foot of the Big Bernardinos. Bingham could understand that wanting to know about the strange river that ran upside-down, and he rented the mules to the new man and wished him well. But Bingham was very wrong. He didn't understand, at all, what that man wanted to know about the Pahquoc River.

After a brief time, the man was back in Willow Springs and he brought with him papers to show that he had filed on the dry lands above and below the irrigated fields along the Pahquoc. He then had other men of the town go into the settlements across the mountains and file on more claims above his, and he bought these claims from the men when they came back to Willow Springs with title to them. Only he didn't call them claims. He said he was acquiring land to run cattle on, as he had an idea the desert in spring would be good browse, if a man owned enough deeded land to build his headquarters ranch and owned enough of the riverbank land to guarantee sufficient water—riparian rights, he called it—to protect his investment in animals to stock the barren range. The townsfolk were pleased to cooperate with him, and file for him, as he assured them he would need the green forage crops, the grains and hay grasses they could grow on their irrigated fields. He would buy from them to feed his cattle when the spring browse was gone from the desert, and between them they would put Willow Springs on the map as a beef and hide center, as well as a field-crop center, and everybody would do better and better all the while.

Somehow, Bingham didn't care for this talk. But he put his misgivings aside, as he well knew that his own likings for solitude and peace were not matched by the desires and needs of his younger neighbors with their growing fields and their growing families and their growing hopes for the town they had founded in the wilderness. So he did not say anything against the newcomer or his ideas about raising market steers where the jack-rabbits had a hard time making out. But there was something wrong, all the same, with the entire proposition, and with the man who had brought it with him to Willow Springs.

It was not long after that, after he had bought up all the deeded land he could along the river, that the inquisitive man rented more mules and scrapers and men and wagons and began building beside the Pahquoc a stamp mill, and then the people knew. The underground river was not only a treasure trove of pure water, but of bright and glittering gold. News of the strike spread as such news always does and within a month there was no more Willow Springs there at the old crossing of the Pahquoc wagon road but a new town called Selkirk, after the man who had rented the two mules from Bingham, and it wasn't a town any more but a city for it had 5,000 people living there in less than thirty days, and the man, now grown old and ailing, who had first come there and stayed by the little springs and helped the travelers who passed his way, knew that it was time for him to move on and to find another place where there were no people, no people at all, and to begin again if he could find the will and the heart and strength to think about it, and to do it all from the very first again. And so he sold his two mules and his homestead by the old crossing and he gave the land to the Selkirk School District for the building of a high school and a normal school and a grade school. Then he bought a small brown burro, a female it was, as they were the more faithful, and set forth from Selkirk to find a better strike. People shook their heads and said that he was crazy, after all, and they promptly forgot about him and about how their town had started and what had made it prosper and become strong.

Greed grew in Selkirk after Bingham had gone, and ambitious men, needing more and more water with which to work Selkirk's four stamp mills and one refinery, which took the gold from the weird strata of quartzite found, as such rock is never found, among sedimentary sandstones and mother granites up at the head of the Pahquoc, and made of this native ore the pure metal in a matter of 48 hours, these men, heeding nothing of the warnings that old miners and prospectors made, planted great charges of powder in deep holes drilled in the riverbed rock. Then they put the match to these charges and blew the riverbed for a quarter of a mile in both directions from Bingham's springs, hoping to fracture the strata and to open it wider and permit heavier and much swifter flows of the water from the mountains above.

The result of the great explosion was something sinister and strange. The river, rather than increasing its flow, ceased to flow altogether, and then the terrified diggers and bull-prod drillmen and powder monkeys and engineers of the Selkirk Mining Corporation knew what they had done: they had fractured the water flow into another, unknown channel deep within the earth. It never rose again in the bed of the Pahquoc River at Selkirk City, which is what they were calling the place at that time. The walls of the Bingham high school and teachers college, already rearing where the original springs had gushed and now were gone with the river, paused in their construction and partly stood and partly crumbled away, and in either case were forgotten of both purpose and pledge.

Selkirk City was returned to the kit foxes, the cactus owls, the pack rats and the white-footed desert mice. Within six months it was standing the way that it stands yet, empty-windowed and forlorn, dust-whorled and weed-grown, sinking into a sea of sand and waiting, as it waits today, for a tomorrow that will never come and for a day beyond that which will come all too soon and stay forever.

"Well," said the old man, "I must go. See, down there, your bus is ready. You better be off down the hill yourself. I've enjoyed the talk, boy. It was kind of you to say 'hello' down below, and to give me the chance to get shut of my tale. How'd you like it?"

"It was kind of sad, mister," said the boy. "But I didn't mind that, really. You see, it seems to me that old Bingham did well, and that was the main thing. He didn't give in and quit, just because things didn't behave the way he thought they should. I guess it worked out all right. What do you think?"

"I'm not sure," said the old man. "Somehow, though, I feel better now. I've got an idea you're right; that things will work out all right. That's because you listened so good, I think. I believe you'll remember."

"Sure I will. I never would forget you or Mary Frances or Old Tap or any of it."

"How's that, boy? What's Old Tap to do with me and the burro? You strung that altogether there as though it went of one piece. You don't want to get the story mixed up with me and Mary Frances. We're just a couple of old desert rats. We come down just to see the folks get off the bus, and maybe have a kind word with one of them now and again, like with you."

"I know. Don't you worry, mister. I've got it all straight. You can trust me."

The old man peered at him, and nodded. "Yes," he said, "I reckon I can. I reckoned I could to begin with. You better go now, lad. Me, too. We got a long way over the mountain, me and Mary Frances. We'll never make it by dark, unless we start right soon."

"How far do you go?" asked the boy.

"A long way." He pointed. "Way up there, where the pines get dark and the snow shows white."

"You live up there? That high? Isn't it too cold?"

"Yes, it's cold sometimes. And lonesome. But it's going to be better now. Maybe I won't go back up there, after all. Maybe I'll just go fetch my things and come back down below. It'll be warmer, like you say, and not so lonely and off the trail."

"Sure," said the boy, "and it'll be closer to home for you and Mary Frances. I wish you'd do it."

Again the old man studied him.

"Yes," he nodded, after a long time, "I think you're right. I believe I will settle in Selkirk City. It's not so crowded any more since the river's dried up. Maybe I could rest here now. There's sure no one to bother me."

"That's so," said the boy, "and your work is done now and no need for you to go on wandering. You're real old. As old as Selkirk City, I think. I would worry about you all alone up there in the high mountains."

"I'll do it!" said the old man, enthused. "I'll go up and fetch Old—" he broke off, stammering a little, then went on, "that is, I'll have to go back up and bring down my dog. I left him on guard up there at the camp in the high timber. He'll be glad to hear the news, too; he always liked it better down here in the desert."

"What kind of a dog have you got?" asked the boy.

"Just a dog," said the old man. "Nothing special. But he's been with me a spell. I wouldn't want to do him any wrong. You get attached out here in the quiet."

"Sure," said the boy, "I had a dog once. He wasn't anything special either. Nothing at all like Old Tap was to Mister Bingham, say. But I loved him pretty hard."

"Goodbye, boy," said the old man. He went over and untied the burro and said, "Come along, Mary Frances, we have many a mile to climb." He started up the trail away from the little sandstone bench and the spring of cold water above Selkirk City and the boy waved and smiled after him and called out, "Goodbye, Mister Bingham; say hello to Old Tap for me!" and the old man stopped and turned and waved back and smiled in his turn, but said no more and was soon gone out of sight upon the mountainside, into the first of the dark pine timber reaching down from the snows above. It was an odd, still moment there on the tawny hillside, and rather eerie, too. But the boy wasn't worried by it, or frightened in any way. If he thought it peculiar that the first of the pine timber was several miles away and above the yellow hills of the Ocatillos, and yet that the old man and the ragged-eared burro had seemed to reach that timber in a matter of minutes, while the boy watched and waved, he never bothered himself or anyone else about it. He was that kind of boy. He took things as they came along to him and didn't examine them until they fell apart and were shredded to nothing.

His spirits rising, he turned away from the mountains and started down the dusty trail to Selkirk City and the waiting bus. He was content with the story of the town and he was no longer disturbed by the mystery of the stillness in which it lay glistening and rusting and dry-rotting in the sun of the near-century that had passed since it was first named Bingham Springs. He believed what he felt was right to believe; and it was thus that the old man was able to light in his heart the beacon of continuing hope, and to plant in his unspoiled mind the seed of desire that would lead him to seek out his own Willow Springs and build it into his own Selkirk City to leave behind him when his own time came to wander on in the search that never ends for a better and brighter next day.

For the boy's part, he was always very sure that he had talked to the old man who had discovered the great underground river nearly a hundred years before. Getting into the big city bus, he did not bother to tell his fussy, work-worn mother, or his fat, perspiring father what he had heard, or where he had been, and with whom. He knew better than that. Parents never believed anything children, their children, told them. Grownups in general never believed what they themselves didn't see, or couldn't see, or wouldn't admit to if they did see.

So he kept quiet and looked out the bus window across the glimmering heat beyond the desiccated rocks of Selkirk City and he saw what he saw—the great irrigated green valley of the mysterious underground river as it bloomed and flourished a century gone—and he knew what he knew, and he could still hear the old man's last words to him as clearly as though the old fellow were saying them once again, right on the bus, but only for him and not for the others, who would not listen, anyway.

"The answer to what built the town, lad? Why, it was faith, boy; that's as clear as the water in the old Pahquoc. . . . One man's faith and the faith of his fellowmen to back it up. When that faith was gone, the town was gone. There never was anything there but faith to begin and to end with. There is never anything but faith anywhere. . . . It's all that a man has ever had to build upon. . . ."

The small, sober-faced boy was asleep on the seat.

The fussy mother nudged the fat father and said,

"Huh, lookit him. Tuckered out, I guess."

The father grimaced. "My God," he said irritably, "who ain't? That damned heat. My feet are killing me."

"It's kind of pretty," sighed the weary mother, looking out the window at the sear ochre of the desert. "Awful dry and hot, but kind of pretty."

The father groaned and pried off his shoes.

"It stinks," he said. "Selkirk City; what a graft! I'll bet some movie outfit built it for a western and let it sit there and rot when they was through. My God, people are sure stupid. The whole thing's a phoney!"

The woman looked out the window again, and shook her head. She was frowning faintly.

"Well, maybe," she said. "I don't know."

The Trap

Canady felt the horse beginning to go rough beneath him. He had been expecting it. On this rocky going no mount could make it for long when he was already ridden out in coming to it. ‘‘Easy, easy,’’ he said to the laboring animal. ‘‘It’s only a posse.’’ The horse seemed to understand the tone of the words, for it slowed and went better and steadier for a ways. ‘‘We’ll rest on the rise ahead,’’ Canady said. ‘‘I can see back a few miles and you can catch some wind and we’ll go on. We’ll make it.’’

He knew they wouldn’t. He knew it before they came to the rise and he got down and walked out on the overhanging spur of gray-black basalt that gave view down the canyon behind them for ten miles. It wasn’t a canyon, really, but a narrowing valley. The canyon proper lay before them. Canady grinned and wiped his streaming face. It was hot, and going to get hotter. ‘‘Hoss,’’ he said, "they're pushing. They mean to take us. They must know the country ahead. They don't ride like there's any hurry." The horse, now, did not respond with its ears and a turning of its soft eyes, as it had before. It stood, head-down, blowing out through its distended nostrils. Canady came back and squatted down and put his hand below the nose of the horse, where the moisture of its pained breathing would strike his palm. "Damn," he said softly. "Blood."

He got his field glasses from the saddle pocket and examined the pursuers through them. "Eight," he said aloud, "and six ropes. I wonder how come it is that they always fetch so many ropes? Never saw a posse yet didn't feel they'd each of them ought to have a rope."

His fingers went to his sunburned neck. They felt it tenderly, and he grinned again. "Son of a gun," he said, "it could happen."

Canady's grins were not the grimaces of a fool, or of an unfeeling man. They were the grins of a gambler. And of an outlaw. And a thief. Canady knew where he was and where he had been and, most apparently, where he was going. It did not frighten him. He would grin when they put the loop over his head. That was his kind. He wouldn't curse or revile, and he wouldn't pray. Not out loud, anyway.

"Hoss," he said, "what do you think?"

The animal, slightly recovered, moved its ears and whickered gruntingly. Canady nodded, turning his back to the approaching posse and glassing the country ahead. "Me too," he agreed. "A grunt and a whicker is all she's worth. We haven't got no place to go." He tensed, as he said it, the glasses freezing on an opening in the rearing base rock of the closing valley. It was to their right. A good horse, fresh and sound, could take a man up to that gap in the cliff. The spill of detritus and ages-old fan of boulders and stunted pine that lay below its lip would permit of perilous mounted passage. There was water up there, too, for Canady could see the small white ribbon of the stream splashing down a rainbow falls to mist up upon the lower rocks in a spume of red and yellow and turquoise green lights, splendid with beauty in the early sun. "I take it back," he said. "Maybe we do have a place to go. Pretty, too, and handy to town. You can't beat that."

Directly ahead was a level sunlit flat, dotted with tall pines and scrub juniper and house-sized boulders. The clear stream from the high hole in the right-side valley wall watered the flat, growing good mountain hay upon its sandy red loam and making a ride across it a thing to pleasure the heart of any Western man.

"Come on," said Canady to his horse. "You canter me across the flat and I'll climb the fan afoot leaving you to pack up nothing but the saddle and the grub sack. You game? Least we can do is make those birds scratch for their breakfast. And who knows? Our luck might change. We might get up there and into that hole-in-the-wall before they come up to the rise, here, and spot us. If we can do that, there's a chance they'll ride on by, up the valley, and we can double back tonight and make it free."

He was talking to Canady, now, not to the horse. It was the way of men much alone and when they needed to do some figuring. They would do it out loud, the way Canady was doing. It sounded better that way, more convincing, and more as though it might really come off. Canady even swung into the saddle believing his own advice, telling himself what he wanted to know, then accepting it as a very good chance indeed. Again, it was his way. A man didn't live by the gun and the good fast horse without acquiring a working philosophy with lots of elastic in it.

"Move out," he repeated to the horse. "It's your part to get us across the flat in time."

The little mustang humped its back and shook itself like a wet dog. Running sweat, and caked, as well, flew from its streaked hide. It's gathering of itself in response to the rider's words was a visible thing. The horse was like the man. It wouldn't quit short of the last second, or step, or shot. They were of a kind with the country around them. It was all the edge they had ever needed.

Canady panted. He wiped the perspiration from his eyes and started upward again. Behind him, the little horse came on, unled, the reins looped over the horn so as not to trail and be stepped on. He followed the man like a dog, panting with him, struggling where he struggled, sliding where he slid, and lunging on as he did, after each setback.

They had made nearly the top of the fan of fallen rock below and leading into the opening of the side canyon. In another four or five minutes they would be clear of the climb. They would be off the slide and safely into the notch in the high wall of the valley. They would be out of sight of the posse, and the posse still had not come into view of them on the rise back across the pine flat.

"Easy, hoss," gasped Canady. "We're going to make it."

But Canady was wrong. Thirty yards from the top, the mustang put its slender foreleg into a rock crevice and drew back quickly. The movement set the slide moving and caught the leg and crushed it like a matchstick below the knee. When the horse had freed itself and was standing hunched and trembling behind Canady, the shattered leg hung sickeningly a'swing and free of the ground, and Canady cursed with tears in his eyes. It was not the luck of it that brought his angry words, but the shame of it. It was his pity and his feeling for a gallant companion that had given its all and almost found it enough.

The hesitation, the wait there near the top of the slide, near the safety of the hole-in-the-wall, was the natural thing for a Western man. His horse was hurt. It was hopelessly hurt. He would have to leave it, but not like that. Not standing there on three legs hunched up in the middle with pain and fright. Not standing there watching him with those liquid brown eyes. No, he couldn't leave his horse like that.

But how else? He couldn't shoot the mustang, for the noise would key the posse to his location. Had he had a knife he could cut its throat. Or had he an ax he could have crushed its skull above the eye-socket and put the poor devil down painlessly. With a rock he might be able to stun the brave little brute, but he could not be sure of killing it cleanly. The same held true for the butt of his Colt or the steel-shod heel of his Winchester. He could stun the horse, likely put it to its knees, but not, still, be able to go on knowing it would not recover and try to get up again and go on, and so suffer as no horse-riding man could think to let his mount suffer. But, damn it, this was *his* life he was arguing with himself about. It wasn't the damned horse's life. If he didn't do something and do it quick, the posse would be over the rise and he and the horse could go to hell together. Well, he would use the Colt butt. He knew he could hit the exhausted animal hard enough with it to put it down for the necessary time for himself to get on into the hole-in-the-wall and for the posse to ride by and on up the valley. That was all the time he needed, or at least it was all he could ask for. He pulled the Colt and started back to the horse sliding and stumbling in his hurry to get to the trembling beast and knock it down. But when he got up to its side, when he looked into those dark eyes, he couldn't do it. He had to be sure. "The hell with the posse," he said to the little horse, and spun the

Colt in the air and caught it by the handle and put it behind the ragged ear and pulled the trigger. The smoke from the shot was still curling upward, and the little pony just going slowly down, when the first of the pursuing riders came up over the rise across the flat and yelled excitedly back to his comrades that the game was in sight, and on foot.

Canady went up the little stream. Behind him, where it fed the rainbow falls leaping outward into the main valley, the possemen were just topping the detritus fan and closing in on "the hole." Back there Canady had made a decision. It was not to stay and fight from the entrance cleft of the hole, where the little rivulet went out of the side canyon. He did not know what lay on up the side canyon, and feared there might be a way by which the possemen, familiar with this territory, could ride a circle and come in behind him. He could not risk that, he believed, and must go on up the creek as far as he could, hoping it would be far enough to find a place where he could put his back to the wall and fight without their being able to get behind him.

Now, going along, the way becoming steeper and narrower and the creek bank little more than wide enough to pass a good horse and rider, he saw ahead of him a basalt dike, or cross dam of rock, which cut across the narrowing floor of the side canyon. Here the stream took another plunge, this of about thirty feet. Above the dike, Canady could see the boles of pine trees and hence knew that the ground above the dike lay fairly level. The cross-laying of rock apparently served as a barrier against which the winter erosions of snow, ice and thaw had worked with the spring floodings of the creek to bring down and build up a tiny flat.

Canady's gray eyes lit up. His brown face relaxed and he said aloud, "By God, maybe this is it," and went on with renewed strength and some hope of keeping his life a little longer. Up there, above that rock cross-bank, a man with a good carbine and plenty of shells could hold down most eight-man posses for several afternoons. Well, two or three, anyway. Or one. For certain, until nightfall. Twelve, fifteen hours, say. It was better than nothing.

His luck held. There was a good angling trail going up that thirty-foot vertical face of rock. It was a game trail, and somewhat of a cow trail, too. He made out the droppings of elk, blacktail deer, range steers and, then, suddenly and strangely, a fairly fresh piling of horse sign. This latter find sent a chill through him. He was on his knees in the instant of the sighting, but then he straightened, grinning. It was all right. The pony was unshod. Moreover, he suspected, from the hard round prints that it left, that it never had been shod and was one of a bunch of broomtails—wild mustangs—that came into this rocky depth for the water that flowed so green and cool in the stream.

Clearing the top of the stone dam, Canady's grin widened. The flat above lay precisely as he had imagined it did. He laughed softly, as a man will who is alone. Now, then, it would be a little different from the way those hungry lawmen had planned it. This was perfect. At the apex of the triangle of the flat he saw the thick stand of sycamore and cottonwood, aspen, laurel and willow, and he knew that the water headed there. A moment later, he made out the source of the stream, a large artesian spring gushing from the native rock under great pressure. The spring was set above the grove some few feet, its stream falling rapidly to plunge into the foliage. Likely it pooled up there under the trees and at the foot of the down-plunge. That's what lured in the wild horses and the other game and the cattle, too, what few of the latter were hardy enough to come this far into the mountains for feed. All a man would need to do, now, was hole up in those boulders that girded the spring, up there above the trees, and he could command with his Winchester the whole of the small, open flat between the spring grove and the stone cross-dam that Canady had just clambered up. Taking a deep breath, the fugitive started across the flat, toward the spring and its hole-up boulders. It was not until he had climbed safely into this haven at the canyon head and laid down pantingly to look back on his trail and get ready for the possemen, that he saw where he had come.

Below him in the trees the spring pooled up exactly as he had expected it would. Also the rim of the pool showed the centuries of wear of the hoofed animals coming to its banks for water. But there was something else—two other things—that he had not expected to see there, and his grin faded and his gray eyes grew taut and tired and empty.

The first thing was the wild horse. It had not gone on up out of the little side canyon as Canady had hoped, showing him the way to follow its tracks and escape over the rim where no mounted man might follow. It was still in the grove of trees that sheltered the spring-pool waterhole, and it wasn't still there because of its thirst. Beyond the trees, back where Canady had come from, and so skillfully blended and built into the natural cover of the canyon that even his range-wise eyes had missed them, were the two woven brush and pole wings of the second thing Canady had not dreamed to find there. Those were the manmade wings of a mustang corral down there. Canady had stumbled into a wild horse trap. And he was caught there, with this unfortunate lone mustang that now cowered in the trees and could not get out of the trap any more than could he, and for the same reason—the posse and the box canyon.

"Steady on," Canady called down softly to the terrified horse. "We'll think of something."

Two hours after high noon the sun was gone from the canyon. Canady could see its light splashing the far side of the main valley still, but in the side canyon all was soft shade, and hot. Canady drank enough water to keep himself from drying out, yet not enough to log him. He noted that the wild mustang did the same thing. It knew, as Canady knew, that to be ready to fight or fly called for an empty belly. "Smart," said Canady, "smart as hell." The horse heard him and looked up. "*Coo-ee, coo-ee*," Canady called to him reassuringly. "Don't fret; I'll figure something for us." But it was a lie and he knew it was a lie.

He had gone down, right after he first lay up in the spring boulders and saw the trap and the wild broomtail in it, and closed off the narrow gate of the funnel-winged corral with his lariat. He had done that in a hurry, before the posse had worked up into the canyon and taken its position along the top of the cross-dam. His one thought had been that the broomtail was a horse, wild or not, and that so long as a man had a horse he wasn't out of it in that country. And he had wanted to keep hidden from the posse the fact that he did have a horse up there in that head-waters timber. The mustang had played with him in that last part of it, lying up shy and quiet as a deer in the trees and brush, not wanting any more than Canady wanted for the men to know that it was there. "It" in this case was a scrubby little stallion, probably too small and old to hold a band of mares. The little horse had not only the fixtures but the temperament of the mongrel stud animal. Watching him lie still in the spring brush and keep his eyes following every move of the men below him, as well as of the single man above him, Canady knew that he and the trapped horse were friends. The only problem was proving it to the horse.

Sometimes these old scrub studs had been ridden long ago and would remember man's smell and voice. He tried a dozen times to talk the mustang up toward his end of the spring pool. But the animal gave no sign that the sight, scent or sound of mankind was familiar to him, or welcome. He bared his teeth silently and pinned his ears and squatted in the haunches ready to kick like a pack mule on a cold morning. He did this every time Canady said more than three or four words to him, or accompanied his talk with any movement that might mean he was coming down to see the horse, if the horse would not come up to see him.

What possible good the horse could do him, even if, by some miracle Canady might gentle him down and put his saddle and bridle on him, Canady didn't know. Then, even in thinking that far, he laughed and shrugged. His saddle and bridle were down there on that rock slide below the hole-in-the-wall. He'd had no time and no reason to take them off his dead mount. So if he went out of there astride that broomtail it would be bareback, and that was about as good a bet as that the crafty old stallion would sprout wings and fly up out of the canyon. A bridle, of sorts, he could rig from splitting and unraveling a short length of his lariat. It would be sort of a breaking hackamore arrangement and might do to give simple directions of right and left and whoa-up. But even if he rigged this Sioux headstall and got it on the shaggy little horse, then what? That was, even if the rascal wanted to be good, or had been ridden in the past, and remembered it of a sudden? Nothing. Not a damned thing. Canady couldn't ride out of that canyon if he had the best saddle mount in Montana waiting and eager to make the try with him. It was all crazy, thinking of that wild stud. But just finding any horse up there was bound to start a man's mind going. Especially when he had just shot his own mount and was fixing to put his back to the best rock he could find and go down with lead flying. But it was crazy all the same. All Canady could do was what the old broomtail stud could do—fight the rope to the last breath he had in him, then kill himself, if he could, before the others did it for him.

The afternoon wore on. The heat in the deep-walled little canyon was enormous. The deerflies swarmed at the spring pool and bit like mad cats. They nearly drove Canady wild, but he fought them with hand and mind and swathed neckband and, when evening came, they lifted up out of the canyon on the first stir of the night wind. In the early part of the waiting there had been some desultory talk between the posse and Canady, talk of Canady coming out peacefully and getting a fair trial, but the fugitive had not bothered to take that offer seriously. He knew the trial he would get. The posse had its own witnesses with it. They would bring up these two or three men who had ''seen'' the shooting and say to them, ''Is that him?'' and the men would say, ''Yes, that's him,'' and the trial would be over. Witnesses! thought Canady. God, how he hated them. It wasn't that he minded being identified if he was the man. In his business no feeling was held against the witness who *had* seen something. It was those devils, like the ones with the posse, who had *not* seen the job and yet who were always ready to raise their right hands and be sworn, who were the ones Canady hated. There had not been any witnesses to what passed between him and that teller. All the other bank people had been on the floor behind the cage, and there had been no customers in the bank, or out in front of it. The shooting had happened and Canady had made it to his horse in back of the bank, and made it away down the alley and into the sagebrush south of town before he had passed a living soul. Then, it was two farm wagons, both carrying kids and driven by women, that he had ridden by well out of Gray's Landing. How those good folks—and they were the only real witnesses, save the cashier and the other teller on the bank floor—how they could identify him as anything other than a horseman not of that area, Canady did not know. As for the three shots that had killed the teller, and they must have killed him or the posse would not have pushed so hard, those shots had been fired *after* both barrels of the .36 caliber derringer that the teller brought up out of the cash drawer had been triggered and put their slugs, one in Canady's chest, and one in the ceiling of the Second National Bank of Gray's Landing, Montana. But the only witness to that fact was dead. Canady had reacted as all men with guns in their hands react to other men with guns in their hands. He had fired by instinct, by pure conditioned reflex of long experience, when that first .36 bullet went into the pectoral muscles of his left chest.

Armed robbery? Certainly. Twenty years in the Territorial Prison? Of course. A man expected that. But to be run down like a mad dog and cornered and starved out and then strung up on a naked cottonwood like a damned Indian drunk or a common horse thief was not right or fair. Murder? Could you call it murder when the other man was a professional in his business and he could see that you were a professional in yours? When you told him he would be killed if he tried anything funny? Then, when on top of the fair warning, you gave him the first shot? Could you call it murder, then, if you shot in answer to his try at killing you? Self-defense was the actual verdict, but of course an armed robber could not plead self-defense. But he was not guilty of murder, or even of assault with a deadly weapon, or even of intent to commit murder, or of a damned thing, really, but to sack that cash drawer and clear out of Gray's

Landing just as fast and peaceably as he and the old horse might manage.

Canady grinned, even as he exonerated himself.

It was no good. He knew it was no good. A man had to be honest with himself. If he was in another business he wouldn't need a gun to conduct his trade. Needing and using a gun, he was always in the peril of being forced to use it. The teller was an honest man. Frank Canady was a crook. The teller was a dead honest man and Canady was a live dishonest man. Canady was a killer.

"No!" he yelled down to the posse. "I won't do it; I shot second; I didn't mean to harm that fellow. He pulled on me and shot first. But he's dead, ain't he? Sure he is. And you say to me to come on down peaceable and you'll see I get a fair trial? With a dead teller back there on the floor of the Second National. That's rich. Really rich."

The possemen were startled. It had been two hours since the fugitive had made a sound. Previously he had refused to come down and they had thought he meant it. Now, did they detect a change? Was it that he wanted to reconsider and was only protecting his ego by the defiant outburst.

"That's right, you heard us right," the leader of the posse called up to him. "You come down here and we'll guarantee to take you back to Gray's Landing and get you to either Cheyenne or Miles City, wherever the court is sitting, by train and under armed guard. You'll get the trial we promised, and the protection beforehand." He waited a significant moment, then demanded, "What do you say? There's no use any more people getting hurt."

Canady's gray eyes grew tired again.

"That's so," he called back. "It includes me, too. I don't want to see anybody else get it, either. 'Specially me. No thanks, Mr. Posseman. I'll stay up here. I don't fancy that you brung along all them ropes just to tie me up for the ride back to Gray's Landing.''

There was a silence from below the cross-dam of rock in the upper throat of the canyon that lasted perhaps two, perhaps three stretching minutes. Then the posseman called back. ''All right,'' he said, ''you'll have it your way. When it's full dark we're going to come for you, and you know what that will mean. There are eight of us, all good shots, and you won't have the chance of a rat in an oatbin. We've got bull's-eye lanterns to light you out. We will set them up behind boulders where you can't snipe them, and yet where they will throw light up there around you like it was bright moonlight. We mean to stomp you out. There will be no trial and no talk of a trial. You're dead right now.''

Canady sank back behind his breastwork of basalt and gray-green granite. He hawked the cottony spittle from his throat and spat grimacingly down toward the mustang stud. The animal had been crouching and listening to the exchange of voices intelligently like some big gaunt sandy-maned dog. Seeing him, and noting his apparent interest, Canady managed a trace of his quiet grin.

''What do *you* say, amigo?'' he asked.

The horse looked up at him. It was the first time in all the long hours that Canady had tried gentle-talking to him that the animal had made a direct and not spooked response to the man's voice. Now he stomped a splayed and rock-split forehoof and whickered softly and gruntingly in his throat, precisely as Canady's old horse had done.

''All right,'' said Canady, for some reason feeling mightily warmed by the mustang's action, ''so we've each got one friend in the world. That isn't too bad. As long as you have a friend you have a chance. Rest easy; let me think. We'll still make it, you and me. . . .''

* * *

It was dusk when the old steer came down the cliff trail. He was a ladino, one of those mossy-horned old rascals that had successfully hidden out from the gathers of a dozen years. He was old and crafty and cautious as any wild animal, but he had to have water and he was coming down to the spring pool to get it. He certainly saw the men of the posse, and winded their mounts, but they did not see him and he knew that they did not. His yellow buckskin hide with the dark "cruz" or cross-stripe on the shoulders, and the dark brown legs and feet, blended perfectly into the weathered face of the cliff, and he made no more sound coming down that hidden trail than a mountain doe might have made. But he had failed to see Canady or to separate his scent, or the scent of the mustang stud, from the other horse and man scents coming from below. He came on, carefully, silently, yet quickly down the wall of the canyon from the rim above and Canady, seeing him, was suddenly lifted in mind and heart. He had been right in the first place! There *was* a trail up out of that blind box of a side canyon. A track up that dizzy sheer cliff, up there, that would pass a desperate man, or a catlike wild mustang, but not a mounted man or a man going afoot leading his tamed and trained saddle mount. "Come on, come on," he heard himself whispering to the old outlaw steer. "Come on down here and let me see how you do it. Let me see how and where you get off that damned wall and down here where we are."

He grinned when he said that, when he said "we," meaning himself and the wild stud, without thinking about it. It was funny how a man took to anything for a friend when he had run out of of the real McCoy and was in his last corner. He supposed that if a sidewinder crawled along at the final minute and that was all he had to talk to, a man would find some excuse to think kindly of the snake tribe. Well, anyway, he was thinking with deep kindness about the animal kingdom just then. Especially the horse and cow part of it. And extraspecially about the latter half. "Come on, keep coming on, don't slip, for God's sake," he said to the gaunt dun steer. "Easy, easy. Let me see you do it, just don't fall or spook or get a bad smell and change your mind. That's it, that's it. Easy, easy. . . ."

He talked the steer down that cliff trail as though his life depended on it, and it did. And the steer made it. He made it in a way that caused Canady to suck in his breath and shake his head in wonderment. He made it in a way that even caused Canady to think for a moment about there being something to the idea of a divine providence, for it was the sort of thing no man could have figured out by himself, the weird, crazy, wonderful kind of a last-second reprieve that no force but God Almighty could have sent to a man in Canady's place. It was a miracle.

The dun steer performed it with an easy quickness that defied belief, too. He came to that place on his side of the canyon where it seemed to Canady that the trail must end. The man could see the sheer face of the rock dropping sixty feet to the creek bed. A giant outcropping of granite hid the exact end of the right-side trail, but Canady could see, and with absolute certainty, that the trail did not continue downward past that outcrop that hid its actual terminus. But as he watched the steer disappear behind the outcrop and as he wondered what would happen next, he saw the lean yellow body launch itself in a graceful leap from behind the outer edge of the outcrop, and sail outward through the thin air of the canyon's dark throat. It appeared as though the leap would smash the ribby brute into the rearing face of the opposite, left-hand canyon wall, which lay no more than fifteen or twenty feet from the right-side wall. But again the steer disappeared, this time seemingly into the very face of the opposing cliff.

There was a tricky turn in the rock wall of the canyon's left side at just that point, however, and while Canady could see the creek's raggedly broken bottom, he could not see where the steer hit into the wall. All he was sure of for the moment was that the animal had made his landing somewhere other than in the creek bottom. Difficult as it might be to accept, that old outlaw steer had somehow made it from one side of the wall to the other. But, even so, then what? Where was he now? The questions were soon answered when the missing steer appeared to walk right out of the waterfall that came down from Canady's elevated vantage to strike into and begin following the brief section of creek bed into the pool grove. While Canady gaped, the animal stole swiftly to the pool, drank sparingly, returned and disappeared again behind the curtain of misty water cascading down from the spring above.

So that was it. As simple and as remarkable as that. A trail ran from behind the waterfall up the left-hand wall. At a point opposite the right-side trail's end, it, too, terminated. But it was obvious that there was room enough for a running jump and opposite safe landing, to and from either wall, with both takeoff and landing spots completely masked from the lower canyon.

Gaging the distance of the jump, Canady knew that he could make it. With his boots off and laced about his neck, or better, thrown over with his Colt and the saddlebags with the bank money, the Winchester being slung on his back, alone, he could make that distance through the air. But, then, what of that? He made the jump safely and went on up the right-side cliff trail behind the ladino steer and gained the rim; then what? He would still be afoot in a hostile land in midsummer's blazing heat without food, water, or a mount. That was the rub. Even if he made that jump and the cliff climb beyond it and got to the rim, he would have to have a horse. Otherwise, the possemen, within an hour or two of dark, having come for him and found him gone, would go back out and climb out of the main valley and cut for his sign on both rims of the side canyon, and they would still get him. They would get him, easy, with them mounted and he afoot.

No, he had to take that broomy studhorse with him.

Somehow, he had to get that mustang to go with him up the cliff. If he could do that, could get the little horse to make the jump with him on its back—it would have to be that way for he could never trust the brute to follow him or to wait for him if he allowed it to jump first—if he could make that gap in the canyon on the back of that little wild horse, then stay with him, hand-leading him up the cliff trail, then, oh then, by the dear good Lord, he would make it. He and the horse would make it together. Just as he had promised the raunchy little devil. Up on the rim, he would remount the tough wiry mustang and together they would race away and Canady would have his life and the broomtail stud would have his freedom and the Gray's Landing posse would have their ropes unstretched and their vengeance unadministered and left to God where it belonged.

The thought of the Almighty came very strong to Canady in that moment of desperate hope. He turned his face upward to peer out of the narrow slit of late twilight far above him where the walls of the canyon seemed almost to touch at the top and where, far, far up there, he could now see the yellow steer climbing the last few steps of the steep trail and humping himself over the rim and losing himself to canyon's view. Canady nodded and said to the dusk-hushed stillness about him: "If you'll let me make it, too, Lord, me and that little hoss down yonder, I will try to set things as right as I can.

I'll take this money, Lord, the bank don't need it and I won't want it any more after this night, and I will give this money to the widow of that poor teller. I will figure some way to do it, Lord, that she don't know where it came from. And I'll turn loose this little wild hoss, if you will let me gentle him enough to get on him and push him to that jump, up yonder. I'm going to try it, Lord. I'm going down there to the pool and try putting my loop on him right now. You reckon you could help me? I surely hope so, as I think you wouldn't send that ladino steer down here to show a man the way out, and then not help him to make it. Nor likewise do I think you would put that little old mustang studhorse down there in that trap by the pool unless you wanted him used. It looks to me, Lord, as if you truly wanted to pull me out of this here trap, and if that's the way it is, why thank You and I'll do my best. . . ."

In the little light remaining, Canady went down from his rocks by the spring to try for the trapped wild horse. He took his rope from the trap gate and closed the gate, instead, with brush and poles, hoping it would turn the stud should he break past him when he came at him with the lariat.

The actual catching went, as such things perversely will, with a strange easiness. Oh, the little horse fought the loop when he felt it settle on him, but he did not do so viciously. The very fact that he permitted Canady to come close enough to dab the loop on him to begin with was peculiarly simple. It made the matter suspicious to Canady and he thought the little stud was merely stalling on him, was trying to tempt him in close where he could use his teeth and hooves on him. He knew the small mustangs would do this. They would fight like panthers in close, using their teeth like carnivorous animals, and their feet with all the savagery of elk or moose fighting off wolves. But this was not the case with the tattered broomtail in the mustang trap. When Canady got up near enough to him, he saw the reason why, or thought that he did. The telltale white marks of the cinch and saddle, the places where white hair had grown in to replace the original claybank sorrel hairs, showed clearly in the darkening twilight. Canady's first thought that this horse had been handled before was now assured. And it certainly explained the change in the animal the moment the man snugged the loop high up on his neck, under the jaw, in a way that showed the horse he meant to hold him hard and fast, and to handle him again as he had been handled years before. Memory is a strong force. The stud made Canady throw him on the ground, using the loose end of the rope to make a figure-8 snake and roll it around the front legs to bring the little pony down, but once he had been thrown and permitted to stand up again, it was all over. This man had gentled many horses. He had spent his life with them. Their smell had become his smell. The very sound of his voice had a horse sound in it. The mustang had heard it the first word of the day. He had sensed his kinship with this particular man, then, and he sensed his mastery of the horsekind, now. He submitted to Canady and stood quietly, if still trembling, while the man stroked him and sweet-whispered to him and got him to ease and to stand without shaking, and without dread or apprehension.

Then Canady cut and wove the makeshift breaking halter, the Plains Indian's simple rope rein and bridle arrangement, continuing to talk all the while to the small mustang. When, in half an hour more, it was full dark and the split-ear hackamore-bridle and its short reining rope were finished and put upon the horse, the animal was to all practical purposes reduced to a usable saddle horse. It was a piece of the greatest luck, Canady knew, that he had been able to catch and work the little brute.

But it was not so entirely luck that it had no sense or possibility to it, and his success only made the fugitive believe that his hunch of higher help was a true one, and this thought, in turn, strengthened him and made his spirits rise.

"Come on," he murmured to the little horse, "it's time we got shut of here. Come along, *coo-ee, coo-ee*, little hoss. That's good, that's real good. Easy, easy. . . ."

They went in behind the creek falls, as the yellow ladino steer had done. The mustang pulled back a bit at the water but once it had hit him he steadied down and followed Canady's urging pull on the lariat as well and as obediently as any horse would have done in similar straits. Beyond the sheet of the falls, the left-hand trail went sharply but safely upward and around the trunklike bulge of the canyon's wall which had hidden it from Canady's view at the spring. Around the turn was the expected straight run at the leap-over. It was better, even, than Canady hoped. There was some actual soil in its track and, here and there, some clumps of tough wire grass to give footing and power for the jump.

"Steady, now," said Canady, and eased up onto the crouching mustang. The little mount flinched and deepened his crouch, but he did not break. Canady sighed gratefully and nodded upward to that power which clearly was helping him now. He took his grip on the rope rein and put the pressure of his bowed knees to the mustang's ribs. Beneath him, he felt the little horse squat and gather himself. Then he touched him, just touched him, with his left bootheel. The wild stud uncoiled his tensed muscles, shot down the runway of the trail, came up to the jump-across as though he had been trained to it since colthood. Canady felt his heart soar with the mighty upward spring in the small brute's wiry limbs. He laughed with the sheer joy of it. He couldn't help it.

He had never in his life felt a triumph such as this one; this sailing over that hell's pit of blackness down there beneath him; this gliding spring, this arching, floating burst of power that was carrying him high above those deadly rock fangs so far below, and was carrying him, too, up and away from those blood-hungry possemen and their winking, glaring, prying bull's-eye lanterns, which he could just see now, from an eye-corner, coming into view down-canyon of his deserted place at the spring above the pool and the peaceful grove of mountain ash and alder and willow there at the head of Rainbow Creek in Blind Canyon, sixty and more miles from the Second National Bank and that fool of a dead teller in Gray's Landing, Montana. Oh, what a wondrous, heady thing was life! And, oh! what a beholden and humble man was Frank Canady for this gift, this chance, this answer to his fumbling prayer. He would never forget it. Never, never, never.

They came down very hard at the far end of the jump. The concussion of the horse hitting the ground rattled Canady's teeth and cracked his jaws together as loud as a pistol shot. He saw lights behind his eyes and heard wild and strange sounds, but only for a second or two. Then all was clear again and he and the little horse were going together up the right-side cliff trail, Canady leading the way, the little horse following faithful as a pet dog behind him. It seemed no more than a minute before they were where it had taken the yellow steer half an hour to climb, and it seemed only a breath later that they had topped out on the rim and were free.

Canady cried then. The tears came to his eyes and he could not help himself. He didn't think that the little mustang would care, though, and he was right. When he put his arms about the shaggy, warm neck and hugged the skinny old stud, the mustang only whickered deep in his throat and leaned into Frank Canady and rested

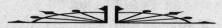